The Drinking Gourd

The Kansas Pirate Series:

Book III

I0673156

S.L. Kotar and J.E. Gessler

Ahead of the Press Publishing
St. Louis, Missouri

Library of Congress Cataloguing-in-Publication Data

The Drinking Gourd
The Kansas Pirate Series: Book III
/ S.L. Kotar and J.E. Gessler / authors
/E.J. Rossi / illustrator

ISBN   Paperback   978-1-950392-04-9
ISBN   KINDLE   978-1-950392-05-6

Manufactured in the United States of America
Ahead of The Press Publishing
St. Louis, Missouri

Table of Contents

SUMMARY OF THE KANSAS PIRATE SERIES BOOKS 5
DEDICATION 8
CHAPTER 1 9
CHAPTER 2 20
CHAPTER 3 28
CHAPTER 4 37
CHAPTER 5 48
CHAPTER 6 61
CHAPTER 7 75
CHAPTER 8 86
CHAPTER 9 96
CHAPTER 10 105
CHAPTER 11 115
CHAPTER 12 124
CHAPTER 13 134
CHAPTER 14 145
CHAPTER 15 155
CHAPTER 16 163
CHAPTER 17 175
CHAPTER 18 183
CHAPTER 19 194
CHAPTER 20 206
CHAPTER 21 214
CHAPTER 22 223
CHAPTER 23 233
CHAPTER 25 253
CHAPTER 26 262

CHAPTER 27	271
CHAPTER 28	282
CHAPTER 29	296
CHAPTER 30	310
CHAPTER 31	319
CHAPTER 32	332
CHAPTER 33	342
CHAPTER 34	353
CHAPTER 35	371
ALSO BY: S.L.KOTAR AND J.E.GESSLER	382

SUMMARY OF THE KANSAS PIRATE SERIES BOOKS

Pirate Treasure

Book I

They said the boy was haunted and the townspeople of Lawrence, Kansas, wanted nothing to do with widower Seth Ward or his two children. In 1857, superstitions run high.

Left alone to raise Patricia and Peter, Seth has been isolated from his neighbors since the death of his wife from a lingering, malignant disease. Nearly at his wits end, a young woman appears in response to an advertisement for help.

Barbara Nelander dared brave the terror of a dead woman's ghost and the haunting of her son because she was not like other women. Born in Nova Scotia, "Nelander," as she was called, had served as a crewman aboard her father's trading ship since early childhood. Used to working in a man's world and handling difficult situations, she signs aboard with the determination to dispel the ghosts of the past.

Transforming the homestead into a figurative pirate ship, she uses her wiles to restore Peter's self-confidence, extract a buccaneer's revenge on those who tormented him and battles drought alongside Seth as the harsh Kansas summer threatens to destroy the family and the relationship that develops between the "captain" and "first officer."

Strawberry Fields

Book II

What is a dream but a fight against the odds? A struggle to rise above the ordinary and express a creativity that encapsulates the soul. When love is shared, that emotion becomes a dual consciousness. As a small child, Seth Ward had seen a valley filled with wild strawberry plants and imagined that one day he would own that land and cultivate those plants. Growing to adulthood and facing the harsh reality of raising two small children in Bloody Kansas of the 1850's, however, life was 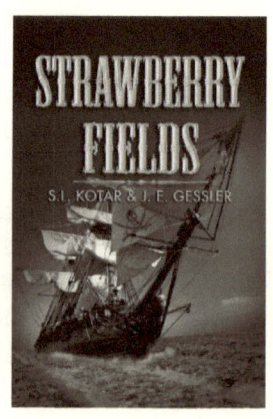 reduced to dreary survival and dreams were tucked away into the recesses of yesteryear.

When love and remarriage came to Seth unexpectedly in the person of a strange, wild, nautical woman named Nelander, he shared his dream and she determined to make it a reality. A sad twist of fate brought the strawberry field into their possession and using the last of her seaman's savings, she bought 5,000 plants to add to the wild variety in the hope the family could make a success growing and selling the sweet berries.

The enterprise faced nearly insurmountable obstacles but as often as disaster struck, the touch of a higher power seemed to guide their way. With the assistance of two former slaves, an elderly woman and her son, the small clan of "Kansas Pirates" persevered, ultimately discovering that one dream had the power to blossom into dozens.

THE DRINKING GOURD

S.L. KOTAR & J. E. GESSLER

DEDICATION

"The Drinking Gourd"

It happened twice: in 1985 and again in 1987. Two St. Louis Cardinals baseball teams, managed by the great "White Rat, " Whitey Herzog, made it to the World Series. They were strange teams, not the power-slugging type that usually ascended to baseball's highest stage, but teams designed around managerial mysticism, pitching, defense, speed and that elusive element known as chemistry. Called the "Running Redbirds," these Cardinal teams boasted inning after inning of brilliant baseball; John Tudor, the otherworldly left-hander; Ozzie Smith, the shortstop Wizard; Vince Coleman, the base stealer with uncanny success; Clark and Pendleton, McGee and Forsch, Daley and Worrell.

They should have been World Champions both these years and were not. Such is cruel fate. To Whitey and John Tudor and all the rest of the St. Louis Cardinals in the era of "Whitey Ball," where the only color that mattered was red, we dedicate "The Drinking Gourd," the story of the "Kansas Pirate," who saw neither black nor white but only one common humanity.

SLK and JEG

CHAPTER 1

The knock at the door came quickly: three sharp raps, a pause, followed by two more. For all the world it might have been a code, yet none in the house rightly spoke the language.

That it signaled danger, however, could not be debated.

Seth Ward rose from his rocker, the Lawrence *Gazette* he had been reading slipping from his lap to the wooden floor. It landed with a soft swishing noise, hardly enough to disturb a sleeping babe, yet he flinched as though the periodical rattled the walls. Hand to lips, he signaled for silence. Barbara Nelander-Ward, his wife, nodded understanding and softly ushered two older children and the sleeping babe into a rear bedroom.

Before completing the tactical withdrawal, a small pup, teeth bared, body quivering in righteous indignation, raced between her legs. Viciously yapping, the animal squared itself by the main entranceway, a narrow line of fur bristling down its back like a solitary row of corn. The hound's sudden silence bore testimony to the fact Seth had slipped a hand around its muzzle.

Inside the sleeping chamber, the children formed a close-knit circle.

"Who is out there?" Patricia whispered. As the elder of the non-commissioned crew and senior able-bodied seaman of the farm called Pirate Treasure, she took it upon herself to speak for Peter, her brother, and their infant sister, Paula.

"I don't know," Nelander responded in a command tone befitting the many years she had worked aboard a real sea-going vessel. "It is best we take precautions..."

... times being what they are.

She did not finish the sentence. In the opening months of 1861, it had already grown old by repetition.

"Shall I get my cutlass?" Peter demanded in a brave, ten year-old's voice. "If it's trouble, I want to be ready."

"Say, rather, it is the unknown," his stepmother advised.

"But I want to be prepared to defend the house. And you and Captain Papa and --"

"Enough. It is an officer's duty to protect. You will receive your orders. In the meantime, stay here. Do not emerge until given the all clear."

Expecting them to obey, she cast a loving glance at her sleeping daughter then tiptoed out, sealing the door behind. Lowering the wick in the kerosene lamp to make she and her husband less of an obvious target, Nelander merged into the night shadows, rejoining Seth by the entrance. The fact he had grabbed the deer rifle from the wall and cradled it in the crook of his arm augmented rather than lessened her discomfiture.

"Have you looked out the window? Who's there?" He shrugged.

"Whoever it is, is standing out of the line of vision. Can't make him out."

Professing ignorance of the summons provided no escape. Granting the stranger had seen the lamp burning through the window, he could reasonably expect the family to be home. Waiting too long might incite ire. Refusing it altogether implied fear.

And cowardice.

Giving their enemy, if so he turned out to be, an edge.

Pirates, as the Ward family had come to be known in landlocked Kansas, were notorious for bravery. And occasionally rash behavior. The newly promoted Captain of the Fleet of the erstwhile ship could not back down even if such were his natural inclination Not in front of his second in command.

Wrapping his hand around the knob, he moved it a half turn, gently drew the door back and peered into the night. Before he had a chance to ascertain the identity of the visitor, the man shoved a foot inside. Blocking any chance Ward might have had to shut him out, shoulders, head and body followed. Once safely within the perimeter, the intruder's eyes shifted toward the sole light source.

"Blow out the lamp. I want no one to see my silhouette. It would not do to have three adults counted within."

As peculiar as the request seemed, Nelander followed the direction. Further lowering the wick, then blowing out the flame, she plunged the room into total blackness. The sudden darkening caused the dog to recommence barking.

"Silence him!"

Unable to control both rifle and squirming pup, Seth handed the hound over to Nelander. Accepting the burden, she copied her husband's example by clamping a hand over the beast's jaws. It struggled madly in her arms. Her grip tightened.

"Are you alone? No one else is here?" the stranger demanded.

The initial preliminaries over and reasonable prudence thrown to the wind, Seth found his voice.

"Who is asking? And why do you want to know?"

"No time for questions." The man appeared annoyed and might not have said more but for the suddenly stubborn obstinacy of the farmers. "Blind Betty and Mute Thomas sent me."

A white man evoking the name of two Negroes elicited more shock than compliance. Drawling closer, Nelander stared at the shadowed, ill-defined features of the interloper. His attire did not make the quest easy, for he wore a broad-rimmed hat drawn tightly past his brow. Any other identifying indicators were hidden by a long, buff-colored, ankle-length coat and workman's gloves. Still, she could not shake the impression of vague familiarity.

"You mention friends' names, yet you have not given your own. What do you want?"

Grinding his foot into the floorboards the way a man might extinguish a cigar butt, he hitched a shoulder, debated, then turned his back. Crossing to the door, he opened it a crack then issued one sharp whistle through his teeth. A moment passed before a figure made its way from the barn. Crouching low, it weaved and bobbed in a hurdy-gurdy fashion, reminiscent of the way a musician played that instrument by turning a crank. Transforming from spirit to substance under the rays of a crescent moon, the suddenly three-dimensional person tread lightly on the porch boards before slipping inside.

Acting on an unseen cue, the second stranger used one hand to draw back a loose-fitting cape from head and shoulders, revealing the characteristics of a young woman. Even in the gloom she could not be mistaken for anything but what she was: an African.

Breathing through her mouth, Nelander nodded.

"All right, sir: you have shown your credentials. Tell us what is desired."

"A place for her to stay. Hidden. Out of sight. No one must know she is here. She is a runaway. The bounty hunters are after her."

"The slavers, you mean," Seth clarified through clenched teeth. For once, the man agreeably nodded.

"Exactly correct. You understand the situation?"

"How close are they?"

"We lost them by wading in the creek. But they are locals. First, they will go to -- the Windsor's farm," he added, astutely watching the Ward's expression.

"Are Betty and Thomas in danger?"

"Not tonight. The men will search their house and then come here." He hesitated, tugged on a sleeve of his coat and added, "It is dangerous for you to become involved. Miss Theresa has a price on her head: five hundred dollars." The enormity of the sum staggered. The guide did not hesitate to underscore the significance. "The same price, I have heard it said, you were once offered for a crop of strawberries." He directed a glare at Seth. "An amount no reasonable man would refuse."

"I am not in the business of brokering flesh."

"I pray God you will have no cause to regret those brave words. You will hide her here?"

"We will."

The use of the pronoun was not lost on the listener.

"I will come back tomorrow at this time to collect her." He hesitated, then added, "If all be well."

The farmer held out his hand. "It will be, Mister --"

"Giles." The two shook, then Giles bowed toward Barbara. "Word is that you are a woman of courage -- and conviction... Nelander."

The fact he knew her name no longer caused surprise. Only one individual outside the family called her that, unadorned by "Mrs." or "Miz." It substantiated his claim.

"You may thank Blind Betty for that testimonial. And tell her we shall do what we can. Come hell or high water."

An apt expression when spoken by a former seaman.

"I am grateful." Refastening a button which had come undone, Giles retreated toward the door. Retreated, in a figurative sense, for no aura of defeat lurked about him. "Tomorrow night, then."

Before husband or wife had a chance to blink, he disappeared. Had he not left a present behind, they might have believed the entire incident to be imagined.

Recovering first, Nelander made overtures toward the woman.

"We are your friends and will do everything in our power to help you. Your name is Theresa?"

"Yas, ma'am."

"I am Officer Nelander and this is Captain Ward. You are not injured -- by a fall, perhaps?"

"No, ma'am."

"Very good. Then we must think of a proper place to hide you. I have stowed cargo before, but never contraband. In the barn, Seth?"

He shrugged, acutely conscious of time pressing.

"If it were filled with hay bales, I might be able to make a den they would overlook in a search, but there is not enough."

"The stalls? In with Blaze or Bessie?"

"The animals will not take well to someone they do not know. A seasoned bounty hunter will detect signs of unease." He looked upward. "Whether we permit it or not, they will force their way in here; look in the loft and under the beds. Out back," he decided. "In the strawberry field. If she lies low --"

The sound of distant braying caught their attention and for a moment, both froze.

"No," Nelander dismissed. "The dogs are on the scent. Once trailing her here, they will follow their noses outside into the patch." Snapping her fingers, her head shot up. "I know of a place."

Grabbing the Negress by the arm, she started to guide her away when another noise, this one closer at hand, arrested further motion. As a new mother, herself, Nelander instantly identified the cause.

"You have a baby."

"Mah chil'."

"Oh, dear Lord. Two of you." The realization heightened her resolve. "You must keep it still."

"Da babe be hungry. Ain't had no milk fo' to feed it."

"All right. We will see to that, afterward. Seth can find a bottle and heat cow's milk. But first we must get rid of those men. They will be here in a matter of minutes. Follow me."

Seth tried to waylay her with an urgent, "Where are you going?"

"To a place no gentleman dare enter without permission. Do your best to 'entertain' our guests. Light the lamp and pretend you are reading. You suspect nothing, remember?"

Making a brief side trip to the pantry, Nelander grabbed a jar, then ushered the runaways out.

Head still spinning from the unexpected encounter and the trial yet to come, Seth reached for a Lucifer, had a change of heart, and tossed it down. Wrenching the globe from the socket of the lamp, he wiped the inside with a shirt tail. For the effort he sustained a deep black, greasy stain and smeared glass. The arrangement suited, however, for he quickly struck another match, re-lit the wick and settled the sphere back under the brass clamps.

Before he had time to settle into his chair and pretend to read, Squash, the hound pup recommenced a new round of barking and howling, matched in intensity by the deep baying of mature dogs. Scratching madly at the door and finding no way out, Squash scampered to the side window. Sticking his wet nose between curtain and glass, he stared outside, body shaking in uncontrollable anger.

"Down, boy!" the master ordered as the sharp click of horseshoes against dried earth indicated riders had pulled up. Getting slowly to his feet, he snapped thumb and third finger together as a signal for the animal to quiet just as a fist pounded madly on the door.

"Open up, in the name of the law!"

"Coming." And then added, although he knew better, "Just a minute, Sheriff." Pulling in the wooden portal, he affected surprise at the two men confronting him. The nearer held the lead to a pair of matched bloodhounds, straining to free themselves from the restraint and enter. Eyebrows narrowed, the farmer remarked, "You're not Will Bochner."

Identification quickly followed. "Dick McConaghie. Brian Clement. I thought you said you were the law."

Determined to shove the farmer aside, then thinking better of it as Seth blocked the archway, Clement tapped a badge affixed to his vest.

"We are. Properly sworn. Step aside. We're on official duty."

"Hold on, there. That's not a deputy's star." Righteously indignant, he bent closer for a more detailed inspection. "It says, 'Agent.'"

"That's right. We're employees of the Simpson Agency."

"I don't recognize that as any duly appointed authority of Douglas County."

"We're bounty hunters. That makes us --"

"Blood suckers."

Dick stuck out his jaw. "We do the work Sheriff Bochner don't have time for."

"Doesn't have the stomach for, you mean. Collecting money on wanted men's heads -- dead or alive. I always figured a bounty hunter was no better than a glorified judge, jury and executioner."

"We've got a warrant for the apprehension of an escapee. Theresa Jones."

"A woman, for God's sake? What'd she do? Run away from her husband an' he hired you to go and tote her back?"

"She a nigger," Dick spat, curling his lips.

"Must be a pretty dangerous one, seein' that firepower you're carrying."

Clement lowered his rifle and shoved a paper under Seth's nose.

"Ever seen her before?"

Accepting the poster, he studied the roughly drawn ink sketch.

"This might be any young woman of color. Not very detailed."

Irritated by the reply, the men grew impatient.

"We've been trackin' her all night; lost her a ways back. Them is tricky bastards."

"I won't have that language used around me or my family."

The warning worked its charm and the bounty hunters backed off.

"Sorry, Seth," Clement apologized. "But we gotta bring her in. It's the law," he added. "You seen her?"

"I have not. Been no one out this way for days."

"You lie to us," the elder of the three McConaghie boys hissed, "and you can find yerself in a heap o' trouble. Yer sentiments is well known in these parts."

"No more so than yours. Where's your father, by the way? He with you, too? I always expect to see Mathis around when there's easy pickings."

"I'm on my own tonight. Now, let us in so we can have a look around."

"I told you -- that woman's not here."

"Then you won't mind us pokin' our noses inside. Right?"

Seth hesitated then stepped aside. Clement tied the leash to the railing and lowered his weapon as he crossed the threshold. Squash leapt down from the window where he had been watching the proceedings and attacked, sinking white fangs into Brian's boot. The man let out a yell and tried to kick the dog away.

"Get that thing offa me or I'll plant a slug between its eyes!"

Before any action could be taken, the pup let go of its own accord and attacked Dick McConaghie. Using the rifle butt, he delivered a blow to the animal's back. It increased its yapping and would have gone after him, but for Seth's quicker movement. Grabbing it by the scruff, he dangled it in the air before tucking the writhing beast under his arm. Dick ran his tongue behind his front teeth.

"That damn hound. You bought him from my father."

"Bartered for him; for a basket of strawberries."

"That was a waste; he's worth twenty dollars."

"He-don't-hunt. That's what Mathis said."

Dick gave the speaker a queer look, then abandoned the subject.

"Theresa? Theresa! You better cume out if you know what's good fer ya. Make it easy on yerself. The longer you hide, the worse yer punishment. You know that." He turned to the homeowner. "She's run off befer."

"Then it would seem to me her... master's better off without her; seein' as all the trouble she's caused."

Clement snorted.

"That one's a Number One prime slave, 'Captain Ward.' You know what that means?"

"She's a human being some men call chattel."

"It means she's worth twelve hundred dollars. Prime breeding stock."

"Kansas is a free state."

The bounty hunters chuckled.

"Tell that to Dred Scott. The Su-preme Court of these U-nited States done decided that issue. A slave's a slave, whether he's in a free state or not. Mr. Jones is takin' her to Texas where he's got property. That male babe she's got wid her'll be worth $1,500 by the time he's growed."

"By the time he's twelve," Seth clarified, shivering in remembrance of the lecture he had heard in town.

Slave children grow rapidly to adulthood. By the age of twelve, boys are fully mature. Their voices have deepened; they have the beginnings of beards. They are capable of a full day's labor in the field. Girls develop womanly characteristics and are ready for reproduction. Yes, my friends, they grow but they are not adults. Intellectually, they remain boys and girls forever, incapable of rational decisions. For those, they must look to the white man.

The babbles of slave holders, repeated in derision by Reverend Thomas Pickering, rang in his ears. The lecture, itself, had been a tragedy, resulting in conflagration, rioting and looting. The Boston preacher had come to speak to the converted; to give them courage and in so doing, had sacrificed his life.

So the men and women in Kansas would have the words to use when confronted by just such a situation as he and Nelander now found themselves. Seth Ward did not think it a fair exchange, but his admiration for the slain abolitionist grew one hundredfold.

"I tell you: she is not here."

Dick McConaghie scratched his ear.

"We seed your place from the fields. Furst there was a light on, then there wasn't, then there was. She cume up to the door, you blew out the lamp to hide where you put her, then lit it back to fool us."

"I did nothing of the sort. The lamp was burning but the globe was too soiled to read by. So I blew it out to clean the glass and then re-lit it." Indicating the soiled shirt tail, his eyes narrowed at the accusation. "See?"

Irked by the rebuff, Clement called, "Theresa Jones! I know yer here!"

Sickened at the addendum of the owner's surname, a common practice denoting the status of property, Seth attempted to regain control of the struggling dog, then abandoned the effort. Crossing the living room, he dropped the puppy into his older daughter's room and shut him in. But not before the bounty hunters pushed inside.

Briefly inspecting behind the bed, they marched into Peter's room and checked before straddling the entranceway to the adult's sleeping chamber.

"We gotta look in there. Where's yer wife an' children, by the way?"

Before Seth could decide whether or not to lie, the door opened from inside and a sleepy-eyed child stared up at the men.

"What's the matter, papa?" Patricia inquired. Pretending to just recognize the newcomers, she smiled. "Hello, Mr. McConaghie; hello, Mr. Clement." Daring to express disapproval, she worked on a frown. "If you're looking for Mr. Windsor, we ain't seen him. He never come back after that night you an' your brothers and your pa came out here, Mr. McConaghie, wearin' hoods over your heads. Peter done asked the spirits to chase him off an' that's what they done, a'right."

Being reminded of that unpleasant event, Dick made a face and stepped back.

"No. We ain't lookin' fer him. It's another -- an African woman. A runaway. We got legal authority... this time. You seen her?"

Patricia shrugged and glanced over her shoulder. Peter slipped up beside her, using both hands to hold the mojo bag he wore around his neck.

"There ain't been no one here tonight. Jest papa an' Nelander an' Patricia an' baby Paula an' me. And mama."

The reference to his dead mother caused the townsmen to blanch. Removing one hand from his magic sack, the boy bit on a hangnail. His fingers were dirty. As though he had recently been digging in the ground. The agents separated themselves from him.

"We'll look outside."

Without daring to turn their backs, they shuffled away, only turning at the edge of the living room.

"We find yer hidin' that nigger, Ward, it'll go bad fer you. You bein' an upright citizen an' all, be a shame if you got throw'd in jail."

"Sheriff Bochner shoulda hanged you and your family when he had the chance. Stealing water from a well when the rest of us were dying from the drought. None of you are any good."

Dick grinned and put a hand out toward Squash. The pup bristled and refused the overture.

"Guess he don't remember me."

"Guess he does."

Raising his rifle, the oldest of the three McConaghie boys drew a bead on Seth. Locking eyes with the farmer over the gun sights, they held one another's glare until Brian Clement finally broke it up.

"He's got her hid in the barn. Let's go collect her an' git outta here."

Reluctantly lowering the weapon, for he had given the idea of pulling the trigger considerable thought, the bounty hunter followed his partner. Detaching the hounds, they allowed themselves to be led away. Seth did not dare take a breath until they were safely away in the yard. Taking that as a signal, Patricia and Peter ran to his side, each grabbing a hand in their own.

"Did we do all right, Captain Papa?'

"I know you said we weren't to come out, but I heard what those men were saying --"

"You did just fine."

"But where is Nelander? And Miss Theresa?"

Carefully detaching himself from their grasp, he put a finger to his lips and shook his head. They rightly interpreted it to mean, I do not know.

And wish to high heaven I did.

Heaven, in this case, being a little too close for comfort.

CHAPTER 2

Seth Ward watched from the porch as the two representatives of the Simpson Agency went through the barn. Muscles twitching as he heard them shout back and forth, his nerves frayed as one gave a particularly sharp holler. Unable to distinguish the words, he crept into the yard, his own rifle clutched between white knuckles. Only after discerning a narrow beam of light coming from beneath the cracks in the walls did he ease up on his grip.

Unable to discover anyone in the dark, they had gone to the trouble of lighting a lantern. If the women were inside, they had done a good job of hiding themselves.

Ten minutes later, the men emerged, bits of hay sprouting at odd angles from their clothing. Clement gave the dogs their head while McConaghie raised the lantern, casting an arc of light over the open space.

"You can put that back where you found it," Seth advised, an edge to his voice. "And I'll be sending a bill to your 'masters' for the oil you've burned."

"You do that, Capt'n Ward. I'll be sure to put my approval on it: ten cents owing. You come collect it in person, you hear?"

Spitefully leaving the lamp on the ground, he followed his partner as he wandered behind the house. This time, Seth followed.

Amazed at the newly cultivated field, McConaghie pushed back his hat and stared into the distance.

"What you got growing back here? Too stunted fer corn."

Hoping that by answering he would dissuade them from further investigation, he truthfully answered, "Strawberries."

"That's right. I fergot. This where you got 'em, ugh? How was the crop this year? Didn't see you peddlin' 'em in town."

"Don't make small talk with me. Finish your dirty business an' get off my property. I'll be ridin' into Lawrence tomorrow to swear out a complaint on you."

Dick chuckled and would have replied when Clement let out a cry.

"Sumethin's wrong wid the dogs!"

Both animals, which had been sniffing the ground with interest, pulled up short and began whining. Tails tucked between legs, ears drooping, they scratched at their muzzles, particles of saliva scattering to the four winds.

"What's a matter wid 'em?"

"Don't know. Got into sumthin' bad."

Dropping to one knee, Clement tried to console one of the hounds when another, more plaintive sound caught his ear. Freezing for a moment, head cocked to one side, he suddenly snapped his fingers. Abandoning the dogs, he scampered toward the outhouse.

"Found her! Listen to this, will you? As sweet a music as I ever done hear!" From within the narrow building, the thin, strident wail of a baby could be clearly distinguished. Reaching the privy, he pummeled on the door. "Come on out, Theresa. I hear that brat of yours! Game's up!"

From his position in the yard, Seth could just make out an amorphous shape behind the woodcut crescent moon. Heart sinking to his boots, he hurried over, debating whether to shoot the men in the back or try and create enough of a diversion for the slave to run free. He had not made up his mind when the door flew open from a kick originating within and Barbara Nelander emerged. Dodging the swinging partition, she permitted the inside hasp to catch before looking around in annoyance.

"What the hell is going on? Who are you, that you disturb a woman at her business?" Scrunching her eyes, she identified the intruders. "Dick McConaghie -- I should have guessed. You haven't got the manners of a pig. And who's that with you? Brian Clement. As low a cur as ever there was one." She tugged at her waist, where an open belt hung. "I knew you weren't gentlemen, but I never suspected you for Peeping Toms. Or were you hoping to catch a glimpse of something equally forbidden?"

Adjusting the baby at her breast, she fussed with her shawl, covering her body and incidentally the infant. The men grunted in consternation.

"Sorry, Miz Ward," Clement apologized. "We was lookin' fer --"

"Yes. I know what you 'was lookin' fer.' And that is a sin."

"No, ma'am. It weren't nuthin' like that."

"They are bounty hunters," Seth clarified, feeling the sweat trickle down his arm pits. "Searching for a runaway."

"Then God help him. Where have you got him tucked away, Captain? Down the well?" The two men flinched, eyes snaking toward the low stone retaining walls. Nelander snorted in derision. "Go look. Satisfy yourselves. Don't want it said we harbor fugitives."

Obliging from shame rather than expectation, they padded to the well and stared dawn the yawning hole. Dick listlessly poked the rope, then dropped the bucket down. It landed with a splash.

"There's no one down there," he needlessly explained to his partner. "Guess we better be goin'."

"You guess right." Seth pointed down the road. "Ride off my property. Next time you come by this way there'll be 'No Trespassing' signs put up. I don't give a damn if you are agents. Bounty hunters have to respect the law, and on this farm, my word is law. And if you can't read," he added in derision pointing to the flags which fluttered in the late night breeze, "then take a good look at them. One's the Skull and Crossbones. The other's called the Black Flag. Tell 'em what they mean."

Only too glad to oblige, Nelander walked toward the twin poles.

"The Jolly Roger signifies that pirates abide below. The other -- that dark standard -- signifies no mercy for our enemies. You've had your warning, Dick McConaghie and Brian Clement. After this, we use ever power at our command -- living and dead -- to protect ourselves." Gently petting the baby's face, she cooed, "It's all right, Paula." The child made a low gurgling noise. Nelander attentively listened, then bobbed her head.

"Children are notoriously close to the spirit world. Being so young, they remember the time before they were born, when everyone around them were spirits. Coming to earth, they retain a memory of that language. That's why Peter can talk to ghosts. It's not a bewitching," she stressed, "but a way of communication we adults don't understand. Spirits get mighty riled when one of their owns in trouble. I'm surprised you never heard Reverend Ginnis speak about that," she concluded, barely controlling her anger. "Seeing as how you're both God fearing churchgoers."

"Jest doin' a job, Miz Ward. We'll be goin', now. Sorry fer troublin' you all."

Scurrying toward their horses, the bounty hunters mounted and spurred the animals, whistling for the dogs to follow. Dried summer dust flew up from eight hooves as they thundered away. Neither Seth nor Nelander moved until the pair had disappeared from sight. Only then, did "Miz Ward" heave a sigh of relief. Seth sprang upon her.

"That was masterful! Pretending that baby was Paula. But where is Miss Theresa?"

"I think, sir, that I would use a word other than 'masterful.' As I have been reminded, 'master' has a far different connotation on land than it does at sea." Handing him the tiny black infant, she strode to the outhouse. Bending over, she peered under the door. "No legs showing. No one here. Or is there?" Prying open the door, she stood back, revealing the Negress squatting on top of the privy seat. A gush of trapped air escaped Seth's lungs.

"Well, I'll be a monkey's uncle!"

"A comment, I am certain, with which Mr. Darwin would agree. We," she indicated, including the young woman, "are all one family. Although, I suspect the naturalist would be inclined to include McConaghie and Clement in a branch of the human race more closely aligned to rattlesnakes than people."

"Ain't that a pisser!" All eyes turned toward the speaker, who happened to be a boy in communication with spirits. The cussing, however, had less to do with the supernatural than of an opportunity seized. His father grunted and pointed toward the house.

"I thought you were told to stay put until called for."

"I was. But I thought I might be needed. I didn't like the idea of them Port Authorities boardin' our ship."

"Peter -- this is not a game."

"No, sir. It ain't."

Seeing little use debating the point at this juncture, he indicated they go back to the house. Once safely within and the curtains drawn, the Wards and their guests gathered at the table. Hesitant to relinquish the greedily sucking babe, Nelander directed Patricia to prepare a cold meal for Theresa while Seth boiled water. Grateful but ashamed of her need, the young woman reached for her offspring.

"Ah take da boy frum yuh, Miz. Ah don' want yuh habe to feed a nigger chil' frum yuhr own breast."

"Let me straighten you out on several accounts, Miss Theresa. First, we do not use the word 'nigger' aboard our property. It is offensive to us as well, I expect, as to you. Second, I do not 'have' to feed him. I want to. It is my choice. You said you were unable to produce milk. Fortunately, I have more than enough for -- What is his name?"

"Samuel, Miz."

"My own baby's needs are adequately met and it is my pleasure to care for Samuel. Before Mr. Giles returns, we will supply you with a bottle and nipple for the journey. How were you feeding him before?"

"Da masta -- Mr. Jones -- had 'nuther... black woman wid him. She be feedin' da babe."

"She, too, had a child?"

"Ah 'spect she did, but Ah neber seed it. Mr. Jones done bought me 'cross da riber. Dat be two weeks 'go."

"Where is your husband? The child's father?"

"Ah dunno, Miz. We was sold at auction on da court house steps. In Liberty."

"Missouri," Seth explained. Nelander winced at the inappropriate town name.

"Mah man wen' to one masta an' me to 'nudder." Tears welled in her eyes but bravery and perhaps a resignation to fate gave her the stoicism to control herself.

"I am terribly sorry," Nelander softly replied.

The conversation lagged as the Wards allowed the woman to eat her supper. Although they might have expected her to use fingers to shovel in the bread and cheese, she demurely employed fork and knife, cutting small, bite-sized pieces and taking pains to chew properly before swallowing. When served a mug of steaming tea, however, she cried in surprise.

"Yuh make a brew ob da African herbs, Miz?"

"We call it tea. It is brewed with dried black leaves to make a stronger cup, although I have also had green tea, which is somewhat weaker and has a different flavor. What you are drinking comes from China. A different continent, entirely, although they may grow tea or something similar in Africa. I do not know."

"Where yuh learn to steep dis -- tea?"

"Aboard ship." Noting the expression of surprise, Nelander smiled. "I was born into a seaman's family and went to work when I was five. I spent most of my life on the ocean before coming to Kansas."

"Yuh been to Af-rica?"

"No. Nor have I ever been to China, although such were my plans before my father, Captain Nelander, was murdered. Many ships serve hot tea. Working outdoors is hard work and in the higher latitudes, it is cold. Getting something warm inside is not only life sustaining, it fortifies the body."

"They serve rum, too," Peter promptly supplied. "That does a bit o' fortifyin', too. Knocks you off your feet if you're not careful. Mebbe Miss Theresa needs a flagon."

"I think in this case, she is better off with tea."

Undeterred, he turned to the newcomer. "Pirates drink a lot of rum. Especially after they've fought a battle. Like tonight."

"I am afraid we had better save off on celebrating until we can fairly say we've won," Seth decided. "You can sleep in Patricia's bed tonight, Miss Theresa. The rest of us will take turns standing guard until daylight."

Again nearly overcome by emotion, the young woman fought off tears.

"Why yuh do dis fo' meh? Yuh put yuhrse'f in mos' terrible danger."

Instead of answering, he drummed his fingers.

"How is it you came under Mr. Giles' protection?"

"And who is he?" Nelander asked, leaning forward, elbows on the table.

"Ah don' know him, Miz." Throwing back her head, her eyes hardened. "Afta dat debil masta laid his hands on meh, Ah know'd Ah had to git away. So Ah waited until he fell 'sleep den wrapped mah chil' in da blanket an' ran. Ah cum out ob da woods in Nigger Hole an' one ob da womens dere hid meh in her hut. She went an' fetched dat Mista Giles. He said he was gonna take me to da Big House, but den he says we couldn't git through 'cause dere was men hangin' round. Dey was gettin' out da hounds to look fo' meh. So we went acrost da fields. And cume out here."

"Speaking of hounds," Seth interrupted, addressing his wife. "What did you lay down to set off the dogs?"

"Chili powder, of course. I figured if it were good enough to pizzon the contestants at the Eatin' Contest, it'd have the same effect of four-legged critters. It wouldn't have done me any good to bluff my way out of the water closet if the dogs kept barking at the door."

"Damn good idea!" Patricia approved. Receiving a scowl, she contritely amended, "Damned good idea." Her parents let it pass, turning back to the runaway.

"Did Giles take you to another house, first? Near here? Where Blind Betty and Mute Thomas live? Two people of color?"

"No, Miz. We went through da fields, den into da long wood. Ah dunno dat he meant to take me here, but onest he heard dem hounds close by, we crossed da stream an' headed in dis direction. Didn't stop nowhere's else."

The adults caught one another's eye.

"McConaghie already knew there were Negroes living at the Windsor's old homestead. Since they were in the vicinity, that'd be the first place he checked."

"I suppose he would. I hope they're all right."

"I'll have to check."

Suppressing her first impulse to say, I'll go with you, Nelander nodded. It would not do to leave their vulnerable guest in charge of children.

"All right. Take the rifle."

"Had a mind to leave it with you. And when things quiet down," he pursued, "it wouldn't hurt for you -- and Patricia and Peter -- to get in some target practice. Much as I hate to say it, there may come a time when you need the skill."

Attempting to put a softer touch on the dire presentment, she gently poked him in the ribs.

"My prowess in shooting Terrance in the chest did not impress you?"

"Might have, had you actually pulled the trigger. Not that I doubt your resolve," he hastened to assuage. "But I was thinking of aiming at a target a might farther away. Even Blind Betty couldn't have missed from point blank range." Absently scratching behind his ear, he stared at the ceiling. "Even if this hadn't happened tonight, I was gonna speak to you. Been giving a lot of thought to what you said."

"Which was?"

"How a man or a boy, who's better able to fend for himself, goes out armed, while a girl or a woman has no instruction in firearms. Not that I'd want Patricia to have to shoot a horse if it broke its leg, but your point was well taken. Don't know what kind of vermin any of us are likely to encounter until this secession matter gets settled."

A second protest died on her lips. The idea of "get settled" meant one thing to him and another to her.

"It is agreed. We will have Patricia draw some likenesses of unwelcome vermin and post them on a board in the field. That will make the stakes more interesting."

"Got anyone's face in mind?"

"We can start with Mathis McConaghie. I am sure there will be others."

Uneasy at the casual bloodthirstiness of the comment, of which he could find no fault, Seth rose and started for the door.

"I'll be back in an hour."

"See to it you keep the timetable. It is four bells, now -- ten o'clock. If you are not home by eight bells, I will come after you. And shoot anything that moves. Nor will I be aiming at the head, sir. It is too small a target. The bastard who runs foul of me shall lose his manhood."

"A point well taken. I will return on time," which she had wisely increased by an hour. Making a bow to their guest, he settled a broad-rimmed hat over his head and shuffled toward the door. Despite the threat, Barbara followed and shoved the rifle in his hand. Feeling the weight drag him down, he addressed the children.

"Crew, behave yourselves. Do as Nelander says. And make our guests feel at home."

"We will be standing guard, Captain Papa."

On another night, he would have relieved them of other duties and dispatched them to bed. Yet, in so short a time, the hours of darkness had become their enemy, no longer a period of innocent repose.

The thought depressed him. No more so when he stepped outside and caught sight of the two flags flying prominently outside the house.

One skull, two crossed bones and a square of black.

Harbingers of death.

CHAPTER 3

No lights shone through the windows. Not, in itself, a warning of danger. Farmers lived by the maxim, "Early to bed, early to rise." Hesitating in the trees just before the yard formerly belonging to the Windsors, Seth tried to remember the rest of the rhyme. He might have summoned the lines more quickly, but he meant the memory exercise for a delaying tactic so that his senses might explore while his mind churned.

> Early to bed, early to rise....
>> Gives the cook time to bake pies.
>> Helps a fella keep his size.
>> Ties his tongue from telling lies.

And those other, less amusing rhymes.

> Early to bed, early to rise...
>> One long prayer that he doesn't dies.
>> And if he wakes, it's one hell of a surprise.

He never did get around to,

> Makes a man health, wealthy and wise.

Which was probably just as well. In truth, it had less verity.

Finally assured by his instincts, if not his propensity for lyrics, Seth hefted the deer rifle which had never actually been fired at a deer, and marched into the open space fronting the house. The action made him an easy target if an enemy loitered in the tall grass grown over the cavity which had once been a barn.

Lacking any clear idea who might wish to take a pot shot, he gave them ample opportunity while crossing the yard. Muscles stiffened, ears attuned for the cock of a hammer, he made it safely to the porch. Pursing his lips in wonder at his luck, he started to knock, then suddenly thought better of it. Playing back the peculiar summons the interloper had used on his own door, he repeated the sounds.

Three sharp raps, a pause, followed by two more.

Before he could set himself, the knob turned and a voice whispered, "Cume in. Quick."

He obeyed with the absolute certainly the invitation had not been meant for him.

Rather than delay the surprise his presence would occasion, he boldly announced, "It is I, Miss Betty. Seth Ward."

An intake of breath confirmed his assumption.

"Capt'n Ward!"

Assessing that the old woman and her grown son had not suffered at the hands of the Simpson agents, he signaled she relax. Although she was sightless, he had enough experience with Betty's powers of divination to expect she would detect and rightly interpret the motion.

Stepping past the threshold, the unintentional co-conspirator politely removed his hat.

"We are all right. There have been visitors to the house."

Carefully guarding her tone, Betty inquired, "Who dey be?"

Suspecting she knew more than the question implied, Seth walked into the room he let to the family and took in the scene. Nothing appeared different than on previous visits. Baskets of all sizes and shapes hung from the walls, while in the center of the room, several freshly hewn planks set atop tree stumps served as a work bench. Piles of reeds for weaving, spools of ribbon used as decoration and thin branches for handles covered all but a small portion. A wicker chair, seat covered by an Afghan, was positioned by the open space where she plied her craft.

"Ah light da lamp."

Adeptly moving through the house, she stuck a thatch of straw into simmering coals from the stove, blew on them to create a flame, then touched the homemade match to a wick floating in a pool of dark liquid. Light, less intrusive than that given off by kerosene, created a modicum of brightness.

Taking the dried gourd serving as a lamp, Betty placed it on the bench. He waited until preparations were complete before answering the previously placed question.

"A man knocked on our door. He used the same signal I gave you. What does it mean?"

Sucking in her cheeks, she debated how best to reply.

"What dis man look like?"

"He wore a long coat and had a hat pulled over his face. It was difficult to determine specific features."

"Giles," she hissed in what may or may not have been approval. "What he want?"

"He was not supposed to come to us. His destination was the Windsor farm, if I guess right."

"Yah, suh." The admission carried no contrition. "Weh been waitin' fo' him." A pause, then, "What he say? 'bout cuming to yuhr place?"

"It is not what he said but what I inferred. Those tracking him were locals -- men of the community, not out-of-staters as expected. They already knew Negroes lived here and thus were likely -- even willing -- participants in his illegal act."

"He'pin' runaways escape."

"Yes. Did they come here? The bounty hunters?"

"Dey did. Ah let dem search da place. Didn't find nuthin' so dey went off." She hesitated, then asked, "Giles habe da woman an' da babe wid him?"

Had he been a lesser man, the audacity would have riled him, for Giles -- and by association -- Betty and Thomas -- had put his family at grave risk. Without forewarning or prior approval.

"He did. Miss Theresa and Samuel."

"Ah." Intuitively sensing the moment lay on her shoulders, Betty bade him sit. "Ah made sume tea."

He did not want to drink, but to rush the interview meant endangering a friendship already strained by common danger and secretiveness. Instead of using the chair by the reeds, he followed her into the kitchen, settling into one at the table. Watching how adeptly the blind woman went about the chore, he waited until water had boiled and been poured over dried leaves before continuing.

Serving him the mint tea with a small crock of honey, Betty opted to remain standing as he drank.

"Dem men -- da ones followin' Giles -- dey make it to da Pirate Treasure?"

Her use of the familiar name for their farm did not evoke surprise for she and her son had duly been recruited as buccaneers. Catching his attention, however, was the omission of the title "mister" before Giles' name. Three times she had spoken it and in no instance adorned it with any form of respect. Habitually well mannered, Seth could put no explanation to Betty's lack of formality.

"They did."

"Dick McConaghie and Brian Clement," she identified.

"Correct. They wore badges from the Simpson Agency. You know of this outfit?"

"Ah do, suh. Dey be slabe hunters outta St. Louis." She pronounced the word in the French style, San Louie. "Da man who operates it be a col'nel in da state militia."

"Kansas is not Missouri. They have no legal authority here."

"Neber stopped 'em befo'. Dey cross ober when dey on da trail ob darkies runnin' 'way. Ah ain't neber heard ob dem recruitin' agents as far 'way as Law'rence, dough. Usual, dey do der own dirty work. Dis be bad."

"I am not surprised at the two they hired. Both are bad men."

"Yas, sur. Dat dey be. Bad men." Wrapping a shawl closer around her shoulders, Betty warmed her thin hands over the steam coming from the tea pot. "Pray da Lor' dey didn't gibe yuh no mo' trouble."

"We let them search the house and barn."

Her foot brushed against a chair leg, making a discordant scraping noise. "Dey fin' da woman an' babe?"

"No, ma'am. They did not. Nelander hid them in the outhouse. When they went to check there, she came out with the baby at her breast, pretending it was Paula. Her... seaman's language frightened them off."

Betty finally smiled. "Dat be good, suh! Real good. But what about da houn's?"

"A bit of chili pepper on the ground rendered them useless."

"Dat chili pepper, ag'in! It be a blessin' frum above."

He matched her grin. "I don't know about that. Nelander would say it 'be' a blessing from Mexico."

"Dat, too." Hearing a nearly unperceivable sound from behind, she motioned Thomas join them. He entered through the rear door, nodding respectfully at Seth. "Set down, boy, an' habe some tea wid da Capt'n."

The assumption of privilege underscored the equality bestowed by the conversation and the officer's complicity in their illegal activity. Thomas reluctantly obeyed his mother. Shoulders rounded, he contemplated the floor for a moment, then shyly reached out a hand and laid it on Seth's. Without words, he expressed his devotion and respect.

Sandwiching the black man's hand between his own, they sealed a new pact.

"Mister Giles is to come tomorrow night and get the woman and baby. Where does he take them from here?"

Purposely using a title, Seth tried to observe a reaction from his tenants and saw none.

"Across da riber into da Nebraska Territory. Frum dere, dey fin' a guide takes dem further north."

"To Canada?"

This elicited a wider smile. "Canada be a mighty fine place, suh. Ah knows ob sumeone hereabouts what cume frum dere. A seaman, Ah heard tell. Wid a whole mouthful ob salty language an' da brass to stan' up to spooks an' bounty hunters. Yuh know dis person, Mista Seth?"

Her use of the word "Mister" was not lost on him.

"I do, indeed. In fact, I married her!"

"Speaks well fo' you, Capt'n." The smile faded and a seriousness swept over her tightly drawn features. "But don' t'ink we meant to inbolve yuh. Giles never had no orders to take Theresa to da Pirate Treasure. He shoulda gone on; went to da riber."

The statement revealed two facts: she would not use a title when speaking of the guide, and that she and Thomas were fully away of the plan, if not its originators.

"The Kaw River is a long way away. The dogs were on their trail and the baby was hungry. Miss Theresa cannot give milk. Before Mr. Giles returns tomorrow evening, we will give her a bottle and... flagon of cow's milk to take on the journey."

"Ah t'ank yuh, suh."

Having ascertained the family survived the incident unmolested and receiving more than his fill of information, Seth finished the contents of the cup, stifled a yawn and spread hands across the table.

"I best be getting back. If I do not return within two hours, the newly promoted Captain Nelander has promised to come looking for me. Discovering I tarried for tea rather than any good purpose, I am likely to find myself sleeping in the barn."

Meaning it only half seriously, the old woman took him at his word and applied pressure to his arm, forcing his attention to her face. Staring into the sliver of glazed orbs just discernible under the permanently lowered eyelids, he absorbed a warning.

"Yuh speak lightly, Capt'n Ward, but heed mah meanin'. Do not eben t'ink ob dat. A man sleeps in the hay, he leaves an impression." Her words assumed grammatical clarity, reminding him again she had the gift of language, though rarely employed. Her use of it now shook him to the core. "An experienced tracker will recognize that and put a different interpretation to it: that you were harboring a slave. No amount of explaining will convince him otherwise."

Gliding from the table, she went to her workbench and came back with a scrap of leather, roughly six inches square. Although he saw no writing, sinuous lines and markings had been burned into the surface, indicating it for a type of crude map. Prominent among the markings were several small images. The image of a butternut squash hung from the top. At an angle which bore a significance he could not place.

"Yuh know what dis be?"

His spontaneous reply left no room for doubt.

"A treasure map."

Betty clucked her tongue, head barely moving. He could not tell whether his identification pleased her or the contrary.

"Yas, suh. Dat it be. Yuh know what 'treasure' be hid?"

"Contraband."

Her reaction surprised him. Throwing back her head, she laughed.

"No, suh. Da runaways, dey mobe too fast to be marked on inny map. What else?"

Seth tried to get another look at the leather remnant but she withdrew it from his inspection.

"I do not know." And then, more coyly, "Let me see it again."

"Yuh seed 'nuf. Mo' den what's good fo' yuh. It be a map ob safe houses."

A cold sweat dripped from under his armpits.

"Where those helping colored people escape live?"

"Dat's it. Yuhr farm on it."

"Did you put it there?"

"Say, suh, yuhr good heart done dat. Dere are odders. Yuh don' need to know who dey are."

"One day I might." The protest fell on deaf ears.

"Ah pray to da Lor' dat neber be da case. To know too much is to endanger all." Her lower lip jutted as a second wave of fear chilled his spine. "But Ah be speakin' ob maps. Da bounty hunters got der own set ob maps. Marked wid 'X's'. Dey put down the homes ob does dey knows to be -- sympathetic -- to da Cause. When dey on da trail, dats where dey start. Yuh don' wanna be no 'X' on dose maps. Leabin' an impression in da straw -- dat tip 'em off. An' yuh marked." Her voice lowered. "One day, dey cume an' burn yuh out. Or hang yuh."

His fists tightened. "I've faced that once, already."

"So yuh did." A hesitation, then, "Yuh was lucky."

"Why is that?" he asked. Betty shook her head. "Because Nelander put a stop to Terrance Windsor before he and the McConaghies could finish what they started? Where is he, by the way? Do you know?"

She started, then frowned. "Who?"

"Terrance Windsor."

"Why yuh axin' me?"

For once, Seth Ward pressed his advantage.

"Because you seem to know a lot more about these things than I do. The sheriff put out a wanted poster on him after the incident at the Pirate

Treasure. I didn't want him to, but Bochner said he broke the law and he'd be punished for it if he ever showed up again. Kind of made me feel...." Not wanting to describe the emotion as "bad," yet finding no suitable word, Seth let it drop. Instead, he leaned over. "I had no idea about maps and X's or any organized resistance against agents plying their... legal trade." If he meant to shock, he did not succeed. "Who is Giles and how do you know him?"

"Mista Seth, Ah knows yuh fo' a good man. Dere are odders knows da same. Sume good men, sume bad men. It be a dangerous worl' in which we libe. Dese times an' da circumstances set men apart. Sume it makes stronger; odders weaker. Ah don' know what happened to Mista Windsor an' his fambly. Ah ax' around, seein' as Ah knows mo' 'bout dese t'ings den yuh do."

"Now, you mock me."

The accusation elicited a deadly serious response.

"No, suh. Neber. Ah lay don' mah life fo' yuh, it cume to dat. So would Thomas. Yuh an' Nelander part human bein', part angel. Ah neber meant to put yuh in harm. Giles, he went to yuh on his own. Ah neber gabe him permission. No, suh."

"All right. I accept you at your word. Nor am I complaining. But I would have appreciated some forewarning of what you were involved in." Her right eyelid twitched. "Is it something new?"

"No, suh. It be as old as slabery."

"Your involvement."

"No, suh."

"I see. Something you did -- helping runaways -- before you came here?"

"Yas, suh."

"And you will say no more?"

"It be better dat way." Thomas began signing but Seth could not interpret the hand signals and Betty could not see them. Frustrated, the grown son crept nearer, taking his mother's hand and drawing symbols in her palm. She replied in a language Seth did not understand, then turned to the captain. "He says we pack up an' leabe."

"No, ma'am. That is not what I want. You and Thomas are pirates; we belong to the same ship. Nelander will never release you from the Articles you signed. Nor will Patricia and Peter. Besides," he tried, working on a twisted grin. "If you go, who will tend the strawberries in the valley? They are vital to our survival. In fact, there are some to be harvested in the field behind the house. The ice storm stunted their growth, but those which survived are just now producing fruit."

"Dat be so?"

He took her to mean hers and Thomas' inclusion in their family as well as laborers, and made an approving noise deep in his throat.

"That be so. Tomorrow -- or the day after -- you must come and help us pick."

"We be dere, suh. An'... t'ank yuh."

"Very well. Good night, mother. Good night, brother."

Waving a farewell, he showed himself out. A breeze had come up and the moving air felt fresh on his feverish brow.

Anyone's guess how long that would last.

Ill winds arose quickly across the plains of Kansas.

CHAPTER 4

Seth saw Nelander coming across the hills. Instead of hurrying to meet her, he waited until she came up alongside.

"You were late getting back."

"I was."

"Is everything all right?"

"I cannot rightly answer that, for... everything... has altered."

Taking her hand, more to reassure himself she existed than to bestow comfort, they made their way back toward the Pirate Treasure.

"Are you going to tell me?"

"It appears our fellow buccaneers are a way-station along the Underground Railroad."

Her fingers tightened around his.

"So that is what all this was about tonight."

"Yes. Giles was supposed to take his charges to Blind Betty. From there, I presume Thomas would take them on to the next stop."

"What happened to prevent that?"

"There aren't many who know we have Negroes living at the Windsor place but the McConaghies do. Once Giles discovered who was on his trail, he had to change plans."

"And Betty knew all this?"

"She did. She and Thomas have apparently been involved in this sort of activity for years."

"Interesting way to find out."

"I thought so, too."

"What do we do next?"

"Pass Theresa and the baby along tomorrow night. And then wait and see."

Turning to stare into his face, Nelander did not need the light of the moon to read his expression.

"That makes us conspirators."

"Yes."

She sighed and swung her legs in an easy seaman's jaunt. "Good. The crew will like that."

Seth stopped cold. Still attached to her, he broke the rhythm.

"Surely you do not mean to tell them."

"Surely I do."

"But they are just children."

"Children with a firm grasp of reality. It is unwise to lie to them, Seth. If we gloss over what we have all just been through -- or are going through," she amended, "careless words may give us away. An innocent comment in town -- at church -- or to some man wearing a badge -- and we are in serious trouble. No: they must be made aware of the danger. In fact, if I may be so bold, Captain Ward, I suggest we hold a Council of War."

"I have been through one of those before," he groaned. "And as I recall, my position was voted down."

"But not without considerable discussion -- and a shared commitment to the consequences."

"What you mean is, I was wrong and the rest of you right."

Stopping so suddenly her shadow collided with his, causing an impact both felt, Nelander planted her feet in the warm, moist earth.

"'Wrong or right' implies that we debated an issue of morality. That was not the case. Say, rather, we weighed the lesser of two evils and by putting our four minds together, came up with a solution temporarily staving off disaster. Besides," she added, resuming their walk, "it was you who saved Patricia's cameo."

His body twitched as though a ghost had walked across his grave.

"By violence."

"'A time for war, and a time for peace.'"

Dismissing, or perhaps silently acknowledging the Biblical quotation, Seth let his eyes roan across the open plain. Ears attuned to the sounds of nature from childhood, he absorbed the rustle of wind bending but not bowing the tall grasses; the scurry of a field mouse furtively seeking sustenance. The buzz of a mosquito; the strident chirp of a cricket. In the distance, the yap of a coyote.

Life begetting death. The survival of the fittest. The triumph of weak over strong.

A scenario appreciated only by the fortunate.

Those which lived to see the dawn, whether by cunning or chance.

Seth Ward did not feel lucky and he doubted his skills.

The world he knew had turned against him. Not in a personal sense, but rather with the disinterest of a third party. Passionless and lacking soul.

The way drought blanketed a landscape.

Or the way a bullet struck an inanimate object.

Guilty or innocent, contrite or arrogant, young or old.

Death stalked the land. It would reap what it had no right to sow; raping laughter, begetting widow's weeds.

"Who did you leave on guard?" he suddenly demanded, shivering in the warmth of the Kansas night.

"Herman. I called him in from the corn field and set him to watch the house."

He had expected a different answer and lacked a rebuttal. They continued in silence.

In the morning Seth unearthed one of the bottles used when Peter was an infant and rigged a rubber nipple to the top. Filling it with warm milk from Bessie, the resident cow, he offered it to Theresa so she might feed Samuel. Greedy lips drawing liquid through the narrow opening proved the success of the experiment.

"Takes to it like a duck to water," Nelander declared. By the time Giles comes tonight, we'll have put together a traveling case for you. More milk, change of diapers and some clothes. We cannot have our young gentleman go about his journey clad only in a nightshirt."

Taking the young mother and her own crew into the bedroom Paula shared with her parents, Barbara opened a drawer and rummaged through the clothes.

"Two pair of socks, a baby shirt long enough to fit an elephant's trunk --"

"What is an elephant?" Peter interrupted.

Nelander affected surprise. "You do not have elephants in Kansas? I thought they were indigenous to the Midwest."

"If we got 'em, I ain't seen 'em."

"You cannot rightly say that, if you do not know what they look like."

"Is it some sort of sea beast?" Patricia inquired. "Like a whale?"

"Not quite that size. Say, between a whale and a horse. In fact, an elephant has some characteristics of a horse. Fetch your sketch pad and you draw what I describe."

The girl hurried to carry out the order and the family perched on the wide, hard mattress, eagerly awaiting a description. Even Captain Papa came in, pretending to be looking for a fresh shirt while watching over his daughter's shoulder.

"Begin with four legs and a massive midsection," the world traveler declared. "No -- shorter legs -- and thicker. This wide," she demonstrated, holding hands apart. "And broad, flat feet. Like dinner plates, but soft on the bottoms; no hooves." Peter gasped in wonder.

"How can it move around wid legs like that? Ain't never gonna win no race wid them clod-hoppers."

"You would be surprised how fast they can move -- particularly if one is charging you. All right," she continued, directing Patricia's pencil. "A wide girth, then a short neck and a large head. No, no -- not ears like a horse but big, floppy ones."

"That can't be real," Seth scoffed, observing the animal's features come to life. "You are making this up."

"I assure you such a creature does exist."

"Where?"

"In northern Africa. In the savannas -- the grasslands."

Theresa's eyes grew as wide as an elephant's feet.

"In Africa, Miss?"

"Yes, indeed. They may live in other parts of the world, as well, but the elephant I saw was brought from Africa."

"Like da slabes!"

Blinking in surprise, Nelander gave the statement consideration.

"I suppose that is true, although it pains me to think so."

"What dese ele-pents do, Miss? Dey work in da fields?"

"I imagine they are used as beasts of burden in their native land. I really cannot say, never having made a study. The one I saw was in a circus. A man rode on its back while it pushed around barrels with its trunk."

Peter scrunched his face. "It brung a trunk wid it from Africa? Like the one we're makin' for Miss Theresa?"

His mother grinned and redirected Patricia's fingers. "A trunk, in this case, is a very long nose. "Here," she indicated. "Draw a curling appendage -- about this thick." Again she demonstrated and the artist adapted the width to coordinate with the image on her paper. "That's right! Excellent. There you have it -- an elephant!"

Seth scraped his foot along the bare floor.

"Looks like a sea monster to me. Sure you didn't see this thing after Captain Nelander'd passed around a mite too much rum?"

"He was very thrifty and I seriously doubt in his entire career he ever dispensed enough to make a jack tar woozy."

"Dis da mos' beautiful ani'mule Ah eber did see. An ele-pent. What color dey be, miss?"

"Grey."

Theresa clapped her hands. "Dat be fine! A'most black! Like colored folk."

"Exactly right."

"An' it be strong?"

"Very powerful. Stronger than any five horses or any ten men."

"Ah gonna adopt dis ele-pent fo' Samuel. Ah gonna pray to da spirit ob da ele-pent to protect him. Yes, Miss," she decided with solemnity. "He gonna be Samuel Ele-pent frum now on."

"A good name."

Glancing at her father for approval, Patricia removed the paper from the hard-cover binding fastened with ribbon hinges and offered it to their guest.

"Then I reckon you ought to have this; to show the baby when he gets older. He'll never believe it if you just try and describe such a magnificent creature to him."

"Why don't you sign your artwork?" Seth suggested. "That way, he'll have an original Patricia Ward drawing. One day, perhaps he will have a house of his own and frame it above his fireplace."

Blushing under the compliment, she hesitated, then made a large "X" in the lower right hand corner. Her father frowned.

"You can write your name. Your penmanship is better than mine. A person only signs an 'X' when he can't make letters."

"Yes, sir. I know. But I was thinking if something happened. If the picture gets lost and a bad man finds it, he'll see my name. Everyone knows the Wards. They might use it against us."

The dire prediction put a damper on the moment. To know they lived in frightening times bore enough weight. But to hear it proclaimed from the lips of a child underscored the omnipresent danger.

"Very well. A good thought," he agreed. Nelander attempted to lighten the mood.

"When you are safe in Canada, Theresa, and in the company of good people, then you may write the name above the mark. 'Patricia Ward.' That will give it dual significance: a flight from bondage and a celebration of freedom."

"Ah do dat, Miss. Ah won' neber fergit dis day -- or what yuh all done fo' meh an' Samuel Ele-pent. Da Lor' He bless yuh."

Holding the child in one hand and the drawing in the other, she stooped to kiss the babe. He smiled in return.

For just a second the Wards could believe her hopeful benediction.

Giles came at midnight. He wore the same clothing and hat pulled low. This time, Nelander took particular note of his gloves. Not the type used by farmers to protect their hands in the fields or by cattle drovers, accustomed to long hours in the saddle. There were -- she could not think of an adequate description. Not fancy dress gloves suitable for gentlemen about town, nor even Sunday-go-to-Meeting gloves. The closest she could come to a descriptive word was "disguise."

Barbara did not doubt that conductors along the Underground Railroad needed to hide their identities. But the Wards already knew his name and that presumably he lived in or around Lawrence. Not difficult to further identify, surely. And then there was the disquieting feeling she had met him somewhere before. Yet a period of twenty-four hours had not jogged her memory.

Shaking off the suspicion, she lunged for Squash which had commenced a frenzied peel of barking the moment his acute ears detected the stranger's presence come up the walk. Scooping him under the belly, still rounded from puppy fat, she passed him over to Peter.

"Lock him in the bedroom."

"Yes, sir."

When Giles seemed indisposed to talk, she ushered their guests into the living room.

"We have made a small bundle," she continued. "A bottle and milk; some clothes for Samuel. And provided Theresa with a new outfit. As a disguise," she tried, fishing for a reaction. His face did not change expression.

"That is well. Her wardrobe was, no doubt, described to the agents. Thank you." He forced the last as if feelings of gratitude were a foreign emotion.

Hurriedly kissing the mother and child, Nelander stepped back, allowing Patricia and Peter to do the same.

"You take care, now. We'll say our prayers for you."

"An' remember that pirates is lookin' out for you. You may make it all the way to the ocean. To Nova Scotia. There's a hot bed of 'em."

"Ah neber fergit da pirates Ah met here. Dem who's brabe enuf to fight off mos' innythin'. An' da ele-pent. When Ah git to Freedom, Ah's gonna put lil' Samuel on da back ob one ob dem creatures, fo' sure."

"You do that."

"Hurry."

Making a low curtsy to Seth and then another to Barbara, she wiped away a tear, then passed through the door left open by Giles. Seth offered to shake.

"Good luck."

The courier hesitated so long he did not think he would accept the gesture. Finally shoving out a hand, he gripped more tightly than expected, then touched the brim of his hat.

"Remember: not a word to anyone." Addressing the woman of the house, a light finally shone in his eye. "You have had a good harvest of strawberries?"

She could not have been more surprised had he inquired of her familiarity with the Man in the Moon.

"For a second season, more than we anticipated. The ice storm put us back, some, but those in the valley survived nicely. The plants in the patch behind the house are ready to be picked."

"How much money did you make?"

The audacity of the question annoyed Seth but Nelander provided the answer.

"Three hundred; plus what we will make in the next few weeks. Fifty dollars, perhaps. Next year," she added from pride, "will be better."

"Ah Sometimes the best bargains are those never made."

Before she could recover, he slipped away, a shadow in the night. No one spoke until Squash finally stopped backing, indicating the man, woman and child had put adequate distance between themselves and the house.

Patricia let the pup out and he scrambled around the room, nose to the floor, tail madly wagging. Finally assuring himself that all be well within, the animal scratched to be let out. Peter went to comply but his father prohibited.

"Not now."

"But he has to do his business, Captain Papa."

"No. He is on the scent. He will trail our friends for miles and give away their position." Frowning, he tugged at his ear. "Mathis said he would not hunt. That's why he traded him to us."

"It appears he was wrong," his wife observed, ushering the crew together. "Time for bed. It is very late and there are chores waiting for you in the morning."

"Seems to be this is a call for rum."

"When we hear Miss Theresa is safely away, then. Perhaps Off you go."

Reluctantly obeying orders, the pair made the rounds for good night kisses, then shuffled off to their own rooms. Barbara indicated the kitchen.

"Peter is not far off but for the wrong reason. Would you like a dram of Captain Nelander's finest to settle the nerves?"

He answered, but not the question.

"A man like Mathis doesn't make a mistake on a dog. Dogs are his livelihood. This one here has a nose as good as any. And an eagerness born into his race. He'd hunt, all right. So why did he give him to us? With the warning we keep him and not give him away?"

"If you are asking me to diving the reasoning of a man no better than a cold-blooded killer, I am afraid you are barking up the wrong tree." Seth did not smile. Retiring to the kitchen, she put the kettle on the stove. "I will make some tea. I am too restless to sleep."

Seth settled into his chair, then finding himself as ill at ease as she, joined her. When the water boiled and the beverage steeped, Nelander placed a square of cheesecloth over the cups to catch the loose leaves as she poured.

"When we are wealthy, I shall surely buy myself a tea ball. A silver one. From England."

"Why England?"

"Because my father once bought one there."

"Your father used a silver tea ball? Hardly the image I have of him."

"For my mother."

"Oh." And then, lacking anything better to say, added, "I am sure she appreciated it."

Barbara started to let it pass, then shrugged. "I don't know what she appreciated. But I surely doubt she could be bribed by gifts."

Carrying his mug to the window, Seth stared out.

"What did she want?"

"For her husband to retire on his profits and live the life of a gentleman. With her at his side."

"Could he have done that?"

"Financially? I don't know. Possibly. But not here." She tapped her heart. "He was a seaman, born and bred. He would never be happy ashore."

"Hard life for a wife."

"One I would not have wanted for myself."

She rubbed shoulders with him at the window.

"But that was your destiny; if Ol' Ned had not taken you for a sailor."

"By gender and 'birthright,'" she agreed. "But I doubt it. I think I would have left."

"And done what?"

"I don't know. At age five, I can hardly say to have weighed my options any further than wanting to get out."

"But that was all you knew," he prodded, curious by the protestation.

"I knew there was a world beyond the confines of that small village. I watched boys go to sea. I couldn't imagine any good reason why I shouldn't follow." She snorted. "Someone would have told me. But I wouldn't have listened. If I couldn't ship out as a crewman, I'd have bought a boat, somehow. Or made one. Just like you're going to make one," she reminded. "For the pond. Done some fishing."

"Could you have made a living?"

"I could have lived." The correction hung like an accusation. She forced a smile. "I never dreamed I'd be doing my fishing in the Kansas Ocean."

"Or growing strawberries on the Kansas prairie."

Nelander stared to reply when her face took on a twisted, startled look. "Son of a bitch!"

Never having heard her use that particular cuss, Seth withdrew in shock.

"What -- son of a bitch?" he repeated to mitigate the damage.

"That man. Giles. Now I remember where I saw him."

"At sea?"

Hurrying away from the window, Barbara crossed the threshold and went outside. Seth followed, trailing her out back toward the strawberry field. She cast an arm in a wide arc.

"Out here."

"Here? On our property? When was this?"

"At a time when it looked as though we would have no harvest. Or at least never recover my initial investment. When we needed money," came the firm emphasis. "Remember? I told you about it."

Stroking his chin, Seth tried and failed to summon the memory.

"No. I do not recall."

Barbara scuffed her foot in unconscious imitation of he to whom she spoke.

"I put it to you as a hypothetical question: would you sell out before ever seeing my wild fantasy come to fruition or would you rather have money in the bank?"

He snapped his fingers.

"And I told you, you were a fool for starting any such project and that if I had known, I would have talked you out of it."

"Yesss."

Crisscrossing the narrow rows, he breathed through his nose, imbibing the scent of earth and growing plants.

"And then we spoke of hope: of how money in the bank disappears but looking toward the future gives a man a reason to go on."

"You got around to that conclusion," she hedged.

"And I decided you done the right thing." Done, not did. Despite his avowal, a man still under stress. "But after that, you said it wasn't true. That there was no buyer."

"I lied."

"You mean, there was? That you were askin' for real?"

"Yes."

"And the man who offered to buy our crop -- and all the crops that would ever grow -- for $500 -- was Giles?"

"Yes."

"Why in God's name would a man like Giles want to make such an offer? What are strawberries to him?" She had no answer. "To do us a good turn? Why?" Silence ruled. "Because we hired Blind Betty and Mute Thomas?"

That seemed to be as good an answer as any. And thus, Nelander did not believe it.

"No."

"Why, then?" She closed her eyes as he worked through the puzzle. "Maybe he was testin' us. To see our resolve. Because he knew we'd get involved in this Underground Railroad sooner or later."

Sometimes the best bargains are those never made.

Nelander said nothing.

Chapter 5

"How many strawberries you reckon we picked?"

Taking stock of the reed baskets supplied by Miss Betty, Nelander wiped her brow and made a rapid calculation.

"Fifty quarts."

"That's one hundred pints," Patricia promptly supplied. "At ten cents a pint, we got ourselves ten dollars."

Brushing back her close-cropped hair, the landlocked seaman took stock.

"Seems like a hell of a lot of work for ten dollars."

The captain ignored the bad word.

"It's ten dollars more'n we'd have if I left this field unplowed. Five dollars to spend in Anson's Dry Goods and five to put away." He winked. "We'll call it our egg money."

Nelander groaned. "Say, rather, our treasure trove for a rainy day."

"Or a drought," Peter supplied. "We gonna go out on the wagon, ag'in? To all them towns, like we did before? We ain't been to Dr. McTree's in a while. You kin pick up ice from his supply an' Patricia and I kin play wid Minerva. I 'spect she's wantin' to hear about her pups, anyway. Wait till we tell her how big Dardanelles an' Mizzenmast are gettin'."

Seth shook his head. "I don't have the time to go traipsing all over the countryside sellin' fifty quarts of strawberries. I've got corn to tend. This much we ought to be able to sell in Lawrence." Removing his hat, he fanned his face. "And if not, the six of us can probably eat 'em pretty fast."

"But then we wouldn't make any money, Captain Papa."

Gazing at the field, picked dry of red berries, he sighed.

"We'll do better next year when folks have more money." Left unsaid lay the fact that the late winter ice storm had destroyed a good portion of the local farmer's crops. "Next year" boded little better than "this year."

"Let's load up the wagon."

"It's already late. Wouldn't you prefer to wait and get an early start in the morning?"

With an awkward shrug, he hefted a basket.

"I've wasted enough time. If we don't go until tomorrow, the whole day will be shot."

"Then why don't Patricia and I go alone? We can set up in the farmer's market and if we don't sell what we have by the time it closes, we'll drive around the streets, going door-to-door. Fifty quarts, Seth. That's ten dollars I'd just as soon earn than see go to waste. There has to be one hundred citizens in Lawrence with ten cents to their name. You know," she prodded, ignoring the skepticism. "Clerks and bankers and post masters and peace officers. Those not related to farmers."

He ticked the occupations off on his fingers. "Yes. A conservative guess would put that number around thirty. Considering we have only two bankers, one mail sorter and one sheriff."

"Thirty times ten cents is three dollars. A dollar-fifty to spend at Anson's store and the same for the kitty."

"Are we gonna get another cat?" Peter eagerly inquired.

"'Kitty, in this case, referring to the empty tea canister on the mantel. It means a small savings you stash away."

"Oh. I'd rather have a cat."

"No, you wouldn't," Seth groused. "Besides, we've already got more than we can afford to feed."

"They're good mousers, papa."

"They'd be better if you didn't sneak them scraps from the table."

"Oh, no, sir," his son innocently piped. "We only do that for Herman and Squash."

The farmer rolled his eyes and turned to his wife. "I don't want you driving home in the dark. Don't like to do it, myself. There isn't much of a moon and a lantern only helps so much."

"We will stay the night with Dr. McTree. That way, if we have strawberries left, we can have a second chance to sell them before we set out for home."

The temptation to make even as little as three dollars carried the argument.

"All right. Leave Paula with Peter and me. No sense rattling her bones over that rough road. I'll put her in the backpack and take her into the fields with me in the morning."

"That's what used to happen to me," the boy happily bragged. "When mama was too sick, papa'd strap me to his back, papoose-style and bring me out to the fields. Learned a thing or two 'bout farmin' that way, I did."

"Did not," Patricia scoffed. "Mostly you spent the day sleepin' or bawlin'."

"I suppose in between, he did absorb his father's love of the land," Barbara kindly soothed. "It's settled, then. Peter, hitch Blaze to the wagon, if you please."

He started to comply, then squinted in thought.

"If you say, 'If you please,' does that mean it's not an order and I can disobey if I want?"

The seaman who had once been second officer aboard the Bottom Dollar gave him a stare from under lowered lids.

"Indeed, not. It is a polite form of speech, correctly interpreted as 'Do as you're told or I'll dress you down in front of the whole crew.'" Surreptitiously sneaking a peek at Seth, she added, "Or, more commonly, 'Ignore me at your peril or I'll keelhaul your damned ass.'"

The crew snickered behind their hands and scurried off, feeling that if one were to obey an order, two carrying it out would be that much more prudent. Seth huffed.

"By the time they're grown, they'll be proficient in two languages -- English and Cursing."

"Absolutely not." He arched an eyebrow, challenging her to defend the denial. Such was the farthest thing from her mind. "I would grade them as well-competent now. No need to look to the future."

He started to spit, thought better of it and choked. She left him to recover of his own accord and after his own fashion.

In whichever language best suited the occasion.

Arriving in town just after the lunch hour proved bad timing. Driving slowly down the main street, Patricia banged a stick on the flat of the wagon seat and called, "Strawberries for sale! Fresh strawberries! Home-grown, Kansas strawberries! Ten cents a pint!"

Receiving several glances but few takers, she took to personalizing her pitch.

"Lookee here, Mr. Wilkie -- nice, sweet strawberries."

He hesitated, then waved her off.

"I would, honey, but I jest ete -- an' in this heat, they won't last till after supper."

Undaunted, the little huckster redirected her comments.

"Mrs. Morley -- it's me -- Patricia Ward. I got fresh strawberries to sell. Only ten cents a pint. That's almost free! Bet if you went over to the Deeds Office right now with a pint of fresh strawberries, Mr. Morley'd be right appreciative. Why, he'd smack his lips over 'em!"

The lady appeared unconvinced but did not wish to offend. Digging into her cloth handbag, she searched the contents, finally coming up with pennies. Shading her eyes against the sun, she offered them out in the palm of her hand.

"I've got five cents here. May I purchase half a pint?"

"That isn't much -- just a cup. Hardly more'n a handful. Mebbe if you look ag'in --"

"I am afraid this is all I have."

"Be a losin' proposition, me selling you a half pint and givin' you a nice, useful reed basket."

Nelander poked her in the rubs.

"Let us not be ungracious."

Pouting over the dubious worth of such a small transaction, Patricia measured out what she estimated to be fair value. Barbara added another handful.

"Here, Mrs. Morley. And we hope you and Mr. Morley enjoy them."

"Most kind of you, ma'am."

Taking her unexpected treasure with the useful reed basket, she carefully cradled the purchase to her breast and hurried out of the sun. Not unaware of the temperature herself, the older Ward urged Blaze forward.

"We are not having much luck this way. Let us set up shop at the Farmer's Market and see if it improves. If nothing else, I can rig an awning over the fruit to keep it in the shade."

Prospects for a quick sale diminished as they drove around to the end of the line. Few customers wandered between the dirt rows and those who did kept their hands in their pockets.

"To prevent buying on impulse," Nelander decided. "They have come to 'window shop.'"

In truth, what produce the sellers offered did not stimulate the appetite. The greens had wilted, root vegetables displayed depressing splotches of dried dirt and large, black flies buzzed ominously over the sole vendor offering smoked meat.

After two hours, they had sold three pints, earning for their long ride to town the paltry sum of thirty-five cents.

Rearranging the few filled baskets they had set out for display, the adult noted a sticky pool of red juice beneath each. Making a face, she held one up to the western sun, critically observing the bottom.

"The heat is causing them to spoil. Those below are weighted by the ones on top and they are --" Weeping came to mind, but she did not care to use it, feeling too close to that emotion, herself. "We might as well wrap up for today and go over to Dr. McTree's. If nothing else, we can treat him to a fancy desert."

"He ought to be able to afford three pints. That's one for each of us."

"Guests may not allow their host to buy them desert. That is both rude and bad manners. We will treat him for putting us up for the night."

"Then you go to bed early and I'll dicker with him over the price. I'll cut him a good deal," she promised, undaunted by the dark look received for her trouble. "Twenty-five cents and I get the baskets back. No sense throwing good money after bad."

Feeling guilty, Nelander asked, "Where in the world did you learn to think like that?" Patricia did not bother to answer and they hurriedly packed their belongings. With a quick wave at the other vendors who could not afford to leave early, mother and daughter set their sights on other, if not greener pastures.

Arriving outside the physician's gate, Patricia slipped off the rear of the wagon and scampered up the walk. Banging on the door, she waited nearly two seconds before turning the knob and sticking her nose through the opening.

"Dr. McTree!"

Enthusiasm undiminished by receiving no reply, she vanished from sight. Nelander waited, expecting to see the doctor's cheery countenance welcome her aboard. A smile died on her lips as Patricia re-emerged alone.

"He's not here, but Minerva is. She says to come on in. He'll be home directly."

Without pausing to reflect that dogs seldom, if ever, spoke in human tongue, Nelander heaved a sigh and wearily directed the horse around back. Taking her time with the unhitching, she searched in vain for a brush before realizing McTree likely stabled his horse at the livery. Gently tousling Blaze's ears, she drew him a bucket of water from the well, allowed him to drink, then deftly applied a pair of hobbles. Turning him out to graze in the open field behind the house, she went in the rear entrance. The faithful friend and guard dog met her with a happy wag.

"Gone out on a call, has he, old girl? But you think he'll be back for supper?" The canine woofed. Assuming her most sincere Midwestern drawl, the guest decided, "Well then, we'll jest have to rustle up some grub an' surprise him when he gits back."

This seemed acceptable. Summoning Patricia to help, the pair removed the strawberries from the wagon and placed them in in a wooden cabinet where the doctor stored his ice. While the cool air would not undue damage already wrought, it would prevent further spoilage until they had a second chance to sell it in the morning.

Although never having eaten at the bachelor's house, preferring to invite him to the farm, Barbara easily found all the utensils required. Assigning Patricia to peel potatoes, she chopped onions, boiling the former and frying the latter from a pool of melted bacon fat stored in the pantry. While the vegetables cooked, she cut a slab of dried meat and shredded it with her pocketknife.

"We makin' scouse?"

"More like a hash."

"Smells good."

"It does, doesn't it?"

Mashing the soft potatoes and nearly translucent onions together, she added bits of beef, stirred the concoction, then dumped the whole into a large, cast iron frying pan bubbling with another generous dose of bacon fat. When the bottom had formed an appetizing brown crust, she flipped it like an overweight pancake and fried the other side.

Just as the mash finished cooking, a booming voice declared, "Danged, if I ain't in the wrong house! I've know'd Hank McTree all my life, or thereabouts an' I ain't niver smelled nothin' so odor-some comin' frum his cook stove!"

Turning around with pleasure, Nelander allowed the doctor the liberty of kissing her cheek.

"Welcome home, sir. I thought since Patricia and I were going to throw ourselves on your good graces for the night, the least we could do is prepare you a welcome home supper."

"It doesn't take much to spoil me, you know," he winked, unbuttoning his coat and tossing it over the back of a chair. Mouth watering, he peered into the frying pan. "Put some nice hot chilies in there, did you?"

"Not this time. I save that for unsuspecting neighbors who've done us a bad turn or for the winter months when the body needs a good spice to warm the blood. Go and wash up; I'll have the food on the table by the time you get back."

He skipped to his task and appeared fresh-scrubbed and pink-eared by the time the last of the hash had been divided. Grabbing a clean plate from the cabinet, he scooped a small portion of the meal from his own serving and set it out for Minerva. The act only served to further redden that which lye soap had begun.

"People who live alone tend to think of their pets as family. I always make enough for two -- Minerva and I. She appreciates it and I feel... less lonely."

"If you are looking for chastisement, sir, you have appealed to the wrong individual. Aboard ship, seamen frequently eat with their fingers and always use the back of their sleeve for a napkin. As for a friend, I would rather a rat from the hold than many of your citizens."

"Well put, sir."

He saluted and plopped down, grabbing for the salt cellar. Using a diminutive silver spoon, he dumped a heaping teaspoonful over the hash, ground it in with the back of his fork then dug in. Patricia officially cleared her throat for attention.

"Aren't you gonna give any salt to Minerva?"

"Ah. Yes. Well...." Grabbing a bit of seasoning with thumb and forefinger, he sprinkled it over the dog's meal. Giving it a sniff, she expressed approval by wolfing it down.

"I chew a mite more'n she does but that's where the difference ends. This is wonderful, Officer Nelander."

"Bit dry," the girl objected, clearing her throat. "Be better if we had some rum to wash it down."

"That I generally save for medicinal purposes." Hank's eyes brightened. "But I do have a bottle of wine."

Leaping from the table, he came back with an emerald green bottle, three-quarters filled with a dark amber liquid. Taking down three scarred glasses, he poured two generous servings for the adults and a smaller one for the child. Without bothering to offer a toast, he sipped, then nodded as his tongue curled.

"Got this from Josh Bayliss."

"What is it? Wine?"

"Applejack; fermented cider."

"Does he have apple trees?"

"A whole orchard. Why? Are you interested in cultivating apples, too?"

She hesitated then let her eyes roam over the ceiling.

"Apples; onions; pickles. Spuds. Beans. Limes. These are foods I know. They give me a... comfort."

"In these trying times, I think we're all reaching out to our past. Trying to regain something we fear is lost forever. Not from growing older or even growing up. But from the simple fact none of us knows what tomorrow will bring."

"It's going to bring war."

"I think growing apples is a good idea. Next time I'm out that way I'll ask from for some saplings. I might put in a few, myself." They drank the liquor, watching in guarded amusement as Patricia tried hers, then made a face and pushed it away.

"Do pirates drink this?"

"Not generally. Like seaman the world over, what they drained out of barrels was more likely vinegar."

"For the scurvy."

"Correct."

"Scorbutus; from the German, schorboet. A putrid disease, thought to be caused by a deprivation of fresh provisions," Hank observed, draining his glass. "I don't know that I've ever seen a full-blown case. But I guess sailors would be susceptible to diseases of malnutrition. I probably don't eat enough vegetables and fruits, myself."

The statement prompted a relief from darker thoughts. Patricia popped up and went for the ice chest.

"We brought fifty quarts of strawberries, hoping to sell them. We'll do that in the morning. But Nelander says we ought to provide you with dessert."

"So that's why you're here. I thought you sold the lot."

"These are from the patch behind the house. The matured later. Didn't get many but I was hoping to make a few dollars."

"We arrived too late. 'Spect we'll make ten dollars outta 'em tomorrow."

She opened the cabinet and he took stock.

"I'm not sure a man can ever get too many strawberries. Put me down for... two quarts."

"That's forty cents --" Quickly catching herself, Patricia retracted the price. "It would be for anyone else. But tonight we're treatin'."

"Oh. I see. Thank you."

The girl doled out generous portions and they went after them with pleasure, creating an impressive pile of leaves and hulls before finishing. The doctor patted his stomach.

"Yes, sir, that was a good meal. Like I say, I spoil easily. Could get used to having people take care of me right well."

Crossing with him into the living room which also doubled as a waiting room, Nelander skimmed his small library, then beckoned for her daughter.

"Pick a book and take it with you to bed. It's getting late and we have to be up early."

"They're all scientific books."

"Try the lower shelf," McTree advised. "I've some poetry books you might enjoy." She selected one and tucked it under her arm. He indicated an ante chamber. "There's a bed in the surgery. No one's using it. Just make it up in the morning and no one's the wiser. Least ways, I've never had a patient complain there were a few wrinkles in the sheets."

Stifling a yawn, Patricia trudged off.

"Can I take Minerva with me? I'm not used to sleepin' in a strange place."

"Go ahead. Just leave the door open a crack so she can get out when nature calls."

"Good night, then."

"Nighty-night."

"Sleep tight. Do not let the bedbugs bite," Patricia finished.

Her departure made the living room more intimate and equally lonely. Nelander attempted to ease the silence by an apology.

"I hope you don't mind us coming in and making ourselves at home. Or of inviting ourselves to stay the night."

"Me casa es su casa," he quoted. "Do you speak Spanish?"

"Enough to get by. I have fluent French and it's close enough. I don't know about, 'My house is your house,' but I can give orders in Spanish and do some pretty fair swearing."

"Bet you can. You and Seth and the children are always welcome here. I'm glad you took the liberty. I don't often admit it, but a man gets lonely living by himself."

"It's a wonder, then, Hank, you don't have any servants."

"For company?"

She ignored the implication, altering the complexion of the conversation. "To cook and clean for you. And maybe even let the younger ones sit on the floor while you read aloud. Everyone can benefit from poetry; especially those with a propensity for metre."

Slapping a hand on his thigh, the doctor appeared relieved.

"I thought I was in for a lecture on the benefits of marital bliss. I see now you are more interested in my views on slavery." The woman gave no acknowledgment. "I would have presumed my opinions clear. You know I regularly go to Little Lawrence and provide medical services. On occasion, a severely injured person of color is brought here." The silence of his listening partner deepened. "I applauded when you and Seth brought Blind

Betty and Mute Thomas out to the old Windsor farm." Leaning toward her, he pantomimed bringing food to his mouth. "I have eaten strawberries picked by freed black hands."

Still, nothing. "I'm trolling here, Nelander and you haven't given me so much as a nibble." He saw tracks of thought weave themselves behind her eyes and deeper still, lingering wisps of doubt. What she wished to hear could not be solicited. "Has there been trouble?" His figurative hook gave a twitch. "What sort? Not a falling out with your -- hands?"

"No." The answer fell short of Certainly not. He bit his lower lip, then to cover the reaction, dipped into his pocket for a pouch of chewing tobacco. Pinching several strands between his fingers, he studiously weighed the amount by some inner process before tucking it in his cheek.

"You are concerned that if there is a war, Seth -- or I -- may take up arms?" An alternation of breathing pattern. Were he not a physician, he might not have detected the reaction. "I will never bear arms against anyone. I abhor violence. And the Captain....?"

After so long a period of quietude, her voice suddenly caught him off guard and he jumped from the verve of her tone.

"I would not hesitate to shoot a man in the back."

"You are thinking of going for a soldier!" He meant to elicit a smile and did not succeed. "I suppose your solution is the safest. I have never been a proponent of the Rules of War or gentleman's agreements, for that matter. War, I imagine, is not a game of survival of the fittest, but rather an ugly, deadly conflict where an individual's fate depends as much on luck as bravery. And of discarding all concept of fair play for continuing existence."

She waited until he spat a stream of tobacco juice into a spittoon before reacting.

"I am sure on one level you condone that philosophy. On another, most civilized people expect honor... among combatants. As though we should be more noble at times of crisis than at dinner parties or board rooms."

He chewed harder. "You have shot someone and are debating whether to turn yourself in."

This finally elicited a scoff. "My conscience does not trouble me. If I had dispatched someone, doctor, a shovel and the application of manual labor would have the corpse fertilizing the strawberries you so guilelessly consumed at supper."

"Barbara, I am not a fisherman nor am I a man of arms. Ask me anything and if it is within my power, I will answer. Keeping both the question and reply a secret between us."

Running hands through her hair, the seafarer finally directed her blue orbs on the physician's face.

"Are you, then, a conductor?"

She drawled out the word.

Con-duc-tor.

He experienced a chill as though the season had suddenly advanced to winter.

"No. I am not a conductor."

"You are familiar with the -- occupation?"

"I am."

"And are aware tracks run through the environs of Lawrence?"

"I cross them gingerly, looking both ways."

"Why is that?"

"For the same reason you could not come out and directly pose your question." He spit again and added more to his chaw. "I am not averse to such... labor."

"Yet you have not joined the cause."

"Say, instead, I have never been recruited."

"Why not?"

"I can only give you speculation." She bade him continue. "I am too public a figure. Too... well known as a man of principle. I have occasionally suspected my domicile of being watched." Settling into a chair, he crossed his legs. "Just the other day, I observed a man outside my gate. At first I took him for someone in need of medical attention. But he did not come in. He exhibited patience, you might say, rather than being a patient."

"What did he look like?"

"Medium height. Sandy hair. Well dressed. With the bearing of a military man. I could not be certain but I thought he wore a badge."

"From the Simpson Agency. A slave hunter who works out of the Missouri Militia."

Less surprised than he should have been, for her knowledge admitted close association, he tried a grin.

"That is the individual you shot? In the back? Have you the body out in the wagon? Is that really why you have come? If so, I will gladly write a certificate, stating the cause of death to be apoplexy."

Remembering a time before her arrival, Nelander arched an eyebrow.

"There are some who say your professional word is not always taken at face value. People believe what they want to, doctor. A tragic accident may as soon be called murder. Or suicide."

"Ah. Yes. Better you planted him in the strawberry field. But how, then, may I be of service?"

Taking out a pocketknife, Nelander worked on excising a hangnail.

"I have never seen the man of whom you speak I have encountered his operateur; say, rather, two of them. He has been in town hiring accomplices."

"Do say. Anyone I know?"

"We had a visit from Dick McConaghie and Brian Clement. Wearing badges. "

"The devil take them. I trust they discovered nothing untoward?"

"By the grace of God. And a bit of subterfuge and chili pepper."

"You pizzoned 'em?"

"Used on the dogs. The four-legged variety. I hid the young woman and her infant in the privy. They were supposed to be... delivered... to the old Windsor farm. Outsiders do not know there are Negroes living there; people clearly sympathetic to the Cause. But the local men do -- especially the McConaghies. When the guide discovered they were the ones following him, he obviously could not go there. So he took them to us."

"Sweet Jesus. I am sorry. Had I known, I would have warned you."

Nelander dismissed the statement. "Who runs the Underground Railroad from town?"

Removing the wad of wet tobacco, McTree dropped it in the spittoon, then wiped his mouth.

"I don't know. I have never made it my business to ask."

"But you have your suspicions."

"I know who I don't suspect. That leaves a wide field. But I will sniff around. Do not do so, yourself; appearances are deceiving and words do not always mean what they say. If I hear anything, I'll ride out on a 'professional call.'"

"Thank you."

She meant that to be the end of the discussion and he obligingly rose.

"Sleep in my bed. I will be more than comfortable on the couch." Seeing she would make no objection, he lit a candle and handed it to her. "So you won't trip on the books on the floor." Taking the light, Nelander had crossed the room before he spoke again. "Betty will not tell you? Or, perhaps, she does not know," he tried to soften.

The interrogative stopped her forward progression.

"Betty knows more than she cares to say. There are secrets far beyond the Underground Railroad she hides."

With that as her closing salvo, Barbara Nelander went to bed. Leaving Hank McTree with the uneasy supposition that as a fisherman, he had tried to reel in a whale with a bent pin.

CHAPTER 6

The morning proved depressingly similar to the preceding afternoon. Several women purchased a pint or two of strawberries for their husband's morning meal, but by ten o'clock, that nebulous period between breakfast and dinner, business had tapered to feral cats and drunks.

"Come on, Patricia. Let's wrap it up."

The child stared disconsolately at the neat array of baskets she had set out on the rear gate.

"We haven't made much money."

"No, we haven't. But I want to get home. My breasts are aching and I should like to relieve the pressure by feeding Paula. And I am certain your father and Peter miss us as much as we miss them."

"I had a good time at Dr. McTree's."

The reply evoked surprise and Barbara drew back to better appraise the speaker.

"Really?"

"It was sort of like an adventure. Sleepin' in a different bed and all. I fell asleep imagining myself aboard a pirate ship. I'm not used to the creaks in his house, so it was easy to believe they were from the ship rollin' on the waves. Minerva played the part of a tar."

"Then I hope she did not jump on your bed," the adult dryly observed.

Patricia started to deny it, then grinned.

"She did, but that's when she turned back into a dog."

"I am relieved to hear it."

Pushing the berries back, Nelander tossed a blanket over the to prevent spilling, then hoisted up the back. Patricia put a hand on her arm.

"What do you say, once around town? Just to be certain we didn't miss any potential customers?"

Not daring to dampen hope, or pass up the opportunity of making money, no matter how slight, she agreed, and they began their rounds. Traveling up and down the parallel roads, hot sun boring holes in their heads, they sold three more pints before Nelander determined to call off the endeavor.

"That's enough. Let us turn our heads for home."

"What about up there?" Patricia pointed to an imposing three story mansion perched on a hill at the outskirts of town. "I bet they have lots of money to spend on strawberries."

Shading her eyes, the seaman sweating under the landlocked rays, appraised the structure. Hardly an expert on architecture, she presumed the white columns and broad veranda representative of a Southern plantation. Set away from the road, a high, cast iron fence, split in the middle by a matching gate, stood guard over the occupants. Two chimneys to either side rose above the roof, while rows of hedges hid the lower windows from closer scrutiny.

Without ever having been on the property, she presumed a series of outbuildings circled the rear of the home. Stable, carriage house, privy, probably even a separate kitchen and smoke house. Unquestioningly the most magnificent estate in Lawrence, the structure bore an aloof, almost unused air, as though the owner and his family were frequently away on trips to the Continent.

Nelander had observed the mansion from a distance but never inquired of its history.

"Who owns it?"

"It's the old Dryfus place. I cain't ever remember there being a Mr. Dryfus. I expect he died a long time ago. Mrs. Dryfus lives there."

The name did not ring a bell, proving Seth had never spoken of the family.

"Have you ever met her?"

"No, sir. She doesn't go to church and the captain says she got servants to do her shopping. Never even seen her at the fair."

"Then, perhaps she does not like to be disturbed. There is the gate -- and it is shut."

"I'll just see if it's locked."

Before waiting to be stopped, Patricia hopped down and ran to the iron bars which dwarfed her by a good two feet. Briefly examining the latch, she yanked upward and discovered it to be unfastened.

"Guess she can't be too fussy who comes to call."

Returning to the wagon, the girl shoved a hand underneath the blanket and took out a quart basket. Winking broadly, she scampered through the opening and high-stepped up the path, inlaid with carefully placed stepping stones. Nelander half expected a pack of hounds or a guard to stop her, but nothing stirred, adding to the desultory atmosphere of abandonment.

Stifling an urge to call her back, Nelander could not shake a feeling of disquietude. If any in the city were likely to entertain a traveler and his colored entourage from out of state, these inhabitants seemed the most probable. If true, that also meant the lady of the house had either summoned or permitted her guest to summon the Simpson Agency when one of her slaves had the audacity to escape.

Patricia did not know Mrs. Dryfus by sight but that did not preclude the matron from recognizing her. Nelander was not at all sure she wished such a person to know a portion of the Ward crew were in Lawrence, selling a most unusual crop Not only would it give Mrs. Dryfus insight into their business, it might prompt her, or her visitors, to dispatch men to the Pirate Treasure.

Along the lines of "divide and conquer."

A tactic worthy of buccaneers.

Leaping to the ground, the captain raced through the gate and up the sidewalk, reaching the door just as it opened to Patricia's summons. A man, dressed in black broadcloth peered out from the interior. He wore white gloves and carried a silver tray. Nelander gasped and pulled back.

"Giles!"

His right eye narrowed but otherwise gave no indication of surprise.

"Miz Ward," he officiously acknowledged.

Although the dress clearly represented a butler's livery, rather than the costume he had worn on his recent visit to the farm, Barbara immediately divined the purpose of the gloves. With a long coat and hat drawn low to cover his features, he had seemed like any other white man. His hands, however, would have told a different story. While not overly dark-skinned, she recognized him now as a Negro.

At a loss to determine whether she had stumbled onto a secret or simply completed a journey he expected her to make, she stumbled over an explanation. Patricia had no such qualms and fell naturally into the patter developed over the course of a growing season.

Holding the produce, close enough to observe but not near enough to snatch, were such his desire, the child adroitly placed a foot in the doorway.

"Good morning, sir! As you can see here, we're sellin' fresh, ripe strawberries. Grown right here in Kansas an' still glistening with mornin' dew. They're as sweet as a candy stick an' we have 'em on sale fer twenty-five cents a quart. That's only fifty cents fer two. A bargain, if ever I heard one. An' if you act now, I'll throw in this nice, fine, custom-wove reed basket. Useful around the house for many purposes."

Embarrassed by the snake oil charm and the inexplicable raise in price, Nelander tried to quiet her.

"Hush, now. That is enough --"

The attempt had no effect.

"You kin go to the Farmer's Market right this minute an' you won't find any strawberries. No, sir. Nary a one. That's because we're the sole grower an' distributor of 'Nelander's Plump an' Juicy Ruby-red Strawberries.' Jest one taste will hearken you back to your days of short pants when you was out an' about, pickin' wild berries kissed by faeries."

"That-is-enough --"

Fearful the extemporized script was not only inappropriate but offensive, her partner tried to stem the tide, but Giles surprised her by holding out a hand.

"You paint a pretty picture, Miss Ward."

"It's actual 'Navigator Ward,' sir, but I forgive you fer not knowin' that. We come from a place just north-east of here called the Pirate Treasure. It's our ship, although it don't actually sail on the ocean. Fergive me fer not introducin' my associate. This here is Captain Nelander. She's got experience on the High Seas."

Giles made a bow.

"Captain Nelander."

Patricia spoke for the silent adult.

"Yes, sir. Back at the farm we also have Fleet Captain Seth Ward and Warrant Officer Peter."

"A small crew."

"Well, there's another; she isn't big enough to be called an 'able-bodied,' but I expect she'll get there. I reckon you could count her as a powder monkey."

"Patricia --"

" -- an' then there's the ship's doctor -- that's Miss Betty. 'Doctor' aboard ship means cook, but she has skill in the healin' arts, too. And then there's Able-bodied Buccaneer, Thomas. But you know them."

"But not their new titles."

"I'm surprised they haven't told you. We're all Wards, together. But as I'm standin' here talkin', these strawberries are gettin' a might peak-ed in the heat. It'd be best if you bought them now and took 'em inside outta the sun. Got any ice?"

"Yes, I believe there is ice in the house."

"That's fine, sir. For jest fifty cents, you own 'em, plus two fine reed baskets. Set 'em in your ice box an' they'll last for days. Not that I expect 'em to. Once you get a taste of 'Nelander's Finest,' you'll devour 'em right quick!"

Finished with her sale's pitch, Patricia rolled back on her heels. Nelander attempted to make amends.

"Mr. Giles, I am sorry if we intruded. I had no idea you lived here, sir, and if I had, we would surely not have come to the door."

"I work here, Captain," he softly corrected. "If you step inside, I will inquire of the mistress if she be interested in fine, plump, ruby-red strawberries for her table."

Stepping aside, he permitted them to pass. Closing the door with a demure effort, he directed them to follow. Settling the pair in the parlor, he bowed again and backed away.

"If you will kindly wait here."

Still clutching her precious berries, Patricia walked around the room, eyes drinking in the wonders.

Bypassing an exquisite embroidered couch and matching chairs, she went directly to the marble fireplace. Above it hung two large oil portraits, framed in gilt. Between them hung a smaller painting, this one a landscape of a solitary tree, created in watercolors. Smaller than those flanking it, it bore an unadorned wooden frame.

"Aren't they beautiful, Nelander? I feel as though the faces could start talking at any minute."

Drawn to the likenesses, Nelander could not disagree. Clearly fashioned by a master, she beheld both faces. The one of the right depicted a man in his late forties. Although the artist had tried to paint the subject to best advantage, a slight drooping of the jowls, the presence of age lines around his eyes and the sweep of grey at the temples stamped him with the scars of maturity. Nelander guessed at the time he sat for the portrait he had been in his early fifties and the artist had taken five years off his chronological age.

Dressed in a businessman's suit, the figure sat in a chair easily recognizable as one still present in the room. Hands crossed, head thrown back, he glowered at the onlookers with an expression of harsh judgment. While easy to imagine he had assumed such an expression to depict worldliness and wealth, Barbara suspected that in real life, he had been no different. She did not like him and could have given a sailor's laundry list of reasons why.

The woman presented a striking contrast. No more than twenty years of age, she, like her husband, bore no smile. The seriousness came neither from superiority nor money, but rather the opposite: a young life already filled with tragedy. Ignorant of specifics, an observer might speculate she had recently lost a baby in childbirth.

Unlike the gentleman, whose clothing came as an adjunct, the artist had spent considerable time displaying the woman's attire. The pale green gown of early 19th-Century European fashion might have been designed for a member of the British nobility. Augmenting the impression, she wore a delicate gold tiara set atop long, dark brown, meticulously coiffured tresses, two jeweled rings and a wedding band. Around her neck lay a necklace of spun gold, gently depositing a glistening ruby at the apex of her cleavage.

Incongruous to the overall effect of husband and wife, the watercolor in the middle seemed to bear no relevance to the desired ambiance. Stark, bare and devoid of color, the black-and-white branches reached out beyond the frame, giving the impression that if left untended, its limbs might eventually overgrow the bonds, engulfing the couple by its side. That created a misnomer, however, for the tree bore no signs of life. Not the slightest hint of green graced its tendril fingers.

Viewed from a near perspective, it presented a picture of twisted and gnarled discord, as if Nature had bestowed the framework of life, then withheld the breath to make it complete. Stepping back and observed from a distance, as Nelander did, the smaller twigs and branches faded to the background, leaving the tall, black upright trunk and a pair of prominent arms, stretched right and left.

Creating the image of a cross.

Struck by the mysticism, Nelander bent to one side. Although never taking her eyes from the tree, one of the crossbeams disappeared, leaving the gaunt wooden structure one-handed. Twisting the opposite way, the faded limb reappeared and the other diminished.

This proved first impressions disingenuous. While the portraits were painted by a master, the tree represented the creation of genius. Without question, its presence made the other two superfluous instead of the other way around.

Before she had the chance to share her observations, the sway of cloth caught her ear and she turned in time to see Mrs. Dryfus enter. Although the passage of time had aged her, there could be no doubt she represented the young woman in the portrait. Patricia drew the same conclusion. With a child's inability to gauge adult proprieties, she boldly approached the gran dame, hand extended.

"You were pretty then, Mrs. Dryfus, but your face has more character now."

Seldom one to place manners over honesty, Nelander shrunk back from the statement. It did not appear to have a negative effect on the woman so addressed, for she readily accepted and shook the hand.

"That is most kind of you to say. I have always prized mental fortitude over physical attributes. One is earned while the other inherited. I suspect you would agree, Captain Nelander?"

Her use of rank for a title did not occasion surprise for the officer had already determined Giles faithfully repeated the dialogue at the door word-for-word.

"I have little regard for that which is not obtained by strength of will. Where I come from, 'pretty boys' are often used for shark bait."

Mrs. Dryfus indulged in a hearty laugh, gripping her visitor's hand with strength.

"Well put."

"An honor to meet you, ma'am."

That comment settled less agreeably.

"Why do you say that? Because I am wealthy and live in this impressive house?"

"No, ma'am. Because you employ a gentleman I regard with the utmost respect. It speaks well for your judgment."

"Oh? Have you met... Giles before?"

Nelander's pulse raced beside her thoughts as she debated whether her comment had been a mistake. Taking for granted the employer knew of her servant's late night activities, she had spoken with undue haste. Patricia readily assumed the thread.

"Yes, ma'am. We saw him at the Farmer's Market. He admired our strawberries and that earned him our regard. We kinda look at them the way other folks are proud of their puppies or kittens." She pulled a long face which augmented her sincerity. "He didn't buy any, though; said he'd have to check with you. Thought we'd save him the trouble of comin' back by bringin' the strawberries to your door."

"It is surprising then, for he made no mention of strawberries. And I am most fond of them."

Nelander could not tell by the tone whether the mistress knew the true state of affairs or not. The mention of a fondness for strawberries, however, rang true and clear.

"Here's a quart I have right with me. Nice and fresh and sweet."

Accepting the basket, Mrs. Dryfus spent a long time examining the workmanship before turning her attention to the fruit. For a moment, her eyes sparkled more clearly than the ruby necklace in the portrait.

"How much for this -- including the basket?"

"Twenty-five cents and we give you the basket for free."

Her voice deepened. "And if I do not want it?"

If she attempted to faze the child, the effort proved for naught.

"Then put them in your own basket and give that one back. It's an 'operating expense,' you know, and we're always glad to save on output."

"Since you put it that way, I do not want to be cheated. I will keep the basket. Have you more?"

"Baskets?"

"Strawberries."

Patricia flashed a grin.

"You bet! We have a whole wagon full."

"So many." Mrs. Dryfus turned to Nelander. "It is a wonder you did not sell them all at market."

"Times are hard. First the drought and then the ice storm. People in Lawrence have very little extra money to spare on... treats."

For some reason, Mrs. Dryfus took that as a cue and bade her guests be seated.

"Forgive me for not offering sooner. Please; make yourselves comfortable."

"But we have only come to sell our produce."

"Anyone who crosses my threshold is an invited guest, Nelander." The omission of title and careful enunciation of her last name jogged a memory Barbara could not immediately place. Annoyed with herself, she accepted, Patricia standing by her side. Mrs. Dryfus sat opposite.

"You have managed to sell the rest of your crop? Or is it yet to be picked? But then, it is late in the season."

This time, Nelander had the distinct impression the woman knew exactly what they had sold and to whom. Yet she did not begrudge an answer.

"We have two fields; one on the corner of our property and the other behind the house. The plants in the valley fared better this spring and we sold that crop in adjoining towns where the weather had not been so devastating and people had more money to spend. Many plants from the second patch were killed or stunted by the ice. Those which survived were set back and we are only now harvesting."

"How unfortunate."

Although she meant to convey a disinterest, possibly even the opposite of what the words stated, Nelander did not believe her. She failed, however, to justify why Mrs. Dryfus muted her concern, unless it be from her superior position.

"Thank you. Although, all things considered, it is probably for the best. Captain Ward does not have the time to spare from the cash crops to travel with us across the state."

"The corn and the wheat, you mean?"

"Yes."

"You would not go alone? With Patricia and Peter, of course?"

No one had mentioned Peter's name. Nelander tensed her muscles.

"I would, but there is also the baby to consider. I would not care to be separated from her for any length of time and taking her with me is hard on an infant."

"What is her name?"

"Paula Nelander-Ward."

"You have given the child your father's surname for her middle name?"

"I have given her my name as a hyphenate: Nelander-Ward."

"I see. And your husband had no objection?"

"He, too, is a Nelander-Ward. As are we all."

"A peculiar man."

Fingering her wedding ring, Barbara's eyes went from it to the ostentatious band depicted so prominently on Mrs. Dryfus' portrait. She did not doubt the precious metal and intricate design cost Mr. Dryfus a king's ransom, yet would not have traded it for her own humble ring of brass.

Not for all the tea in China.

Unconsciously glancing back at her host, she saw no wedding ring. Astutely following the train of thought, Mrs. Dryfus held up her right hand.

"My husband is dead, Nelander. It is a European custom for a woman to move her band from the left to the right to signify widowhood."

Accepting the statement on face value, Barbara nodded with the assurance Mrs. Dryfus had performed the act with more satisfaction than grief.

Nor did the use of her name, Nelander, escape unnoticed. Nelander. Again, it touched a nerve. Again, she could not place the significance.

"But we were speaking of strawberries. Patricia, how many have you in the wagon?"

"Fifty quarts," came the deliberated reply.

"Fifty quarts. At twenty-five cents a quart? Plus baskets?"

"Yes, ma'am. That is --"

"Fifty dollars." The miscalculation started both sellers.

"No, ma'am. It isn't but twelve dollars and fifty cents."

"I have said fifty dollars. I do not make statements lightly, Navigator Nelander-Ward. Fifty dollars for all the strawberries and baskets you have in the wagon. Is it agreed?"

Torn by the glaring contradiction, Patricia sadly shook her head.

"No, ma'am. It wouldn't be fair." Overcome by guilt, she scuffed a foot along the carpet. "In fact, I didn't really quote you fair. It was only on account of you having such a nice house that I told you the quart basket cost twenty-five cents. It doesn't, really. It's ten cents a pint. That makes it twenty cents a quart, not two bits."

"I see."

"So, if you still want what we have, I'll go out and make a count. The number may be closer to forty quarts than fifty. That'd be eight dollars, total."

Mrs. Dryfus looked from mother to daughter, ruefully shaking her head.

"I can see the apple does not fall far from the tree. Or in this particular case, the strawberry runner takes root near the mother plant. Do you know to what I refer -- Nelander?"

"You are saying Patricia and I are poor salesmen." The matron smirked and Nelander took offense. "I fail to see why you include me in your assessment. I have said nothing."

"Oh, but you did not have to." Gracefully swirling the long skirt about her person as she crossed to the window, she bade the girl depart. "Go, child, and count the strawberries. So we may have an accurate judgment."

"Yes, ma'am."

Patricia scooted away, glad for the chance to make amends. Nelander divined the dismissal as having a dual purpose and justified her opinion as

Mrs. Dryfus took her time watching through the glass before pulling on a bell cord. Giles entered, too quickly to have been in another part of the house.

"We will take refreshment. Bring us a bottle of rum." She cast a casual glance at the guest as Giles backed away. "That is the preferred drink of seamen, is it not? When they have business to discuss?"

Because she did not understand the veiled reference, Nelander chose not to answer in the manner prescribed.

"I had presumed we were finished discussing business."

"Whether we have or not depends entirely upon you."

The servant returned carrying a silver tray with a crystal decanter, two matching glasses, a bucket, a small covered container and tongs. Since showing the guests into the parlor, the man had not spoken a word and did not do so now.

"Do you take sugar with your rum, Captain?"

"That depends on whether it is available."

Mrs. Dryfus gave consent and Giles added two cubes to each glass.

"Ice?"

The officer finally smiled. "I prefer to skate on ice rather than have it dilute my liquor."

Giles offered her the glass and a similar one to the mistress. Duty accomplished, he retired.

"You wondered why I accused you of having a poor head for business. How much money did you make from the sale of strawberries this season?"

Although the question might have been taken for impertinence, Nelander did not begrudge the answer.

"Slightly less than $350. Including the eight dollars you are going to pay."

"What amount were you anticipating?"

"Considering circumstances, I feel grateful the crew and I earned as much as we did."

"But a far cry from $500."

"Next year will be better."

"Next year, madam seaman, this country will be at war."

"I hope that is not the case. But if it be so, then the farmers will have more money than usual." Taking a stiff swallow of sweetened rum, Mrs. Dryfus rolled the liquid around in her mouth before swallowing. Nelander did the same, finding the flavor far superior to that which Seth had purchased at the Tankard's Draft. "This is excellent rum."

"From Barbados. An island nation in the Caribbean. Have you been there?"

"I have not. Have you?"

"Indeed. I have traveled extensively." She drank again, coyly observing the guest through the rivulets of alcohol lining the glass. "Why do you suppose the farmers will have more money?"

"To engage in armed conflict, armies must be raised. Soldiers must be fed. The government -- any government -- must buy local produce. The need for corn and wheat will be great. That will necessarily raise the price."

"An astute observation. I commend you. But have you taken inflation into account?"

"I have not."

"Something to consider. Will you have more rum?"

"No, thank you."

"I thought sailors were renowned for their drinking prowess."

"I am an officer, ma'am."

Adding to her own drink, Mrs. Dryfus began a short circuit around the room. Nelander silently decided the woman had been used to living alone and in select company, for in no way could the action be considered genteel or ladylike.

"I consider you a bad businessman because last year when the opportunity presented itself, you turned down an offer of five hundred dollars, cash. Money you could have had without the trouble of 'hawking your wares' from town to town and ultimately earning substantially less."

Drawing air through her front teeth, Nelander reeled from the statement. With effort, she controlled herself.

"That is not a fact you could have known, were you not the one making the offer. But how could it be? We did not know you, then. Nor was it commonly known we had planted such a crop."

The heiress smiled at the mystery.

"I am the wealthiest woman in Lawrence. It is said and likely true that I have greater riches than any man, woman or child in Kansas. Money has its advantages, Captain. I occasionally use it to buy information -- as well as strawberries."

Deciding she would have another drink, Nelander refilled her glass, this time omitting the sugar.

"Your offer, although generous, was entirely one-sided. By accepting, we would have received no more than what I paid for the plants. At the time, I agree, we desperately needed money and it appeared my -- scheme -- to be foolhardy. Not the first I have made since coming here. But to have sold the crop and all subsequent harvests for a one-time payment of $500 deprived us of any expectation for future profit. Or hope for a better life."

"You may have made a rash decision. One, I suspect your husband would not approve."

"In that you err, for it was his decision."

Stopping shock still, Mrs. Dryfus expressed genuine surprise.

"You discussed it with him, then?"

"Of course."

"Do not say 'of course.' I do not know many women in your place who would have done the same."

"Then I pity them, for theirs is an unequal partnership."

"That, Mrs. Ward, is the nature of marriage." Resuming her walk, but coming closer to her guest, she inquired, "Why do you suppose I made such an offer?"

The idea had not occurred to her, but hearing Patricia knock on the outside door, she envisioned a silent Giles answering the summons. A cold shiver slipped down her spine.

"To put Blind Betty and Mute Thomas out of work."

The child's entrance abruptly terminated the discussion if not the speculation. Having run up the pathway, she puffed from exertion.

"Forty-four baskets! If you want them all, that is $8.80."

Carefully laying her glass on the tray, Mrs. Dryfus shot Nelander a pointed look.

"I have already made an offer. Fifty dollars. Take it or leave it as you will."

"With-or-without-the-baskets?"

Their eyes met in standoff.

"With them. Of course."

Of course. When she had so recently admonished, Do not say "of course."

On another subject.

Or not.

CHAPTER 7

Cradling the gold coins given her by Mrs. Dryfus, Nelander directed the wagon slowly down Main Street. Several women nodded greeting. One or two men, either out of work or perpetually unemployed, touched the brim of their hats. To each, Patricia gave a friendly "Hallo!" or a quick wave. Content to let her daughter distribute the social amenities, the officer paid scant attention. With so much money aboard, she did not wish to be delayed.

Slowing the conveyance at the fork in the road, she debated delaying their return long enough to deposit the fifty dollars in the bank. While prudent, such an action would deprive her the pleasure of dropping five ten-dollar coins in Seth's hand and seeing his eyes sparkle.

This hesitation proved her undoing, for as Blaze came to a temporary stop, a man stepped off the boardwalk and approached. Grabbing the bridle in a display of ownership, he placed himself in such a position as to prohibit any counter move.

"Morning, Nelander," he greeted, evoking disgust rather than familiarity.

Deciding her distaste of the man and his arrogant dominance superseded politeness, the officer gave him a curt direction.

"Kindly let go the reins, Mathis, and step aside."

"What's the hurry? I seed yer wagon an' wondered if you got inny more strawberries to sell, is all."

"I have not."

"Didn't figure you to dispose of all them you brung in yesterday. Not much luck at the market, was there?"

The awareness of her activities stirred concern. Although not specifically looking for Mathis, father of the slave tracker Dick McConaghie, she had not seen him, either. That implied stealth on his part. Digging a fingernail into her palm, she silently cursed and promised increased vigilance.

"We sold most by going door-to-door."

"That a fact?" Scratching the front of his thumb across a week's worth of stubble, then listening to the noise as though it conveyed a private message, he appeared to consider her statement. "That old witch on the hill buy the lot? How much she give you fer 'em?"

Too stunned to think of a reply, Patricia saved her.

"We got five dollars an' a'ready put it on account at Mr. Anson's store. You know how it is, sir, when you have to pay what's owin'. Got me and Peter some peppermint sticks, though. Them's a penny a piece."

"Did you, now? Buy yerself some candy? That's good. I got a bit of a sweet tooth, myself. Cost a penny, you say? And you got two?"

"Yes, sir."

"How's about I offer you... fifty cents fer one of them peppermint sticks?" Fishing in his pocket, he withdrew a handful of change. "I got a mind to suck on one jest now. I'm thirsty an' it'll wet my chops."

Caught in a lie, Patricia drew back.

"No, sir. Can't do it. If I come back without one for Peter, he'd be mighty disappointed."

"Then sell me yours. Fifty-to-one is a mighty fine profit. And I hear yer one wid a head fer business."

Another reference to information he had no right knowing. He not only spied on them, he had somehow overheard or been told the conversation taking place less than half an hour ago. Circumstances demanded she trust Giles and Mrs. Dryfus. Neither would have cause and less reason to confide in Mathis McConaghie, who not only had a son working for the Simpson Agency, he likely accepted commissions, as well. That meant another in the household had hurried outside to relay the information.

Whether that servant was black or white remained an open question.

Nelander slapped the leather in an attempt to break away. The horse surged forward but Mathis held him close.

"Get away from the wagon and do not tempt the child with an unholy bargain."

"How's that, now?" He grinned, revealing a mouthful of dirty, crooked teeth.

"It teaches a bad lesson. One does not find such... generous odds... in real life."

"Oh, I dunno know, Miz Ward. Sumtimes a blessing jest falls in yer lap. How's that dog I sold you? Gettin' big, I expect. Eatin' good, is he? And a yapper?"

Remembering again his warning not to sell the animal, she again wondered why. And determined to be rid of it before whatever nefarious plot its breeder hatched came to fruition.

"We must be going. I ask you to release the horse and step aside or I fear you may be trampled."

He did not appear to fear anything.

"What's the hurry? You don't git into town much. Don't hear the news."

He wanted her to ask "What news?" Sensing he had something of importance he did not wish to openly announce, she reluctantly obliged.

"What has happened?"

"Been a riot in St. Louis. You know where that is?"

"Yes."

He acted as though she replied in the negative.

"Missouri. It's a port town on the Mississippi. Steamboats put in there. Some all the way from New Orleans. Others go up river. To St. Paul, or thereabouts."

"For a landlubber, you know a lot about waterways."

"Then, there's the railroad." She bit her lip and said nothing. "Ever been on a railroad?"

"No."

"Fearsome noisy. There's a railroad runnin' acrost Ill-a-nois: the Chicago, Alton and St. Louis Railroad. Takes you to Chicago. Frum there, it's a hop, skip an' paddle over Lake Michigan to Lake Huron an' then into Georgia Bay. Then," he concluded, "yer in Canada."

"Your geography astonishes me, Mr. McConaghie," Nelander admitted with awe akin to dread. Only slightly recovered, she added, "Are you trying to tell me to go back where I came from?"

"Now, why would I do that? I'm a man who likes his sweets an' yer the onlyest seller in town. Fer one, I'd hate to see you pack up an' depart."

He pronounced the word "de-part," with emphasis on the first syllable. She could not determine whether that stemmed from his regional dialect or contained a more subtle warning.

"You were saying? About a riot?"

"Big brouhaha 'tween the U-nited States soldiers an' the state militia. Them volunteer boys is what you might call pro-secessionist."

"Is that supposed to mean something to me?"

"Seth got a brother in the army, don't he? Where's he stationed? Hate to think of him mixed up in anything like that."

"Norman seldom writes and Captain Ward has no idea where he is; or even if he is still in uniform."

Removing his hat, McConaghie scratched his long, dirty hair.

"There's lots gettin' out, I hear. Resignin' their commissions an' waitin' to see which way the wind blows. By that, I mean," he continued without prompting, "what states'll break away frum the Union. Thought mebbe 'Norman' would drop by your place. Settle in a spell. Until he de-cided which side to join."

She would not take the bait.

"Who won the battle?"

"Hard to say. I only hear bits an' pieces Captain Lyon marched his bluebellies to Camp Jackson an' faced off against General Frost. Frost surrendered peaceably enuf, an' the Federal boys got themselves some armaments saved up fer... well, you know. Used fer various an' sundry purposes. Stirred the locals up sumthin' fierce. They took to shootin' one another. Guess you could say the nigger-lovers against the slavers. Killed nigh onto thirty before it was all over." He replaced his hat and petted the horse. "Put me in mind of what happened in Lawrence -- what wid the fightin' broke out over that preacher fella's incendiary talk."

Nelander would have bet real money Mathis McConaghie did not know the word "incendiary." Hearing it come out of his mouth left her feeling ill.

"Then we have suffered two tragedies in a short time."

"That's what I'm thinkin'."

"No doubt for different reasons. But since you have been so good as to inform me of the riot, I must get home. To be on the lookout for Norman."

"You do that. An' if he comes by yer way, give him my regards An' if he's lookin' fer a huntin' dog -- a good tracker -- you send him my way, you hear?"

"Why would a soldier need a dog?"

"Mebbe he's given up sodgerin'. Like I said -- there's plenty what have. He might be needin' a job."

Stomach muscles tightening as she realized he was recruiting for the Simpson Agency, she pursed her lips. Taking that as an end to the discussion, he obligingly relinquished the bridle and stepped away.

"Say howdy to Seth fer me. An' you enjoy them peppermint sticks, little miss."

Averting her head so as to avoid further sight of the man, Nelander urged the horse forward.

"Gid up!"

Leaving McConaghie in the hot sun, the wagon made double-time out of Lawrence. Despite the heat of the day, she did not slow down until they had put two miles between them and the town. Only then did Patricia speak.

"He caught me in a lie, didn't he?"

"He already knew the truth. He was just pushing to see how far we'd go."

"How you reckon he figured we hadn't been to the general store?"

"He was following us. Him, or one of his boys. No doubt they were aware we spent the night at Dr. McTree's and hung around to see where we'd go after that."

"Even up to Mrs. Dryfus'?"

"Most certainly. I pray we have not put either she or the good doctor in danger."

"Why would we have done that?"

"You heard McConaghie speak of the 'railroad.' That man is dangerous."

She said no more and they hurried home to the Pirate Treasure, arriving just as Peter rang the ship's bell eight times.

"Four o'clock. Hope they got supper started. I'm starved."

"Me, too."

It seemed a safe thing to say.

Bolstering her waning enthusiasm, Nelander waved as Seth came out to meet them, Paula cradled in his arms. Gladly taking the baby, she bestowed a dozen kisses on its tiny brow before offering the same to him. He pretended to pout.

"I see now the proper order: baby first, husband second. Which of us did you miss most?"

"I missed you all. More than I can say."

Before he could correctly interpret the statement to infer a brush with danger, Patricia tugged on his sleeve.

"What till you see what we have, sir!"

"Rum?" he guessed.

Being more astute and less hopeful, Peter inquired, "Peppermint sticks?"

The question evoked an unpleasant association and Nelander shuddered. Rather than speak, she allowed the girl to break the good news.

"We sold all the strawberries, papa! Guess how much we made?"

Clearly surprised, he stood on tiptoe, peering into the rear of the wagon. Seeing no returning produce, he could do no better than take her at her word.

"Ten dollars. And if you say 'aye,' I'll toss my hat in the air."

She giggled and made a face. "You're not wearing one. Try again."

"Eight dollars."

"The-other-way."

Seth tapped his nose in contemplation. "Twelve?"

"No."

"Thirteen?"

"Keep going."

His head swung from side to side.

"You didn't have that many berries with you. Unless you found a faerie godmother, I don't know how you coulda made more than ten."

She clapped her hands. "That's just it! We found a faerie godmother."

Staring at Nelander for confirmation, she motioned he hold out his hand and dropped the five gold coins into it. He whistled, then blew on the money as though believing it to be magic and burning hot.

"Fifty dollars? Sweet Jesus! Who in the world gave you such a princely sum for eight dollars' worth of produce?"

Nelander took up the narrative, albeit it in an abbreviated version.

"We'll tell you all about it after we eat."

Hopping down, she almost escaped but Seth grabbed her arm and gently swung her around, money clenched in his fist.

"Fifty dollars? Is it real?"

"As real as any you'll ever spend."

Belief slowly steeped in.

"Then I'll have to let you market the corn and wheat, too. You're a hard bargainer if ever there was one."

"I think not."

Leaving him with the enigma, she hurried into the house. By the time he returned from seeing to horse and wagon, Paula had been fed and put to bed. After a hurried meal, Peter dragged them into the living room.

"Show the money, papa. Spread it out on the floor, so we can count it."

He obliged and for a long moment, the family stared at the minor miracle. Leaving the boy to play with the coins, Seth assumed, rather than settled, into his rocker.

"You going to tell me who paid you, or is it going to be another guessing game?"

"Mrs. Dryfus."

"The old lady who lives on the hill?" Running his tongue behind his teeth, a grin worked through the surprise. "Sounds like the start of a limerick.

> "'The old lady who lives on the hill;
> she's so rich, she can eat her fill.
> Paying with coins as heavy as lead;
> Nelander's strawberries, as sweet as they are red.'"

"Yes: that lady. You know her, then."

"Know of her," he corrected. "Gossip, mostly."

"I would like to hear it."

Stretching out his legs, Seth tickled Peter's back until the boy scooted out of range.

"Who was it who told me? Probably Hector Anson. Or maybe Able Billup. Vickie -- must be short for Victoria -- was the only offspring of a merchant; stiff necked old buggar named Dillinger. Always held himself above the rest. I won't say 'the rest of us,' because all this happened before I ever moved here."

"Go on."

"He owned a factory; manufactured tinware. All sorts. 'From Cans to Canteens.' That was their motto; still is, I suppose. You've seen the adverts pained across the sides of buildings. There's one on the western side of the livery, if I'm not mistaken."

Nelander slowly nodded. "I have seen it. And several more around town. The Wingate Factory. That's where most of the men in town work."

"Right. I have no idea where that name came from." Peter inched his way back and indicated an itchy spot. Seth obligingly scratched it with his toenails. "Must have been thirty years ago, or thereabouts, that another fella came to town. He started a glassware production line. Jars; globes for lamps. They weren't really in competition but for whatever reason, they partnered up. Probably to keep wages down. Kept the name Wingate, and started selling tinware and glass throughout the Midwest. Shipped a lot to St. Louis and from there, down the river to New Orleans. Made a pretty penny."

"Good for them."

He grinned at the sarcasm. "Rumor has it that Vickie and her father never got along. But anyway, one day old man Dillinger up and married her to his partner. Forget his first name; Dryfus was his last."

"And she moved into his mansion?"

"No. That was her pa's. Dryfus was a lot older'n her; closer to her father's age, I'd guess. They tell me she was a pretty girl. The couple did a lot of socializing. Not here, in Lawrence, but over in Topeka. Did some traveling, too, especially after her father died and she inherited his wealth. If I'm not mistaken, her husband died overseas. Vickie came into that, fortune, as well."

"And then she came back here?" He nodded. "Why?"

"No one knows. Everyone reckoned she'd stay away, not having any family or any particularly good memories about the town."

"Why is that?"

"They say she was always standoffish; never hobnobbed with the locals. Maybe she thought she was too good for them. But she did come back. Holed up inside that house and never really comes out."

"Does she still socialize? Do people from Topeka -- or St. Louis -- ever come to visit?"

"Not as long as I've lived here. Leastways, I've never heard anyone speak of her receiving fancy folk. She's got servants to do her shopping so she never has to poke her head out. Once in a while she gets big shipments; probably furniture or fashions or some such. Comes in special delivery."

"What do you mean?"

"Not by stage or anything like that. On a wagon from Down South; all decked out with a lot of men working on it. Hector calls it her 'entourage.'"

"Why is that?"

"He's put outta joint because she doesn't place any orders through him, I guess."

"What kind of entourage?"

"Never thought to ask. Just workers, mostly. And guards. Furniture and crystal and lamps are expensive. Probably cheaper in the long run to bring it in herself, than to have it insured by shipping agents. What's your interest?"

"I don't know. Her home was very nice, that's all."

"Maybe you brought in some of her things on the Bottom Dollar. Sold them in Charleston and she had them delivered to Kansas. It's a small world, after all."

Itch sated, Peter joined Patricia on the floor. Together, they had developed a game whereby they rolled the coins on their edges, trying to score points by getting their pieces closest to the wall. Nelander watched them play, wondering if the money had ever brought its former owner such joy.

"Is Mrs. Dryfus known to be generous?"

"I suppose she gives her share when the mayor's collecting for a church, or a new city building. Other than that, she's sort of like a ghost up there. No one ever sees her and honestly, no one much talks about her. Still runs the factory, though; or hires men to do it for her. Still makes a pretty profit."

"Enough that she should pay $50 for forty-four quarts of strawberries?"

Seth snorted. "Enough to pay $50 a quart."

"But why would she do that?"

"I have no idea. But I can't say I'm not grateful." Leaning back, he rocked awhile, then directed his attention to the crew. "Enough of these games. Give the coins to Nelander so she can mark 'em in her ledger."

"That's right. I had almost forgotten. It doesn't seem right, though. I didn't really earn the money."

"You sure as Kansas did," he protested, curling his toes against the floorboards. "Mrs. Dryfus didn't give you that $50 for nothing. She bought strawberries. If you hadn't had any to sell, you wouldn't have made anything. Never hear me complain if I sell the crops for more than I judge they're worth, do you?"

"No."

"All right, then. Next year, after we sell more, you'll have paid off your initial investment. Not counting labor, everything after that is gravy."

She glanced at him to see if he meant "black" as opposed to "white" labor and saw that he did not. Gratefully, she returned to the kitchen to clean up. Sometime after eight bells, equating to 8 P.M., they ushered the children to bed and sat out on the porch to catch a breath of night breeze.

"Mrs. Dryfus thinks there's going to be a war," Nelander began after a long time studying the sky.

"Some people do; some don't. I've heard about as many sides as there are. I guess it comes down to whether President Lincoln will let the Southern states go or if he'll fight to preserve the Union."

"Mathis McConaghie stopped me in town. He said there was a riot in St. Louis. Between the state militia and the Federal soldiers."

"Strikes me as an odd conversation to have with a woman. Even one who wears trousers," he teased.

"Having any conversation with Mathis McConaghie strikes me as odd." Her eyes drifted back to the heavens. "He said it was really about slavery."

"Don't know why he'd care."

"I suppose he's afraid of losing his livelihood."

"Raisin' hounds?"

"Catching runaways." Seth grunted as Nelander shifted her gaze. "Mathis knew where I'd been in town. That Patricia and I tried to sell strawberries at the market; that we stayed over with Hank McTree. He even knew we had been up to the Big House."

"Probably doesn't have anything better to do with his time."

"You know who we saw there? Besides Mrs. Dryfus?"

"Who?"

"Giles."

"Doing what?"

"Working as a servant." The captain sucked his cheek. "I had a good look at him. He's a Negro."

"That explains why he helped Theresa and the baby."

"I think McConaghie has a spy in the house. He undoubtedly knows Giles works for the Underground Railroad. That may be why his son and Clement got onto them so fast."

"What do you want me to do about it?"

She expected some reaction but not that.

"If Giles has any more 'passengers,' he may take them here. For all we know, the McConaghies and Clement are out there now," she indicated, pointing toward the hills. "Watching us. Waiting. If they come again and catch us trying to help, we could be in trouble." He said nothing. "It's against the law. I don't want you going to jail."

"You want me to speak to Blind Betty? Ask her to have Giles give us a wide berth?"

His use of a nautical expression caused her to shiver.

"I don't know. I want to help but I don't want to be involved.... If you know what I mean."

If Seth knew, he did not say.

Overhead, an array of twinkling stars shone around the Man in the Moon.

He did not vouchsafe an opinion, either.

Leaving them all in the dark.

CHAPTER 8

If silence were truly golden, Nelander and Seth Ward could have bought themselves a clipper ship filled with Spanish doubloons. Having no intrinsic value in the real world, however, the cold barrel of the pistol shoved between them carried a reality as vivid as the breaking of a marriage vow,

"Not a word," a harsh voice warned. "Git up."

"Who the hell --?"

"No questions. Obey as if I were yer captain an' you two able-bodies."

While not out of synchronization with the dialogue usually issued aboard the Pirate Treasure, hearing it from a foreign voice doused familiarity with a bucket of cold water.

Following the warning with alacrity, the married couple slipped out of bed, he to port, she to starboard. Anticipating this physical separation would give them some advantage over the night raider, the man dashed hope by jabbing the pistol butt under her chin.

"Do exactly as I say. You," he directed at Barbara, "Git yer clothes on. No light!"

Seth pulled away from the table lamp, fingers scalded as though the globe had been red hot rather than stone cold. His intent had been a diversion; not for illumination but to seize the heavy brass base as a weapon. Whether that purpose had been divined or if the invader merely wished to remain cloaked in darkness went unanswered.

Nelander glossed over their shared disappointment with a hissed interrogative.

"How do you expect me to 'git dressed' with that damned gun under my chin?"

Seth's muscles tensed, expecting a violent confrontation, but the intruder surprised him by backing off. Lowering the pistol to his side, he used it as a directional.

"Shirt, trousers, socks, boots. An' jacket."

The final command, coming as an afterthought, elicited surprise.

"It's July. Too hot." No answer. "Where are you taking us?"

"Not 'us.' Jest you."

It required no deep introspection to draw dire conclusions. With a cry, half anguish, half rage, Seth reached across the bed, attempting to knock the weapon from the man's hands. Had he been a hunter, on equal footing with his prey, he might have succeeded. But the devil in darkness saw the blow coming and dodged sideways. Unabashed, Seth raced around the foot of the bed, ready to continue the confrontation.

"You're not taking my wife anywhere!"

"Ain't got time to argue." Leveling the gun at a point between Nelander's rib cage, he made clear his intent. "Git dressed. And be quick about it. I ain't got nuthin' to lose." Hearing truth in the avowal, she did as directed. When Seth attempted to follow suit, the deadly weapon meandered over toward him. "Not you." Voice dripping with contempt, he added, "It's too hot. Hate to git you worked into a sweat."

Throwing her arms into a farmer's shirt, then fastening the middle buttons over the cotton undershirt worn as a night dress, Nelander drew a pair of pants over slim hips. Leaving the outerwear untucked, she jammed her feet into socks, then the workman's boots she wore in the fields.

"All right. I'm ready."

"Let's go."

Standing back, he allowed the pair to precede him into the living room. Not a scintilla of light penetrated the interior, indicating the curtains had been drawn before the perpetrator entered the bedroom.

"Are you going to tell us what this is all about?"

Before finishing the question, Seth tripped over Squash, as the small hound wiggled its way between his feet. Hope sprang anew as he anticipated the dog would attack the intruder, or at the very least, explode into a frenzy of barking. With that diversion, he and Nelander might have a chance to wrestle the weapon away. Crouching into an attack position, he nearly leapt before realizing his mistake.

If Nelander and he were to fight, it would be without the assistance of the dog.

Instead of raising voice or baring teeth, the animal whinnied in pleasure, rubbing its wet nose against the stranger's ankles. Awareness struck with the power of lightning.

"Son of a bitch! It's you, Mathis, you dirty pig! No wonder you traded us that damned hound -- and demanded we keep it. Whatever it is you're up to, you've had it planned all along."

"Aye," he mocked. "You've hit the nail on the head. I've had you an' the missus in my sights."

The confrontation in the street flashed before Nelander's eyes as clearly as though she and the elder McConaghie stood there yet. Ears ringing with his nefarious knowledge, stealthily obtained, her fists clenched.

"So, that's why you followed me around Lawrence. Watched us at market; trailed us to Mrs. Dryfus' house." Shame at not following her intuition by putting the money in the bank came back to haunt. "You missed your big payday, didn't you? We sold the bulk of the strawberries out of town. A pity you and your boys weren't on the road back with hoods over your heads. You still have them, I suppose? The hoods?"

She could not see him grin but heard it in his voice.

"Niver know when sech a thing might come in handy."

"But you did find out the old lady paid me in gold and you had your second chance. All right, if that's what you want, you can have the coins. They're here. I will get them for you."

He smacked his lips. "We kin talk about that later. Fifty dollars is a lot of money. But right now, I got other things to tend to."

"Don't think you can get away with this," Seth warned. "You didn't count on us recognizing you, but we have. You lay a hand on Nelander, I won't bother reporting you to the sheriff. I'll kill you with my bare hands. And then I'll send the ghosts on this place out to haunt you. You'll never have peace, alive or dead." Sensing the man waver, he pursued his only option. "But if you leave now -- go away and never come back -- I won't say anything."

"Oh, you won't be sayin' nuthin', one way or 'tother."

Desperation rose. "I mean it. Take that damn dog of yours and get out." Sweat poured down his jaw. "We'll pretend none of this ever happened. You can even have the damn money. Just leave us alone."

"Cain't be doin' that."

"Then you'll have to murder us both."

McConaghie shifted weight from one leg to the other.

"Oh, not jest the two of you. I'd have to kill them young'uns, too. Murder's a hangin' offense. Wouldn't want to leave inny witnesses."

Shrieking in fury, Seth lunged at the slave catcher. In the inky blackness he misjudged the distance, striking a blow to the side, rather than full in the chest. With the agility of a hunter, Mathis recovered quickly, bringing the butt of the pistol across the back of his head. Crying in pain, Seth slumped to his knees. Nelander would have been next, but a growled warning kept her away.

"I don't want to have to shoot. Wake up them 'crew.' They cume out here, all sorts of devils is gonna be unleased."

She believed him.

"All right. I'll go with you."

"Now," he urged, relieved. "Quick."

"No --!"

The point of the gun to his back silenced further protest from the distraught husband.

"You -- go back to bed. Git under the covers. Pull the sheet over yer head. Don't cume lookin' fer me. Don't follow. Got it? If you do, likely you ain't niver gonna see yer wife ag'in. Understand?"

"Yes."

"Yes, what?"

"Yes... sir. You bastard."

"Been called worse. Remember what I said. You don't know nuthin'. Nuthing. Not one damn thing. You been sleepin' all night. Yer wife," he ominously added, "is in bed. She took bad wid a sick headache. Innyone asks, you don't want to wake her. Can you remember?"

"Yes. I can remember."

"Ain't no one been here."

"Please, if it's money you want --"

"Shut up! Ain't got time to argue." To Nelander, he growled, "Let's go. Quiet."

Slipping out the door, she waited as he stooped to run a rough hand over Squash's head before joining her. The action stirred no affection in her heart. When this night reached a conclusion, she would shoot the animal.

With luck, she would shoot both animals.

"West," he said. "Through the fields."

A creepy-crawly sensation of dread spread down Nelander's back and into her vital organs. Rationally, the command carried no more a threat than having the barrel of a gun jammed in her face. On a lower, more basic level, however, her instincts as a woman rebelled from a fate more insidious than death.

Occasionally aboard ship, she had been confronted with unwanted attention from one of the sailors. More rarely, threats of a singular nature were directed at her female constitution. Those, she had managed to fend off through threat and once, violence. Alerted by her struggle, the crew had responded, coming to her defense. The perpetrator had been apprehended, taken before a spontaneously assembled seaman's court and convicted.

Had his crime been the actual commitment of rape, a sentence of death would have come swift and sure. Without appeal, he would have been set adrift on a yawl, provided enough food and water to last three days. In the middle of the ocean, the punishment was less merciful than immediate drowning by tying bags of sand to his ankles and tossing him overboard.

Attempted rape carried only slightly less punishment. Captain Nelander brought out the cat o' nine tails and ordered the attacker bound to the mast. Lashing the naked body until the felon fell insensate, he was then dispatched to the hold where he remained for the duration of the voyage. Rather than hand him over to civilian authorities when they reached port, the captain reported the incident to the Harbor Master. That worthy entered the criminal's name and description in a ledger, made available only to ships' officers. For a tar, that amounted to the kiss of death, for no reputable captain ever hired an individual so inscribed.

Barbara Nelander-Ward had no such redress available. Standing alone with a man threatening violence, no vengeful crew within shouting distance, she had little chance of escape by matching her physical prowess against his. That meant survival depended solely on wits.

"I do not take orders from inferiors."

The audacity did not deter her captor.

"Suit yerself. I shoot you here, then wait fer everyone to come runnin' outta the house an' shoot them, too. Like varmints comin' outta a flooded hole. That what you want?"

He knew the answer and it made her desperate.

"Mathis, for God's sake, what is this all about?"

"Mebbe more about 'God' than you think. Git movin.'"

The cryptic reply in no way soothed her nerves, but did prompt compliance. Striking a westerly direction, she plunged into the darkness, shoulders slightly bowed, legs striding with purpose. If nothing else, she would save Seth and the children, confronting her own mortality when the time came.

They traveled an hour before he called a halt. Leaning his back against a tree, the bulky man panted heavily, removing his hat to fan his freely perspiring face. Better conditioned from a life at sea, and stamina sharpened by repeated trips to and from the valley, Barbara more easily caught her breath. Feigning undue weariness, however, she dropped into a squat near him, attempting to position herself for an attack. If she were able to grab the pistol from his hand, the tables would turn.

He proved a more adept predator than that which she gave him credit, by prodding her back with his foot. He might have done so with violence but settled for intent.

"Easy, missus. I hunted enuf bear to know all the tricks."

The warning elicited anger.

"Shoot me here, then, if you've a mind. We are far away with no one to hear."

"Got farther to go befer dawn."

"Where? Where are you taking me? And for what purpose?"

He stared at her from under brushy eyebrows.

"Who said there were inny purpose?"

"A man does not track -- or lead -- a 'bear' for sport. He intends to kill."

"Then, you've answered yer own question."

"But not your reason." Stomach upturning, a vague premonition availed reason. "Further north is the Kaw River. You do not mean to... sell me into slavery?"

Even in the blackness she could see him grin.

"Now, that'd be illegal, wouldn't it? Pawnin' off a white woman as a Negress." He replaced his hat, then patted the breast pocket of his shirt. "I'd need papers; certifyin' you to be the product of a white man an' a darkie." Reaching out, he brought a hand near her face. "Yer young enuf to be my daughter."

"Only if you began fornicating before you were old enough to skin a deer."

She had not meant for him to laugh but he did, round and jolly.

"That comes close to a compliment, Miz Officer. How old are you?"

"Eighty."

Too late to take it back.

Retreating a safe distance, Nelander appraised what she could see of the man.

"You know, I have never heard you laugh."

"Cain't say I've had much occasion."

"So kidnapping amuses you?"

"I don't find nuthin' involvin' money to be funny." Checking the pistol in his belt, he motioned they move out. "You make a lot of money, runnin' that ship you was on?"

"I did not own it."

"Git paid good?"

"A fair wage."

"Have niggers aboard?"

"My best friend was a Negro."

Bending beneath an overhanging branch, he did not look back to see if she were following.

"That where you learned to tolerate 'em?"

"That is where I learned to judge a man by his heart and skill rather than the color of his skin." Instead of stooping, Nelander pushed the branch aside so she could pass. "Where did you learn your hatred?"

"You 'spect a man kin hate what he makes money on?"

"I've known sailors who hated the sea."

The reply puzzled him, for he stopped and glanced over his shoulder.

"Why is that?"

"They are afraid."

She passed and took the lead. He followed without protest.

"Of dyin'?"

"All men, I suppose, are afraid of dying. It is the manner of death as much as anything else. Falling from the topmast. Being washed overboard in a storm and drowning. Suffering from scurvy. Running afoul of the captain and being mistreated. Some men are even afraid of hard work." She meant the barb for McConaghie and he grunted in acknowledgment. "They dream about riches but have no legitimate way of obtaining them. That embitters them and drives the most craven into lawlessness."

"I'd like to be rich."

"It does not appear your present occupation offers much opportunity for that."

"Oh, you'd be surprised. A nice, fancy yella gal could fetch upwards of one thousand dollars."

The amount staggered. "You lie."

"No, miss, I ain't lyin'. Courst, a good, strong yellar man's worth more."

"More than a full-blooded black man?"

"That's the way of it."

She had no specific reason for keeping him talking. In the back of her mind, it simply made him more human. Whether that represented a good thing or a bad remained to be seen.

"Why?"

"Plantation owners thinks a slave what got white blood works harder." He tapped his head. "Got more brains."

"I would hardly think that a qualification for working in the fields."

He chuckled again, between a guffaw and a snort.

"The prevailin' theory is a darkie's stronger but more likely to try an' flee. That's an expense, gittin' him back. A half-an-half figures he'll niver git away an' so he stays on till he drops."

"That is the 'brains' of which you speak? I would rather a man with spirit who tries to escape than one resolved to his fate."

Eerily, they both had the same thought. Nelander bolted, darting to her right. Head down, she raced through the low brush, attempting to outdistance him and then lose herself in the taller wood. Reacting simultaneously, he followed close behind, catching her as she attempted to double back. Wrapping thick, iron-hard fingers around her arm, he jerked her back, making her teeth snap.

"Easy," he whispered. Then, "Easy," a second time. Taking quick bearings, he drew her into a thicket. "We're right about there." Wiping a hand across his upper lip, he ground a foot into the earth. "Take off yer clothes."

"Go to hell."

Squinting at her, or so she thought, Nelander brought up both arms in an attitude of defense. Mathis seemed not to notice, eyes shifting upward and beyond.

"It'll be light soon."

"The better to see your dirty deed?"

Snapping back to attention, he slapped a hand against his thigh.

"I ain't kiddin'. Get outta them clothes."

"I have refused once. What is it about 'Go to hell' you don't understand?"

Brave talk notwithstanding, Barbara felt sick. While she had no credible explanation for his actions, the idea he contemplated rape before selling her as damaged goods to an equally despicable slave trader brought her squarely to a conundrum. In all probability, she could anger McConaghie enough to force a confrontation. With a perverted claim on luck, he might kill her before achieving either.

Being dead, she would not care what happened to her body. On the other hand, she no longer claimed sole right to her existence. Within her existed a strong loyalty and dedication to Seth and the children. Surviving whatever horrors Mathis had in store, she might conceivably make her way home. If not for herself, she owed them that chance.

Slowly taking off the jacket he had specifically demanded she wear, Nelander swung her arm, trying to appear as though she were casting it off. Maintaining a firm grasp on one sleeve, however, she used the heavy material as a whip of sorts, cracking the bulky lower end across his face. Caught unaware, he arched his neck, deflecting some but not all of the blow.

"Bitch!" he grunted, temporarily blinded by the cloth. Dancing backward, he caught his balance, lashing out with a leg which caught her in the midriff. Breath knocked out, Nelander doubled over. Straining for air, she dived head first, using her weight to counteract his more formidable strength. They fell together, she on top.

Fingers to his eyes, she gouged, then ripped her nails across his face. Maneuvering too close to the open mouth, he bit down, sending shivers of pain up her wrist and through the arm. Refusing to let go despite another attempt to blind him, McConaghie tore at the flesh, bearing into bone. Forced to abandon any further attack, Nelander went limp and the teeth parted.

Freeing her hand which throbbed an agony in both temples, she jammed her lids closed to cut out an inferno of exploding color, then rolled to his side. Anticipating further blows against her exposed spine, she rolled again, curling into a fetal position, crossed arms covering what she could of chest and head.

"Jesus! Damn hell cat!"

Rubbing his face where she had broken the skin, he pulled himself up to his knees, spat a mouthful of saliva, then peculiarly went after her discarded jacket. Clutching it close, he appeared to be straightening it of wrinkles, before snarling, "The rest of your clothes. Hurry. Or else."

Barbara Nelander did not want to ask, Or else what?

Knowledge, in this case, being tantamount to hell.

CHAPTER 9

Finger aching with the power of a sledgehammer driving a stake through her hand, Nelander found she could not unfasten the buttons of her shirt. Pain making her defiant to the point of madness, she tore at the placket with the intent of ripping it, when a gruff, almost anxious voice arrested the gesture.

"Wait! Don't rip it!"

The command made no sense. He could not very well expect to violate her, then return her home, pretending, by outward appearance, nothing had happened. Nor could she believe a slave buyer would give a fig whether she came to the block fully dressed or stark naked.

Unable to reason further, Nelander abandoned all attempt to comply. Catching herself from swooning as dark mists gathered behind her orbs, the captive made a gesture of defeat.

"You just about tore my finger off."

"Damn me if I did." A second or a third or the tenth assertion of nonsense. She had lost count and did not care. Retreating two more steps, an image of her father, standing alone in a San Francisco saloon, battered, bloodied and outnumbered, came to her in a flash. The old, familiar face she knew so well, turned slowly, staring at the daughter whose reputation he defended.

Choked with emotion, Barbara felt her throat constrict as she willed him to hear, You did it for me. Dutchy said so. You against the world. I never had the chance to say thank you. To tell you... how much you meant to me. How much I loved you. Tears came to her eyes. You died, Captain Nelander, before I ever knew what happened. Not fair. Not fair. We were going to go to China.

One blackened eye seemed to twitch; the other, swollen shut, drooped at the corner. A bubble in blood formed at the apex of his broken nose. She could hear the wheezing from his lungs. One, if not both, had been punctured.

An ugly way to die.

A smile curled along the edges of his smashed lips.

No, Nelander. You judge too harshly. Appearances are not always what they seem. I am drowning, you see -- drowning in my own blood. If a seaman is going to die, he ought to drown. I have gotten my wish. Gone down defending the ship. As a captain should. No regrets, Officer Nelander.

I was not ready to have you die.

Neptune never asks; he takes at will.

Then his will is that I join you.

No, Nelander. His smile widened. She saw the gap where a tooth had broken. His tongue came out to cover the hole. I never called you daughter. I shall not do so now. Your fight has just begun.

I have fought him and lost.

Neptune is not ready to take you.

The hair on the back of her head bristled in indignation.

I did not mean Neptune.

Who else can claim one of the sea?

A devil of the land.

You know better than that. He cocked an ear. She could see a trickle of blood and knew the ear drum had shattered. Listen on the wind.

Listen for what he heard.

Through the senses of a dead man.

A captain who had drowned on shore.

That realization made all the difference.

She heard the noise. Far off. In the bushes. Several hundred yards away. Forcing down her eyes which had rolled into the top of her skull, Nelander listened. Footsteps. One pair. And then a second. Two strangers approaching.

A rendezvous.

Three against one.

Ned Nelander had fought greater numbers.

And lost.

Neptune is not ready to take you.

Concentrating on the sound sharpened her senses. The hurt in her hand faded.

A cry. Not her own. Seamen did not cry. They abandoned such sentiment when signing the Articles.

A woman's voice. Low. A muffled apology.

Listen.

She listened.

A hand rested on her shoulder. Her body did not flinch.

"Git them clothes off. Quick, like a bunny."

She no longer felt afraid.

The strangers came into the clearing. Two, as she had guessed. A man unknown to her and a Negress. The woman drew near and touched her hair. Nelander supposed it to be a gesture of sisterhood. The man approached McConaghie.

"We have to hurry," he said. "Is everything agreed?"

She expected them to exchange money. They did not. Perhaps the stranger had already paid for her.

Everything hinged on what she did next.

Run -- quick, like a bunny.

Obey orders and undress.

Fight like a hell cat.

An obvious choice. Unfortunately, she had no idea which to pick.

The newcomer rubbed his hands together. He had not anticipated delay.

"You won't be goin' far," he tried. "It's me an' Lolly who'll be followin' the drinking gourd."

Feeling her pupils expand, increased vision peeled back layers of night which hung on one another like dual skins.

"What?"

"Look," he explained, pointing upward. In the pre-dawn heaven she beheld a bevy of distant stars. Seamens' friends the world over. Constellations used for navigation. With a chart and a sextant, a man could measure the horizontal and vertical angular distance between objects above the horizon, determining longitude and latitude.

"You know the sky?"

"I know the sky," she repeated.

"We're goin' one way, you an' Mathis the other."

It's me an' Lolly who'll be followin' the drinking gourd.

She formed the shape in her mind. Slightly curled, like a comma. Or a butternut squash Revelation came with awe.

"The Big Dipper. You'll be going north."

"That's right; once we git to Topeka, we go north as far as Nebraska City. Then east."

Using the stars as guide.

There's a railroad runnin' acrost Ill-a-nois: the Chicago, Alton and St. Louis Railroad. Takes you to Chicago. Frum there, it's a hop, skip an' paddle over Lake Michigan to Lake Huron an' then into Georgia Bay. Then, yer in Canada.

Two separate routes.

Along the Underground Railroad.

One given her by Mathis McConaghie. A slave catcher. The other by a stranger. A slave buyer.

It did not make sense.

But, of course, it did. If the world had turned topsy-turvy.

Shaking in rage, Nelander directed a pointed stare at her nemesis.

"Son of a bitch. You expect me to believe you're an abolitionist?"

He grinned and his smile had a lopsided configuration. Like a comma. Or a drinking gourd.

"No, ma'am. I raise hounds fer a livin'. Do a bit o' plantin' on the side; fer times when I gotta give a dog away. The kind that don't track."

Does he have a name?

Squash.

"Why did you trade us that pup? There's nothing wrong with him. His nose is as good as Herman's. Better."

"Finally realized that, did you?"

Facts tumbled in on her the way baby animals romped with one another.

"But it didn't bark to alert us when you broke in the house."

"Smart dog, ain't he? He took to learnin' real quick."

"You told me not to sell it or give it away -- so you could steal inside when we thought ourselves protected."

"Barkin' dog kin be heard a long ways off. Men trackin' me 'ill follow the sound right to yer doorstep. There's some what knows you got a hound.

They don't hear no yappin', they figure ain't no one up yer way. They keep lookin' through the woods."

"Your sons," she accused. "Working for the Simpson Agency."

"That's right."

Them dogs is sorta like my family. Worth more'n the boys, sumtimes, I think.

"And you don't."

"I work the other side, you might say."

The insinuations, the vague references, the carefully laid plans made her brain ache.

"And who is your 'boss'?"

He winked. "Mrs. Dryfus. I thought you mighta figured that."

She might have, had not her reasoning fallen along a different track.

"Why, in God's name, didn't you make your intentions clearer?"

"Don't like people thinkin' bad of me."

By "bad," or course, he meant "good." Which brought nothing into sharper focus.

"Your sons -- don't know?"

He scoffed. "Course they don't. Come to it, they'd put a bullet in my back."

"Why?"

"They got their life, I got mine."

"But surely they... learned from you."

"Their ma. She has a way wid her. A'ways snoopin' round. Found herse'f a good payday, onest. The boys took to that real good. Better'n trainin' dogs or growin' corn."

"What... payday?"

"Ain't fer me to say. Now you know an' you kin use it ag'in me."

"That, I would never do." Nelander ground her foot in the earth. "You know that."

"Don't know nuthin' 'bout trustin' people." Putting a hand to his own shirt, he indicated she do the same. "We gotta hurry. You change clothes wid the miss, here. Good thing yer a one fer wearin' trousers. She gotta look like a man."

"A man?"

"Agents on both sides of the river is searchin' fer a female. That," he added with a grin, "be you."

The bizarre situation finally revealed, Nelander quickly exchanged clothes with the young woman. After making the exchange, the Negress reached out a hesitant hand and tried a shy smile.

"Yuh a good woman."

"And you are a brave one, Miss --?"

"Lolly. No, miss. Ah ain't. Mah man be waitin' fer me." She puffed with pride. "He 'scaped a year ago. He be waitin' fer me."

"I wish you well."

Giving her a hug, the white woman quickly threw on the rough homespun, worming into the dress opposite of how a butterfly would emerge from a cocoon. The garment proved too small, compelling her to force it over wide shoulders and long legs. While an astute eye could easily detect some shenanigans at play, most men would pass her by without a second glance. Hopefully, such indifference would be enough to allow Barbara to pass.

Without pants, her legs felt bare and the open construction felt drafty, if not downright indecent. It had been a long time since she wore anything resembling a dress and standing in the open with two men, she wondered why anyone would willingly choose so revealing and un-protective a style.

Bracing herself for a crude observation from McConaghie, he merely indicated she more carefully lace the light sandals taken in trade, then nodded.

"I'll be takin' you to the river. It ain't far."

"And then what?"

He indicated she wrap a kerchief over her hair. "That way, you won't be so easily spotted fer white. We want 'em followin' you a good piece befer they learn they're on the wrong trail." He waited until she did as directed before continuing. "If there ain't no disturbance, then we go up into the Territories a might. Camp out, mebbe, one night. By that time, I reckon one or two of them boys frum the Simpson Agency'll be around. They'll move in, try to make an arrest. Only, you won't be who they think you is."

"But what about the dogs? They'll lead your sons and Clement away from our trail and right after these two."

"Hounds cain't be fooled by color. Yer right about that. They'll follow the scent, a'right."

"Then the plan cannot work --"

"The same scent they been followin' all night. Yours."

"Mine? But how? You mean, because they picked it up at the house? But surely Dick has something of Lolly's --"

"That he do, Nelander. He got a rag she hid under; outta the wagon used to smuggle her into Lawrence."

"Well, then?"

"Peculiar thing, it looks 'zactly like a piece of cloth you used to cover them strawberries you sold 'em to Mrs. Dryfus."

The magnitude of the plan caused her to shiver.

"You switched them?"

"Why not? A man cain't tell the difference. He cain't smell no scent. So when he's tolt this is what the runaway curled up in, he has no reason to believe otherwise."

"Is that why... she bought the fruit?"

He shrugged. "I don't pry into her business." Which may or may not have been all the truth. "Let's go."

Pausing to shake hands with the second operative of the Underground Railroad, Nelander followed Mathis, this time with a spring to her step. After traveling for an hour, a subtle change in air alerted her senses. It did not take much to put an interpretation to the effect.

"We are near the river."

"Glad to hear it." He swore and shook a leg. "This walkin' is killin' my feet."

Although unintended, the complaint finally solicited a dry laugh.

"You risk your life for a cause I still cannot believe you espouse, then fuss over so simple a matter as your feet. You, sir, are an... odd duck." Grinning with intent, she added, "I was going to call you 'peculiar,' but that word has forever been linked with poor Master Peter. I should think you would not appreciate it."

Curious to see how he would react, McConaghie digested the comparison, then waved a hand in front of his face as if whisking away unwanted spirits.

"You jest see he don't sic none of them ghosts after me when you git back. Or rather," he clarified, uncomfortably clearing his throat, "Tell him to call 'em off. I been feelin' them goblins ticklin' my nose since we left yer place."

"Do you, now?"

"I do. Don't be tellin' 'im why, now, mind. Don't want my involvement gittin' out. Them boys of mine'll skin me alive, they figure I crossed 'em."

"I am sorry to hear that. But I will say nothing -- to the children. As for Seth, I must offer some explanation or your life won't be worth two cents. And the hell with spirits," came the afterthought.

Parting a tumble of thickets, they made their way through and came out at the river bank. Enough light filtered from the newly rising sun to make the land and the expanse of water clearly visible.

Stopping short, he cast her a sideways stare.

"You ain't afraid to go on by yerself?"

"You are not coming with me?"

The accusation caused him pain, for he grimaced.

"Cain't. They'll be another fella on t'other side. He'll pick you up and take you a ways. Like I said."

"What will you do?"

"Hightail it back. Say I lost the trail I were followin'. Cuss sumthin' awful about it, too. Missin' out on that re-ward money. A damn terrible shame."

Quietly appraising him, Nelander paused a long beat before finally speaking.

"You play a most dangerous game, Mr. McConaghie. One I hope is well rewarded -- I will not say 'in heaven,' for I doubt that holds much significance. Mrs. Dryfus is generous?"

He spat and looked away.

"Not as much as if I was sellin' strawberries."

"Then I will have to save you some cuttings from my crop. An industrious man who tended to his farming ought to be able to harvest a small crop in a year or two."

Jerking his head back up, he squinted, then blew air through his nose.

"Spare yerself the trouble. Over there." He raised a hand and waved it across the river bank. "You'll find a man wid a boat. He'll row you over an' then leave you. Jest start walkin'. The next conductor'll find you."

"What does he look like? What is his name? How will I know him?"

"You jest say one thing -- you ask 'im fer a drink frum his gourd. That'll be enuf."

"And after this -- adventure is over and I prove I am not the runaway they seek -- how do I get back?"

"Same way you come."

"Thanks a lot."

Tipping his hat, Mathis stepped into the water and she followed. After walking several hundred yards he raised a hand in farewell and made it to shore.

"I see you ag'in," he mumbled over his shoulder, "you think I'm the devil's poison. Remember."

"That, sir, I shall have no trouble keeping in mind."

This time, he evinced no humor.

Not when Peter Ward's hobgoblins were dogging his footsteps.

CHAPTER 10

A ten minute walk down the coastline took Nelander through a tangle of bushes and scrub trees. Coming through the other side convinced no good could ever come of wearing a skirt, she confronted a white man wearing what more closely resembled swamp grass than headwear. Permitting herself a moment to appraise the newcomer, she decided "nondescript" suited and turned attention toward the boat dragged on shore.

Clearly homemade, the craft showed signs of long wear. Splinters protrudes from around the edges, the hull revealed scrape marks from too much contact with unfriendly shore rocks and the oars, hanging with a desultory air from either side, might have better served for kindling. Yet, it had been four years since last she faced the prospect of a water craft of any type and she embraced the chance with open arms.

Barely able to contain mounting enthusiasm, she riveted her eyes back toward the stranger.

"A sip from your drinking gourd, mister?"

Dropping his hand toward a dried squash water-vessel carried on a sling over his shoulder, they confirmed identities. Satisfied, the former seaman stepped boldly toward the row boat. Showing aside the proffered help, she leapt aboard, settled in by the oars and gave him a quick nod.

"Shove off, master riverman."

The command took him aback.

"You ain't afeared of the water, miss?"

"There 'ain't' no 'miss' about it. While the Kaw River makes a mighty poor sea, I have dreamed of such a moment. I have been too long separated from the ocean."

Unable to account for the sentiment, he pushed the boat into the water, then hopped in. Nelander refused to give up her position.

"I will row."

Had circumstances been otherwise, she would have laughed at his tortured expression.

"I don't cotton to bein' dumped," he hiccupped.

"While I am out of practice, I have never yet lost a crewman."

Adeptly maneuvering the oars, she redirected the boat toward the opposite side and threw herself into the task. It took no more than three deep cuts of the blades to propel them into the depths. Another half dozen and the conductor settled back, finally daring to brush a strand of loose palmetto away from his face.

"You row like a man."

"No, sir. I row better'n a man."

"How'd that happen?" he sniffed, as if expecting that beneath her female attire lay the anatomy of a male.

"I was born to it -- same as you, I expect. By the time I was five years old, I had signed aboard the Bottom Dollar. She was a ship outta Canada. Worked my way up to second officer. Never took any favors, never gave any." Realizing too late the double entendre, Barbara shot him a warning. She need not have bothered, for he never made the connection.

"How is it a seaman comes to find himself in Kansas?"

Debating how much to say, she opted for a half truth.

"I was shipwrecked in San Francisco; was making my way overland back to the Atlantic when I ran out of money. Got as far as Lawrence and took a different berth."

He seemed to accept the explanation and she worked in silence, only regretfully reaching the shallows and bringing their trip to an end. Without waiting for him to get out and drag the boat ashore, she jumped into the water and performed the task.

"Now, yer all wet," he exclaimed, casting a furtive glance around the shore.

"Never known a seaman to melt. Besides, it's hot. I'll dry." Wringing out the hem of the dress, she made a face and shrugged. "What's next? Are you coming with me or will there be another?"

"I'm gone. Got work to do. Be back here in a day or two. Jest this spot? Kin you remember?"

Taking stock of the landmarks, she nodded.

"But there must be danger for you: helping a runaway escape."

"No, sir. I didn't help no runaway. I took a white lady acrost. An' she paid me a dollar fer my trouble. Didn't say who she was an' I didn't ask. Nothing illegal about that."

"But surely those slave chasers will catch on."

"Then, we change operations. Best be goin'. You'll be met up wid."

Wiping a hand on his shirt front, he offered it. Nelander took it and they shook. Not like men, but equals in a very deadly game of cat and mouse.

"See you by-and-by."

Drawing up the wet, heavy material of the dress, Barbara set out, moving with the long, assured strides of someone set on a course. She did not look back, but heard her unnamed conspirator row away.

Soon, another stranger fell in by her side and they walked together without exchanging particulars for nearly ten hours. As the sun reached a settling angle in the west, he made a low grunt and indicated they stop.

"Fer enuf. We'll make camp. You hungry?"

"About enough to gnaw on your leg -- raw."

Dropping a shoulder pack to the ground, he quickly assembled material and made a fire. Feeding it dry twigs, then larger sticks and finally logs, the fiery, orange, blue-tipped flames vigorously thrust aside the growing shadows. Without prompting, he explained.

"Got no need to hide. We want 'em to find us."

She had forgotten and the words sufficed to allay her concern.

"I wondered what it would be like -- being a slave and running for my freedom. Never knowing who to trust; always looking over my shoulder, listening for the sound of baying dogs. Putting miles behind me and knowing that one slip -- one mistake -- and one of them would find me. Living without legal recourse -- seeing the law as an enemy and not a friend. Facing certain punishment and worse -- the loss of hope. Now, I know."

Casting her a strange look, the man rested back on the flat of his feet. These were the first words either had spoken and they struck a chord.

"You are a poet."

Articulated without his previous gruffness, the sentence revealed not only a capacity for wonder but sentience and education. Beyond that profundity, the speech revealed him for an outsider, causing her to shiver.

"You are not from around here."

He grinned and wiped his face, clearing away an accumulation of grime and perspiration. Somewhat neatened, Barbara more accurately guessed his age at twenty-five where before, she had supposed him older.

"Philadelphia. And you are not from around here, either."

"Nova Scotia."

"That gives us something in common. Neither of our places of birth tolerate the onerous stain of slavery."

"Indeed, they do not." Dropping into a squatting position, she watched as he dropped a pound of bacon onto a frying pan and adeptly settled it over the fire. "Got any coffee in there?"

"Coffee comes next."

"Coffee, sir, ought to come first."

Digging out a battered pot, he filled it from a canteen and added rough-ground beans. Settling it alongside the pan, the air soon filled with the delicious odor of sizzling fat and boiling java. The aroma encouraged familiarity.

"What's a man from Philadelphia doing in Kansas?"

"From an early age, I was always moved by injustice. I heard a preacher come through the city one day and he spoke of such atrocities, I was moved to tears. Gave up my teaching position and joined a Society. They sent me south. What I witnessed there scared the bejesus out of me. Sane, rational men defending the enslavement of human beings on the basis of bettering the race. Yet seeing nothing wrong with working them to death in the cotton fields or the gin mills."

Nelander poured coffee into a pair of dented, black-speckled tole mugs and they drank.

"I have had some exposure to that way of thinking. There was a minister from Boston and a plantation owner from Charleston debating in Lawrence. What they had to say was chilling -- made worse by the reception, which turned violent."

"I am afraid there is no talking our way out of this curse."

Not wanting to agree, they ate in silence, dipping hard crusts of bread into the fat and chewing fried meat before she finally came back to conversation.

"Why did you come this far west?"

"It was an accident, really. I was out walking late one night -- in Charlotte. I heard a scuffle between a white man and a Negro and dared intervene. I left the fellow with a cracked noggin. Since that meant I had to depart in a hurry, I decided to take the slave with me. As a servant, as it turned out. No one questioned that relationship. I ended up here and luckily fell in with some good people. They sent him along the Railroad and put me to work."

"Did you ever hear from him, again -- the man you saved? Did he get away?"

"No." He did not elaborate on which interrogative he answered. The one word negative spoke for itself. "My name is James Best, by the way."

"Barbara Nelander; Captain Nelander to strangers; Nelander to friends."

"I'm just plain Jim."

"Not so plain, sir. You do dangerous service for the oppressed."

"Someone has to care." Lips pursed, he might have gone on when the muffled sound of a tree limb moving unnaturally in the quiet drew his attention. She read his expression.

They are here.

Adding pretend to her repertoire, Nelander pulled up her hood and reached for the coffee pot.

"I will have more --"

"Leave yer hands where they is!" a stern command warned.

Two thoughts flashed simultaneously through her mind: she did not recognize the voice and if she had a weapon, she would whirl and discharge it. The awareness of her propensity for violence came as no surprise. The regret at being unarmed did.

Two men rushed the inner circle of light, one shoving the barrel of a shotgun in Best's face, the other taking advantage of Nelander's immobility to grab her neck. Hands pressed firmly across throat and voice box, she could neither breathe nor speak. The instant deprivation of freedom and lack of oxygen caused a reddening of facial pigment.

"Don't move." Directed at Plain Jim, the youth unfroze enough to let arms drop listlessly to his side. Seeing he would not struggle, the speaker glanced at their valuable captive. "Give us a merry chase, you did. Yer master'll be glad to git you back. He says spunky ones fetch a higher price. You'll go to the block -- but not," he winked, "widout a taste of punishment."

A third man, holding a pair of muzzled bloodhounds on a long leather leash, broke into the camp site. Using all his strength to hold the animals back, he panted heavily before dropping to one knee. Deftly removing the cloth straps around the dog's jaws, they began a loud, insistent barking.

"Looks like we found our prey, Reeder," he grinned.

Pulling her feet away from the snapping teeth, Nelander nearly choked before the tracker loosened his grip.

"Wouldn't want to leave no marks on you, little miss darkie."

Stifling a natural impulse to curse, the so-called slave displayed a white woman's indignation.

"How dare you, sir! I am no more colored than you -- less, I say. Take your hands off me, or my husband will press charges."

Stunned by the clearly Caucasian enunciation, if not the demand, the bounty hunter readjusted his grip, moving upward so he held her hair. Using that as a tether, he led Barbara closer to the fire. Without permission, he yanked back the head covering, staring angrily into her face. His partner cursed.

"Son of a bitch!"

Jumping back as if stung, Reeder shook his hands from the offending contact with a white woman. While Akins, the man with the shotgun, aimed the weapon at Best, Hoskins, the dog-handler, crossed toward Nelander, corner of his mouth drooping.

"Cain't be no mistake," he huffed. His partner shot him an accusing stare.

"What do ya mean, cain't be no mistake? She's white as the driven snow!"

"The hounds followed her trail --"

"Picked up the wrong one 'crost the damn river."

"Ain't possible. Jest ain't possible." He shoved his unshaven jowls into her face. "She's the one we tracked. It were her scent the dogs was on."

Without giving them time to reason out the puzzle, Nelander stomped her foot.

"Let me go -- do not touch me. I do not know who you are or how you have been so mistaken, but you insult me. The authorities shall hear of this." Realizing full well that neither she nor Plain Jim were in any position to report anything to the law, she gave him the opportunity of putting her to rights. "Where is the closest sheriff, Herbert? This atrocity must be brought to his attention. Surely they have rules and regulations --"

"I don't know. I warned you when we left Kansas City this was a new land --" Affecting innocence, Jim tried, "You, sir. Kindly inform me where the closest town is and the name of the sheriff."

"Not likely."

Clearing his throat then spitting on the ground, the rough-shod man reluctantly lowered the shotgun. Nelander remained obstinate.

"Then, surely an apology is in order."

"We're more sorry than you kin know." Lashing a foot out at the closest dog, the animal yipped and withdrew, ears flattened, tail tucked between its legs. "It don't make no sense. None of this." Reluctant to give up the quest, Hoskins stared harder at Nelander, as though imagining she might somehow have conjured magic to lighten her skin. Begrudgingly abandoning the idea, he turned to Best. "How'd you come to be out here?"

"The answer is none of your business, but I will tell you. My wife and I are traveling to the Nebraska Territories. To start a new life. I am, sir, an apothecary."

"A tonic maker."

"I gave up a very lucrative practice --"

"And would not have had to drag me to this place if you had been able to keep your eyes in their sockets," the erstwhile wife complained.

She succeeded in lessening the tension and the three trackers rocked back on their heels.

"We got us here a 'fee-landerer,'" Akins scoffed. "Sorry to have troubled you, miss, seein' as how you got trouble enuf." Making a lunge at one of the hounds, his nose crinkled. "I'm gonna shoot them mutts. Ain't none of 'em inny good. Lost the scent at the water, they did, an' took up another. Wasted us a whole day."

"Dogs don't do that. They're trained better'n that."

"Then mebbe who-some-ever trained 'em done it wrong. Or sold us some bad ones. Twenty dollars each fer them mutts and cain't one of 'em smell a nigger from the hind end of a jackass." Spitting again, he rested the shotgun in the crook of his arm. "Now, we gotta start over. Damnation!"

Motioning the rest follow, he plunged back into the encroaching darkness. Reeder followed, leaving behind only the man with the hounds. Not as quick to give up his chance at a payday, Hoskin's hand twitched.

"Dogs don't make no mistakes."

Nelander bristled.

"The quotation, sir, is 'God doesn't make any mistakes.' You and your animals are a far cry from that."

"You tricked us. Got a mind to bring you back, innyway. Have someone take a look-see at you."

"Do that and make yourself the laughing stock of Douglas County. See who will hire the likes of he who cannot tell the difference between a white woman and a Negress."

"Them dogs tracked you." Shaking his head, he wandered around the campsite, determined to solve the mystery. "No. You was the ones we was after. No doubt about it." Dropping down, he grabbed the nearest dog and shook it by the head. Removing a cloth from his back pocket, he shoved it out. "Smell this, boy."

Quickly obliging, for that was its nature, it sniffed, then rolled wide, black marble eyes toward Nelander. Mouth slightly parted, the animal quivered and would have leapt forward, had the tracker not prevented.

James Best slid to his left, putting distance between himself and Barbara. Whatever his intent, he erred, for the slaver took it as an aggressive gesture. Rising too fast, he let go the hound, which immediately made a dash at its prey. Sixty pounds of instant fury struck Nelander full in the chest. Losing balance, she toppled backward, arms crossed over her throat to fend off the snap of fangs.

Ignoring that scene which bore no relevance to his payday, the slaver drew a hunting knife from his belt, waving it at Best.

"I knew I were right; she is the one. There's some trickery here." His eyes lit. "Back in town. They put us on the wrong track. Slipped that nigger out another way an' sent us on a wild goose chase. That's what they done, a'right. When I git back, I'm gonna see about it." He winked. "Ferret out that rotten apple."

Even a man called "Plain Jim" realized the implication of that threat. It would not take much ferreting to discover who lay behind the deception. Bringing Mrs. Dryfus down meant losing a vital link along the railway.

Making a dash for the fire, Best grabbed for the coffee pot, intending to fling the boiling contents at his enemy. Stung by the sizzle of flesh as his fingers wrapped around the red hot handle, however, he cried and spilled half the contents before blocking the pain. Amid a small cloud of steam and choking ash, he heaved pot and all at the dogman's face. The projectile missed, but droplets flew in every direction, temporarily giving him an edge.

Screaming with pent-up rage, Jim lowered his shoulder and ran the few short steps, striking his enemy in the gut. Amid a gasp of foully exhaled air, both men fell to earth, one astride the other. Madly pummeling face and neck, the former teacher's advantage evaporated nearly as fast as the coffee. Having the edge in size and training, Hoskins cracked the back of his hand against Best's ear, temporarily stunning him. Roaring in anger, the tracker scrambled out from beneath, kicked Jim in the head, then directed a heavy foot into the other's chest. A shriek, cut off in mid cry, attested to the fact ribs had been broken.

Leering superiorly at his vanquished foe, Hoskins wiped a sliver of reddish fluid from beneath his nose, then lunged for the dog. Grasping both ears, he yanked back, managing to hoist the snapping jaws away from its victim's airway. Bruised, shattered and bloody, Nelander curled into a ball, desperately sucking air into starved lungs. Oblivious to anything but the instinct to survive, she made herself as small a target as possible while shattered nerves recovered some semblance of equilibrium.

Tussling with the dog, the slaver managed to wrap a strip of cloth over his muzzle before finally letting it go. Delivering another kick to the prostate man, he crossed to Barbara, giving her the same to the lower back.

"Still breathin', are ya? Then, you'll be a'right. Git up an' tell me yer name."

Although still breathless, the "Go to hell" came out with remarkable clarity. The oppressor chuckled.

"Almost got away wid it, didn't you? Now, you're gonna tell me where that nigger woman really went. She cain't be fer ahead. That prize money belongs to me and I aim to git it."

"I-don't-know-what... you're-talking-about."

"You two ain't no husband an' wife frum Kansas. Yer helpin' blacks git away frum their masters. Better tell me what I wanta know or thems you left behind is gonna have a mighty long wait befer they sees their loved ones ag'in." His tone turned ominous. "Or mebbe they'll niver see you ag'in. You, miss, was the one askin' about the sheriff. Mebbe what I outta do is turn you in. Aidin' an' abettin' a fugitive slave is against the law. They put abolitionists in jail fer that. A nice long stretch. How'd you like that?"

She would not like it at all.

Without choice, Barbara Nelander had been recruited into the ranks of those conductors working the Underground Railroad. She could not lay the blame for her present predicament at the feet of Mathis McConaghie or Victoria Dryfus, however. Even knowing what she knew now, Barbara Nelander would have committed to the Cause.

Thus violating the first rule of seamanship.

Never volunteer for anything.

CHAPTER 11

"Let's go."

Hoskins did not carry a gun, but the threat of setting the hounds loose worked the same as though he did. Jim groaned, attempted to comply, then sunk back down, wheezing heavily for breath. First conveying she meant no aggression and thus sparing herself possible violence, Nelander rushed to his side. It did not require medical training to deduce the dire nature of Best's injury.

"He cannot travel. A lung has been punctured. One of us will have to go for a doctor -- and a wagon to transport him. Without delay."

"I don't think so."

Her temper flared. "Do you want him to die? He is a man convicted of no crime. That, sir, in any jurisdiction, is murder." She read no contrition. "There are no posters out on him; no 'Wanted Dead or Alive.' You have no excuse not to help."

She might have added, No human reason, but did not. Appealing to Hoskins' better nature did not cross her mind.

"I don't owe you nuthin'. In fact," he considered, rubbing his chin, "if I was to leave now, I'd just be savin' the circuit judge a trip. Cuz if I turn you in, there'd sure as hell be a trial." He squinted and leaned forward. "This close to the Missourah line, you think he'd get a fair trial? No-sir-ee, Bob."

Nelander broke out in a sweat. "Please. In the name of God." And then, more adroitly, "I have money."

"Show it."

Bluff made, bluff called.

"When I get home. I will send it to you. Give me an address."

"How's about you give me sumthin' I kin believe. Like the name of the man who set this run up."

"You are entirely mistaken --"

"No, I ain't. So don't let's play games. Tell me where the real darkie was taken."

"I have no idea." Realizing she could not hope to convince Hoskins of their lack of complicity, Barbara resorted to half-truth. "We are given no more information than is absolutely necessary."

His eyes dulled and she might have pulled it off, when one of the dogs barked. Stomping a foot in annoyance, the slaver put down a hand. The hound sniffed it, then crept away, choosing a position behind the woman. Tail wagging in confusion, it pawed the earth.

Hoskins snapped his fingers.

"Sweet Jesus! No wonder there was so much fussin' down by the river. Reeder blamed the dogs but it weren't their fault. Why didn't I think of it sooner?" Pointing a finger, he displayed a crooked grin. "They was confused, a'right. Picked up yer trail an' followed you, but sumthin' was wrong. They had two scents: the one from the cloth outta the wagon an' another. You changed dresses! That's what it were."

"No --"

"Right as rain. You take it off. I go back an' start ag'in. On the other side'a the water. That's what they did, a'right. Dressed her like a white woman an' you like a brown one. Make it easier fer her to pass."

"It wasn't like that."

"Sure it was. Take it off, I say. Strip down to yer drawers."

"I will not."

"Oh, you will. Or I'll rip 'em off. Don't make any difference to them dogs Do it now, miss. Befer you got real reason to regret what you done."

Jim Best rolled, trying to find a position which afforded him a better chance of breathing.

"Do as he says," he pleaded. "No more trouble."

"I will tear a corner off," she tried, fearful of leaving herself unclothed.

"All of it. That way, you're a might more shy about showin' yer face in any town. Might have friends there; those sympathetic to yer cause. Time you figure out what to do, I'll be long gone." Grinding a boot into the earth, he nodded in agreement with himself. "I'll send you a letter to Lawrence general delivery. Tell you how I'm spendin' my re-ward money."

"I won't undress."

Hoskins raised a foot and delivered a blow to Jim. The man cried and rolled on the ground, writhing in a fit of coughing.

"All right, damn you."

Without bothering to unbutton the fastenings, Barbara raised the dress over her head and tore it off. Disdainfully flinging it toward Hoskins, she fell to one knee, gently cradling Jim's head in her arms. The slaver whistled. She did not look up.

"Pretty female flesh. A shame I ain't got more time to do it justice."

Gathering the hounds together, he tucked the dress inside his shirt, then directed them back the way they had come. Jim groaned again and she withdrew her hands, fearful of doing more ill than good. The action served a dual purpose, for the clamminess of his skin turned her stomach.

Waiting until their enemy had gotten a safe distance away, she asked, "Do you think you can walk if I support you? We have to get out of here; find a doctor."

"No." Even so short a negation cost him and he choked, clutching his side as waves of pain shot through the chest cavity. Air flow severely compromised, the exchange make low, ominous wheezing sounds. Blood trickled from his mouth. He made no attempt to wipe it away.

"Then, I must go myself and bring one back."

He tried to answer, shrieked in agony and pulled away. Spasm after spasm wracked his frame, causing a deep gurgling. Spitting a mouthful of saliva, his knees curled upward and his back arched. Nostrils flared, mouth agape, one hand pulled his hair in a random act of violence, while the other pounded at his ribs. Confused at the reaction and frightened that he inflict more damage, she flung her arms around his shoulders, holding tight.

Whether that pressure aided his air exchange or merely the simple touch afforded a momentary release from terror, Jim's body went limp. Afraid to move, Nelander tensed her muscles and froze. Without saying so, the offer of going for help was rescinded. Even if she found a surgeon before dawn, bringing him back would be too late.

Time dragged so slowly, it might not have passed at all. The only way Nelander had of proving such were the case was to watch the stars. Eyes affixed heavenward, she exerted all her concentration on the celestial bodies. Limbs aching from immobility, her mind strained harder, first counting, then merely attaching themselves to the distant points of light.

Heat of day reluctantly faded from the ground, replaced by a gradual cooling. A breeze sprang up. She imagined herself on a ship, standing watch. In her mind, she paced the deck, stretching her legs, swinging her arms. For an hour, perhaps two, the ruse worked. Her head nodded and eyelids drooped.

She might have remained that way until daylight, but a sudden shift brought her to alertness. Jim moaned, flailed about, then started coughing. This time when blood began to flow from his mouth, it did not stop. The warmth of it over her bare skin served to take off the chill, but as quickly turned cold. Ice cold.

Barbara Nelander had seen men die but never had one perished in her arms. The ugly, tortured manifestations, witnessed at close range, revoked any fantasies she may have harbored on the concept of final reconciliation and slipping gracefully into the arms of waiting angels.

Augmented by rays of the full moon, Jim Best's teeth shone an unearthly white, reminding her that they represented an outward look at the inward skeleton. Gums receded, lips bleached pale, pinkish-blue, they appeared twice normal size; too large, in fact, to fit inside his skull. She tried, unsuccessfully, to quell an unreasoning fear he might spit them out at her.

Perhaps by a trick of light, his hair appeared to have gone grey, with long, colorless strings hanging about his brow the way sea foam gathered along the shore. The stench of copper and iron reminded her of rotting fish. The whistle in his lungs solicited memories of boatswains blasting out signals to the crew.

Lower the mast.

Furl the sails.

All hands on deck.

Orders Plain Jim Best would never heed.

Lacking any plan deeper than seeing to her newly found friend's comfort, even that failed as sensation, returning to numb limbs, became an overwhelming pain. Needle jabs of pain shot through cramped muscles, finally forcing Nelander to move. Stretching out one leg and then the other, even this slight readjustment elicited a cry of anguish. Guiltily, she suspended further movement.

"Easy," she intoned, suspecting any sound above a whisper would hurt his raw nerves. "Easy."

Easy to say. More difficult to obey.

It took five minutes for her arms and legs to wake and cease their throbbing. She guessed half an hour, and only then from experience. Gauging by emotional time, it seemed longer. By a day or a week. Or a month.

"Jim." His eyelids fluttered. "Is there someone you wish me to notify? Back home? Do you have family?"

He mumbled something. The words slurred, rendering them meaningless. She tried harder.

"A name? An address? I will write them. Tell me."

"Red," he said. Red. A nickname? A color? A locale?

Red Best? Red, as in blood? Red, Pennsylvania?

Red, rhyming with bed? Or dead?

Red haired. Red Indian. A book, long ago read?

"Tell me. I am listening."

He tried. Another spasm, a cry, dry retching. His entire body shook. An arm waved, fingers grasping. She took it in her own and held fast.

"I am here for you."

Whatever good that may be.

The coughing persisted, the exchange of air more labored. She turned her head so as not to see those teeth. And felt herself a coward.

In order to preserve her sanity, Nelander turned her mind to the future, summoning all the anger she could muster. It proved a simple task. Rage at the three men who had caused so unnecessary a tragedy. Fury at the law and those who wrote it. Biting contempt for those who enforced it. Bitter recrimination for men and women alike who turned a blind eye.

Concentrate. Think. Plan.

No point going after Hoskins. He was long gone. She would have to warn someone. But who? The man at the river crossing? She did not know his name. What could he do? She doubted there existed a way to alert Mathis' associate and his charge.

Tell whoever had set them on their journey. Victoria Dryfus. The image of the woman came back to Barbara with surprising clarity. Although knowing little about her, Mrs. Dryfus had emerged as a startlingly important person in her life. Why had she paid $50 for the strawberries? And why had she become involved in the Underground Railroad?

Beyond common gossip and a handful of facts, no one knew anything about her. What, in God's name, had possessed such a woman to take a stand? Who was she, that she dared rebel against the law of the land? And who was Giles? Her servant, certainly, but clearly more than that. An individual intricately involved with this escape route. Someone who worked with and likely recruited Blind Betty and Mute Thomas.

Or had it been the other way around? Had Betty and her son found Giles? Where? In Little Lawrence? The connection between them was important. Perhaps vital. Nelander would know more. She had earned the right. As had Seth. They deserved to be leveled with, told the truth. Behind their backs, their names had come up. Go to them. Use them. They can be trusted.

They are fool enough to step forward when no one else will. Knock on their door in the middle of the night. Leave an escaped runaway in their house. Give them a bloodhound puppy so it might not bark when another agent invaded their sanctuary.

Stealth is the order of the day. Follow instructions. Risk life and limb.

Anger turned to gall. She and Seth had been set up from the beginning. Long before they realized a way-station even existed in town, those behind the scenes had already chosen them for participation in this most deadly game.

Their inclusion bordered on audacity. Why them? Why she and her husband? Because Seth had allowed his children to play with those of darker skin? Had it gone back as far as that? Because he occasionally hired black men to work for him? Because she and he had attended an abolitionist's meeting? What made them think she would go along? Her origins as a Canadian? Her position aboard ship? Because a black man had been her best friend? But no one knew.

Unless they had been listening. All along. From the beginning. It had not been one single factor which brought a conductor to their doorstep but a dozen, dating back months.

Years. To the recruitment of Mathis McConaghie. Of all people, he would have been the last she suspected. Did he actually have pure motives, or did he act from greed? Or where there other factors involved? What were they? She had taken him for an oaf; a lout. A bully and an antagonist. Seth did not like him. Mathis had spoken against him at the trial when the townspeople tried to condemn a poor, innocent farmer in the death of his wife.

McConaghie feared Peter and his spirits. Or had that, too, been an act? Just as his presence at their home when Terrance Windsor came calling.

Don't like people thinkin' bad of me.

Now you know an' you kin use it ag'in me.

Come to it, they'd put a bullet in my back.

His sons were on the other side. And his wife, a'ways snoopin' round. Found herse'f a good payday, onest. The boys took to that real good. Better'n trainin' dogs or growin' corn.

What payday? What did Mrs. McConaghie know that no one else did?

And how did that tie into everything else?

Too many questions. No answers.

Save one.

A man lay dying in her lap.

Death did not come easily. The spirit fought the inevitable, writhing, crying, suffering and enduring. Jim Best talked again, rambling words dissociated from circumstance. Some she made out, others were obscure. Barbara stopped trying to make sense of them. No matter. What he had to say was comprehended -- or not -- by God. Whatever meanings they conveyed would have to be acted upon -- or not -- by that same deity.

Making a difference lay beyond her control.

Gurgling, then trying to swallow, Jim struggled as fluid swept back into his lungs. Fists clenched, neck veins distended, he hacked and rallied, combating weakness with a dying man's strength. Lifting him to a sitting position, Nelander pounded his back as if he were a child and a bite of meat had gone down the wrong way. No dislodging this obstruction, however, as eyeballs rolled to the back of his head and his torso stiffened.

Whistle wheezing, chest moving, nostrils wide, mouth rounded in silent scream, then a quiver, a tremor, a slow, all-encompassing shake and stillness.

"No!"

An impotent protest against the unstoppable; a cry of dismay for that which she had been praying. A denial of reality. One second without compassion before mercy asserted itself. If mercy could fairly be said to come in the sharp of the Grim Reaper.

Barbara Nelander would not have bet on that before last evening.

Good thing. She would have lost her stake.

Slowly, painstakingly, she disengaged herself from the stiffening corpse. No need, yet she acted from habit. She would not have called it duty. Her regard for those passed over had perished an ungainly death.

She felt the expression, "a lump of clay" in her bones.

Ashes to ashes, dust to dust.

No consolation there. And never would be, again.

Lips curled back in the self-protection of the living, Nelander stared around the campsite. Day had well advanced. Time to leave. She could no longer think clearly about what ought to be done. Beating a hand into her brow, her mind worked through the web of nothingness.

A dead body must be buried.

Death had always been a distant concept. If a men perished at sea, the captain had him rolled in his blanket and dropped overboard.

No ocean to swallow this body.

A grave. Landlubbers were buried in the earth.

She did not know whether Jim Best would appreciate being called a "landlubber" or not. And did not have the strength to care.

It had been meant kindly.

Or not.

Even that remained unclear.

Grasping the coffee pot which had so lately been utilized as a weapon, she used it as a tool of a different sort, attempting to dig in the earth. Three jabs in the hard ground and she discarded the implement as useless.

The lid, although sharper along the edges, proved no better. With a sigh of resignation which might have been a curse, Barbara realized the futility of the act. It would take the rest of the day and probably into the next for her to carve out a hole deep enough for a body. Being alone that long with the remains of a murder victim, even one with a pure heart, did not settle. She must leave. Go home.

For whatever reason.

"Seth and the crew are waiting for me."

As good a reason as any.

And just as hollow.

Civilized people did not leave bodies to rot. They took care of them; bestowed last respects.

She could not imagine why.

Burials were for the living. To offer comfort for those left behind.

Nothing would console her now.

Barbara Nelander turned her back on the corpse and had crossed into the trees before realizing her error. Not in leaving Jim Best unburied. In her own nakedness. The bastard Hoskins had taken her clothes. She could not appear in public undressed. Men would take her for a beggar. Or worse. That, she could not risk.

Not when she had no answers to supply.

Resigned to the only course open, she crept back, jaw locked in place. Setting her mind to the open sea and the lapping of waves, she worked blindfolded, unbuttoning his shirt, slipping trousers down bent legs. Working arms through stiff cloth, legs into bloodied pants, she fitted herself into a dead man's outfit.

Even with thoughts fixed upon the ocean, significance reared its ugly head.

She had changed into a dress owned by a slave and now wore the clothes of a dead freedom fighter.

Bad choices all around.

CHAPTER 12

Seth listened to her story on the porch over a pot of tea. He had suggested rum, but Nelander pointed out they saved that for special occasions and this hardly qualified.

His protest that her returning alive "from the bowels of hell" failed to persuade her and he had let the matter drop. In the long run, it made no difference whether they drank rum, tea, milk, water or any combination thereof. He had her back, safe and relatively sound.

Or sound and relatively safe.

Barbara had only smiled once since her return a full twenty-four hours ago. That had been when she told him Mathis McConaghie was one of "them." His sputtered exclamation, "You're a bald-faced liar!" had been agreed to while she rubbed her beardless jaw. His next comment, spoken with resignation had been what turned the trick.

"I suppose this means I'll be expected to buy a pup from him every year from now 'till eternity."

Her facial expression settled him down and they had gone to bed without further conversation. The fact he had completely misunderstood her emotion passed away like so much else.

Their conversation had lapsed into uneasy silence when she startled him by announcing, "Sunday after church, we'll have to go into town and see if we can have an appointment with Mrs. Dryfus. There is much to discuss."

"You mean about that boy -- Jim Best?"

"No. I left word with Giles before I came home last night. It was he who drove me in from town."

"Was it? I didn't recognize him."

"He is a man of many faces."

"What did he have to say?"

"That he would see what could be done."

Exasperated that she held too much close to the vest, he slapped a hand against his thigh.

"What does that mean? That he -- or they -- will notify his next of kin? That they'll send someone out to give him a Christian burial, or they will notify whoever's conducting Miss Lolly that their plan has been compromised?"

"He did not elaborate."

"Didn't you ask?"

"If he wanted to say, he would have. The only way we're going to learn more is by going to the source."

Seth whistled and rubbed his fingers together.

"Who woulda believed? A woman like that, with all the money in the world. And no one having a hint about it."

"Someone had more than a hint. Our 'dear friend' Mathis."

"He's another bag of bones." She flinched at the expression and he reached out a hand in apology. "I'm sorry. What I meant was --"

"I know. It's all right."

To make up for his error, he tried, "We can go into Lawrence tomorrow, if you want."

"I do, but it would look suspicious and the last thing I want to do is raise eyebrows."

"How so?"

"In the middle of the growing season farmers do not simply drop into town. We don't need any supplies and you have no work for the blacksmith. We might be excused some window-shopping on Sunday but not on a weekday."

"We could say you was expectin' a letter --"

The lapse into poor grammar caused her to shiver for it underlined the tension he felt.

"I am expecting a letter. One I do not care to receive."

"Oh. Yeah. From that slaver." His foot shook. "But he didn't know yer name."

Nelander let the statement fade away before speaking again.

"Strawberries."

"What?"

"Strawberries. Whatever ties us to Mrs. Dryfus has something to do with strawberries."

"I figured her buyin' them was just a sham -- an excuse to invite you in."

"Then why pay fifty dollars?" She found her own foot matching the tempo Seth set. "And why send Giles out a full year ago to buy a crop that had not yet come in?"

He surprised her by his quick response. "That's easy. As a bribe. Or an insurance policy."

"How so?"

"In case one of us died, the other'd have something to live on."

For a year, she thought. Not long. Not nearly long enough.

The explanation made perverted sense but also reeked of pessimism. She could not fathom how people involved in such a scheme would be fixated on the darker outcomes. To survive, the enterprise required optimism. And faith in a better tomorrow.

"I don't like any of this... not knowin'." His voice broke into her rumination. "I 'specially don't like them presumin'. Sendin' that devil out in the middle of the night -- scarin' the heebie jeebies outta me. An' the crew."

This finally elicited a second smile in as many days.

"What's a 'heebie jeebie'?"

"A nice word for 'crap.'"

Her guffaw rewarded him for his delicacy.

"I don't have to ask what that is."

"Cow poop."

The small voice behind them caused both to jump. Snapping his fingers, Seth summoned the boy out of the shadows.

"You ain't supposed to be listening to grown-up's private conversations."

Unabashed, Peter crossed his arms behind his back and puffed out his chest.

"It ain't private if'n it's held in public."

"Now, you're gettin' smart with me. You was supposed to be in bed."

"I ain't sleepy."

"I am not sleepy," Nelander tersely corrected. "Get into bed and close your eyes. You'll be surprised how fast you fall asleep. And if you don't, there are always chores to do."

"In the middle of the night?"

"That's why we have lamps. You can read from that book I assigned, or practice your sums."

"What about Patricia?"

Seth groaned and peered into the darkness.

"I should have known. Where there's one, there's always the other. Come out and show yourself." Patricia did as directed, joining her brother. "You weren't sleepy, either?"

"No, sir." Two pair of eyes bore through the falsity. "What I mean is, we wanted to hear what happened."

"Does this mean we gotta give up Squash?" Peter added before the Hand of Authority swept them off to bed.

"No, we are not giving up Squash. And if we wanted you to hear everything, we would have held a council."

"Reckon we have time for that before the cock crows."

This time Nelander interceded.

"What the captain and I are discussing has serious repercussions. That means there are things you are better off not knowing."

"We won't tell."

"Don't you trust us?" Patricia put less delicately.

"Neither your father nor I know who to trust. Things are very dangerous right now. We are only trying to protect you. What you don't know you can't say. Leave it at that," she warned.

"Will you tell us one day?"

"I hope we have the chance."

Sensing they had pushed their luck far enough, Patricia poked her brother.

"Come on. Good night."

"Good night."

The adults waited until the children disappeared into the house, but the moment had passed and they did not resume the thread. After half an hour of quiet, they mutually rose and went inside. Contrary to Nelander's prediction, neither found closing their eyes a recipe for slumber.

In the morning Seth took Peter with him to the fields while Patricia went out to work in the garden. At noon, Nelander gave her a dinner pail and set her out to find them.

"There is enough in here for all three of you. Once you've eaten, see if you can help with the weeding or whatever else needs doing."

Giving the commanding officer a snappy salute, the girl scampered off, proud to be assigned "men's work." Twenty minutes later a scratching knock on the door brought Barbara out from the living room where she had been working on the books.

"No weeding to be done?" she called. "Didn't tell me --?" The question died on her lips as she opened the door and beheld a tall man standing outside. Reacting spontaneously, she jokingly inquired, "What's the matter? Forget your key?"

Only after speaking did she realize her error. The man on the porch was not her husband but a watered-down version of Seth Ward. Drawing back in surprise, she scrutinized his features. Lighter-haired than Seth, with locks reaching to his collar, he had a smattering of freckles over a small, muted nose. Smiling politely, he revealed a mouthful of crooked teeth, similar to Seth's but more pronounced. Deeply tanned, he carried with him a swagger unlike that of any farmer of her acquaintance.

Reaching a hand to a tan, wide-brimmed hat with a high crown, he doffed it before inquiring, "Mrs. Ward?"

The words were clipped and sharp, despite an attempt to soften them. She marked him immediately for a military man.

"Norman?"

While enunciated as a question, no doubt existed in her mind as to the identity of the stranger.

"Yes, ma'am. Norman Ward. Seth's younger brother. They told me in town he lived out this way. The clerk wasn't much for giving directions, though and I wasn't sure I had the right place."

"I know," she sighed, too well recalling her original inquiry. "'There's a sort of a road,'" she quoted from memory. "'Leastways, it goes on about a mile or so an' then peters into a track. It's called 'The Road Outta Town.'"

"Yes, ma'am. Almost to the word." His face darkened. "Damn foot sodgers."

The curse did not surprise her nearly as much as hearing her own sentiment, slightly paraphrased, from the mouth of another.

Standing back, she swung her hand toward the interior.

"Come in, won't you, please? Seth is not here -- he is out in the fields. But I can send for him --"

Accepting the invitation, Norman removed his hat and allowed her to precede him. Nelander's first instinct was to close the door. She did not heed it and left it open.

"No need for that, ma'am. I can wait for him. Don't mind takin' a load off my feet, though." Whether or not he guessed the rocker belonged to Seth, Norman settled into it and stretched his legs. "My feet ache. I'm not used to walkin', but my horse gave out on me awhile back and I let him go. Carried the saddle over my shoulder about fifty miles, I guess. Left it in town."

"I'm sorry. About the horse."

"He was a good ol' boy But he took a rock in his frog and cut it bad. It'll heal but I didn't have time to wait. Woulda led him but he wasn't one for followin'. Got antsy an' fought the bit."

"I see."

"Have to buy another... unless Seth's got one to give me?"

"We only have one and that's used for plowing."

"Oh. Too bad. No saddle horse?"

"We cannot afford the luxury."

He glanced around the room with undisguised curiosity.

"Doin' bad, are you?"

Suddenly, Nelander did not wish to confess the state of their finances.

"There was a drought and then a flood. Most farmers around here are just recovering."

"He never was much of a rider, anyhow. Got any grub?"

"I was just making something for myself. I shall be glad to include you." Crossing into the kitchen, she went about the business of slicing ham and bread. That done, she added roasted beans to the grinder and whirred the handle. The noise overrode any other in the room, but a sixth sense urged Barbara to glance over her shoulder. She was not caught unaware, therefore, to see Norman had gotten up and crept behind her. If he thought to surprise, therefore, he failed.

Effecting a wide, boyish grin, the man who looked so much like Seth Ward, inhaled deeply.

"Smells good." This time, she erred, for she presumed he meant the coffee. "Don't have many females at the post. None of 'em wear long pants, either."

Meeting him with a calculated offense, she replied, "If I 'smell,' sir, that is because I have not bathed in a dog's age. And as for trousers, I have been accustomed to such attire from an early age."

Easily withdrawing, Norman did not lose the grin.

"Not from around here, are you?"

"No more than you."

He grunted. "Been away a long time. A 'dog's age,' as you say."

"I referred to the fact you and Seth were born in a different county. As I have learned from the locals, your invisible boundaries separate foreign countries."

"That's true, I expect. Been a lot of grumbling lately about such things."

"Is that why you are no longer in the army? Because of the political situation?"

Dropping a half cup measure into the pot of boiling water, this time the room did fill with a pleasing aroma.

"What makes you say that?"

She did not like men who spoke in vagueness or answered questions with questions. It bordered on obfuscation.

"You are out of uniform."

He inspected his clothing as if the fact had escaped him.

"Oh, that. It's gotten to be a fella don't know who's liable to take a potshot at him. Wearin' the blue's like wavin' a red flag at a bull."

"So, you have not resigned your commission?"

Removing a red handkerchief from a rear pocket, Norman wrapped it around the coffee pot handle and poured himself a cup from the set hanging from a mug tree on the counter.

"Good."

Biting off the retort, Coffee comes dear, Nelander indicated the meat and bread.

"Help yourself."

Grunting a second time, a habit soldiers, like seamen, developed when receiving an order they did not particularly appreciate, Norman adeptly piled ham between two slices and ate standing. Discovering her own hunger mitigated and not unaware of the impropriety of officers supping with jack tars, Nelander drew her own coffee and quaffed a long swallow without waiting for it to cool. She meant the act to convey disdain, if not superiority. Until observing how Seth would set the tone, she would create her own standards.

She had not lived eighteen years aboard a ship without learning that to give the crew the upper hand meant losing command.

"Have you left the army?"

"Well, I didn't bring the platoon wid me, if that's what you mean." Pretending he had actually answered, Norman wandered around the room. "Bunch of boys like that'd ride roughshod over a nice place like this."

"I asked a direct question, mister, and I expect an answer." His hand jerked back so fast an amount of hot liquid spilled over the side of the cup. Instead of cleaning it, he rubbed the coffee in with his foot. "Use the rag in your pocket," she advised. "You'll find it amazingly porous. Maybe soldiers don't give a damn about their barracks, but you've come to a private home. Consider it the quarters of your commanding officer while you're here, and we'll get along just fine."

He obeyed for to refuse meant open disobedience.

"Who are you, anyway?"

"The captain of this ship we call Pirate Treasure. And as such, I expect all invited guests to behave themselves."

"Yes, ma'am." Stuffing the wet handkerchief back in his pocket, he flashed the innocent grin he clearly knew how to use. "Seth caught himself a live one, did he? Forgive my rough talk, ma'am. I'm used to bein' wid men. Troopers."

"Yes. Dragoons. I know."

"Seth told you about me?"

"What little he knew. It has been a long time since we have had word of you."

"I ain't much fer writin'. Kin you read?"

"Better than your general."

He puckered his lips but did not whistle. "Cain't say I've ever actual seen a general. Colonel's more like it. They're paper-pushers. Captain, now. He's the one we follow."

"Oh, I don't know. A colonel or a general give you an order, you'd hop to it faster'n bacon sizzles in a hot fryin' pan."

"Seth teach you how to talk like this?"

"I'm teaching him."

"Where'd you learn it?"

"Finish up yer 'grub,' and then why don't you take a nap? After the long walk you've had, I expect you're plum tuckered out."

"I am, at that. When you say Seth'd be back?"

"Suppertime."

"Right."

"Where'd you leave your kit?"

"How's that, again?"

"Haversack. Bedroll. Rifle."

"What makes you think I got that with me?"

"Soldier doesn't go anywhere without his weapon. Since you're not wearing a sidearm, I expect you left that with the rest of your gear. Behind the tree in the front, was it?"

"You saw me," he marveled. "You got Injun eyes, ma'am."

She had not seen him hide his kit but accepted the compliment, realizing its worth.

"There's an empty room in the loft." Indicating upward so that he would not infer she meant the barn, Nelander strode into the living room. "I'll pull down the ladder and you can bunk up there."

"That's right kind."

Waiting for him to stuff the remaining sandwich in his mouth then amble outside, Nelander grabbed an iron staff and looped the curled end around a ring in the ceiling. Hauling down the long unused steps, she planted the feet along the floor, then awaited Norman's return. He appeared quickly, a gunbelt slung over his shoulder, rifle in one hand and rolled blanket in the other.

"You'll find it dusty up there, but better than sleeping on the ground."

"Ain't no stranger to either." Shifting the bedroll from one hand to the other, he offered to shake.

"Didn't mean to get off on the wrong foot. I'm mighty glad to be here. Haven't had what you'd call a home in too many years. Always movin' from one fort to the next; livin' hard. It feels good to be with family, again."

"In that case we're glad to have you."

For the moment, neither quite meant what they said. But as a beginning, it settled better than first impressions and created a middle ground. How that field would be plowed depended on many factors.

Not the least of which included Seth Ward's own interpretation of his long-lost brother.

CHAPTER 13

She met him outside, standing by the well. Waving a friendly "hello," Seth tossed down his work gloves and waited while Nelander drew water. Gratefully dunking his head in the bucket, he sighed at the cool relief, then doused himself with the rest.

"Hot enough to fry eggs in sand."

Normally predisposed to exchange playful banter, she assessed that the children had been waylaid in the yard playing with Squash and Herman before cutting to the chase.

"We have company."

His eyes rounded. "Who?"

Unable to bring herself to evoke a family tie, Nelander replied, "Norman Ward." His surprise could hardly have been greater if she had said, "President Lincoln."

"My brother? Norman? Here?"

Three questions in one breath, amounting to the same thing. She answered all with one terse word.

"Yes."

"What's he doing here? He quit the army?"

"You will have to ask him."

Absorbing the tension, he retrieved his gloves and shoved them in a back pocket.

"You don't like him."

"I don't know him."

Leaning against the well, he gazed at the crew.

"Can't say I know him any better. It's been a long time. Where is he?"

"I put him up in the loft. He's asleep. Or, at least he was. He hears you come up, he'll be down. I just wanted to warn you."

"Appreciate that. Haven't seen him since we was little more'n boys. What's he look like?"

"You."

"Younger, though," he tried.

"Except for Norman having softer features, I'd have taken him for being older."

"Do say. Mebbe bein' a soldier didn't set with him."

"You be the judge."

He shrugged, hesitated, then narrowed an eye.

"Is he harsh-spoken? If he is, I don't want the children exposed to his language."

"He spoke nicer that I expected."

"But?" he prodded, hearing more. Nelander arched an eyebrow to counter his lowered lid. "I know. Judge for myself."

Running a hand over his shirt to shake away loose dirt, Seth scraped a foot in front of him, then nodded.

"Let's face the prodigal."

She did not say but nevertheless conveyed, Hardly that.

Without having been summoned, Normal Ward waited just beyond the arc of the door, so that when Seth swing it inward, it barely passed the tips of his light leather boots. Nelander noted they had been freshly cleaned. Without blackening they lacked shine, but considerable attention had been paid to detail.

His wardrobe, too, had been brushed and straightened. They appeared so natty, in fact, she wondered if he had changed clothes. She did not condemn him for wishing to make a good first impression; the surprise came from the fact he had made no sound upon rising. What she beheld took time. Not five minutes or ten, but thirty. Barbara swore she had heard him snoring no more than fifteen minutes ago.

In future, nothing could be treated at face value.

"Norman," Seth identified, eyes wide with wonder.

"How are you, Seth? Long time, no see."

"I'm fine. And you are the same, I see." Holding out a hand, the two men shook. "When I didn't hear from you, I wondered... didn't know what to think."

Norman winked and stepped back to let them enter.

"Reckoned I'd gotten shot? Or scalped?"

"Promoted to lieutenant, or something, and gotten too fancy for us."

"The only way a dragoon gets bars on his shoulders is when one of his officers gets put under the buffalo dung. We had a good bunch of boys. Dead shots. Not many of us went that way."

Recalling the one letter he had received so long ago, describing how five or six Union troopers had been killed by a war party, Seth could only speculate that the company had gotten better with time or his brother had forgotten what he wrote. To consider him a storyteller or at worst a liar did not occur to him.

"And you've... resigned?"

"I'm on a leave of absence." Not so charitable, Nelander presumed that while he spit-polished his boots, Norman had come up with a neutral explanation for his unexpected arrival. "Haven't been home in quite a while. Had a lot of leave built up. No sense lettin' it go to waste, so I put in for three months. When they approved it, I just set out. Didn't figure to come here, exactly, but here's where my footsteps took me."

"Well, I'm glad to see you. Glad to know you're all right."

"Them your young'uns out there?"

Seth nodded and gave a holler. "Patricia! Peter! Come here." The pair scrambled in through the door then stopped cold as they beheld a stranger. Their father motioned them in. "This here's my brother; your Uncle Norman."

"How do you do, sir?" Patricia offered. Peter made a bow.

"Where's your uniform?"

"I'm on holiday. And a good thing, too, for I see you must be some sort of officer by that saber hanging from your side."

Peter lovingly withdrew it for inspection.

"It's a cutlass. I'm a crewman, but my official title is warrant officer. Patricia's a full-fledged navigator, Nelander's a captain and papa's Captain of the Fleet. We're pirates."

"Are you, now? I seen those flags flying. Death's head and bones; black standard. Thought mebbe someone'd died from the plague and you were warning people to stay away."

"We're warnin' 'em all right. Come here and be on your best behavior. Or else."

"Else what?"

"We either lop off their heads or sic the spirits on 'em."

Norman laughed and held his belly.

"Then I'll watch my manners, 'cause I don't want either one of them things to happen to me."

"You're damned right you don't."

Embarrassed at his son's curse word, Seth stomped a foot.

"Enough of this kind of talk. Norman, you're welcome to stay as long as you like. Nelander said she put you up in the loft. Find it accommodating?"

"Better'n a hotel room and a sight finer than making a bed on the prairie."

"Good. We'll eat, then, and you can tell us about your adventures afterward."

Taking the children with her, Nelander went into the kitchen to prepare supper. Frying a beefsteak alongside potatoes, she sliced raw onions and served them on a dish. Adding beet greens to boiling water, she waited until they were tender, then set them in a bowl. Peter poured each a glass of milk freshly gotten from Bessie and Patricia prepared the table. When called, the men appeared.

"Sit beside Peter," Barbara directed before it became an issue. Taking her place at one end, Seth assumed his opposite. The positioning left no doubt they shared the head of the table together.

Seth cut and distributed the meat and the family helped themselves to vegetables. Norman stared at the onions with surprise.

"What are these, now? A test of bravery? Or are you young 'uns trying to see if I'll take the bait an' try one, just to see my eyes water?"

"Onions keep away scurvy," Patricia explained.

"If we wanted to do that, we'd pizzon you with chili," Peter glibly informed.

"Chili isn't pizzon."

They sucked in their breaths.

"You know how to eat chili?"

"Sure I do. It's a 'Mex' dish, hotter'n -- Hades. Burns your tongue off, you're not used to it. But I never had any chili in Kansas."

"Nelander ordered it special. Captain Papa won the eatin' contest when no one else could get down our stew. That sure was a great day."

"Bet is was. How is it, ma'am -- 'cuse me, I don't know what to call you."

She would have answered for herself, but Patricia spoke faster.

"Nelander. That's her name. Captain Nelander, formerly of the Bottom Dollar and now of the Pirate Treasure. "

Norman appeared to consider, yet she saw by his eyes that her previous reference to the farm by its proper title had not gone unnoted.

"Ships' names. You... owned a ship... Nelander?"

"I served aboard. As second officer."

"That explains the nautical talk. I wondered. And the pirates. Were you a buccaneer, ma'am?"

"No. But I am, now."

"Where's your buried treasure?"

"Out back, Uncle Norman," Patricia excitedly explained.

"Out back?"

"She means the strawberries," Peter helped. "Nelander bought them an' we helped put 'em in. We had a good crop this year an' we'll have a better one next!"

Seeing that he would say more, the junior captain quickly interceded.

"Too much talking, young man! When you dine with the officers, it is they who make conversation and you who eat with eyes directed on your plate and tongue in your mouth."

Taken back by the harsh tone, Peter's eyes grew wide. They always chatted at table. Having little experience with guests and less with outsiders, her reasoning defied protocol.

"But he talked to me, first. Ain't I supposed to answer an officer?"

"We have not yet ascertained his rank."

All eyes turned to Norman. Seth reluctantly spoke for the crew. His wider familiarity with the world offered no more insight than the boy's when it came to rationalizing his wife's reticence.

"Tell us, Norman, so we can finish our meal in peace."

"I wear the stripes, sir, but not the shoulder boards."

"Then you are not an officer," Captain Nelander rightly interpreted. "He is, master Peter, a non-commissioned officer."

"Like me!"

"Yes. Now finish your meal."

That ended all hope of further revelations and they ate quickly. Norman passed on the onions.

After the dishes had been cleared, the soldier went outside to smoke and the two adults dismissed the crew to their studies while they finished clean-up.

Keeping his voice lowered, Seth began the interrogation.

"What was that all about?" On the questioning look, he added, "No speaking at the table."

"It wasn't that which bothered me; it was the subject."

"Which was?"

"Strawberries."

"You got no reason to be ashamed --"

She slapped him with the dish towel. "Nothing of the kind. Quite the contrary. I don't want him making any judgments about our finances."

"Or our affairs?" he guessed. She nodded and Seth restated his first impression. "You don't like him."

"I don't know him. Neither do you. He is more -- and perhaps less -- than he seems."

"You think he's quit the army to come back here and make trouble?" No answer. "To borrow money?"

"He's already asked for a horse."

"It's only natural, him wanting a mount. Being a dragoon an' all. He probably expects..."

"... that his brother will help him out."

"Won't I?"

"Not if you don't have it."

"Tinker'll probably have a horse and let me pay it off slow."

"He can pay his own horse off. There's nothing wrong with him. He can get a job."

"Jobs are hard to come by these days."

"Then what about his savings? What's a soldier do with his pay?" She noted the glint and hurried on. "Yes. I know. Gals and whisky. Let him sell his rifle, then. I got a good look at it. New. And the pistol. One or both ought to buy him a thoroughbred."

"What's the matter with you?"

She did not choose to answer. "And then there's the connection between Mrs. Dryfus and the strawberries. I didn't want Peter inadvertently mentioning that."

"Why not?"

Nelander closed her eyes and rolled them, sight unseen.

"Because she paid fifty dollars for a crop worth ten. The children are aware of that. Because she's a link to the Underground Railroad. I don't want Norman sniffing around."

As if to confirm her suspicions, Herman and Squash came up, tails wagging. Stooping to pet both, she fed them as Seth watched.

"What makes you think Norman'd find out anything, even if he were interested? No one else in Lawrence has ever been able to put it together."

She washed a dish and handed it to him for drying.

"Hasn't it struck you as a bit odd that he shows up after all these years just when we get recruited for the Cause?"

"No. I believed him when he said he was on leave. Besides, that only happened a week ago. Even if he were part of a conspiracy, he couldn't have gotten here that quickly."

"We really don't know where he was stationed, Seth. Or if he were stationed anywhere at all. He might have been out of the army for years; or at least months. A man with military experience... tracking Indians... would be a welcome addition to the Simpson Agency. Or one like it."

"What makes you think his sentiments aren't the same as mine?"

"What makes you think they are?"

"Because we grew up together."

"True. But your real exposure to Negroes came after you moved to Douglas County. Who knows what his have been? Hating one race easily translates into hating another."

"I don't know that he hates Indians."

She conceded the point and moved away. Washing several more dishes, she maintained her distance and lowered her tone of voice.

"I keep thinking about that meeting in town. What the Reverend Pickering said. And what I've read, since."

"About what?"

"The argument that ridding the land of Indians for the benefit of the white man was decreed by God. Pro-slavers use the same justification to dominate the black race. The name of the Lord is evoked for so many evils." She finished up and waited while he dried the last of the glasses. "I'm not saying I know what's in your brother's mind. Perhaps his arrival here is purely coincidental. I hope so. It's as likely as not that he's on leave; and that when it comes to choosing sides, he will go for the North."

"Maybe he won't 'go' anywhere at all. Maybe he's had enough of soldiering."

That, Nelander could not let pass.

"No, my beloved. A man who arrives with a new model rifle and a pistol hasn't given up the army. He didn't come to settle down. And I seriously doubt he came to renew old family ties."

He brought his cheek close to hers.

"What did he come for, then?"

"To see which way the wind is blowing. To get a feel for the temper of the town." She sucked in her cheek. "To get a promotion; to wear the shoulder boards."

"You lost me."

"You know yourself they're recruiting all over the state; in this one and every other. Troops are being raised; companies assembled. Who's to command them? The butcher or the blacksmith or the career 'non-com'? Norman could step into any one of those units and be elected captain. Or colonel."

"If he's for our side, that wouldn't be a bad thing."

"And if he's not?"

Seth bounced on his toes.

"Then I won't take out a loan to buy him a horse."

"Which probably explains, dear husband, why he hasn't said."

Seth gritted his teeth while draping the damp towel over a drying rack.

"Then, I guess we'll just have to ask him."

"Carefully. And speak to the crew -- in private. Not to make them suspicious but just warn them. He would have found the strawberry patch by himself, so there's no harm there. But Betty and Thomas -- that's... another kettle of fish. Best none of us mention our... lodgers."

"All right. I take your meaning." He hitched up his suspenders and sidled away. "But if he's as sneaky as you think, he'll find out, anyway."

For that, she had no counter.

Norman slept in the loft and in the morning arose before Mr. Noise Box had begun his crowing. By the time Seth and Nelander made their way into the kitchen, their guest had washed, shaven and put the coffee on to boil.

"Thought you'd sleep in today," the senior captain observed. "Taking advantage of your holiday. Doubt dragoons are left to linger beneath the sheets when they're on duty."

"Was planning to, but I'd actually forgotten all the different sounds around a farm. Not that I heard them so much as felt them: chickens in the coup. Cow in the barn. The way the leaves blow; how the house settles. Even the... sense of children around."

"I suppose that would make a difference."

"Not that there weren't some young'uns about the fort," he explained, motioning they sit while he prepared breakfast. "Some of the officers brought in their families. Never liked the idea much, though."

"Why not?" Barbara asked, taking her place at the table.

"It's dangerous, for one thing. No matter how high the walls, a fort isn't secure. It can always be attacked. Burned down, even. And the privation. Man doesn't mind eatin' corn bread and venison but a woman's got more refined tastes. And she needs company -- of her own kind. There may be a few females around, but there ain't nothing for them to do all day. They're better off at home, in a town or a city."

"Maybe they get lonely."

"I expect they do." Cracking the last of a dozen eggs into a crockery bowl, Norman broke them with a fork, then added the liquid to the pan. Beside it, he fried bread in bacon fat. "But better safe than sorry."

Seth cleared his throat and set the table.

"What are your plans? You're always welcome to come out with me and tend the crops."

"Thought I'd ride your horse into Lawrence and see about getting a mount for myself. Then I'll have a look-see around town. Anything you want me to bring back?"

"No. We're fine." Within the denial rested tacit permission for Norman to borrow Blaze. Nelander turned away from the pair. "You might drop in at the gunsmith's though. I promised Jake Dale that if you ever took leave you'd pay him a visit."

"All right. I'll do 'er. What's the town like, anyway?"

"Like most others, I expect. Mostly good people."

Serving the scrambled eggs and fried bread, Norman nodded a friendly greeting as Patricia and Peter joined them.

"Morning, crew. I was askin' about the town. What it's like."

"Don't you know?"

"Nope. Your father an' I were raised a fair piece from here. Never got this far east." Waiting until the captain sat, he plopped into his own chair and began eating, talking with his mouth full. "Ever get back to the old homestead, Seth?"

"Have no reason to."

"Anyone from those parts ever write?"

"Can't say that they do."

"You go back for the funeral? Of Rick, I mean. Funny to think of him bein' dead. In a fire, too."

"What makes you say that?"

"I dunno. Just thought he'd go on forever. Sorta like you an' me. Dyin' in a fire... that's a hard thing. Ever go by the graves? To leave flowers, or anything?"

"No."

"Thought I might. Pay last respects. If I get me a horse, might ride out that way." He turned to the children. "You two ever meet your Uncle Rick? Or your grandma?"

"No, sir."

"What about you, Nelander?"

"I never met them."

"What about your own folks?"

"My father died in San Francisco. My mother lives in Canada. Too long a trip to ask her to make."

"Maybe you'd like to see her: show her the grandchildren." He ate some more, then wiped his mouth on the back of his sleeve. "I heard a baby squallin' durin' the night. Boy or girl?"

"A little girl. Her name is Paula."

"How old?"

"She was born in March."

"Nice family you got here, brother." Suddenly remembering his napkin, Norman took it out and absently refolded it. "What happened to Belinda?"

"She died. Some years back."

"Sorry to hear that. I know how much you liked her."

"Loved her," he corrected. Norman hitched a shoulder and glanced at Barbara.

"He wasn't hardly dry behind the ears when he decided to marry that gal. That's all I can remember him talkin' about: marryin' up an' getting himself a place of his own. You sure was a hard worker, Seth."

"Still am."

"Don't doubt it. Nice place you have here. Always wondered why you didn't settle closer to the old homestead, though."

"This was the land I wanted. What about you? Ever think of settling down? Got your eye on anyone?"

"I'll let you know after I come back from town." He grinned, a boyish, playful expression. "Now, what's this about strawberries? Never heard tell of anyone growing berries in these parts."

"It was Nelander's idea. To supplement the corn and wheat."

He gave her an eye. "What's a Canadian know about strawberries?"

"I read about it."

Seeing she would say no more, his attention seemed to wander.

"Hope it works out for you." Quickly finishing his meal, he pushed the plate aside and got to his feet. "All right if I take the horse?"

The extra assurance settled well with Seth, who nodded.

"Sure. Don't ride him too hard, though. He's old but I'd have a hard time replacing him. Sorta like he's one of the family."

"That's the way a dragoon feels about his horse. Like he's an extra arm or a leg. I'll take care. See you this evening, then."

Waving a friendly farewell, he slipped away. Nelander waited until they heard the barn door open, then got up and crossed to the window. In less than five minutes, Norman reemerged, astride Blaze. Confirming for herself one salient fact, she returned to the table.

Norman Ward had his rifle affixed to the saddle and his gunbelt around the horn. Since he had not taken them with him, he had brought them to the barn while the family slept.

The revelation came as no surprise.

She did not bother informing Seth.

Blood flowed thicker than water. He would have to paddle his own canoe.

CHAPTER 14

"When is Uncle Norman coming back? I thought he would be here by suppertime," Peter complained. "I put on my pirate uniform just to show him and he's not here."

"He has to come," Patricia decided for the group. "He has taken Blaze and he must return him."

Stretching her legs over the edge of the porch and into the dirt of the yard, still warm from the heat of the day, Nelander wondered if she had ever truly been young. As a thought to ponder, it reoccurred often since she came to the Pirate Treasure.

Because of my exposure to children, she mused. Before that, any contemplation had been confined to future speculation.

When am I going to get taller?

How soon before I reach my majority?

When will I earn the right to command?

If childhood meant dressing up or reasoning with simple logic, Nelander could not be certain whether she had been immune or not. On state occasions, her father wore a dark blue suit with brass buttons, decorated with embossed anchors. He had looked every inch a seafaring officer and behind his back, the crew called him "Admiral."

Yes, she decided. His uniform was just as much dress-up as Peter's costume and I wished one day to earn the right.

And how different my own thought process from that of Patricia's? When we set to sea, I had every faith the ship would return to land. Between the two points, lay an entire realm of probability: storm, a hole in the keel, running aground on shore rocks. Scurvy. Even being attacked by pirates.

Not entirely wayward from the belief that if a man gave his word to return with borrowed property, he would stand by it.

"You are smiling," Seth observed, poking her gently in the ribs.

"Am I?"

"What are you thinking?"

"About pirates and horses."

"A strange combination."

Her aspect altered at his expression. Strange, not peculiar. The crew of Ward's ship used the word "strange" to describe an odd occurrence. "Peculiar" they saved for people. Or rather, "peculiar" was reserved for use by other people. To describe them.

"I suppose Norman will return," she declared. "He is a man of honor."

Until he proves otherwise.

As if her sentiment were heard by the stars and whispered to the gods, the whinny of a horse reached them from over the hill. All heads turned expectantly as the silhouette and then the substance of a man on horseback come into view.

"Look, Captain Papa! It is Uncle Norman."

"With two horses!"

Sharp eyes proved correct, for Norman Ward rode one steed while leading another. A hand raised in salutation.

"Hallo!"

Peter raced into the yard to wait, impatiently fussing with his black jacket and eye patch as the younger of the two Ward brothers increased pace. In a matter of moments, he arrived, slipping easily off the back of his new horse before it had come to a halt.

"I was afraid you'd all be gone to bed and wouldn't be up to see my new accusation!" Reining in his own enthusiasm, he kindly took time to note his nephew's wardrobe.

"What have we here? A blackguard, if ever there was one. For a moment I took you for a highwayman until I remembered where I was. This farm is set upon the high seas, and you are a pirate."

"Yes, sir! We waited up for you."

"There -- stand in the moonlight an' let me get a gander at you." Directing Peter, he watched carefully as the boy took out his cutlass and made jabbing motions in the air. After one particularly vicious stab, Norman clapped his hands. "Very good, young sir!" Pretending he held his own weapon, the adult parried with the boy, using his arm to thrust and parry. When Peter managed to inflict a blow, he howled in feigned pain. "Got me, boy!"

"That's how I take over treasure ships! I leap aboard an' cut them scalawags down -- those that don't give up when they see the Skull an' Crossbones," he bragged.

"That's the way I fought Injuns. Hand-to-hand combat. I'd use my cavalry saber and they'd have tomahawks. We'd go at it pretty vicious, too."

"Did you always win, Uncle Norman?"

"Got the scars to show I got struck more'n my fair share, but I'm here to tell the story and them Red Men ain't. So I guess you could say I won."

"That musta been glorious!"

"It had some glory to it, I suppose, but killin' a man is grim business, boy. You don't think about that when you're cheek to jowl wid 'im."

"What do you think about?" came the hushed query.

"Stayin' alive. An' prayin' God you got more strength an' agility -- and luck -- then he's got."

Peter stuck out his jaw. "What's luck got to do with it?"

"Pretty nearly everything. Then Injuns don't know no quarter. They never give up an' they're strong as buffalo an' jest as cunnin' as a wolf. They train with them tomahawks from the day they're old enough to walk. None of 'em can call himself a brave 'till he's passed a test -- a ritual of manhood, you might say."

"What's it like, this ritual?"

Picking Peter up and placing him on the back of his new mount, Norman led the boy around in a circle.

"Sometimes, it's bein' set out alone an' havin' to live off the land. Sometimes, it's killin' your first white man. Depends on the tribe. Those boys, they don't flinch, sir. And they don't quit once they get riled. You take one on an' it's a fight to the death."

"But where does luck come in?" Peter demanded, surveying his kingdom from the exalted elevation of a fiery stallion.

"Say you're evenly matched, man-to-man," Norman began, more thoughtfully than that which Nelander would have credited him. "He hacks at you, you stab at him. You're both bleedin' and pantin' like dogs. Fighting is a terrible tiring business, boy. Gets so you don't have the strength to lift your arm. But you gotta, 'cause your enemy ain't never gonna give in."

Seeing Patricia out of the corner of his eye, he reached for the girl and set her behind her brother.

"You've matched strength-for-strength and agility-for-agility. That's where luck comes in. You trip over a rock and go down. Ahhh!" he cried, making a sweeping motion. "He takes a swipe at your noggin an' gets your scalp. Or, mebbe the head of his tomahawk works loose. It ain't no good to him anymore an' you run the steel of your blade through his heart. That's what you call luck. It runs good an' bad."

"And that's why you're here -- because you have better luck?"

"Something like that," he chuckled. "And superior numbers. Mustn't ever forget that. Two-on-one is a sight easier than one-on-one."

Chilled by the rendition, Seth approached, putting a hand on the horse's neck.

"Where'd you get him?"

"Blacksmith in town. Jest like you said."

"Good looking animal."

"Dropped in to see your friend, the gunsmithy, too. Jake Dale. He knows a thing or two about firearms. Bought some ammunition off him. He said I look jest like you. Woulda know'd me anywhere."

"Glad to see you're spreading your business around. Town can use the economy. Got any more dragoons coming in?"

"Not from my troop. They've all gone their separate ways. No one knows what's gonna happen. Mostly, they've gone home to wait. See what their state does. Which way is Kansas leaning, by the way? I've been gone so long, I don't have a finger on it. She came in free, though?"

"That's right. A free state," Nelander informed. "Which way are you leaning?"

"Can't say 'till it all settles out."

He watched while Nelander took both children off the horse and pointed them in the direction of the house.

"All right you two. Enough is enough. It's past bedtime."

"But I want to ride Norman's horse. What's his name, uncle?" Peter demanded. Norman scratched his chin.

"Haven't rightly gotten that far. What'd you pick?"

Putting off his dismissal to bed, the boy walked around the horse, hands behind his back.

"This here horseflesh's a might different than ol' Blaze," he declared with a farmer's appreciation. "A ridin' animal; not fer plowin'. He's two hands higher'n Blaze an' he ain't got the girth for field work. Long legs, though. Fer speed. We ain't never had no horse like this. Kinda brings to mind Mr. Windsor's Brandy, don't it?"

"Yes, son. It does. But we never needed a riding horse," Seth added, shamed in front of his brother.

"Who's Mr. Windsor?"

Peter spoke before his parents could prevent.

"He used to be our neighbor. Over that way," he indicated. "He was plannin' on breedin' horses but the drought took 'im out. They moved away. Captain Papa and Nelander bought their place."

"They did, did they?" Norman carefully considered, staring into the night sky rather than at the others. "Musta set you back some. What'd you buy it for?"

"There was a piece of land I wanted."

"For the strawberries?"

The pointed question could not be ignored. But it gave rise to how Norman's mind worked.

"Yes."

"Good for you. But from what I'm hearin', you'll do better puttin' in corn."

"Why is that?" came the defensive query.

"If there is gonna be a war -- and I'm not sayin' there is -- soldiers'll need food. Lots of it. Might be the government -- either one -- will be buying wholesale."

Barbara blanched and turned away, having already heard that dire prediction from another source -- one equally suspicious and unappreciated.

Patricia interrupting the line of talk by demanding, "But what are you going to call your horse? He's got to have a name."

"Right you are. You pick one. A good, strong one."

Patricia allowed Peter the lead.

"If I had a horse, I'd call him Rum."

The incongruity, coming from so small a boy, elicited a loud guffaw.

"Rum?"

"That's the pirate's drink."

"And a fair number of cavalrymen, too, I'd wager. Rum, it is. Right in keeping with the 'spirit' of the moment."

Nelander grimaced and would have objected but the time had passed too quickly for interjection. She did not appreciate having the animal named after anything associated with pirates but gave in rather than having to explain her motives.

"All right. Now that that's done, into bed. Now."

Patricia and Peter saluted and trudged toward the house.

"Good night, Uncle Norman."

"Good night, you two. Sleep tight."

Teeth clenched, Barbara waited for the crew to finish the sentence, ... and do not let the bedbugs bite, but fortunately neither did. It would have seemed a bad omen, tying Norman in with their innocent ritual. While he had given her no overt reason to distrust him, there had been just enough provocation for doubt.

Even if he were Seth's flesh and blood and recited the same childhood phrases.

Between them lay a league of difference.

Yawning prodigiously, Norman scratched behind the ears of "Rum."

"Guess I'll go rub down the horses, then turn in. Sorry if I kept you up late." He led the animals away, then hesitated as he remembered something. "Here, ma'am. Got a letter for you. Fella at the post office mistook me for Seth. Came runnin' over to give it to me. Sorta felt foolish, I reckon, mistakin' us two, but after I explained who I was, he was real friendly. Figured I was trustworthy enough to deliver this. Next time you see him, you tell him you got it, won't you?"

"Of course."

Receiving the paper with a firm grip, Nelander glanced at the writing. Even if the moonlight had not been clear enough to read the personalization, the vibrations received would have conveyed the message.

I'll send you a letter to Lawrence general delivery. Tell you how I'm spendin' my re-ward money.

Chilled to the bone, her first instinct was to lie.

It is a letter from my mother in Canada.

It was sent to me by the man from whom I bought the strawberries.

The Windsors wrote.

Postmark aside, Norman would know any explanation for a falsehood. Hoskins had addressed it, "To the Lady what Give up Her Dress."

Hardly something her mother or a businessman or a neighbor would pen.

To the Lady what Give up her Dress.

How could Pete Erlinger know the letter was meant for her? He could have surmised the reference to a dress reflected on her penchant for wearing trousers, but the stretch was a long one. Had he been as sure she was the recipient as Norman made it sound? Or had Pete hedged, explaining that he knew of no other woman in Lawrence for whom it might be intended?

Had it been a lucky guess or was the postmaster somehow involved?

And if so, on which side?

"Sides" having taken on a completely new and dire meaning.

The idea came to her in the middle of the night. Waking from a sound sleep, Nelander sat bolt upright, eyes wide, senses alert. Seth lay beside her, not wakened by her sudden movement.

Pausing long enough for her heart to stop pounding, Nelander listened to the dark sounds: those noises only audible in the hours between midnight and dawn. And heard nothing.

Silence did not allay fear. It only augmented suspicion.

Rolling out of bed, bare feet touched floor. Blindly striking a hand, she found the cradle and touched the wood. Using that to orient herself, she dipped inside, fishing first for the blanket and then the baby. Two covered legs, one exposed arm, the round warmth of a head.

In her mind, the singsong cadence of the Bottom Dollar came back to her.

All's well.

Aboard ship, the universal reassurance of the watch brought relief. Not so on land. No sentry here to be believed.

Already dressed in a loose-fitting pullover shirt and pants, testimony to the uncertainty of the times, Nelander tiptoed out the bedroom and into the main body of the house. Feeling completely alone and adrift, for the dogs were out in the fields on guard duty against gentle deer and raccoons, enemy to plants but not to people, she felt their loss. Not for protection so much as company. With the entire world asleep, she might have been the only one awake.

Yet, if such were true, she had no cause for worry.

Creeping up the ladder to check whether Norman resided within his bed must not be entertained. Being a woman, the action would appear untoward and no amount of explaining would lift the stain of suspicion. If detected, the dragoon would either assume her motives to be impure or nosy. In either case, it would give him an edge to hold against her.

Waking Peter and asking him to creep into the loft presented a better alternative, but she doubted that scenario would wash. Even if the boy pleaded an eagerness to speak with his uncle, it would necessarily involve him in intrigue, for she had no doubt the slightest intrusion on his privacy would wake the soldier. A man living with the threat of Indian attack did not slumber heavily.

She could not even be certain the threat resounding in her bones represented their visitor. There stood an equal chance Mathis McConaghie lurked around the corner with another passenger riding the Underground Railroad. Or worse, one of his sons, snooping about. If Pete Erlinger had figured out who "the lady what give up her dress" might be, others could do the same.

Standing alone, bare feet absorbing the vibrations and undercurrent of noises stemming from innocent house settlings, it occurred to her she ought to return the letter, professing innocence.

I am not to one to whom this is addressed.

I do not understand the veiled reference.

Some mistake.

Whether or not she fooled anyone, the act would stand for itself.

Two can play this game.

To do so, however, meant reading the missive. That, she had not done. Receiving it had been message enough. The bragging of a murdering slave hunter would only elicit hurt. And anger.

Nelander could do nothing, however, without first ascertaining whether Norman Ward were in the loft, or had sneaked out. Two horses in the stalls would answer the question.

Feeling her way toward the kitchen, Barbara found the letter left on the table and shoved it in her pocket. Thus armed, she went outside. More at ease in the open space, she unerringly crossed the yard, reaching the barn. Raising the latch, she slipped inside.

Manure. Hay. Wood. Familiar smells. Quiet. Reassuring. A low snort; air through the nostrils of a horse. The shifting of weight from one leg to another. The scurry of a mouse. And then something else. The brush of warmth across her ankle.

Nerves turned to ice, Barbara froze. Only her mind worked.

Cat.

Dardanelles.

Nearly spasmed with relief, she bent down to catch the orange feline. Clutching the kitten to her face, she scratched it behind the ears, eliciting a series of purrs loud enough to stand any two- or four-legged creature on guard.

Not from the sound of contentment but from the human's presence.

"Pretty cat. Good cat. What are you about? Hunting mice? The captain says you are better at bumping the top off the milking pail than you are at foraging for your supper. What have you to say?"

If purring were an answer, Dardanelles evinced no concern. Likely, she did not feel the need to defend her actions.

Nelander placed the feline back on the floor. The cat made a narrow circle around her feet, then positioned herself within easy distance. Tail raised, back arched, she expected her person to use cat's eyes to divine the need.

"I see. You need a good scratching."

Bending down, Barbara dug her fingernails through the fur, seeking the elusive itch. Moving in synchronization with the constantly turning gato, she completed a one hundred and eighty degree circuit before declaring the deed accomplished.

"Never say we are not a good team."

Smiling to herself, the officer retraced her steps toward the barn door. Instead of pulling it further back as a normal person might do when departing, she firmly grasped the wood and shoved it away.

Having detected the pair of boots while stooping to pet the mouser, the man's presence behind the door came as no surprise.

Removing the paper, she offered it out.

"I am glad I found you. As it is more likely you will be in town before I, kindly return this to the postmaster. He erred in thinking it meant for me." She smiled, aware that even in the gloom, he could see the white of her teeth. "I am certain there is some young woman in town eagerly awaiting its arrival. No doubt it is a love missive from a young man. You note, I did not call him a gentleman."

Norman chortled and took the letter.

"I thought the same thing, myself." His fingers ran around the edges. "But you did not open it."

"That, sir, would be snooping. If the young man used a first name, I might, perhaps, guess the identity of the intended. Being a church-going person, I would rather not know."

"Hear no evil, see no evil. I would have taken you for a believer in 'Know thy enemy.'"

"At sea, there were many sailors who believed the storm clouds and the high, choppy waves to be their enemy. My father felt differently. He said they were just as likely to befriend us in times of calm. It is all a matter of perspective."

"In that case, one could be both enemy and friend. Good and evil."

"Most things are like that, are they not? Coins have two sides, but they all spend the same."

"Well put. I shall have to remember that."

"Good night, brother-in-law."

"And the same to you, sister-in-law."

Nelander let herself out, well satisfied with the encounter.

And grateful to a mysterious grimalkin named after a strait.

Which had allowed her to draw a line in the sand.

CHAPTER 15

In the morning, Norman announced his intention to leave.

"I hope you don't think I'm ungrateful, but I've a hankering to ride over to the old homestead -- what's left of it -- and pay my respects to Ma and Pa's and Rick's graves. Must be getting old. Don't suppose you'd like to come with me, Seth?"

"I've got work to do here."

"Only be gone a few days; mebbe a week. You could have someone come over to keep an eye on the crops."

"Have to pay 'em and that's more than I can afford."

Not surprised by the denial, Norman went up to retrieve his bedroll. Emerging with it tucked under his arm, he waved a farewell.

"I'll say a prayer for you if you want."

"You do that."

Stopping in mid stride, Norman shot him a quizzical look.

"Seth, you're a hard-nosed man. I would have figured different of you, somehow."

"Why?" Nelander asked, joining her husband in the living room. Norman squinted as though trying to track down an elusive idea.

"As a boy, it seemed to me Seth always went with the flow; he bent, you might say, but never broke. Whatever happened, he was able to adapt. Never complained. When Rick inherited everything, I was mad as hell. I figured we deserved our share. But Seth never said a word. Then, when he got thrown outta the house so's big brother could have it alone with his bride, he just packed up and went out into the barn. Rick was full'a gall and Seth was the quiet one."

He bent back an ear, calling in memories. "I was the one who never forgave. Now, I'm figuring to make amends an' Seth's the one with a rod down his back."

Fleet Captain Ward took in a deep breath and let it out. Slowly.

"I always knew what I wanted and I never asked anything of anybody. That doesn't mean I've forgiven. Pa was a loveless man. He always thought he was right. He shot my dog." Glancing at his wife, she nodded.

"He was wrong to do that. He was wrong about a lot'a things. I've had a chance to love and be loved. That helps a man learn when to take a stand. Gives him something to defend."

"They're recruitin' in town for 'Mr. Lincoln's War.' Companies bein' raised all over the place. You gonna join up?"

"No."

"To defend the Union?"

"What about you? You swore an oath to the flag."

"I heard there'll be a new one."

"Not one flying over Washington. That'll be the Stars and Stripes."

Norman leaned against the door. "They say this'll end up bein' a war against slavery. What do you think?"

"I don't own any slaves. Neither do you."

"You want a Negro votin' in the next election?"

"Right alongside Nelander."

Norman did a double-take, then whistled.

"No, sir. I don't know you, at all."

"Yes, you do. The man you don't know is yourself. Have a safe journey. Make your amends. Say your prayers Do some thinking along the way. Might be surprised what you come up with."

"Wish I'd have found someone to love. I love myself. Does that count?"

"You love life, brother. That's not the same thing."

"Damn sure I do, 'cause that's all there is. See you when I get back."

He winked and slipped out, shutting the door behind him.

Neither of the Wards made comment that for a man going off to pray, his sentiment about the finality of death made a poor traveling companion.

After church service, Seth settled on the wagon seat beside Nelander and gave her a look. She knew what it meant. Although they had discussed the trip into town, neither looked forward to it with great anticipation.

"Yes," she reluctantly agreed. "Today is the day."

"Perhaps we ought not to go if you -- we -- are hesitant."

"And perhaps Mrs. Dryfus will not see us and the long ride will be for naught. But we have to try. After all," she pursued, voice growing more resolute, "ultimately, it was she who involved us. If nothing else, she owes an explanation."

"And then there is the letter; and the warning it conveys."

"We must go."

"Are we going to see Mrs. Dryfus, papa?" Patricia inquired, scrambling up from the rear of the wagon. "Is she going to buy more strawberries?"

"We have none to sell. You and your brother and Paula are going to visit Dr. McTree."

"But I want to go with you."

"Not this time."

She sullenly returned to the back where Peter had set out a game of dominoes. Aside from the occasional howl when one of the crew scored a particularly good play or a bump in the road caused the wheels to dip, shaking the pieces out of order, they maintained a stoical silence.

Arriving at the outskirts of Lawrence just after one o'clock, the Wards discovered much had altered since last visiting. Two separate army camps had been established, already filled with men. Some were performing rudimentary exercises to the barking instruction of an officer. Others pitched tents, groomed horses or wandered around, hands in pockets while attempting to absorb the whys and wherefores of military life.

"Norman mentioned some such, but I hardly imagined this," Seth grunted. "How many do you think are here?"

"A thousand. Maybe fewer. But more men than I have ever seen together. Except, perhaps, in San Francisco, crowding the wharves when a ship came in. But they were not dangerous. These are."

"Surely they have come to support the Union."

"Even so."

"Look," he pointed. "Old Glory."

Taking in the sight of the familiar flag, Nelander found her heart catching. While not a citizen of the United States, she had always looked upon the standard of blue stars and red and white stripes with awe and respect. This afternoon, however, the colors held new meaning.

The hue of a dead man's lips; the spilling of crimson blood; ashen faces turned upward to the sun.

"And over there?"

At a separate camp five hundred yards distant, the same flag, flown upside-down.

Another line in the sand.

Grunting with a combination of fear and disgust, Seth slapped the reins over the horse's back and they moved on without further comment.

Maneuvering carefully through the streets clogged with newcomers, they finally came out at Dr. McTree's residence. Baby in her arms, Nelander got down and walked up the path. After several knocks, she tried the door and found it locked. Disturbed at this unexpected setback, she traipsed back and resumed her seat.

"Why would he have locked up the place? He never does."

"Maybe with all the strangers around he figured it wasn't safe. He's got instruments and medicines inside. Valuable."

"We can stay in the yard," Patricia volunteered. "And wait for him to come home. If Minerva is out back we can play with her."

"Not today."

Seth made a clicking sound and Blaze strained against the harness, moving the wagon forward with a herky-jerky motion before getting in rhythm. Another ten minutes took them to the mansion on the hill.

"Shall I go up and inquire if the lady will see us?"

"We shall go together," Nelander decided, having seen Giles face at the window. "If they turn us away, then we are done with this business."

Noting the cutting edge to her words, Seth guided the children out then led the way. Their suspense ended quickly, for the servant met them before he could raise a hand to knock.

"Good afternoon," Giles greeted. "Mrs. Dryfus has been expecting you." The reception, more chilling than inviting, prompted them to enter. Both adults on guard, they followed the man into the same parlor as before. "Please be seated. May I bring you some refreshment while you wait?"

"We are fine, thank you."

He bowed and disappeared. Hands clasped, Seth whistled.

"I never thought to see a room so grand. Always wondered what it was like in here; how rich folk spent their money. Look at the couch!" Hardly daring to sit, he ran a hand over the cushions. "Fine. Just fine. A man could put his feet up and read the newspaper and feel like a grand old fellow!"

"I was thinking the opposite," Barbara confessed. "It is rich but without warmth. While it has the appearance of comfort, I find it repelling."

"Why?"

"It reminds me of a museum. A place people view the wonders of what they are so far removed from. It is more a display of fossils or ancient artwork. When the lights go down and the gates are closed, no one lives there. There is no... lingering laughter. No stories to share by the fireside. No... cat fur or dog hair on the rug. No toys for children. No place for a baby to crawl. All it lacks is a sign, 'Do Not Touch.'"

"Very well," he grinned, not insensitive to her objections. "When your strawberries have made us wealthy, I will live in a palace such as this and you may have the Pirate Treasure, with the creaky rocking chair and sagging sofa cushions. And the rag rug which Dardanelles has used for a scratching post and the legs of the chairs Herman has chewed since puppyhood."

"And the library of carefully chosen and beloved books? And the game of jacks; the India rubber balls, Patricia's water color paintings and Peter's corncob scarecrow family? The lithograph of the world, removed from the jacket of an atlas? All your hand-ruled ledgers dating back to the Flood? You, sir, would not last a week without such comforts."

"Well, you could visit me --"

"And the first time Paula spittled on your priceless Oriental rug, or Peter spilled rum on your French chair or Patricia knocked off an Italian sculpture from the mantel, or the cat shed or Herman gnawed or I dug my heels into your marble dance floor --"

"Stop! You have convinced me. But might I not have...." He faltered for one precious object. "One golden urn?"

"Yes. For your ashes."

His stomach turned and Seth no longer felt like touching anything.

"You paint an ugly picture."

The voice, coming from behind, startled them and they guiltily turned toward the source. Mrs. Dryfus stood in front of a concealed entranceway. Contrary to expectations, she wore not a scowl but a sad smile.

"It might have been different," she continued, sweeping into the room, the hem of her elaborate dress flowing over the priceless Brussels' carpet, "had my life turned out the way I hoped. But, alas, others took control and I must now live in a showcase, having nothing more to show the world than my vast riches."

Nelander made a quick bow with her head. "I did not mean to offend."

"You did not mean for me to hear. I understand the difference. Nor would I disagree with your assessment. I find it astute and honest. Honesty is something I am seldom exposed to. People fear -- offending me. As well they should, for I punish with impunity."

"Then we shall go, and I apologize for disturbing you."

"Sit down." Not a request but a command. And then, more softly, "Please. You are most welcome. I prize truth over all things. Except, perhaps...." Her voice trailed off. "Loyalty. And love." Before considering the ramifications, Seth arched an eyebrow. She took his meaning. "Yes, Mr. Ward. I do know something of both. Or, rather, I have been in love and exhibited loyalty. This room, you see, represents both."

He shifted his gaze from the stately woman to the portrait hanging over the fireplace.

"Your late husband. I see."

"You do not see, sir. Mine was an arranged marriage. I hated Mr. Dryfus with every fiber of my soul."

"Oh. I am sorry."

"Not more so than I. Will you take rum?"

The question proved rhetorical for Giles made an un-summoned appearance, carrying a tray with a bottle of liquor and six glasses. On his mistress' silent command, he poured two fingers into each glass, then offered the first to Barbara.

"You see, I remembered, Captain Nelander." Her emphasis on the last name again solicited a vague recognition and again, that so-named failed to identify the source. "Sailors drink their alcohol straight. And without sugar."

"You have a good memory."

"I-never-forget-anything. You will permit the children a sip? Between... shipmates?"

"Put like that, I could hardly refuse."

She took a glass, then Seth. Peter eagerly grabbed his and Patricia obliged. Mrs. Dryfus accepted hers from Giles' hand, leaving one. The madam waited, astutely aware she had set the scene for her own purposes.

"The last is for... the baby?" Barbara finally inquired.

Well satisfied at the query, Mrs. Dryfus shook her head.

"No, captain. Even a -- barren woman -- knows you do not offer rum to an infant." The chilling effect of her words briefly dropped a pall over the chamber. "Mr. Giles shall join us. That is, if you have no objection?"

Mister Giles.

Referring to a Negro.

A servant.

A former slave.

Nelander checked herself. Slave. While circumstances might indicate otherwise, she had no way of knowing if Giles were free or not. Although the men of Kansas had voted to join the Union as a free state, old ways lingered. What Sheriff Bochner would not ask would go unrecorded in the city ledgers.

"Of course not."

"And you, Captain Ward? Or is it Nelander-Ward? Do you approve?"

"There are those who say a brown man cannot hold his liquor. They are like the Red Men in that regard. 'Fire water,' I believe is the term used when selling liquor to the Indians. They call it 'red eye' in the Tankard's Draft and serve it to white men." He turned to the woman by his side. "What do we call it?"

"Rum."

"Ah. Served in moderation for a difficult task, well done, and at celebrations. Which occasion is this, ma'am?"

She rose to his challenge by deflecting the shot.

"One question to my three. I asked first."

"I have always found people call you whatever they wish. In town, I am known as Seth. Occasionally, murderer. Or Sire of the Devil. With money in my pocket, they nod and call me 'sir.' One of Nelander's first acts was to christen me captain. On the day of our marriage, I became a Nelander-Ward. What I prefer depends on who is speaking to me. Between friends, it does not matter. 'Papa' serves as well as 'Captain,' and 'Nelander-Ward' as well as 'Ward.'"

"And the third question?"

"I believe I have already answered it."

"Say it out. For Giles to hear."

Warming the glass in his hands, Seth glanced from one resident of the grand old house to the other.

"Mister Giles already knows. It is you who wish to hear my thought spoken."

This time, he caught her unawares. She recovered quickly.

"I grant you that -- sir."

"I believe all people are the same. Brown, white, red -- male and female. God judges us by our deeds, not outward appearance, which is, at any rate, transitory. In fact, I would go farther than our late acquaintance, Reverend Pickering. Separate, ma'am, is not equal."

Sliding away, he inched across the room, eyes fixed on the oil portraits.

"In my life, I have been blessed with the love of two good women. I can think of nothing more tragic than a loveless marriage. This painting -- the one on the right. It is of you?"

"It is."

"When you were recently married?"

"Within the year."

"The love has not gone out of your eyes."

"I hated him."

"And I do not doubt for cause. And your father?"

"I hated him, as well. For what he did."

Still cradling the glass, Seth met the gaze of Mrs. Dryfus.

"I have told you what I am called." A soft light radiated from his countenance. "Of all the names and titles, perhaps 'Captain Papa' suits me best, for it encompasses the bond shared between my wife and my children. What do you call Mister Giles? When you are alone and there is no one but God to hear?"

"Son."

Without registering the slightest shock, he grinned. "Then we will have our toast, for you have finally answered my question as to the occasion: parents, celebrating their beloved offspring."

Hands trembling, Mrs. Dryfus laid one on Giles' arm.

"For the first time on my life, Antony, I welcome you publicly into my family. A family of two."

Tears rolled down the cheeks of the formerly stoical man.

"I thank you, mother."

Six imported Irish crystal glasses clinked together.

Seamen's rum sipped from a dead man's treasure.

CHAPTER 16

Setting the empty glass down, Mrs. Dryfus poured herself a second drink. Taking this more from defiance than symbolism, a smile of a different sort crossed her wan features.

"Mr. Dryfus is rolling in his grave."

"No, he ain't, ma'am," Peter promptly supplied, smacking his lips from the bite of the liquor. "The dead don't move around in their graves. I oughta know. I've dug up enuf of 'em to know."

The childlike bravado startled the adults, who took a moment to digest the portentous avowal. Mrs. Dryfus reacted the hardest and with the greater sincerity.

"Is that so, child?"

"Yes, ma'am. The bones lie there, still."

"And what of the spirits?"

"Oh, they kin talk to you, all right. Not all of 'em. Jest a few."

"And the rest?"

"They go on."

"To hell?"

"I never asked. The spirits don't talk about the dead. Only about the living."

"What do they say, boy?"

"Mostly, they say 'I love you.' An' 'keep faith.' An' 'I am with you.'"

She cried and lowered herself into a chair. Giles knelt beside her, fanning her face. Grabbing his hand with hers, she held fast.

"And you have never encountered bad spirits?"

"No, ma'am. I say I do to scare people off, 'cause they believe a bad spirit kin get 'em. Don't like to lie, but sometimes, you gotta do it."

"You do not believe the dead are vengeful?"

"They watch over and protect. Like mama. She's a good spirit. She loves me. I ain't never encountered no other. I expect the bad move on to make their peace."

Mrs. Dryfus' expression hardened.

"And if the living do not wish the dead to have peace?"

He shrugged "It ain't up to us. God sees to it."

"And is God vengeful?" An arm shot out, finger jabbing toward the three paintings above the mantel. "Does He make the evil suffer?"

"Heaven's like school, I guess. There's a lotta lessons to be learned. Jest when you reckon you'll never learn your sums, it comes to you. The sevens are the hardest. Seven times six. Forty-two. I about yanked my hair out over that one. But I got it."

"Your God is kinder than mine."

He dragged his foot over the priceless carpet.

"There's only one. Like it or not, we gotta share."

She surprised everyone by laughing.

"All right then, boy. Yours may teach arithmetic but mine carries a hickory stick."

"I'm a boy, a'right; my name is Peter." He grinned at his parents. "Warrant officer Peter Nelander-Ward."

"And my name is Victoria. Victoria Giles. No hyphen. You may call me Vickie." The revelation carried less surprise than the offer of familiarity. "I was married to a Negro, you see. Marc Giles. He was a... slave in my father's house. I loved him more than God permitted."

"No -- Vickie," Nelander protested. "God did not object. Human beings did." Her voice grew gentle. "He gave you a child to love."

"And took away my husband." The muscles in her jaw twitched. "All right. Men did that. My father and Mr. Dryfus. They conspired against me. My sin offended their righteousness. White women do not love brown men." Her tone deepened. "'That is the same, my dear, as a woman copulating with an ape. It is against God and nature.'"

Barbara stared long at the picture -- not the ones on the end but the stark depiction of a naked, barren tree in the middle -- before making a move toward their hostess. Mrs. Dryfus divined her meaning of comfort and recoiled.

"You will forgive me, but I dislike being touched. By Caucasians. I appreciate your care, although I need none. I have learned how to survive... as a widow." Her look hardened. "Mr. Dryfus thought me cold as ice and so I was. He wished an heir and I did not provide one. The son I brought to the marriage was unacceptable."

"He knew about it, then? Your marriage?" Seeing her shudder, Barbara quickly retracted the question. "You need not tell us. I did not wish to pry."

The older woman's head shot up.

"Of course you meant to pry. What you meant was you did not want to inflict hurt. Speak honestly to me, Captain Nelander. I thought we had an understanding."

Ashamed, the officer retreated, mind wrapped around the pronunciation of that one word which so affected her. This time, with more pieces of the puzzle, the explanation jumped out at her.

"Blind Betty!" Seth jumped from the boom of revelation as Nelander clapped her hands. "That is who speaks my name with such an intonation. You say 'Nelander' exactly as she does!"

"Do I? Really? Then you flatter me, Nelander, for she is a great woman."

The lone white man blinked, played back the manner of speaking between the two women, then nodded.

"Just so. But you need tell us no more of your history, ma'am. We have not come for that."

"I know the purpose of your visit. Perhaps I have answered some of your questions, already." She smiled dryly. "Why a matron with all the money in the world would run one way-station along the Underground Railroad. I have a vested interest, you see, for I identify far stronger with the oppressed than with the masters. And another answer, as well -- why you were selected as conductors."

"Because we hired Betty and Mute Thomas. That meant we could be trusted."

"It also marked you for 'nigger lovers,' but I had no choice. It was, in fact, Miss Betty's decision. She chose you. I might have hesitated, yet I never go against her judgment. Or her wishes."

Mrs. Dryfus gathered her skirts around her and stood. "I will tell you my story, but it is long and I do not care to speak freely in front of...." Her lips curled. "That bastard, whose portrait I 'hang' in my parlor. It makes this room distasteful to me."

"If you hate him, then why is he here?"

"He is, you might say, the ember which keeps my fire lit." Crossing to the hearth, a hand rested on a poker, suspended through one of four ornate brass arms holding shovel, brush and tongs. "There used to be a third likeness there -- in the middle. Of Adam Dillinger, the patriarch. His portrait I could not endure and consigned it to the flames. I wished nothing of him to survive -- save for a daughter and a Negro grandchild."

The bitterness ran so deep neither Nelander nor Seth knew how to react. Patricia spoke, not for them but for herself.

"I am glad you did not burn the oil of yourself."

"Because I was beautiful?" the matriarch sneered.

"No, ma'am." Turning to appraise the living face, she considered. "You still are, so you need no reminder. Because the artist has captured your determination. And more than that. Papa is right. There is love behind your eyes."

"I felt no love when I posed for it, for it was taken shortly after marriage."

Patricia swelled with certainty. "Love for your real husband. You may have tried to hide it, but I see it there. I hope, someday, to have that same skill."

This peeked curiosity. "You like to paint, child?"

"Yes, ma'am. I have a set of colored pencils and a sketchbook at home. I made all the signs we used to sell the strawberries. But I also like to draw people and landscapes. Nelander and Captain Papa bought me some water colors."

"What do you think of my tree?"

The girl drew in a deep breath. "You made that?"

"I did. Once I destroyed the symmetry by consigning Mr. Dillinger to hell's flames, I needed something to take its place. The tree has... significance to me." She scanned the image with deep introspection. "It is dark and without leaves. All around it has died. I saw one like it once and it... inspired me." Rather than pursue further, she pulled back to a lighter subject. "Have you never painted with oils?"

A reverent, "No, ma'am."

"Then you shall, for I have an entire set which has gone untouched these many years. And an easel and many canvasses, stretched and mounted but never used."

"I cannot take your paints."

"You may consider it a gift; one hardly worthy of the title, for I will never touch them again. If they bring you pleasure, you have given me a blessing. And you, Warrant Officer Peter. What is it you like?"

With the unabashed honesty of a child, he promptly supplied, "Considerin' it ain't likely you got a boat around here, I would like a pony."

His father nearly doubled over while his mother laughed. Mrs. Dryfus, alone, remained serious.

"I have no boat and I have no pony. But there are horses in the stable. I suppose a filly would not do? Born this year and not yet broken to halter. Can you perform that service for me?"

Eyes as wide as starfish, mouth agape, he gasped, "Yes, ma'am!"

"Then go to the pasture and find her. If you manage, you do me a great favor."

"What's her name?"

"She has not yet been named. You select an appropriate one."

"Well, it can't be 'Rum,'" he decided with a whistle. "That's a'ready taken." He hitched up his pants, then fussed with a suspender strap. "I'll take a look at her, first, ma'am. An' let you know."

"You do that. The fields are out back. I am sure you can find your way." Receiving permission from his parents, he raced away, arms flying. The matron turned to the second crewman. "Navigator Patricia, the oils are in the attic. Come. I will show you the stairs." Leading the way from the loveless room, she directed the child toward the sweeping staircase. "Up there, three flights. The door is unlocked. You will find my oils by the window. In my 'garret,' you might say. Paint me something... nice."

"But I have never used oils and might make a mess."

"Young woman, that is precisely what garrets are for! Go and have fun and create a masterpiece. Giles will come and get you when it is time to leave."

"Mister Giles," came the stern but friendly reminder. "You're with friends, Mrs. Giles. Friends are always respectful of one another." She rolled her eyes for comedic effect. "That is, mostly. When you have a little brother, it's not always easy. Sometimes he stinks worse than Herman." Victoria bit her lip.

"Who is Herman?"

"The dog!"

"Thank God it is no worse." She turned to Nelander. "You have read Jane Eyre?"

"We have both read it," she replied, including Seth.

"I would have thought it a woman's book."

"Just as periodicals of scientific farming are men's domain. I light up a Stogie while perusing them while Mr. Ward sips sherry and writes critiques of the Brontes for Godey's Lady's Magazine."

"Well put, and I stand chastised." Directing Patricia up the stairs, she led the three remaining Nelander-Wards to the dining room. "We shall take a light meal."

Another brown-skinned servant assisted her with the chair and she sat at the head of the table. Seth and Barbara sat by her side, Nelander maneuvering the baby from left to right in order to free her dominant hand. Mrs. Dryfus immediately responded.

"Please. Might I hold Able-bodied Paula while you eat?"

"She is an able-bodied-in-training. But then how will you sup?"

"When one can afford the best of everything, food soon loses its appeal. But a baby -- it has been a long time since last I cradled one. In fact, I cannot rightly say I have ever held an infant to my bosom."

Barbara gladly handed her precious bundle over and Victoria Giles rested her cheek against the soft, chubby cheeks.

"She is beautiful."

"God never created an ugly babe."

"No. But He allows the procreation of those perceived to be."

Paula's parents let the observation go and the butler served them a repast of fresh melon, pared apples and grapes. In the center of the table a set a silver tray filled with various cheeses and biscuits.

"Will you take tea, as well?"

"Most certainly." Nelander winked at Seth. "This, sir, is called 'low tea.' You will take note for next time we dine with the Queen."

Grabbing a knife two-fisted, he jabbed out a pinkie and groaned in Midwestern dialect, "Aw, dang it, ma'am. I never did git the hang of eatin' like this. An' what about this 'u-tensil'? It ain't hardly got an edge to it. How's a feller gonna cut his beefsteak?"

"We are not having 'beefsteak,' sir."

He professed shock. "You mean, this is all there is? Is a man to starve?"

"By the looks of you, you will hardly perish."

"Mah stomach's growlin' an' mah teeth is itchin'." He poked at the platter. "What's this? Are we feedin' ants?"

"Goat cheese."

His nose wrinkled. "I thought goats was used fer wool."

"That is sheep. And if you do not mind your manners, I will have the Royal Guard deposit you in the sheep dip."

"What's that? Raspberry syrup?"

"A chemical compound used for delousing."

"No call fer you to use cuss words at me."

Mrs. Dryfus clapped her hands. "Oh, you are wonderful. And I am only sorry I have no strawberries for you, as well. But I am led to understand they are out of season."

"Just a few in the back --"

"And you did not bring them for me? Knowing how fond I am of them?" Her smile faded. "But you do not know. Not really. Do you? And I must tell you."

"Please do not feel obliged to share what is painful."

The older lady grew suddenly serious.

"But I must. So we might have a better understanding of one another. I have told no one. There are those who know my story, but only because they were intimately involved."

"Miss Betty."

"Yes. Miss Betty knows it all. For many years she was my only confidant." Holding the baby close, she kissed Paula's forehead. "Betty was a slave in my father's household when I was a girl. Since I had no others, she became my playmate. After lessons I taught her all I had learned. She was a better student than I."

"You, then," Nelander whispered, "are her grand lady."

Mrs. Dryfus dismissed the compliment with a wave.

"She has always referred to me in that way. I do not know why."

"Betty was not blind from birth?"

"No, but even as a child a film grew over her eyes. Yet, you would never know it incapacitated her. She saw with her hands and her senses. As we got older, the condition worsened. I would have pitied her, but even then I knew there was little beauty in the world."

"I am sorry."

Waiting for her guests to help themselves to "low tea," she began her narrative.

"My father, Mr. Dillinger, married a woman from high society in Philadelphia. She came west with him when he opened his business in Lawrence. Why he chose this place I cannot say. Because it is close to water, I presume and St. Louis was already too commercialized for his taste. He built a factory: employed many men. Soon he was producing tinware to be shipped further west. Eventually, he took on a partner -- Mr. Dryfus -- and they expanded into glassware. Jars. Window plate. The team of Dillinger-Dryfus garnered many large contracts and money rolled in. Unfortunately, my mother died shortly before this house was completed, so as a very young girl I became its hostess."

She stopped to pet the baby, whose sleepy cries diverted attention for a moment.

"I had many beaus but my father discouraged them all. He always said he desired to take me 'home' to the city of his birth and marry me off to a 'civilized' gentleman. For all his wealth, he was never comfortable here and looked at the people as rabble rather than peers."

In the awkward silence, Seth pointed to the tray.

"Is that really goat cheese?"

"No. You may feel safe to try it."

"Wouldn't want to get above my station."

The matron smiled. "The Queen may not forgive you, but I do." She settled back in her chair, rocking gently. "Of course, I was raised with a full and complete awareness of the differences between brown and white men, but I am afraid my father's teaching and his desire to shield me from the local boys had a very unlooked-for consequence. Young, rebellious and isolated, I sought those at hand for company. And fell madly in love with a boy -- a man -- named Marc Giles."

"One of your father's slaves?"

"Indeed. He was the most beautiful human being I had ever seen. Tall and straight and broad-shouldered with flashing eyes and a brilliant smile. And a sharp wit. Of all the people I knew, he was the only one who could make me laugh. And I had very little of that, as you might imagine."

As the baby fussed, she got up from the table and began a slow trek around the room.

"Despite our differences, I could not help but falling in love with Marc. No one knew about it, of course. Except Betty. She warned me but I would not listen. When one is sixteen years old, one believes they can change the world. Or at least ignore the naysayers If we could not live in Kansas -- or Philadelphia," she added with scorn, "then we would marry and travel to France where men of color were accorded much more freedom. He and I spent hours sitting beneath the rose arbor discussing our plans. It all seemed so simple. So innocent."

"And so it was."

"Not so, Nelander. Neither simple nor innocent. Say, rather, naive. Terribly, horribly naive. I had no money, you see; no means of escape." Her mouth drew into a tight line. "Not even enough to buy Marc's freedom."

"Your mother left no trust fund for you?"

"She did; a considerable one. To be dispensed when I reached the age of twenty-five. Or upon my marriage. A proper marriage -- to a proper man. An acceptable man. I had not realized there was a... difference, you see."

They saw.

"Telling my father of my plans was out of the question. And I would not be put off, so Betty arranged for a minister -- a Negro man of the Gospel -- to perform the ceremony. Legal in my eyes. And in Marc's. It was beautiful. I wore a white gown, purchased for a ball but never worn. Betty stood by my side. Afterwards, she made me promise not to tell my father --

to keep the marriage a secret until I had collected my inheritance and fled. I thought her overcautious."

Paula began to cry and Victoria Giles laid her across her shoulder and patted the tiny back.

"I packed my bags for our journey and went to the bank. I would not tell the president whom I had married, only that I had taken vows. I expected him to take my word, but being merely a female and underage, he demanded proof. The testimony of the minister. Or the registrar from the church. I promised to bring them and never returned."

"I am so sorry."

"As was I. Sorry, bitter and confused. I had followed the dictates of my heart. How could that be wrong? But it was and my husband and I crept back here and resumed our places. Nothing was said and we might have lived that way for years. But I came with child." Her eyes closed as the memory filled her with horror. "I tried to hide my condition, kept out of Mr. Dillinger's way, pleading one illness or another As he spent most of his time at the factory, I had little difficulty and might have concealed my 'sin,' but that, too, was a naive hope. My condition was not unknown among the household staff and one told him." Her voice hardened. "All hell broke loose."

Fearful the rest of her tale would contaminate the baby, the lonely woman offered Paula back to her mother. Nelander might have refused but for the steely glint to Mrs. Dryfus' eyes.

"My father had a fit; he was furious. Indignant. Slighted. Humiliated. He called me anything and everything; words I had never heard before and comprehended from inference rather than meaning. I know them, now. Quite well."

Seth shuddered and took the baby from Nelander so she could concentrate on the story.

"Marc, my husband, fled. What else could he do? It was death to stay and death to run. They called him an escaped slave. Mr. Dryfus let it be known Marc had stolen money and placed a bounty on his head. One thousand dollars. A fortune, by anyone's standards. It was then I learned of honor among thieves; the 'thieves' in this case being white men. The explanation was accepted and no word ever leaked about 'Giles' true crime. The bounty hunters tracked him with dogs. And captured him."

She stopped walking and resumed her place at the table. Hands folded, the attitude belied the intense emotion of events relayed.

"Of course, there was no thought to justice. A Negro was not entitled to a trial. He was guilty as charged. I went to him -- they held him in a small jail west of here. It was fall and bitterly cold. Leaves had fallen from the trees."

A bleak reminder of the painting in the parlor.

"For the bribe of one gold ring, I got in to see him. I, swollen with the result of my fornication and he, a rapist by any other name. My husband. My love." Tears came to her eyes. "Not a dozen gold rings would have bought his freedom and time was short. I asked what I could do and he said, 'Bring me some strawberries. I wish to eat strawberries before I die.' But it was nearing winter and fresh strawberries were not to be had."

"Oh, God," Nelander wailed.

"I gave him a jar of strawberry jam. From the local store. Why they even had any I cannot say. God's small mercy." The words did not convey belief. "I gave it to Marc and he ate the jam with his fingers for I had neglected to bring a spoon. I was so forgetful in those days."

The self-deprecation implied she forgot nothing ever again.

"After he had finished eating, they took him out and hanged him from a tree. I stood by and watched. He died bravely for a crime which was no crime. My lamb... sacrificed for white man's justice." She brushed aside pity from her listeners. "In the spring I gave birth to a baby boy. I anointed him Antony. For the great Roman warrior, Marc Antony, who shared a first name with his father." She coughed into a handkerchief. "Of course I could not be permitted to raise such a... yellow bastard... and my father would not have the child in the house. God knows what he would have done with him, but I had nothing to lose. I threatened to go back east and tell his family and friends what I had done -- that I had married a brown man and borne his child."

Finally, a look of triumph burned like coals behind her orbs. "We reached an agreement. Betty was to be freed and she was to take my son with her. She had her own child, Thomas. Another would not raise eyebrows. My father sent her to 'Nigger Hole,' and there she lived, raising two sons. Teaching them to read, as I had taught her."

"A good deed, rewarded."

"Say no more. What use a 'nigger' for an education? There can be no advancement. No hope of advancement. Until," she stated with an unusually cutting enunciation, "You took Betty and her son and gave them a home. And a job."

"To our mutual benefit. And you took Antony Giles."

She gave slight acknowledgment. "Years before. But only after my 'widowhood.'"

"What happened? Will you tell the rest?"

"After the child was born I was tainted, and certainly could not be wed to a stranger, for fear word of my misdeed leak out and humiliate my father. That disappointed him terribly, for I would never be the belle of Philadelphia society. Mr. Dryfus was an old man -- never married and in search of an heir. Since I had proven my childbearing ability and because he and my father were bound by partnership as well as conspiracy, I was given to him in legal wedlock. Yet, I swear by the God of Vengeance, he never touched me. I would have cut my throat, first."

Having come nearly to the end, her shoulders straightened.

"My father died and Mr. Dryfus took me away from here. I suppose in hopes I might put the past behind. We traveled extensively." Her voice waivered but not from irresolution. "I chose the destinations. We always lodged in separate rooms. When he died by the mercy of that same God, I returned here. To be near my son. Not that I could ever acknowledge him as such. He is my... good servant."

Nelander turned and observed a shadow lurking in the hall. It required no guess to identify the person behind the darkness.

"And now you know why I have cared to involve myself in the Underground Railroad... and my -- affinity for strawberries. Imagine how I felt, learning that you not only took my best friend and my adopted nephew and placed them in their own home, you also grew strawberries. How could God have spoken more plainly?"

Which begged the question: which god?

The god of vengeance?

Or the god of mercy?

CHAPTER 17

"Your fate was sealed," Mrs. Dryfus reiterated, "when I learned of the strawberries. That drew you into a very small and select family circle. I will not ask if you are pleased, or the contrary, for indeed, you have no choice."

Although touched by the woman's story, this arrogance rankled and the darkness of Seth's tan faded as his ire rose.

"Do not take us for granted."

The matron batted her eyes the way she might, had he been a brazen suitor and she not disinterested in his amours.

"I was about to say the same to you."

"How so?"

"You are the ones who fly the flag of dissent, sir."

"You mean the Skull and Crossbones? But that has nothing to do with aiding escaped slaves."

"Does it not? Come, Captain Ward. The Jolly Roger is known as a symbol of defiance the world over. Of flaunting authority; disregard for the rules. The universal warning of violence over diplomacy."

"It is a children's game --"

"It is a man's game you play. Whether meant innocently or the contrary, you have marked yourselves."

"No one hereabout knows of pirates."

"The worse for you. My choice of standard," she continued, growing stronger, "is the old Revolutionary flag: 'Don't Tread on Me.' A fighting stance. But we are all fighters here, are we not?" When he made no counter, she completed her original thought. "I meant, Fleet Captain, your heart is ruler of your soul. You can no more turn your back on events transpiring around you than your... friends in town."

He paled at the implication but could make little sense of it.

"What are you saying?"

"That the times are changing and with them, individuals who once thought themselves immune."

"Speak plainly."

She beamed with pleasure. "Another admonition from our favorite authoress. You would make a splendid Edward Rochester, Seth Ward. You even have the mysterious wife in the attic. A bit Gothic, I confess, but a tragic character who works well in our Victorian times."

"And I, madam?" Nelander demanded. "Am I to play Jane Eyre?"

"Far too tall. I see you more as Heathcliff, the wild boy of the moors."

"We were speaking of my brother," Seth inferred.

"No, sir. We were speaking of your heart. I did not choose you for this work. You volunteered yourselves. We all do what we can. And if we are to succeed, we must help one another."

"The way we aided Jim Best?"

For a moment the name brought a pall to the small gathering, but Mrs. Dryfus would not let it stand.

"I am deeply sorry for him. He is a hero in our new revolution. The risks are great and the rewards... sometimes intangible."

"I received a letter from Hoskins -- the slave trader who killed him."

"What did it say?"

"I did not open it. But I took its meaning. He caught Lolly and returned her to her master for a large reward. We have a spy in our midst, Mrs. Giles. Someone identified me as the woman who helped her escape. A person in your household, perhaps?"

"No."

"Mathis McConaghie, then?"

"He is one of us."

"Before he revealed himself, I would not have taken him for an emancipationist. I do not trust him, yet."

"He is an old friend of mine."

The statement shocked.

"How so? You would seem to have little in common."

"Many years ago he worked for my father. It was he who defied Mr. Dillinger by taking me to see Marc whilst in captivity. Stayed with me during those last horrible days. Otherwise, I would have missed the closing... ceremony. He who found the jar of strawberries."

"So he knows that much."

"He knows more and owes me much. It was his wife who told my father of my condition. Who pointed the finger at my husband. For which," she gritted through clenched teeth, "she received great reward. She, Nelander, is a witch. And has raised three devils. Beware of them."

"We have had our encounters."

"They are the enemy. But Mathis keeps them far afield when he can. When he cannot, he goes along. To mitigate damage."

Seth slammed his fist against the table, rattling the dishes.

"He spoke against me at that mockery of a trial. When I was accused of murdering my wife."

"I did not say he is a paragon of virtue. Only that he is no traitor. And besides, you have the ghosts to protect you from him."

"Who, then, is the spy? Pete Erlinger?"

"I trust no one and it is as well you follow the same policy. I have laid out those on the side of right: myself, Antony, Betty and Mute Thomas. McConaghie. The Nelander-Wards. I vouch for none other in Lawrence."

She might have said more, but Patricia burst into the room, eyes wild with eagerness. Fingers covered in paint, she might have been taken for a spirit, recently escaped from a field of dirt and grass.

"Mrs. Giles! You must help me! There is something wrong!"

"What, child?"

"I have made a picture, but the paint will not dry. I tried blowing on it but when I touched it --" The girl displayed her hands. "It was as wet as when I first put it on."

The adult laughed with a sweet, singsong cadence.

"I should have told you: oils and not like water colors. They take days to dry. A week, perhaps, in this hot, humid weather. In fact," she smiled, "the only time oil dries quickly is when you wish to blend color."

"Oh."

The interruption being a welcome one, Mrs. Giles-no-hyphen-Dryfus, crossed the room, eagerly summoning her guests.

"I must see this production."

Walking with a speed and agility neither Nelander-hyphen-Ward would have attributed to her, they followed Patricia as she led the way upstairs. Bypassing two levels, they arrived at the upper, or attic destination.

Pushing aside the door, the girl entered, taking the group into an open space caught somewhere between the higher and lower regions of human existence.

Warmer than the rest of the house, the roof slanted toward the sides, leaving only enough headroom for an adult at dead center. By a small but adequate garret window a long-ago artist had set up an art studio. A high, three-legged stool sat before a large wooden easel. To the right, three stacked crates served as a table. Upon the uppermost lay pallets, two dozen or more brushes, some pointed downward in jars with dried turpentine residue, and innumerable containers of paint. Rags littered the floor, the painter's equivalent of crumpled manuscripts.

If that were not enough to stimulate the senses, a score of artist's renderings lined the walls. Many were landscapes, similar to the barren tree hung in the parlor, clearly first, second and tenth tries at perfecting the scene. Some trees had the remnants of dried leaves; others nothing but one solitary branch jutting from the black trunk at right angles. One, and only one, depicted the lightly sketched image of a man suspended from a rope.

Opposite, in an entirely different vein, were portraits of people. Lacking the finishing touches of a grand master, the faces nevertheless leapt out with a life undiminished by time. Many depicted Negroes: a woman with round, jolly features, wearing a red kerchief. An aged man with a profusion of snowy hair. A tall, thin boy in dungarees holding a toddler wearing a bright yellow shirt. A profile of a maiden, hair decorated with beads. The stark clarity of the jaw line, the tilt of the head, the steady, introspective gaze identified her more surely than the haze of white about the eye.

"Miss Betty!" Nelander cried in delight, forgetting, for the moment, the purpose of their quest. Hurrying to the painting, she stood before it with awe. "You have captured her brilliantly, Miss Vickie! I feel as though I can feel her breath. This, then, is how our Betty looked as a young woman?"

"I did my best," came the humble admission. "I was never satisfied but my dear friend told me I had painted her better than she deserved. Not true," she added, "for Betty was a beautiful woman."

"And these others -- the two boys. This is surely Thomas."

"Yes."

"And the other?" Stooping closer, Nelander observed that unlike those of the standing boy, the child's features were vague and poorly detailed. "Is this Giles? Your Antony?"

"Not drawn from life," came the testy response. "For I never saw him. Not as an infant and not as a child. I had to... use my imagination."

Nelander steadied her resolve. "Well, you have him, now. What does he think of it?"

"I have never shown him. I have not been in this room since... I satisfied myself with the Hanging Tree."

"But you must have spent many happy hours here before that. It is a shame you did not return to it."

"I forswore happiness." Moving further in, the way a penitent crossed the threshold of a church, Mrs. Dryfus looked around herself with a commingling of tortured emotion. Standing, half in shadow with lips drawn down, wrinkles of age and sorrow accentuated her dark side, while a fresh bloom of youth sprang from the light. Panting rapidly, the moment caught her in the cross-hairs of memory. "I would have thought this place to be covered in dust." Awareness struck and she flinched in surprise. "You," she directed at Patricia, "have set it to rights."

"I did some dusting, ma'am. I could not sit down to paint with all these beautiful pictures neglected. It didn't take long." Seeing the deep-set eyes, she hastened to add, "It wasn't much."

"It was a great deal. But we have not come to speak of me and my minimal talent. Let us see what you have done."

Tiptoeing across the freshly swept floor, she rested a hand on the girl's shoulder as she took in the new oil.

"It's not finished...."

"No, but you have made a brilliant start. Bringing new life back into this place."

Nelander and Seth joined her by the easel. Patricia had begun a landscape of sweeping hills cut by a deep valley. Rows had been tilled along the sides and a profusion of green plants sported headdresses of red berries. At the bottom, a sparkling blue stream bubbled its way to a stand of light green willow trees and a jagged but shallow waterfall.

"It is papa and Nelander's dream," she identified.

"Come to life as surely as though you had snatched it from nature. You have a gift, child."

"I will never be as great as you."

"Much greater, for you are able to instill love into your work."

"I see love in yours, too."

"That love has died, never to return. Where once my art was an amusement, now it is the harbinger of evil. I will never paint again. But you, my girl, are gifted."

"Thank you."

Mrs. Dryfus turned to the parents. "She must have lessons; and the finest material. Hers is a talent to be nurtured."

"We cannot afford --"

Victoria Giles' head snapped back.

"Do not tell me what you can afford and not afford. I have spoken. Patricia must be encouraged. What she needs I will supply."

"We are already beholding to you for the fifty dollars --"

"And now you know why. Strawberries occupy a very special place in my heart. I did not give you money for your own paltry purse but for myself. In recognition." Her expression changed to one of deep introspection. "Not the same reason I once sent Mister Giles to buy your crop. But of that, we will speak no more of for the present. If you will not accept my -- charity -- than Patricia must stay here."

"Stay here?"

"To paint. To learn the medium of oils. It has been so long since there were children about. And never the one I wanted," she added in a whisper so low the words were nearly lost. "But now I have another. An artist whom I may inspire." Seeing doubt, she hurried on. "At least give her to me for several days. So that I may instruct her in the fundamentals. Then we may speak again."

"She has chores to do. And her studies."

And we will miss her.

"Warrant Officer Peter may carry her load for such a short duration. And as for school work, it is summer and classes are recessed." Her eyes assumed a hint of amusement. "And even Patricia's teacher, Miss Barbara, allows for holidays. Or so I am told."

"For a woman who seldom gets out, 'Miss Vickie,' you hear much. But I will not make the decision and defer to the principal, 'Mr. Seth.'"

Disappointed at having been included in a conversation he sought to escape, the parent deferred to one of two students attending Pirate Treasure Academy.

"You are old enough to make your own choice, Patricia. Would you like to stay here?"

"I believe I would, sir."

"Very well. But what of a change of clothes?"

"Rest assured I have clothing here, 'Captain Papa,'" Mrs. Giles noted. "And what I lack may be purchased in town. As a gift to the girl. And if you will not accept that, when she is not painting I will put her to work around the house. With the salary she earns, she may buy her own."

His eyes widened. "If Patricia is going to earn that much within a span of four days, then I may hire myself out to you, for you pay good wages, ma'am. Far better than what a farmer earns."

"As to that, we shall see."

Which put a new dimension on his jest.

"We accept, with gratitude. And now, we must collect our son and take leave, for there is work to be done at home. And return -- at the beginning of the new week." Stooping down, he placed both hands on his daughter's shoulders. "If, for any reason, you do not wish to stay the entire time, go to Dr. McTree's and he will bring you home. Is that clear?"

"Yes, sir."

Reluctantly retiring downstairs, the group passed through the parlor and went outside. Seth whistled for his son and after a protracted delay, Peter finally presented himself, cheeks red from exertion, face aglow with joy.

"Papa, you should have seen the horses! And my filly -- she is the most beautiful horse in the world!"

"It is not your horse --"

"What have you named her?" Mrs. Giles spoke over Seth.

"Fleet." He swelled with pride at his cleverness. "On accounta she's so fast -- an' because 'fleet' means a group of ships."

"Very good! I approve!"

"And you, papa?"

"Naming a filly does not make it yours. Just so you understand."

Peter turned to the rightful owner.

"But I can ride her, can't I? When we come to town and visit?"

"Ride him? Have you already broken her to saddle?"

"Not yet. But I will."

Seth grunted and steered Peter toward the wagon.

"Seems as though my crew has found shore leave at your home very agreeable. But we do not want to be imposing."

"On the contrary, Fleet Captain Ward. They have given me what I always desired -- the sound of children's laughter. Their excitement rekindles my soul. I had thought it... dead."

She offered her hand and he took it. After shaking, Virginia Giles extended it to Nelander.

"You are a woman of extraordinary strength. I never thought to find another who matches my nerve. Having backbone is the realm of men, is it not?"

"Backbone comes in all shapes, sizes and colors. Women often display remarkable resolve and courage, although it is often mistaken for diffidence. The same may be said for our brown brothers and sisters. I welcome you aboard our ship as an honorary crewman."

"And what must I do to become a full-fledged member?" A part of your family. "Like Betty and Thomas?" She detected a flicker of emotion across Nelander's bow but could not interpret the change in climate. "All my worldly possessions?"

"No, Miss Vickie. A captain does not have the right to ask that. What you bring aboard and what you earn belongs to you. How else support those left behind? The world to a seaman may be bow and keel and mast but neither the captain nor his crew must ever forget their dependents, for theirs is a far different reality of landlords and bill collectors."

"And waiting?"

"Always that."

"Then I would rather go for a sailor."

The two women clasped hands, sealing a pact. Where it would end depended on the tides. Not only those dictated by the ebb and draw of the moon, but the waves of civil discontent.

Between the two, a far more unstable element.

CHAPTER 18

"Let us stop by Dr. McTree's before we head home," Seth suggested, reining Blaze to the left. "I wish to put him on the alert if Patricia needs him."

"I think that a good idea."

"And leaving her behind?" His voice reflected sadness. "Did we do the right thing -- allowing Patricia to make the decision? She is so young."

"I was five when I went to sea."

"But it was your father's choice, not yours."

"I would have volunteered and gladly."

"You knew your father better than we know Mrs. Dryfus."

"Say, rather, we had ties of blood. I am inclined to favor friendship over more traditional bonds."

He did not ask her to elaborate.

They found Mr. McTree at home, but not in the manner prescribed. Standing in his yard, he held a mallet in one hand and a wooden sign, fastened to a stake, in the other. His mouth bristled with a profusion of nails.

"Good afternoon," he greeted. Or words to that effect, for the hardware obscured the syllables.

Leaping from the wagon before it had fully stopped, Seth hurried up the path. Not to help but to grab the placard from the physician's grasp.

"What is this? For Sale? You are moving? Leaving Lawrence?"

Seth verbalized questions, answers to which Barbara had already ascertained for herself. Abandoning his usual black coat and silk vest, Hank wore a dyed wool coat with gold buttons.

A uniform.

"I've gone for a soldier. Joined the Union Volunteers."

"A soldier?"

"A six-month enlistment. Not as an infantryman but as a doctor. I figure the boys'll be needing my services more than the folks of Lawrence." He winked. "Pay's better, too. What do you think of my outfit?"

Dropping the sign in horror, Seth pulled back to stare at what his senses had rejected first time around.

"They gave you a uniform?"

"No," he scoffed. "I ordered if from Mrs. Debasio."

"The dressmaker?"

"Not much call for ball gowns these days; but she's working overtime on military dress. Coats; jackets. Trousers. Vests."

"Sudden, isn't it? A week ago, you scorned the idea of joining the army."

He turned to look at the speaker who had come up beside her husband. In his euphoric state of mind, he misread her condemnation.

"Yes. Very sudden. I guess you could say I got caught up in the enthusiasm. Went to a recruitment meeting; not with the intent of joining but just to listen. I confess to being swayed." Running his fingers over the buttons, he grinned like a boy. "I didn't have any rank put on because I wasn't sure what I'd be given." His chest puffed. "They've made me a captain." His eyes widened. "Of course, unlike a ship's captain I won't have command responsibilities. Except for those in the Medical Corps. I've already been assigned an aide. And an orderly. Imagine that? Around here, I couldn't find a nurse if I paid in gold."

Nelander nodded, trying her level best to quell the butterflies in her stomach.

"Congratulations."

The word fell flat. Hank did not notice.

"Thank you. There's going to be a war and I want to have a hand in it."

"And that means you have to sell your home?" Seth asked, tossing down the board. "Won't you be stationed here? To protect the city?"

"I expect we'll be sent to Missouri. President Lincoln's already chosen a commander -- General Fremont. There's a lot of unrest over there and he's to put it down."

"What interest do you have in Missouri?"

"My interest lies in preserving the integrity of the Union. That's what President Lincoln says is the purpose of the war. He just addressed the Twenty-Seventh Congress; word came in on the telegraph," he breathlessly added. "There's going to be a big celebration in town. You gonna stay and watch the fireworks tonight?"

"Tonight?"

"July 4th."

His face turned grave. "A farmer doesn't have much call for remembering specific dates. Is that what all the fuss is about at the camps? We passed a number of them coming in. Beehives of activity."

"I expect so. Companies have been drilling all week. They've got red, white and blue banners up, too. The soldiers are going to march through town later this evening. Before the fireworks. Ought to be a grand sight."

"What about the other side? The Rebels? We saw them gathering, too. Is there gonna be trouble?"

"They're supposed to have their own parade. I don't know about fireworks, though."

"I don't give a tinker's dam about fireworks," Seth snarled. "I can't believe you signed up."

"You will, too, before it's all over."

"I got a family. And a farm."

"So have lots of the other men. But patriotism before family, sir."

Seth reacted by drawing back a fist, but Nelander stopped him with a quiet stare.

"When are you leaving?"

"Haven't received my orders, yet. Supposed to know in a week; next Thursday."

Barbara Nelander cringed. Already, the man she knew had changed. Instead of the soft-spoken, sedate physician, his brief exposure to the military had altered his demeanor. Even patterns of speech had changed. With new enthusiasm and more than a touch of arrogance, Hank McTree had already abandoned Hippocrates, Father of Medicine, for Mars, god of war.

Whatever his fortunes, their relationship had changed. Were he to return six months or a year hence, they would begin anew, acquaintances with no more than history between them to ward off strangeness.

Trying to guess her thoughts, the altered Dr. McTree stiffened.

"What's the matter? You're not supporting the wrong side, are you? You would have me choose the other?"

Since he knew better, she saw no point answering. That prompted her to exaggerate a half truth.

"God, no. I was worried... about your dog. What of Minerva?"

"Ah, yes. I was hoping you'd take her. You've got two of her pups. It would be a reunion of sorts."

A sidelong glance at Seth and then, "Yes. We will take her."

"Good. Then it's all settled. How'd you like to buy a house in town, while you're at it?"

"We have enough obligations. But why not just shut it down? Surely you'll want to resume your practice when -- the war is over."

"I'm afraid the military will commandeer it if it's empty. Use it for a headquarters, or even a hospital. Tear it up. For that matter, there's no saying there won't be significant fighting here about. If it's shelled, I'll lose everything. Rather have something in the bank to make a new start than a worthless piece of property."

Nelander might have agreed, save for the un-emotion in his voice. Now a man without ties to the community, he worried more about his savings than the potential destruction and loss of life.

Ill-concealing anger, she retorted, "I wouldn't worry, doctor. The first thing the enemy will go after is our financial institution. If they don't 'shell' it, they'll have Mr. Provost open the vaults. If I were you, I'd send my money as far east as it will go. New York. Boston. Montreal."

He missed the sarcasm.

"That's a good idea. I'll do that." Stooping down to pet Minerva, the animal wagged her tail, sensing her life about to change and seeking comfort from the only source she had ever known. "When will you take her? Today?"

"We will be back in town early next week." She started to explain the actual reason for their visit, then cut off the words. If Patricia needed him, he would not be here. No sense divulging their connection with Mrs. Dryfus for no need. One day it might be used against them.

"Are you going to stay for the parade?"

Tempted to ask, Which one? Seth saved her the trouble.

"We have to be getting back. There's the cow needs milking."

"She can wait until tomorrow. There'll be big doings."

Ignoring the cruelty, Seth retorted, "If, as you suggest, Lawrence is in danger, we'll have more than enough exposure to soldiers marching through town. And fireworks of another kind."

"Suit yourself." He held out a hand. "If I don't see you before I go, this is good-bye. Take care. And pray for me."

Lacking courage to say Doctors are never in danger, so we expect you home safe and sound, Barbara merely took his hand and shook. Going one step further, she reached out and gave him a hug. Not for protection but as a means of sealing off the past from further contamination. Having already lost two friends when the Windsors packed up and left, McTree made three. If she had not solidified a relationship with Victoria Giles Dryfus, Nelander would have been as isolated in Kansas in 1861 as she had been in 1857.

Not counting Seth and the crew.

Whose existence she must now consider as tenuous.

Returning her affection, McTree kissed Barbara on the cheek before wrapping his arms around Seth.

"See you before next spring," he whispered. "Six months."

"I hope it's sooner than that, and you kick yourself for selling the house," Captain Ward muttered. Coming by the title ceremoniously and not actually being a military man, one of the onlookers forgave him the errant wish.

"Thanks. Take care."

Failing to ask why they had dropped by, a fact the civilian would never have overlooked, McTree walked them to the wagon.

"If you're already gone by the time we return, leave Minerva with Anson at the dry goods store and we'll pick her up there."

"All right. And Seth --" The farmer raised an eyebrow. "Hate to say it, but you might think of putting winter wheat in that field behind the house. And maybe corn or potatoes in the valley. No one's going to want strawberries. It's 'fodder' for man and beast that'll bring in the money. Soldiers have to eat. Good idea: wrong time. Sorry."

The farmer's eyebrow met its mate, forming a scowl.

"I thought you said the war would be over in six months. That being the case, returning soldiers'll want nothing more than the sweet taste of home. Sorry," he added, using McTree's intonation.

Sorry, in this case, meaning exactly the opposite.

The Wards might not have spoken on the way out of town, but as they reached the turn-off, a blue-coated sentry with a musket blocked their passage.

Holding the weapon across his chest, legs spread, cap shading his eyes, he reminded them of Todd Bakke, the deputy. The difference being, during the drought, Bakke had kept them out of Lawrence. This man clearly intended to keep them in.

"Halt where you are."

Reining up, Seth pushed back his hat.

"What's this all about?"

"There's gonna be a military procession down this road. Ain't no civilians allowed to block passage."

"I have no intention of getting in the way. Just let us pass. I have a farm outside town. I just want to go home."

"Cain't do that. Got orders."

"What orders, for Christ's sake?"

"The general don't want no disruptions."

"Disruptions? What disruptions?"

"Civilians shootin' off firearms."

"I'm not even armed." Seth held up his hands to signify a lack of weapons. When the soldier remained obstinate, he peered closer at him. "Who are you, anyway?"

"Billy Butler." Stiffening, he corrected, "Private Butler, First Kansas Volunteers."

There were several families named "Butler" in town. Seth could not remember to which this youth belonged.

"What 'general'?"

"General Daly."

If Billy Butler's name rang a bell, Daly's elicited goose bumps.

"James Daly? The newspaper publisher?"

"That's the one."

"A general?"

"Yes, sir."

"When the hell did he get to be a general?"

"He was elected, sir. Raised the company, himself." A grin lit his too-young features. "One hundred strong. Bought us all these uniforms, too, with his own money. And issued me two pair of socks, drawers an' printed up the Regulations for distribution. Took 'em from a book, he did. The Army Manual."

"When was this?"

"Few days ago. Although he's been recruitin' fer a month or more." His grin widened. It made the freckles on his face stand out, like spots on a cow. "We held meetin's in the back room of Tankard's Draft. Got free beer, too. Wanta join? All the officer's positions is already filled, but if you know General Daly, I reckon he could make you an adjunct."

Nelander poked Seth. "Who wouldn't want to be an 'adjunct'?"

"I'd rather be a general."

"That's a'ready taken," she replied in exact synchronization with Billy Butler. "Besides," she continued alone, "you never bought anyone a beer. At least not in recent memory. Have you?"

"About as recent ago as you handed out drawers."

"And socks," she reminded him.

"I'm a captain," he grumbled to the private. This elicited immediate respect.

"Oh. Yes, sir." The boy saluted. "What company?"

"First Naval, Kansas Seamen."

"Kansas got a navy?"

The idea awed but not greater than Jim Daly being a general.

"I am in the process of raising my own company."

"Then I'd have myself upgraded a rank or two," the lowly private advised. "There's already a lot of captains around."

"Thank you. I will keep that under consideration. Now, may we pass?"

"I meant it when I said there's going to be a procession. Wagons an' carts an' men on horseback. Before an' after 'em come the soldiers on foot. That's me," he added, serious enough to elicit laughter had the implications not been so serious. "And a band! The town musicians got together and joined up as a group. They'll be somewhere toward the head of the parade an' afterwards, there's gonna be a concert in the square."

Stepping closer in a friendly sort of way, he grinned at Peter. "Yer pa's a'ready an officer. Bet he'd let you go along with him as a drummer boy."

Instead of outright denying the youth's guess, Seth made a clicking noise and began the slow process of turning around the wagon.

"If I let him enlist, then who's to do his chores? Someone's got to grow corn to feed the army," he added in dark reference to Dr. McTree's words.

Billy Butler pushed the cap back on his forehead, revealing a stock of sweaty curls.

"Never thought of it that way. That's why you're an officer, I suppose. Got an eye for the big picture."

Stomach muscles tightened, the fleet officer glanced at his captain. It required no introspection to envision General James Daly standing on a packing crate, working his arms in an up-and-down motion while lecturing the uninitiated in the Big Picture.

"Guess we'll stay for the ceremonies."

"Thought you might. Good luck with the navy. Sir."

Leg shaking in annoyance, Nelander waited until they were out of earshot before expressing her own views.

"Seth, how can this be happening? Boys from town joining the infantry; a doctor giving up his practice. A newspaper editor being elected general. Privates recruiting drummer boys. Do they think this is all some sort of -- outing?"

"Yes."

Expecting an argument and receiving a blunt confirmation, she put a hand on her leg to stop its irritated movement.

"How can they all be so naive? McTree and Daly are educated men."

"For patriotism, I suppose. And glory. No one wants to be left out. Talk is the war will only last a fortnight or two. If they don't join now, they'll miss the excitement."

"Do you believe that?"

Fanning his face with his hat, Seth's lips drew taught.

"I keep thinking of what Norman wrote. About the Indians. How, after the battle the soldiers lined up the dead dragoons and buried them in a common, shallow grave and left the dead warriors out to rot."

"I doubt 'General Daly' will mention anything like that in his address this evening."

"I can picture Norman's scene. Feel the hot of the setting sun; see the waves of heat distorting the distance. Hear the buzzing of black flies swarming over the corpses. Smell the blood. Taste the sweat in my mouth."

"Doesn't make a pretty picture. Where's the glory?"

"Then, I kinda pull back from it an' see the flag wavin' on a pole. Set in the ground by one of the troopers. Maybe it's got a hole or two in it from arrows or lance points. Maybe one of the dead soldiers was carryin' it. That'd have to assign a new man to carry it."

For a display of triumph, it missed the mark.

"Is that your idea of patriotism?"

Blaze worked his way back down the road without guidance.

"Then I see another scene. Men in starched white collars and black suits with long, split tails. Shaking their fists in the air. Spittle comin' outta their mouths. Red-faced and colicky. All shoutin' at once. Some wavin' papers, others readin' speeches. Mebbe they wrote 'em, mebbe a clerk penned the words. It all sounds the same comin' outta their mouths. Men in the galleys; some leanin' forward, others fannin' themselves. Around the room, flags hangin' from staffs. Can't tell what flags they are. Might be the Stars an' Stripes. Might be state flags. Another's held by a fella up in the top row. What he's displayin' ain't never been seen before. Could be what they call the Confederate flag." He sighed and replaced his hat. "Saw a drawing like that. In Harper's. "

"All right."

She would wait for him to get around to telling her about patriotism.

"Then, my mind goes off. To a railway depot. Crowded with people; so packed a man couldn't move his elbows. Men dressed in fancy uniforms. All of 'em is smilin'. Women hangin' on to 'em." He paused and wiped his nose. "They all look adoring. Some has got little children by the hand. The boys dressed up in uniforms to look like their pa's. The girls wearin' dresses: red, white an' blue ones, with stars cut out and sewed on to make 'em look like flags."

He leaned forward, staring through the "V" of the horse's ears. "If I look real close, I kin see the faces of some of the soldiers through the coach windows; them who's already got seats. They're starin' out. These are a different bunch. They been to war; they've... tasted battle. Their uniforms are all ripped an' tattered. Their caps -- they call 'em kepis, I guess -- are ripped at the brim. Saggin' down. Coverin' sockets where eyeballs used to be. Some are missin' arms. Others got crutches propped up against the sills. None of them are smilin'. Up front, on the locomotive, there's a banner. It reads, 'All Aboard for the Train of the Dead.'"

He did not say where he derived this image. She already guessed.

From a daily published by the Underground.

Not the same organization for which they worked as conductors.

"Lastly, I see a field. Stretching out as far as the eye can see. All plowed but spotty, like; green corn an' weeds. Big, tall, vigorous weeds. There's a farmer out there. He's got his hands on his hips. Talkin' to a fella on horseback. Man wearin' a uniform. Can't tell what color it is. Blue or grey. Don't make any difference. He's holdin' out a wad of bills thick enough to choke a banker's mouth. One thousand dollars; mebbe ten thousand."

Seth patted his pocket. Not wistfully, but in resignation. "Behind this officer -- way off in the hills, behind a clump of trees -- but not outta sight -- is a band of soldiers. Mean lookin' -- dirty. They got a wagon an' it's filled with...." He shrugged. "Anything.   Fodder.   Wheat.   An' ham. Smoked ham. A picnic basket, taken from a pantry. Last of that farmer's canned goods are in there."

He shifted positions as if his legs had gone to sleep. "Behind the wagon them soldiers have got milk cows, tied by rope. Five or six, at least. Mebbe a calf or two. An' chickens; One of 'em looks like Mr. Noise Box. He's gonna be them soldiers' dinner. A few of them boys are carryin' sickles. The farmer knows they're there. He knows if he don't sell his crop they'll take it. 'But all that money, you say.'"

She had not said.

"One thousand dollars. Mebbe ten thousand. That's a lot of money. A fortune. Only, funny thing. That money ain't got no value. The bank in town just printed it; the ink's still wet. Take five thousand to buy an egg. Only there aren't any eggs in town. They all been conscripted."

He smiled at his play on words. Nelander felt faint and took the reins from Seth's hands. He did not seem to notice. Like the farmer in his story, he saw a different reality.

"A man can't spend what don't have any value, he can't buy what isn't there an' he can't feed himself or his family on corn stubble. He knows there's gonna be trouble."

He finally grunted and blinked. They were almost to Lawrence.

Back where they started.

"Six months," he whispered. "How many 'six months' before it's all over?"

How many changed?

How many mutilated?

How many dead?

Barbara had her answer about patriotism.

CHAPTER 19

In the short time they had been away, much had happened. Men, woman and children gathered in the streets. All brimmed with excitement. Banners were woven through balustrades; flags suspended from roof tops, colored bits of paper strewn from over-eager hands.

The batwing doors of the Tankard's Draft had been propped open, allowing for easy ingress. A large, handwritten sign advised, "All is Welcome," and beneath it, in smaller letters, "Don't Ask Management if you can hang your FLAG from the stairs!"

Most businesses remained open. Depending on the political persuasions of the owners, Old Glory flew right-side up or upside down. The First National Bank of Lawrence had been locked and barred, proving either neutrality or fear that love of country might translate into greedy violence.

A team of women were setting up tables for food. A lad, banging the flat of a frying pan with a wooden spoon, the civilian's idea of a drum, walked back and forth, loudly proclaiming, "Eats free fer soldiers; all others pay cash!"

His casual placement of warriors over peacemakers did not bode well for either side.

Detecting the error, not in phraseology but in placement, Sheriff Bochner hustled over toward the well-intentioned gathering.

"Not in the middle of the road, ladies! You've got to move these tables; there's a mess of marchin' men gonna be coming right through here."

Mrs. DeWitt, the first woman in Lawrence who had ever spoken to Barbara and who had, out of kindness or pity, referred her to a farmer named Seth Ward, confronted the peace officer.

"We were told the parade would end at Anson's General Store."

"You was told wrong. They're gonna go all the way to the end of the street."

Hands akimbo, she refused to back down.

"I received my information from General Daly."

Bochner matched her defiant posture. Normally a polite spoken man, the tension of the moment got the better of him.

"Jim Daly don't know his arse from a hole in the ground."

"He is coordinating the festivities. And you had best watch your mouth, Sheriff. I do not cotton to such bad language."

Taking a swipe at an overhang of red tablecloth, he grunted, "This is war, madam. You'll hear worse outta the mouth of your own husband before this is over."

"I should think not! I will wash his mouth with lye soap."

Grinning broadly, for the image caused considerable amusement, the lawman remained obstinate. And foul-tongued.

"Remove the damn tables."

"You do it, then, if you're so set on disrupting our celebration."

Another kick, this one harder, shivered the bowls of baked potatoes and plates of corn bread.

"Gonna make an interesting headline in tomorrow's paper: Local Ladies Trampled by Troops." Appreciating the sound of his alliteration, he threw up his hands, washing himself from the matter. "Only hope 'General' Daly kin take time away from his arduous duties to write it up."

Spinning on his heels, he saw the Wards and sauntered over. "Get a move on, Seth. No tarryin' in the streets. Unless you've a mind to join the parade."

"I think not. I'm only trying to get out of town. There's a sentry posted on the road. He turned us back."

"He did, did he? He ain't got no call to do that." Scrunching up his face, he spat on the ground. "Damn play-sodgers has taken over. Everyone thinks they're in charge. Hear that Jim Daly got himself elected general?"

"We were told at the outpost."

"Who ever heard of a newspaper man being a general? What kinda war is he gonna run?" His eyes twinkled. "Hold on a minute, boys: the battle cain't begin till my sketch artist's got a rendering.' Or, 'How's it feel to git yer arm amputated, private? Speak up, now, boy. I've got a deadline to meet.'"

"Dr. McTree joined up, too."

The news came as a surprise.

"Do say. What side?"

"Union."

"Bad news fer Lawrence. There's lots of others, too. Both my deputies an' Tinker Taylor. He's a'ready closed his smithy. Don't know how these boys is gonna get their sabers sharpened." He spit again. "Abel Billup, too. He went to the other side. What's a hotel clerk know about guns? Heard he bought himself a 'sidearm' from Jake Dale. His business stands to make a mighty good profit from all this. Him an' Dick Duggan. The saloon's been sellin' beer since 6 o'clock this mornin'.'"

"What about the McConaghies? Any of them volunteer?"

He shrugged. "Those bad apples? Haven't seen inny of 'em about. By my way of thinkin', they'll stand behind the lines an' shoot deserters fer bounty." His eyes narrowed. "What about you?"

"Not me."

"Glad to hear it. Everyone else's gone crazy. They all think they're gonna shoot the tarnation outta one another and come back heroes. Most of 'em don't even know what it's all about. Cain't say I rightly do, either. Seems like a lot of hot air in Washington got everyone riled." Hand on the wagon, he peered around the adults to the back. "Good thing your boy ain't any older or he'd be gone, too."

"No, sir," Peter asserted, pleased to finally be a part of the conversation. "I got crops to tend an' chores to do."

"You're a right sensible lad." He turned back to Seth. "Go to church last Sunday?"

"We didn't get there. Why?"

"Reverend Ginnis gave quite a sermon; all about the God of War favoring those who do His biddin'. Afterwards, he did a little side business: he's hired on an extra boy to help him keep coffins in stock. Kinda turned my stomach."

"Yeah."

Standing back, Bochner waved them along.

"Put the wagon in behind the warehouse at the end of the street. Outta be safe there. I'm hopin' this'll be all over by nine. Then you can drive on home. Anyone tries to stop you then, come an' get me. I'll take you through, myself."

"Thanks."

Urging Blaze forward, Seth kept the animal at a walk, mistrustful that a drunken man or an unwary dog might dash in front of, or under the wagon. Reaching the warehouse in relative safety, he got down and hobbled the horse.

"No sense unhitching him. I want to get out of here as soon as we can."

Nelander agreed and the three made their way back to the street. Rows of chairs had already been lined up along the boardwalk.

"I got the best place in town to watch the proceedings," a man with a large slouch hat advised. "Only five cents each. Save yerselves the wear an' tear of standin'."

"No, thanks."

Seth turned to his wife. "Do we really want to watch this?"

"Probably not but we can't stay in the wagon and hide. As long as we're here, it might be interesting to see who marches against the Union."

"Anyone in particular you're looking for?"

"No." Which meant "Yes," and he let it go.

The opening procession, scheduled for 5:00 "sharp" began at 5:45. Rumor had it that the ceremonial fifteen-gun salute to begin the parade "Had spooked the General's horse" and it took three quarters of an hour to secure another. None of his officers, aides and adjutants apparently wishing to sacrifice their mounts for the occasion.

Riding ahead of his newly assembled troops, Volunteer-General Jim Daly sported a new, double-breasted Union uniform, replete with brass buttons, yellow sash, sword belt, knee-high cavalry boots and freshly blocked hat, dyed Yankee blue. Unfortunately, it did not match the color of his coat but only minimally detracted from the grandeur.

Behind him came the recruits, marching in columns four wide and four deep, so they presented a natty square. The first three companies bore rifles over their shoulders; those following apparently arrived too late to be issued weapons. Their arms swung by their sides.

Riding along the peripheral were a dozen mounted soldiers, all wearing an assortment of clothing decorated for the occasion. Lacking uniformity, some had gold braid around the crown of their hats while others wore it at collars and cuffs. One had a purple ostrich plume in his hat band, another a sprig of flowers through a buttonhole.

Separating one half the company from another, a fine band performed popular music. Their repertoire being somewhat short of martial music, they began with the Star Spangled Banner and included Camptown Races, Oh! Susanna and a less than appropriate but nevertheless popular, Listen to the Mockingbird.

Pulling up the rear, two-team horses drew artillery wagons, dog carts and farm wagons, the latter filled with wives of the officers. Dressed in white frocks with red and blue ribbons, they waved to the crowd and tossed favors to bystanders.

Catching one, Seth stared at the paper tube, tied at both ends with string. Turning it in a circular motion, he read, "Stephen A. Douglas for President." Running after another which had fallen in the street, Peter proudly showed his.

"Mine says 'Hang the Missouri Compromise.'"

"Obviously, our citizen-soldiers reached into the outdated political war chest for these," Nelander dryly observed.

"Shall we save them?"

"Not unless you plan on using them for kindling."

Seth grunted and tossed his back into the street. Like a good puppy, Peter ran and fetched it.

"What'd you do that for?"

"I want a collection. Can I go after them, papa and get more?"

"All right. But if someone tries to recruit you, the answer is 'no.'" Watching the boy scamper off, he spoke to no one in particular. "An hour ago he had chores to do. Now he's collecting memorabilia."

"That's what parades and uniforms and brass bands are all about," Nelander answered. "To inspire the children and the childlike."

"Don't think he'll run off, do you?"

"If he does, we'll go and get him."

"They can't make him sign a paper or anything, can they?"

"I don't care if he inscribes his name in blood, they're not going to have him." Steeling a glance at Peter out of the corner of her eye, Seth's vigorous nod reassured her that, for the moment, he stood on his word not to become involved. Realizing that promise for what it was -- a vow made in cool deliberation -- she let the moment pass. Later, whether that meant six months or a year, they would come to it again. She could only pray he would hold to his word.

Pray and arm her arguments.

Another way to fight a war.

As the strains of Star Spangled faded and the last of the Union militia rounded the bend, another band began a different tune. Starting slowly then picking up volume, they began a spirited rendition of Dixie. More curious than angry, all eyes trained toward the east road into town as the marching Rebels made their appearance. Their band headed the procession, followed by a company of men, all singing the lyrics.

> "I wish I was in de land ob cotton,
> Old times dar am not forgotten;
> Look away, look away, look away,
> Dixie Land."

Like their counterparts, being ill-versed in war-themed music, they also played My Old Kentucky Home, Nearer, My God, to Thee and the cheerful, if inappropriate, The One Horse Open Sleigh. Some in the crowd grumbled annoyance, but most sang along with Jingle Bells while eagerly leaning forward to catch a glimpse of these other soldiers: the ones casting their lot with the Confederacy. The mood quickly changed, however as a standard-bearer came into view holding aloft a strange flag that had not been seen in town until that moment. Many in the crowd pointed and whispered to one another. Some men spat. Others looked away as the standard-bearer passed bearing a flag with three equal horizontal bars, red-white-red. The blue canton extended two-thirds the height of the flag and bore a circle of seven five-pointed white stars.

"It looks like Old Glory," a woman standing by Nelander observed. "How dare they?"

"Wadda they call it?" another hissed. "Jeff Davis' Stars and Stripes?"

Overhearing him, or responding to any number of other taunts, one of the Confederate officers responded, "We call it the Stars and Bars."

"'Bars,' no doubt," an old man remarked, shaking a fist. "You might as well call it 'Bars an' Taverns,' 'cause I seed you fellas over to the

Tankard's Draft all mornin'. You ain't niver gonna beat our boys. We got God on our side. He been supportin' this country long as she's been a country an' I don't see that changin' now."

Whether from the insinuation they needed liquor for courage or the pronunciation of the Lord's favor for the Union, the Rebel broke ranks. Three long strides took him to the antagonist.

"Take it back, or you'll be sippin' supper frum a spoon the rest of yer life!"

Undaunted, the local spat in the man's face.

"You ain't even frum these parts. What's a matter? Ain't you got enuf innocent folks' houses to burn yer side of the river? Kansas's is goin' for the U-nited States, mister."

"Tell me where you live an' I'll burn yer house, sure."

The patriot spit. A stream of tobacco juice landed within an inch of the the assailant's boots. His face colored in indignation.

"You hawked on my uniform!"

"If I'd a wanted to hit them rags you's wearin', wouldna speck a landed on the boardwalk."

The enemy combatant's fingers went around the old man's throat and he made a valiant effort to choke the life out of him. Already tensed from the argument, Seth gave a roar and sprang forward. Delivering one punch to the Rebel's back from sheer anger, he wrapped an arm around his throat. To increase pressure, he affixed his left hand over his right-clenched fist, effectively cutting off oxygen. Losing his grip, the Rebel brought both arms upward, first knocking off Seth's hat, then digging into his scalp.

Onlookers backed away as the entangled pair stumbled into the street. Those men in the parade rushed forward to help their companion, but Sheriff Bochner pushed between them, effectively separating the fighters from those who would make it an uneven contest.

"Back!" he ordered, leveling his rifle at the grey-clad company.

"Dirty rotten law dog," one hissed. "We're only protectin' our own."

"Twenty-on-one ain't what I'd call a fair fight," Bochner retorted, teeth clenched. Deftly sidestepping the fighters as they blindly grappled one another, he cast a wary eye on the blue-uniformed men who raced to even the contest. Foremost among them, Tinker Taylor identified the man representing his side and shouted encouragement.

"Get 'em, Seth! Knock 'em to Kingdom Come!"

Others took up the call.

"Beat the tar outta him."

"Gouge his eyes so's he cain't see when we put a bullet in his head."

"A knee in the jimmies, Seth. That'll take the wind outta his sails."

"You -- back off, too," the sheriff warned. "Anyone who lends a hand is going to jail."

"They started it," a boy from the crowd charged, pointing at the rebels. "That one fightin' Mr. Seth tried to kill ol' Dickens."

"He did, Sheriff. He did!" the old man claimed. One of the soldiers pointed a finger.

"You was the one begun it, worm-eater. You spit on him. Man's got a right to defend hisself."

Scrambling to their feet, Seth and the officer sparred, throwing and dodging punches. The farmer sported a swollen lip; the Rebel, a bloody nose.

More soldiers arrived, unconsciously making a circle, those wearing blue making shoulder contact with their opposites. Aside from some light pushing and shoving, they seemed content to watch the opening volleys of the War Between the States fought by a legion of two.

Grabbing a handful of dirt from the street, the officer threw it in Seth's face. Head thrown back to avoid the blinding missiles, Seth threw himself off balance. Taking advantage, the fighter dove headfirst into his stomach. A loud expulsion of breath, then a snarled curse came before he flew backward, into the bystanders. Hands outward, they righted the fighter and threw him back.

"Sic 'em, Seth!"

"Give 'em one for the South, Bill!"

Panting and in obvious pain, Seth lunged at Bill, missed with a right hook, and took another blow to the face. Dropping to one knee, he shielded his face as the other attempted to end the fight with a kick to his jaw. More from instinct than training, he grabbed the boot in mid-air, twisted the ankle and shoved backward. The officer howled and went down, the force of landing temporarily stunning him.

Once more on his feet, but nearly doubled over from exhaustion, Seth heavily panted, hands on his knees.

"Finish him off!"

"Crush his windpipe."

"Git up, Bill."

Before Bochner could call a halt to the proceedings, if such were his intent, another man, also a Confederate officer, bust through the ring of spectators. Purposely crossing near Seth, he shot him a sidewards glance and their eyes met.

"Go on. Get outta here," the stranger mumbled, too low to be heard by the caterwauling crowd. "We've had our first blood." And then, more quietly still, "Good fight."

Unable to interpret the larger implications, Seth backed away as the man in the single-breasted grey jacket offered a hand up to the soldier in the street.

"Come on," he ordered. "Break it up. Enough. We promised the sheriff no violence."

"He came at me," Bill protested before the superior officer restrained him. The latter whispered something in his ear and Bill quickly assented. Freeing himself from the other's grip, he dusted off his coat before hurrying from the circle. Those at the perimeter made way and he passed without further incident.

"Sorry about the fracas," the Confederate continued, addressing Bochner. "We'll be pullin' out tonight. After the fireworks."

"Go quiet and that's all right."

Unspoken was the latent fact that if soldiers on either side determined to make a stand, the local authorities would be powerless to stop them.

Accepting his hat from one of the onlookers, Seth straightened his own shirt, then wiped a stream of blood from his face. Ignoring the pats on the back and friendly well-wishes, he made his way back to Barbara and Peter.

"That was some fight," the boy whistled. "You gave him what-fer, Captain!"

"Never mind," he dismissed, fully aware that if the altercation had been prolonged, the outcome would have been quite different.

"You all right?"

Resting against Nelander until his breathing regulated, he nodded.

"Shouldn't have done that; just seemed... someone had to help ol' Dickens."

"'ol Dickens ought to have kept his mouth shut. What did that man say to you when he broke up the fight?"

"I dunno. Something about 'first blood. And then he congratulated me."

"That doesn't make any sense. You beat one of his own men."

Seth started to speak, thought better of it and hitched a shoulder. "He gave me a look."

"What kind of look?"

"Like he knew me."

"Did he?"

"Never seen him before. Come on. Let's get outta here."

Taking Peter by the hand, they worked their way down the uneven sidewalk, disregarding those who would delay them by conversation. Making it safely back to the wagon, he allowed her to wipe his face with a wet cloth, then make a quick inspection.

"No broken bones. How do you feel?"

"Like I've been run over with a wagon."

"But you showed him, papa. You whupped him, good."

"Didn't mean to, boy. I'm not a fighting man. Neither are you. We're farmers. This is someone else's war. Those who think they know what they're fighting for," he added.

"It's for the Union, sir."

"That's a part of it, Peter. But it seems to me men outta settle that difference in Washington, instead of callin' out the troops. Arguing over States' Rights on the battlefield only leads to a lot of men dying."

"They seem ready for it," Nelander observed, breaking off her sentence as the first of the fireworks exploded overhead.

Effectively ending the conversation, the three perched on the tailgate of the wagon, heads craned back to watch the sky. Fired in rapid succession, flaring streaks of yellow soared upward, developing into an astonishingly bright glow that captured the imagination. Achieving its apex somewhat short of God's private night lights, the missiles mutated into balls of ripe-corn yellow before finally beginning their downward trek. Long before particles of ash reached earth, they burned themselves out.

"Sure is pretty, Captain Papa," Peter observed in awe. "Do you suppose Patricia and Mrs. Giles are watching?"

"Mrs. Dryfus," the father-officer corrected. "That other is her private name, never to be spoken outside the walls of her home."

"Yes, sir. I'm sorry. I forgot."

Stifling a twinge at the pain he experienced from his daughter's absence, Seth spoke to Nelander.

"We did right, didn't we? Leaving her there?"

"We gave her a chance to experience an entirely new world. Nowhere else could she be exposed to oil paints and artwork -- and a teacher who needs her nearly as much as we do."

"Do you like Mrs. Giles?" Catching himself in the same mistake his son made, he tousled Peter's head. "Mrs. Dryfus?"

"Very much."

"And trust her?"

"Yes."

"She won't involve Patricia in any... activities, do you think?"

"She'll never see or hear a word."

He fidgeted as a particularly loud explosion rocked the ground.

"But with McTree gone for a soldier, she has nowhere to go if she's unhappy there."

A day ago, it would have been "Hank." Or "Doctor McTree." Volunteering for a soldier had somehow changed the relationship; placed an unutterable wedge between their friendship.

"There are other places she can go. To Sheriff Bochner. Or even Hector Anson's."

Like Hank McTree's trust, the list had whittled. Before war came calling at Lawrence, Kansas, he might have added "Able Billup," or "Tinker Taylor." But they, like the doctor, had gone. If not physically during the seven days of Patricia's visit, then mentally. No more time to devote themselves to a little girl's plight. Thoughts now only for uniforms, regulations and enemies.

Barbara Nelander-Ward had never felt at home in the city, but its overnight alteration sent chills over her body, underscoring the meaning of impermanence. Gone any ease she once felt; disappeared her sense of security. Lawrence might as well be a ship under new management with an entirely different crew and a manifest which would compel it to travel uncharted waters, all familiarity vanished.

Although the decks and the bulkheads, the masts and quarters remained the same, one life had been exchanged for another. Nothing would ever feel the same again. And while she might grow accustomed to a new way, the old could never be recaptured. One spirit fled and another took its place. Reflecting back to the man standing in the yard with a sign in his hand, she knew that was how she felt about "McTree." As though another identity had crept into his outer shell. He appeared the same and sounded the same but the soul had altered course.

Re-routed to the West Indies. Or China. Not to grow wiser but more worldly.

She felt his loss of innocence acutely.

Or, perhaps, more accurately, she grieved for herself. And for her family.

"What are you thinking?" Seth gently prodded. Shaken from reflection, Barbara shrugged. To say, How few friends we truly have would be an accusation and she were as much to blame as he. In the four years she had lived in Kansas, Nelander had kept aloof from most of the population. She knew many by sight, a lesser number by name. Some were church acquaintances; other people were business associates. None had ever been invited to the Pirate Treasure; neither she nor Seth had gone to dinner in their homes. Only a handful were trusted enough to send a child in need to their doorstep.

A "handful," which had once been four, now found itself reduced by half.

"I hate this war."

She might more correctly have said, I am reprimanding myself, for she had held steadfast to the belief she commanded destiny. Needing no one but Seth and the crew, she falsely assumed faith, hard work and unswaying determination would carry them through any storm. Now that the clouds had lowered, the falsity of that assertion crashed against her keel in potent warning.

No ship is a world onto itself.

A lesson learned, perhaps too late.

CHAPTER 20

He gently tapped her arm.

"Are you awake?"

Roused from a doze, half sleep, half musing, Nelander came to full consciousness.

"Is it over?"

"No more fireworks. I heard Sheriff Bochner tell everyone to break it up and go home. Once the crowds thin we ought to be able to get back on the road."

"No. Not the road." She had a bad feeling. "Can we cut across the fields and pick it up closer to home?"

"We might have done that in the first place."

Softly caressing his swollen cheek, Barbara demurred. "No; there were too many soldiers about. God knows whose camp we might have run into. I want to avoid that at all costs."

"The Rebels, you mean?"

"Either side." Stifling a yawn, she turned back to inspect their sleeping son. Seth had placed his jacket under the boys head and the simple gesture made her smile. "Have I told you how much I love you?"

"Not lately," he grinned. "It's always nice to hear." They kissed, then he stretched his legs, addressing the horse. "Come on, ol' Blaze. Time to go to work."

The animal swished its tail, blew air through its nostrils, then pricked its ears. As the reins flopped lightly against its back, muscles tensed and the wagon lurched forward. Both parents glanced worriedly at Peter, but he did not wake. Each repeating a silent prayer, they settled in for the long ride home.

Maneuvering over uneven ground and grass-strewn land, progress continued at a snail's pace. Half an hour later, they had only gone one mile and had three more to go before connecting with the cleared and hardened dirt which passed for "the road out of town."

Nerves on edge, Nelander suddenly stiffened, head turning sharply to the left.

"Shhh. Did you hear that?"

"What?"

"Someone in the bushes."

He drew up and waited, hoping the noise Blaze made did not forewarn an enemy. Without being directly involved, war had come to the Wards.

What began as a distant sound, hardly more than the rustle of a raccoon on a nighttime prowl, grew in intensity.

"Horse," Seth whispered. "Rider on horseback." And then amended, "Riders."

Within sixty seconds, a pair burst into the clearing. Surprised to encounter a wagon, they slackened pace, scrutinizing the passengers. Unable to make out any features under the night sky, one pulled back the shield from a dark lamp he carried, directing the piercing beam into Seth's face.

"Oh. It's you, Capt'n," he mumbled. "Thought you had gone ahead."

The statement made no sense, compelling Seth to respond with vagueness.

"I'm taking Mrs. Ward back to the farm. She was caught in town; road leadin' out was blocked by a sentry. He sent her back -- till after the parade."

Tipping his hat, the cavalryman nodded. While the gesture might have been one of respect for a lady, it could also have held other meanings. Words did not clarify.

"Take care." Turning to his companion, he nodded and averted the light. Replacing the shield, the night fell into blackness. "Let's go."

The light rattle of spurs indicated haste. In a moment, they plunged forward, quickly lost from sight. Waiting until the sound of hoof beats faded, Nelander put a hand on Seth's arm.

"What was that all about?"

"I have no idea."

"What color uniform were they wearing? Could you tell?"

"Too dark. Not sure they were wearing any. Just jackets," he decided.

"Soldiers?"

"Men on a hunt."

"Hunting what?"

Seth had no more insight than she. With a shrug, he urged Blaze forward, leaving the question unanswered. That, and another she had not asked: why had he referred to her as "Mrs. Ward"? She found Kansas manners strange, but when it came to a woman, certain standards rang true the world over.

"Mesdames" implied a female's married status.

"My wife" erected a barrier.

Go beyond this and there will be trouble. She belongs to me. I will defend her to the death.

Norman Ward reappeared at the Pirate Treasure the next day. Lifting one leg over the military saddle, he hopped down with practiced ease. Grinning broadly, he fanned a reddened complexion with a buff-colored, wide-brimmed hat.

"How'd the trip go?" Nelander inquired, coming out of the house to greet the new arrival.

"Hot." Peering into the cloudless blue expanse, Norman took a long look reading the sky before continuing. "Funny," he finally decided.

"What is funny?"

"How things get tangled up in a man's memory. When I was out west, I used to stare up and think about what it was like back home. Always seemed to be clouds. Big, fluffy white ones, or just streaks, spread out as far as the eye could see. Not promising rain: just there. In patterns. Never could figure out what they meant." He glanced across at her. "You read the clouds?"

"At sea," came the guarded acknowledgment.

"What'd they say to you?"

"What kind of day it'd be. If there'd be a breeze. Which way it'd come from."

"They ever tell you what tomorrow'd bring?"

"Sometimes. On the ocean, weather changed fast. One minute it'd be clear, the next, darkened for storm. You always had to be on the lookout."

"Like Injuns," he approved, stomping his feet to clean his boots of trail dust. "In the Territories, it was always open sky. No clouds. I missed that. I told myself when I came home, the sky'd be full of clouds. And now I see it ain't so. Just blue, stretchin' for all eternity. I wonder which of us changed? Me or the sky?"

The inflection of his voice made it a question but she did not see fit to speculate. The omission did not appear to bother him.

"Ever try and tell the future from the clouds? You know. Not the weather. Like a fortune teller."

"No."

Grasping the bridle, he walked the horse in a wide circle to cool it down. Out of politeness or necessity, Norman raised his voice.

"Maybe that's because you had no cause. You knew where you was goin'. It was right there on a map. The port you left an' the port you was goin' to. Never changed." She noted that like Seth, he slipped in and out of casual speech and wondered if he had picked up the technique from his brother. And if such a habit indicated stress or merely carelessness.

Completing one rotation, he began another.

"I reckon fer most people, the horizon holds a might more mystery. They wanta know what's gonna happen. Who's comin' over the next hill." He reached the apogee of his short journey. "Can you navigate? Read the stars?"

"Yes."

Being served monosyllabic answers did not put him off.

"Must come in handy."

"At sea."

"Stars are stars, ma'am."

Forced to carry the thought to fruition, her lips pursed.

"That depends on where you are. The Southern sky has different constellations than the Northern. You need to know longitude and latitude before you can chart a course. Or you'll never get to 'port.'"

"Ha. Ain't that the truth, now." He stopped to caress the horse's ears. "But knowin' -- havin' a feel for that sort of thing -- gives a man a sense of security. Bet if you woke up an' found yourself in a strange place, you could look up an' rightly figure out where you was."

"Were," she corrected, suddenly annoyed at his grammar.

"Were? Ah. You're correcting me." He winked. "Shoulda been an officer."

"I am an officer."

"So you are." He began loosening the cinch, taking his time, as if the task required delicacy. "Lead men, did you?" Rather than reply, she nodded. "Takes guts -- courage -- to do that. Ever git boarded by... pirates?"

"We weren't that kind of ship."

"Treasure's where you find it."

"So are pirates."

He finally laughed.

"Ain't that the truth. What's treasure to me don't mean squat to you." Curling a finger around his neck, Norman removed a thin leather thong from beneath the collar of his faded blue blouse. A small artifact hung from the center, darkened by perspiration. "Ever seen an arrowhead before?"

"No."

"This here is from an Apache arrow. Struck me right here," he indicated, pointing to an area above his left collarbone. "Hurt like hell." Nelander did not react to the use of a curse word and Norman continued as though he were speaking to a man. "Surgeon cut it out. Arrow's a lot like a cactus barb. It's gotta be worked out the right way -- not pulled straight up. Got a hook on the end." He demonstrated the technique. "If you've never been shot by one, you don't know. Jest try an' yank it out. An arrow's got three points: the tip an' the sides. Pullin' straight up rips a lot of flesh. Sometimes does more damage than the impact."

Swaying back to indicate force, he meant her to flinch at the graphic depiction but she only raised an eyebrow.

"Dangerous."

"Painful," he underscored. "I lay a week with that wound, wonderin' whether I was gonna live or die. I lived," he added with a grin Nelander did not match. "Asked the doc for the arrowhead. I wanted it. Know what for?"

"No."

"As a talisman. Injuns is superstitious. So is soldiers. I figured that I had been struck once but I didn't die. The magic in that arrowhead wasn't powerful enough. So I put my own in it an' turned it around. See what I mean?"

"To ward off other arrows that were powerful enough."

Norman clapped his hand down on Rum's flank. Despite the long journey, he stirred no dust from the short hair.

"You've got it! I knew you'd see. You're one with a feel for such things." His eyes narrowed. "Got your own charm?"

"God."

The shot deflected wide.

"Bein' on the side o' right don't always mean you're gonna win. Ma'am," he added. "Jest like followin' the stars. You may know where you are an' where you're goin' but that don't mean you'll get there. Between one port an' another, there's always sumethin'. Know what I mean?"

Nelander shaded her brow from the rays of the hot sun.

"If I ever ran into Apaches at sea, I'd have been surprised as hell." Meeting him tit-for-tat, Norman burst out into a loud guffaw. She granted him a moment of levity before pursuing, "Find the graves of your father and mother all right?"

"Had to do some lookin'. Land's changed. Who woulda thought?"

"Everything changes."

"Don't it, now? Pulled up weeds an' cleaned 'em up a might. Neglected. That's what they were. No one there to remember." She gave no indication of caring, one way or the other. "You reckon they knew? Saw what I did?"

"Peter's the one who speaks for spirits around here. You'll have to ask him."

"You know, I heard that. In town. Folks think he's touched in the head. Talks to his ma, does he?"

"Oh, he does much more than that."

As if that ended her participation in the conversation, Barbara went to the well. Back to him, she lowered the bucket. Abandoning the horse, Norman followed.

"Do tell. Who else he speak to?"

"To anyone, if they address him. He is a well-mannered boy."

"I mean, what ghosts?"

"They come from all over."

Norman whistled. "How he learn how to do that?"

"It's not a learned thing. The talent just came to him. Something he was born with."

"You believe it?"

"As sure as I believe you and I can navigate by the stars. Maybe less so than I believe an amulet can hold back a killing arrow -- or a bullet."

"Don't say that. I gotta lot of stock placed in my arrow." Leaning over, he stared into the well. Taking offense at his nearness, Nelander moved aside. "Kept me alive all this time. I seen others take a hit an' go to their Reward. But not me. I'm still here."

"Were they better men than you?"

The interrogative puzzled him and he stroked his chin, not entirely without apprehension.

"Some was. Mebbe."

Cranking the handle, Nelander hoisted up the bucket.

"I expect, then, God had other uses for them."

"What you mean?"

"A company of dragoons to fight His battles."

Norman wiped his nose on the back of his sleeve. "Now, you've given me the creeps. What's God need a company of spooks for?"

"To protest those on the side of right," she quoted him.

"I always thought when a man was dead, he stayed dead."

"Then you have no reason to worry about who Peter speaks to."

Didn't say I was worried. Ain't man nor beast I've done harm to what'd come after me. Spook or no spook."

"Except the Apaches."

He snorted, averted his head and spit.

"Now, you ask the U-nited States government about that. They was the ones sent me out there. I was doin' their business."

"I'll make a fresh pot of coffee, you want."

The abrupt change of topic caused him to stand back.

"No, thanks. I ete in town before comin' home. You don't mind me callin' this place home, do you?"

"You're Seth's brother. That makes you family."

He tugged the hat lower, hiding his eyes.

"You ain't 'recruited' me, yet."

"No. But we recruited your horse. Rum."

"Gonna give me a nickname?"

Deftly maneuvering the pail, Barbara began her trek toward the house.

"Thought you already had one."

He did not follow. "What'd that be, now?"

"Capt'n."

Stuffing the arrowhead back under his shirt, Norman did a double take.

"Thought you an' Seth were the captains around here."

"And so we are. And 'baby' makes three." He did not know how to take the statement. She elucidated.

> "Pat a cake, pat a cake,
> Baker's man!
> Bake me a cake as fast as you can.
> One for Tommy and one for me,
> And then another,
> For baby makes three."

"What is that?"

"A children's rhyme."

"I am the baby?"

"You are whoever you want to be."

"I was a sergeant in the army."

"And what are you, now?"

He flashed a grin. "Just a fella come home to do some remembering. To look for clouds."

"I hope you find some."

Leaving open the interpretation.

CHAPTER 21

She heard the sound in the middle of the night. It could not fairly be said she woke from sound sleep, for her repose had been light. Even in her dreams, she had been listening for it. A smothered cough; a tenuous footfall on the ladder. Nelander knew every floorboard creak, hinge squeak and each separate sound the house made as the structure minutely expanded or contracted according to temperature. The noise represented none of those.

Half an hour passed before she dozed. The sound had never reoccurred. In the morning, therefore, she expected him to lie when confronted with his late hour ramblings.

She underestimated her lodger: the one who called Pirate Treasure "home."

"Did I go out? Last night? You caught me," Norman confessed with a grin. It reminded her of Seth's description of his baby brother.

Sassy.

Not precisely in the way Norman replied, but by a latent superiority.

"It must have been one o'clock."

"I tried to be quiet. Didn't want to wake anyone."

Captain Ward the Elder glanced up from his soft-boiled egg.

"What's this?"

"Hate to say anything; no reflection on your grub, ma'am. But I had a call of nature. The runs." He winked at Peter. "Paid my compliments to Mr. Privy. We had quite a conversation."

The boy giggled at his uncle's play on words with Mr. Noise Box's name.

"What did you talk about?"

"Things a man would only confess to a padre."

"What does that mean?"

"'Padre,'" Seth explained, "is the Mexican word for priest."

"You'd tell a padre your bowels was actin' up? An' no one else?"

"Norman is making a joke."

"Oh." He sounded disappointed.

"After that, I had the cramps so bad I had to walk 'em off. Settle my stomach."

Peter went back to eating. "Guess it worked. You ete enough breakfast fer two men and a boy."

"That's a soldier's life, Pete. You never know where your next meal is comin' from, so you shove down whatever's offered."

"Bein' a pirate's better. 'Cept in times of drought."

"Well, I don't guess there's too many droughts at sea."

Seth wiped his lips on the checkered napkin and tossed it on the table.

"I've got work to do. You gonna help this morning, soldier, or are you livin' the life of leisure?"

Norman stifled a yawn, then stretched.

"You go on ahead. Thought I'd catch me a nap. I'll be out this afternoon."

Grunting in reply, the farmer got up from the table and motioned toward his son.

"I'll be diggin' tree stumps out beyond the strawberry field. Why don't you an' Nelander amble over to the pond an' do some fishing? Got a hankering for some fresh whale meat this evening."

"Whale?" Norman yawned again, exaggerating the action to make it appear insincere. "You got whales out there?"

"Not whales, exactly," the boy demurred. "But bass almost as big. Want to come with us?"

"Got a rod for me?"

"No, sir. But I can make you a line with a lead sinker an' a hook."

"The Injuns, now -- I've seen 'em fish with spears. It's a peculiar thing to watch. They stand in the water as still as a statue, starin' down. Sorta like mesmerizing the fish. When one gets near enough, he lets go. Don't know that a white man could do it."

"You know a lot, Uncle Norman."

"I know about horses an' guns an' trackin'. But I don't know anything about farming. Never liked it as a young'un and I got no taste for it, now. But your pa -- he was always the one for the land. He knows a lot I don't. That's how we're different." Standing up, he watched as Seth went to collect work gloves and hat, then redirected attention toward Peter. "You know things I don't know, too."

Wide-eyed, he demanded, "Like what?"

"Your readin' and writin' is better'n mine, for sure. An' this 'bells,' thing. I can never get the hang of how eight bells makes midnight. It outta be twelve."

"Nelander taught us all about that. It's on accounta the shifts at sea. They're four hours long. That's why everything goes in fours. And eights."

"Twelve is just four rung three times."

"Too many to count," the seaman interjected, oddly ill at ease with the discussion. "Peter, I think we will go fishing, although it's awfully hot out there. We may not get many bites."

"Any day's a good day fer fishin', even if we can't catch a whale."

Excusing himself with a flourish, Peter dashed outside, letting the door bang behind him. The adults watched with a bemused expression.

"Nice to have a family around," Norman finally spoke. "I never could think of Rick with a wife, but you, brother, was meant for a husband and a father."

"What about you? You act as though you're past your prime. There's lots of young ladies in town who'd like a husband with your prospects."

Following Seth outside, Norman squinted into the western horizon although the sun rose at his back.

"What prospects would those be?"

"Must have money saved up from your army pay. Might use some of it to buy a business. Or a farm."

"What makes you think I saved my money?"

"Bought a nice horse. Cash, I heard. Seventy dollars."

"You been goin' through my saddlebags?"

"Word gets around. Heard it in town."

"I heard you got in a fight."

"Wasn't nothin'. A mistake more'n anything else." He crossed the yard, Norman trailing behind. "Ever think about settling down? Or are you going back to the army? Seems your leave ought to be just about up."

"Not yet." Which might have answered either question. "If I did think about buying a piece of property, I'd want one with a house on it. Like that land you bought; from the Windsors, wasn't it?"

"Bought it from the bank," he replied with an edge.

"Sell it to me?"

Stopping dead in his tracks, Seth eyed his brother.

"You serious?"

"I don't know. Just asking."

Letting the moment pass, Seth shrugged and rested a hand on the barn door.

"You're welcome to stay here as long as you like. But I'm holding onto that property."

"Lot of acreage for one man."

"I got the boy. He's big enough to be of help. I have no quartermaster handing out my pay. I sell crops. The more I grow, the more money I make."

"I warned you about that corn, now. The Army needin' food to feed its troops."

"The war hasn't come to Kansas. Pray God it won't. They say there'll be fighting back east."

"It'll come here, don't you doubt that for a second, big brother. And crops -- you put 'em in a wagon and bring 'em to the train depot. Ship 'em out. All the way to Virginia, if needs be."

Seth tossed a pickax onto the wagon.

"Then why'd you want to buy my land? Being a bad time and all."

"Just making inquiry." He watched as Seth added two saws and a sharpening stone to the load. "When's Patricia coming back?"

"Monday."

"She's gonna be mighty sorry she missed out on the fishing."

"Guess she will."

"Where's she staying in town?"

"Woulda thought a man who heard I was in a fight would know that."

"Some reason you don't want to tell me?"

Called out, Norman deprived him of the right to evade the question.

"She's with Mrs. Dryfus. Taking painting lessons."

"Painting lessons?"

"Patricia's got a talent. The lady is by way of being an artist, herself. Nelander saw some of her artwork when she sold her a load of strawberries this spring. Mrs. Dryfus saw the signs Patricia made. They got to talkin' and showed her the studio. Up in the attic, it is. Oils and canvas and easels. I think maybe Mrs. Dryfus was lonely, but it's an opportunity we couldn't afford to pass up. Once the harvesting was done, we let Patricia spend some time with her."

Norman surprised him by laughing.

"Who would have thought?"

"Thought what?"

"That the old lady's giving art lessons. That how you got to know her?"

"Never spoke a word to her before that."

"Mystery solved."

Seth frowned. "What mystery?"

"Where your daughter is, of course. And what she's doing."

The older did not appreciate the levity.

"She has talent. Mrs. Dryfus said so. She might be an artist one day."

Norman slapped him on the back as a means of hurrying him along.

"No offense. She comes by it naturally. You were always a bit of a dreamer, yourself. I'm right glad to hear someone's taken an interest. Someday when one of her paintings hangs in a museum I can say I she's my niece."

Appeased, Seth nodded.

"That's all right, then. Sure you don't want to dig out stumps?"

Norman patted his arm. "You need the practice." Receiving a snort for his trouble, he watched as Seth hitched Blaze, then drifted away. "See you this evening. We're having whale for supper."

"Are you asleep?"

"Nope."

"You look asleep. What if a leviathan comes and nibbles on your worm? If he decides to take it and chomps down, you'll get hauled overboard."

Opening an eye which had been narrowed to slits but not fully closed, Nelander grinned.

"And if you ever manage to hit a bass with that spear of yours, you're going to have to jump in to retrieve it."

Delicately balancing himself on the edge of the raft which Nelander had created by tying logs together after last spring's thaw, Peter made a sound between a hiccup and a cough.

"Hadn't thought of that. I guess Injuns fish from shore."

"Indians," came the stern rebuke.

"Uncle Norman calls 'em Injuns."

"If he called them bloody savages or damn redskins, is that what you'd call them?"

"No, sir."

"I should hope not." Shading the sun from her face, she watched as he hefted the homemade lance, hoping for a target close enough to strike. "I thought you were supposed to lure the fish in with your eyes."

"I tried that but none of them fell under my spell. I guess I ain't got the knack."

Hardly persuaded by his own admission, Peter bent at the waist, weapon at the ready. Watching with interest, Barbara mused on the effect Norman Ward had on his nephew. She could hardly blame him for wishing to emulate so worldly a man, but the idea did not please her. The longer Norman stayed and the more stories he told, the greater chance he had of capturing the boy.

She had often speculated on Seth's mysterious brother, but never in the context of war. In her imagination he arrived at their door on a cool fall evening, wearing the snappy blue of a Union officer. Face aglow, he would regale them with adventures of capturing wild mustang ponies, standing on a hillock counting a herd of buffalo ten thousand strong, or teaching them the craft of stringing brightly colored red, blue, green and yellow beads into a headdress.

Occasionally she envisioned him driving a wagon into the yard, stocked with chairs, tables and bedframes. Beside him would be a shy, dark-haired woman wearing a wedding ring and going by the name of "Mrs. Ward." There might even be a tow-headed child in the rear, or a babe in its mother's arms.

Another scenario had him surprising them in town, coming upon the family as they shopped for supplies at Anson's Dry Goods Store. Wearing a Philadelphia suit and a black stovepipe hat, the stranger would doff his headwear, make a low bow and introduce himself.

May I inquire if you are the Wards? There seems to be a resemblance and the last I heard, my brother Seth lived in Lawrence. My name is Norman Ward, lately retired from the United States Army and now a fully-fledged member of the Bar Association. I am visiting your fair city investigating the possibility of opening a law firm. Wiggons, Bartlett and Ward we shall call it. Specializing in insurance investigations.

More often, and not to her credit, Nelander speculated receiving a letter, postmarked Washington. Addressed to "Mister Seth Ward," and signed by the Secretary of War, although penned by an underling, the official document would begin, "I regret to inform you...."

Sergeant Norman Ward dead. Killed in a nameless skirmish with Apaches.

Corporal Norman Ward wounded and recovering in a hospital somewhere on the east coast.

Private Norman Ward cashiered for stealing the company payroll. Sentenced to ten years hard labor in Fort Leavenworth, Kansas. Near enough to visit, if a brother had a mind.

None of the stories Barbara Nelander-Ward concocted had come close to the truth.

In reality, she liked her visions better than the one she received.

Breaking off her musings, she turned just in time to see her adopted son hurl his spear into the water. Exerting too much force, Peter lost his balance, hands waving wildly above his head, legs going out from under him. With a yelp and a splash, he landed head-first in the pond.

"Oh, crap!"

Greatly amused at his plight, Barbara shimmied to the edge of the log raft.

"Given up fishing and taking a swim, instead?" she merrily inquired of the sputtering boy.

"Missed 'em!"

"So you did. Luckily, I had caught enough for supper with my simple rod and line. Swim to the shore and I will meet you there."

Doing his best to dog paddle, a great improvement over his previous lack of aquatic skill, he gratefully reached the shallows. Feet firmly planted in the mud, his face radiated with innocence.

"I may not be as good as an Indian, but I'll make a seaman," he promised.

"You bet."

Taking the trolling pole in both hands, Nelander guided her craft through the waves Peter had set in motion, rapidly joining him at the short pier Seth had constructed for "launching the Kansas Clipper into the great blue beyond." Tossing him the rope, he fastened it to the mooring as she jumped off.

"You won't tell Uncle Norman, will you?" he pleaded, scurrying aboard to retrieve her cache.

"Not a word. As far as he will ever know, Brave Peter of the Ward Clan secured his supper with the adroitness of a chief-in-training."

The compliment pleased him, and he slung the line of bass out in front of him.

"Can I clean them? With your boning knife? At least then, I can say I did some of the work."

"You may."

A stiff twenty minute walk took them to the farm. Arriving earlier than expected, they caught Norman with his saddlebags thrown over his shoulder and blanket tucked under his arm.

"Hello!" he greeted. "One, two, three bass," he counted. "Makes me hungry, already."

"I'm going to get them ready for frying," Peter bragged, hoping for a compliment. But Norman had taken his eyes off supper and turned them onto Nelander.

"Are you leaving?" she asked.

"Nothing of the sort. I just thought that with my late night visitations to Mr. Privy, I had disturbed your sleep."

"Nothing of the sort," she easily mimicked

His fallback came easily. "It's the baby, actually. My little niece, Paula. Being a bachelor and a man used to hearing coyotes and night owls, her crying... unnerves me. Gets my heart to pounding. Thought I'd take up residence in the barn. Don't mean anything bad by it," he apologized. "Just, well... you know."

"I had not thought of that. To us, her cries are the natural rhythm of life. But I can see why they would bother you. Seth and I certainly want you to be comfortable. By all means sleep in the barn, but let me bring out some linen so you might have a proper bed."

He debated the issue, then nodded.

"That's kind of you. I haven't been much help around here --"

"No need for that. You are a guest. And a welcome one."

The sincerity seemed to catch him off guard and he dragged his foot, making a shallow indentation in the dirt. He had learned that, she guessed, from his brother. Yet, they were a long way from being two peas in a pod.

Had they been, her suspicions would not have been aroused.

She could understand the wailing of an infant occasioning discomfort. Truer to the mark, she comprehended Norman's desire for privacy. A man with a past -- or likelier still, a man with a present -- did not care to have his comings and goings detected.

"Let me stash my gear, Peter, and then I'll watch while you bone the fish. Then I'll show you how we cook it on the prairie. If that's all right with you, ma'am."

"Be my guest. Preparing victuals," she drawled in a Midwestern dialect, "has never been my strong suit."

He started at her change of enunciation as much as the expression.

"You a gambler, too?"

"I've been known to play for some pretty high stakes."

Not the least of which is serving as a conductor along the Underground Railroad with a stranger in the house.

Or in the barn.

Or even in the state.

"Takes a steady hand." He spoke without blinking, daring her to meet him or look down.

She accepted but played the game by her own rules.

"Ah. There is Seth, coming home early."

Reacting without thinking, Norman turned his head. Seeing no one he realized he had been had. He played his loss with good humor.

"Just a dust cloud. No matter. I need time to make a fire pit. And I need some nice green leaves; corn leaves ought to do the trick. Think he'll mind if I strip a few off?"

Graceful in triumph, she remarked, "You might as well pick a dozen ears while you're at it. Look for the ripest ones and we'll have them with supper."

"I'll do 'er."

He hurried toward the barn and Peter headed for the house. Alone for the moment, Barbara's orbs wandered toward the Jolly Roger. Hanging listless in the still air, it made her debate who had actually won and why she had bothered. More immediately arose a question: if those aboard the Pirate Treasure would ever have occasion to be "jolly" again.

CHAPTER 22

Seth arrived home at two bells: 5 P.M. Two moons just setting under his armpits corresponded to the time. Matching the western horizon, his florid complexion displayed an array of reds merging into pinks, highlighting the blue of his eyes and the dusty, streaked hues of his long locks.

Raising an eyebrow at the activity in the front yard, he paused, hands on knees.

"I dread to ask." The words came slowly, as if he were too tired to articulate. "Are we putting in a moat?"

Planting the shovel in the hole he had been digging, Norman used the shaft as an aid in rising.

"More like a fire pit, old man."

"For what purpose?"

The younger winked. "First, we set out a front line of sharpened pikes. Like this," he demonstrated, using the digging tool as a display. "Three dozen ought to make an effective barricade. When the enemy comes, they are forced to dismount. Second, we fill our trench with combustibles: tumbleweeds, dried grasses. Then we light it. No soldier ever willingly crosses a fire line."

Observing the discomfiture on his father's face, Peter quickly intervened.

"We are going to cook fish like they do on the prairie, Captain Papa. Uncle Norman is gonna wrap them in leaves an' put them in the coals. The corn, too!"

"Sounds more appetizing than eating Indians."

"Let me give you a hand with the wagon," Norman offered. Seth waved him away.

"Better keep at what you're doing." Guiding Blaze toward the barn, he called over his shoulder, "You're not really going to put up pikes, are you?"

"No. That was just a story I was telling. Wouldn't be a bad idea, though."

If the farmer agreed, he did not say so.

Thirty minutes later after washing and changing clothes, he and Nelander sat on the porch observing the festivities.

"Glad to see your fishing expedition brought on so much activity from the younger set." Crossing one leg over the other, Seth tapped his foot. "If Norman had a job, he'd be dragging his tail like I am."

Observing Peter run and jump around the pit, then drop to one knee and fire off a round from a make-believe rifle, Nelander rocked on the two rear legs of her chair.

"He's had quite an influence around here."

A low grunt served as reply while Seth chewed on the statement.

"'Around here' meaning more than you're saying?"

"He's moved his belongings into the barn."

"What for?"

"He said Paula's crying disturbed him."

"Might be true."

"Might be."

"What else might be true?"

"Keeps his comings and goings secret."

"That's so."

She gave him a quiet appraisal. "Tell me that wasn't your first thought."

"Why would he care? He's free to leave any time he wants."

"Where he hightails off to and for what reason is the question."

"Don't know that's any of our business."

"I don't know that it isn't."

He grunted again and this time did not follow it up with a reply.

After the pit had been dug and the fire burned down to glowing embers, Norman Ward, wilderness explorer and Federal dragoon wrapped the fish into corn leaves and buried them alongside the freshly picked ears of corn. Soon, commingling scents of roasting food filled the yard.

"Whet your appetite?" Norman asked, joining the adults at the porch.

"Sure does. Never figured you for a man with any cooking skills, though."

"Out in the prairie, food's always scarce, big brother. You learn to take what you can find and make the most of it. A fella can always fry fish over a spit but then the juices drip into the fire and burn away. And you can't boil corn if you don't have the water to spare. Makin' do is what survival is all about."

"I always figured you had a chow wagon or something."

"If you're moving whole columns of infantry, you do. Commissary wagons pull up the rear. Beans; flour; jerky. Coffee. Soldiers eat a lot." He laid emphasis on the word and Seth flinched. "Men who ain't fed git surly. Don't obey orders like they should. Progress slows to a crawl."

Plucking a piece of wild grass which grew at the corner of the porch, he sucked on the sweet end. "I seen a foot soldier shot, once, fer just that reason. Years ago," he added as if to mitigate the horror. "We'd been out on patrol fer weeks. Six full companies. Lots of officers." Rounding his lips in disgust, Norman sent the stalk flying. "West Pointers, they were. Fresh outta school. Thought they knew everything. All spit and polish; by the book. No one told 'em 'the book' don't apply west of the Mississippi. Them that learned made it back. Earned some respect. Those what didn't we buried along the trail. No great loss."

He pulled another grass but this time absently wound it around his finger. "I 'spect it's the same thing in the navy, ma'am. Probably, you've heard stories. Some new captain given a command. Maybe in your case, he's the son of the owner. Walks around with those damn white gloves an' inspects the brass."

Nelander nodded and addressed her comment to Seth.

"My father had a pair of white gloves. He put them on when inspecting the submissions at the Arts and Crafts Exhibition."

He chuckled in remembrance. "Must have been quite a sight."

"It was. Once in a while he wore them on shore, but only to impress the buyers."

"That's just what I'm sayin'," Norman broke in. "Dress uniforms are for parades and balls. Not for the field." He tapped his head. "It's what's in here that counts. Leadership comes from brains, not shoulder boards. A man's got to know how to handle a situation. Like that firing squad. This captain was a seasoned buggar. When he saw the men were discontent, he called out the leader and had him shot. That caught everyone's attention. Brought 'em right back in line. The colonel, though -- he was all runny-nosed over it." Norman spat. "Said you rule men by example. De-mean-or.

Guess that's what they taught 'em. All fuss 'n feathers, he was. Feathers never brought a man back in line."

"Were you one of the malcontents?"

"Not me. No, sir. I wasn't one of them donkey-followers. I was on the scouting party. We had just come back to tell them school boys there wasn't anything out there: no Injuns in a week's ride. But the colonel's orders was to make a statement; bring back a few scalps. So he didn't want to hear what we had to say. Kept pushing forward. Into the desert."

He surprised them by laughing and slapping his knee. "Only thing we found was a small settlement of squaws an' children. Motley bunch. Don't know whether they had been left behind, or what. There was this padre there runnin' the show. You know the kind. All pious and holy-like in them robes. Day was hot as hell an' he was out there wrapped in brown blankets. Well, I knew him. Not him, specifically, but 'holys' like him. Tried to tell the colonel but he wouldn't listen."

Norman lowered his voice. "'He's out here bringing religion to the savages,' he said. 'Good man.' Him and that Bible-thumper went into pow-wow. He come out all red-faced an' eager. 'The man tells me there is a band of braves north of here. We're changin' direction."

Norman's leg shook in annoyance. "Now, north is a whole 'nother kettle of fish. Different breed of Injun. Bad sort. 'Best to leave 'em alone,' my lieutenant said. 'We ain't come fer them.'

"'An Injun's an Injun,' the colonel replied. 'The padre tells me they ain't expectin' no soldiers. If we hurry, we can catch 'em with their guard down.' Now, the sun never rose on the day a white man caught a red man wid his guard down. We tried to tell him but he wouldn't listen."

Peter came up and curled beside Norman. The former dragoon put a hand on his head.

"Off they went. Another week, due north. Came upon 'em, a'right. I was out front -- me and the other scouts. Seen 'em. Seen more, too." He stared at Peter. "Know what we saw?"

"No, sir."

"Liquor barrels. That damn padre had a sideline. He was in cahoots wid the fire water salesman. Them who made a pretty penny sellin' hard liquor an' muskets to the Injuns."

"Why would a priest work with men like that?" Seth demanded.

"Raisin' money for that Pope in Rome so he can line the streets with gold." Norman shrugged. "So they wouldn't shoot 'em. Who knows? Innyway, no man in his right mind wants to fight Injuns what been liquored up. Or one lookin' down the barrel of a U.A. Army issue rifle. So we turned south."

"Without telling the colonel what you found?"

"Oh, we told him. Then my lieutenant -- he was a fine fella -- he says, 'I'll take my boys an' circle round. You can do whatever the hell it is you want. We'll flank 'em for you. Only peculiar thing -- it took us so long to git around, we missed the whole damn fight."

He chuckled and ran a hand over his mouth. "This wet-behind-the-ears West Pointer attacks straight on. He weren't afraid of no red men with bows an' arrows. No, sir. He knew how to fight by the rules. Frenchman wrote the rules of war, they say." He leaned back against the post. "Don't know about that. The only Frenchies I ever met were buffalo hunters an' they could cut the hide off a carcass before it ever stopped quivering."

Appraising Nelander out of the corner of his eye, he saw he had not managed to disgust her and continued, albeit it with less enthusiasm.

"Time we circled back, the fun was over."

"Was it fun, Uncle Norman?"

"I say 'fun,' meanin' shootin'. Not 'fun' fer the boot-draggers. Not 'fun' for the colonel, either."

"Did the Indians shoot him?"

"Wish they had. Shot everyone else, though." He snorted. "That teetotaler lived to write a report. Terrible thing, he said, when the padres are in league wid the Injuns an' the red-eye salesman. Sent it to Washington. Only thing ever came out of it was my lieutenant lost his shoulder boards. Seems he were 'derelict in duty' when it came to flankin'. Didn't matter, though. He stayed on an' the Secretary of War sent that chicken shit colonel back to New York to sit on court martial boards. Once he had hightailed it out, my lieutenant took up his old rank. That's the way it is in the army, boy."

"Don't think I'd like it much."

"Survival of the fittest. Ain't that what they say? The army's no different than anywhere else, Peter. You fight when you gotta an' stand down when you have to. Common sense. No one wants to die."

"What about honor?" Seth asked and Norman spat.

"Honor's for story books, Seth. There's the difference between us three brothers. Rick had dirty playing cards under his bed and got messed up with bankers an' investing. You an' Belinda sat under trees in the grove an' read highfalutin' stories to one another. You became a farmer. I learned to shoot an' joined the army. There's two of us left. Which one you think pa'd be more proud of?"

"Rick."

The reply caused Norman to choke.

"By Gawd, it must be time to eat."

Leaving the three at the porch, he went to retrieve his "camp supper." And enjoyed it more than the rest.

Later that evening after Peter had gone to bed and the adults remained to garner whatever of a cool breeze they could, their contemplations were broken by the sound of hooves. Seth shot Nelander a worried look, fearing the messenger might be on an errand of mercy from Mrs. Dryfus, but she shook her head.

Not this time.

Getting to their feet, the three walked into the yard to confront whatever news might be conveyed. Reining up well before them, Will Bochner politely tipped his hat to the woman before addressing the small assemblage.

"Evening, folks."

"Sheriff. What brings you out tonight?"

"News. And it ain't good." Squinting at Norman, he hesitated, leaving Seth to do the introductions.

"This is my brother, Norman. He's on leave from the army."

"Thought I saw you in town. Thought at first there was two of you, Seth."

"People tell me we look alike." The idea might or might not have pleased him. "What's the problem?"

"Marauders. They burned Louis Willingham's place. To the ground."

The grim information stirred the latent sense of unease into full-blown heat lightning.

"Who?"

"Don't know."

"For what purpose?"

Will's nose twitched. "Horses. Took every one he had. The whole herd. Twenty, he said."

Stepping beyond the men, Nelander asked, "Was anyone hurt?"

"They shot Louis' dog, then fired in the air. Once the family took to running they torched the house and then the barn."

"Shot the dog?" Norman picked at the whiskers on his chin. "More business for Mathis McConaghie."

"This isn't a time for joking," Seth snapped.

Hands held up, the soldier pleaded innocent. "Didn't mean any offense."

Seth took control of the conversation. "When was this?"

"Just at sunset. I've got deputies following the tracks, but I figured it was best to make the rounds an' warn other folk to be on the lookout. Haven't seen any riders out this way? Or mebbe just one or two ridin' by? They might be checkin' out the area -- see who else has horses."

"No one." He turned to Barbara. "Anyone been past this way?"

"No. But I was gone all day; out at the pond."

"Norman? You see anyone?"

"All quiet here."

"You sure?" Bochner probed. "I seen tracks on the road. Couldn't tell how many -- more'n a few."

"If they came here, they didn't knock," Norman persisted. "I slept most of the day; out in the barn. Don't think I coulda missed horses, though. Hoof beats woulda woke me up. Besides," he argued, "if these were locals, they wouldn't waste their time out here. I reckon everyone in Lawrence knows Seth don't have but one horse and that's a plug."

The lawman gave a noncommittal shrug.

"What makes you think they're locals?"

"Think about it. Who needs horses? Cavalry -- or those pretending to be cavalry. The new recruits." He did not let the sheriff interject before adding, "Either side. They're all prancing around town like they had smelt gunpowder before."

"Most of 'em is gone. Less there's somethin' you know I don't."

"Why would you say that?"

"You bein' a soldier, and all."

"I don't have any business with amateurs, Sheriff. A newspaper editor pretending he's a general. A hotel clerk and a smithy wearin' the uniform. No. That makes my blood run cold." He pointed at Seth. "I was just telling him about how I feel: West Pointers. Men who earned their commissions studying French. Ain't worth more'n a bullet between the eyes -- like you'd put a rabid dog outta its misery."

"You're pretty familiar with who's joined up," Bochner pointed out. "I'm just wondering what else you know."

"He's my brother, Will," Seth objected. "He's been here all day -- at least I can say all evening. And if he knew something, he'd speak up. He's not a thief and he's not a Rebel."

"That so, Mister Ward?"

"You askin' for my word, Sheriff?"

"I am. And I'd ask the same of Seth if I didn't know him as well as I do."

"Then you may believe him. I'm no thief and I ain't no Rebel. Anything else you want to ask? Spit it out because this is the last we're gonna speak on the subject."

"What'd you come to Lawrence for?"

"I'm on leave. Haven't taken any in as long as I can remember. Haven't seen my brother; never met my new sister-in-law. Never seen my nephew and nieces. That's one reason. Other one is my company broke up. Some went to fight for their States. Others, to Washington to offer their service to the President. Wasn't anyone left."

"Which way you leaning?"

"Don't know that's any of your business. Could be I'm just sick of the army."

"You picked a bad time."

"And then again," Norman objected, taking a step closer the lawman, "it may be that I picked the right time. There's gonna be a lot of bloodshed.

Killing. Brother on brother, they say. I'd hate for that to happen to Seth and me."

"He's not going," Bochner persisted.

"Oh, he's going. Maybe not for a soldier, but he's involved. Just by living here. People say Kansas is a long way from Virginia, and they're right. But there'll be other battles. Along the Mississippi. It'll spill all over the place. Nowhere's safe."

"And you didn't see anyone out here?"

"I already said so."

"That'll be it, then. Sorry to have had to ask. But the place is crawling with strangers. Most left, like I said. But others stayed. Ain't wearing any uniforms but no one knows what they're up to. Might be 'quartermastering' for the army. If you know what I mean."

"Yes, sir. I do, indeed."

Will Bochner switched the reins from one hand to the other and began a tight circle to turn his mount around.

"You folks be on the alert. Don't trust anyone you don't know. That's my advice. Report any suspicious activity to me." Completing the maneuver, he looked back over his shoulder. "And I'd sleep with my rifle by my pillow if I were you. Just in case. Those marauders didn't kill Louis Willingham, but maybe next time they'll be a little more bloodthirsty. There's a war on," he added in sarcasm.

"And maybe they didn't kill Louis because he didn't fight back," Nelander offered.

"That's one way of looking at it. Be on guard. That's all I'm saying. 'Night."

Offering a hand in the air, he spurred the horse, urging it into a gallop. A moment later and they could have believed no one had ever actually been there.

Except for the lingering smell of smoke from the cook pit. That left a reminder louder than words.

Wood fires seldom make the distinction between fish fries and buildings.

Whistling under his breath, Norman swung at and missed a mosquito.

"Guess I'll turn in. I'll clean up in the morning; cover in the hole." Almost wistfully he added, "Don't suppose there are too many more whales in Ward Pond."

"It was a good supper," Seth called after. "Don't let what Sheriff Bochner said upset you --"

"About him not trusting me?"

"-- about Louis' farm."

Spoken simultaneously, the glaring mismatch in sentiments held awkward sway before Nelander interjected, "They're both hurtful things. But they'll work themselves out. The rest of us will gather together and help Louis rebuild. You can come along, Norman. Let people see where you stand. And as for Will's suspicions, Seth put him at ease. He won't question you, again."

Shifting weight from one leg to another, Norman stared down at empty hands.

"How long's a man have to live here before he's considered a friend and not a stranger?"

"When I reach that point, I'll let you know."

Her honesty caught him off guard.

"How long you been here, anyway? I never asked."

"Four years."

He groaned, partially for effect.

"I don't think I have that much time. Good night."

"Good night."

Hands naturally finding one another's, Seth and Barbara waited until Norman had slipped into the barn and closed the door before speaking.

"It's awkward. Isn't it?"

She thought she knew but asked, anyway.

"What is?"

"Not knowing. About Norman."

"You spoke strongly for him."

"So I did."

"Any regrets?"

"I'll let you know. In four years."

His grasp tightened and she leaned against him.

"Time for bed."

Lying side-by-side, covered only by a thin sheet, Barbara had almost drifted off when Seth finished the conversation.

"Blaze is not a 'plug.'"

She might have laughed. But did not.

CHAPTER 23

"Coming to church with us?"

Norman poked around the fried egg on his breakfast plate and shook his head.

"Not much for religion."

"We're going over to Louis Willingham's place after service. If we all pitch in, we ought to have the framework on a new house up by nightfall."

"I'd only be in the way."

"Might be a good way for you to get acquainted," Nelander pointed out.

"Yeah," Seth agreed, finishing up the last of the coffee. "You might even see your friend Mathis McConaghie there... bringing over a pup."

Norman's fork cut through the egg. Although it had been cooked well done, those watching could almost feel the runny yolk leak over the plate.

"I never said he was a friend. In fact, I don't even know him. Just read his name on a sign in the General Store is all."

"In that case, I'll stop lying," the elder captain agreeably offered, pushing away from the table. "Never knew him to give anything away in his life."

Straightening Peter's Sunday suit and wiping a crumb from the boy's lip while his wife went to get Paula, Norman watched in stoical silence. Trailing the family outside, he waited until they had gotten aboard the wagon before thrusting something into his brother's hand.

"Here. Take this."

"What is it?" A glance supplied the answer: money. "What's this for?"

"Buy the old man a dog."

"From Mathis?"

"I don't care who you buy it from. I told you: he's nothing to me. I don't know him. Buy a pup from the doctor."

"The doctor?"

"Isn't that where you got yours? From the sawbones? That's what Peter said. You got two of 'em. Squash and Dardanelles. Although," he added, training his eyes on the doghouse shunned by puppies and Herman, alike, "they're hardly brothers, are they? One's a bloodhound and the other's a mutt."

Biting her tongue too late, Nelander asked, "Which one are you?"

Norman covered up what might have had unpleasant connotations with a gentle guffaw.

"The hound, to be sure. I'm a dragoon, remember? A tracker. But if I'd'a known you was goin' to ask, I'd have called the other a terrier and not a mutt."

"Why is that?"

"'cause if I'm a bloodhound, you're a terrier, big brother. Ain't nothing in the whole world more stubborn than a terrier. 'Cept mebbe a man."

"Is that a compliment?"

"Nope."

"Then I'll settle for being a mutt. See you some time after dark. Make yourself some dinner and we'll eat supper together when we get home."

"Thanks. Watch your thumbs. Don't know when a man with a hammer'll land the head on your finger." He shook his hand. "Hurts powerful much."

"I'll remember that. And if you get bored, there's always stumps to uproot."

"I'll find ways to amuse myself."

"See you."

With everyone at church buzzing about the marauders and the men eager to get on with the work which lay ahead, Reverend Ginnis hurried his sermon. An hour ahead of schedule he concluded with an admonition against sin and a prayer that the Heavenly Father protect "the boys in blue and President Lincoln."

Rewarded by a rousing "Amen," the congregation assembled outside. Those who had brought lumber for the housing project struck out first while the other men quietly arranged assignments, so that no time would be wasted when they arrived at Willingham's. Having no place in the discussion, Barbara and Peter went to wait in the wagon.

"Don't see Mr. McConaghie here," he observed, kicking his feet against the footrest.

"Why are you looking for him?"

"So's we can buy Mr. Willingham a dog."

She had almost forgotten.

"I'm sure we'll see him around. In town, most likely, when we go to pick up your sister." On sudden impulse, she added, "Why don't you go ask any of the other children if they have a new litter? No sense wasting money if we can get one free."

Eager to be of use, Peter slipped off the seat and hurried into the crowd of boys who had gathered under a tree to play with a ball while the adults made plans. Unaccountably restless herself, she followed him close enough to ascertain there would be no trouble, then wandered around the back of the church. Standing between a row of graves, the names of those interred as unfamiliar to her as they would have been to Norman, she started as a shadow fell over her path. Head snapping up, Nelander beheld another who had not attended church service.

Dressed for field work in tattered trousers, faded red undershirt and heavy boots encrusted with mud, Mathis McConaghie bade her welcome with a slight nod.

"Tonight," he whispered.

A feeling of anxiety caused a sharp intake of breath.

"You can't bring anyone to the house. We have company. Seth's brother."

"I know. Meet me out beyond the strawberry patch. In them cluster of trees. What time you be gettin' home tonight?"

"I don't know. Six or seven. Then we'll have to eat supper. Sit up awhile."

"Make it late, then. Say... 2 A.M. Kin you get out widout being seen?"

"Yes. But I'll be missed if I'm not there in the morning."

"Have yer man make some excuse. I'll git you back by noon. That good enuf?"

"He can say I went... fishing. Fish bite better in the morning. But if Norman comes looking for me --"

"Tell him you went fer a walk; took the long way back. He won't have no reason to disbelieve you, will he?"

"I don't know."

McConaghie shrugged and had almost slipped away when she whispered, "Do you know him?"

Turning back with a puzzled expression, Mathis shook his head.

"No. Ain't ever set eyes on him. It were Bochner told me you had a stranger staying with you. Seth's brother, you say?"

"He is." She almost let it go, then added, "You're sure? You never met him? He never came to you... inquiring about buying a dog?"

"Ain't got none to sell."

"Then why is there still a flyer in Anson's window?"

"I took it down."

"When?"

"Month or more ago. My bitch came in heat but I didn't let her out. Case I might need her. She's the best I got."

"A month ago?"

"That's right. Got another -- might breed her. But not right away. Why? You lookin' to buy?"

"No. Yes. I was only asking because Mr. Willingham lost a dog. The men who stole his horses shot it. He'll be needing another."

"Takes a bastard to shoot a dog."

"Takes a whole... troop... of bastards to burn a man's home. And steal horses."

McConaghie's lips curled in anger.

"That's a hanging offense. We know about hanging in these parts." She did not know how to take that statement and let it pass. "You'll be there? Tonight?"

"I will."

He tipped his hat and backtracked through the grave markers. Although walking backward, he managed to avoid every one. She wondered how. And decided she did not like him any better because of it.

She did not tell Seth of her encounter with Mathis McConaghie until they were on their way home from the house building. Beginning vaguely, for that was how she felt, Nelander said, "Tonight."

Whether from the finality of the statement, or because his own mind had been working along the same lines, Seth swallowed down a penetrating dread.

"I sort of thought we were done with that. Don't know why. The war, I guess." He made a low "Gee! Gee!" under his breath. Blaze responded by quickening the pace. "It's a damn shame that kind of work is still needed."

He might have chosen a more descriptive word to replace "work."

Risk.

Sacrifice.

Nelander would not have argued. Nor did she hold the cuss against him. Either one, for his terse command to the horse served two purposes.

Giddy-up.

Hells' bells.

"I am to meet McConaghie behind the strawberry field. At two o'clock."

She matched him tit-for-that. Two o'clock. Not "Four bells."

"Bells" being the common thread between them.

"Who is it this time?"

"He did not say."

"What am I going to tell Norman?"

Previous excuses seemed lame. "I am to be back by noon."

"We are to go and get Patricia tomorrow."

"I will be back. Nothing must prevent us from bringing our daughter home."

They had little else to say. And much upon which to speculate. Privately.

Arriving at the Pirate Treasure as evening shadows deepened into night, Peter jumped from the wagon, calling, "What time is it?"

The question caused the adults to exchange guilty looks, for the passage of hours weighed heavily upon them.

"What do you want to know for?" Seth growled.

"Five minutes past nine," a cheerful voice from the house advised. Stepping out onto the porch, Norman waved a greeting. Peter returned it while running for the bell. Tugging it twice, he returned to his parents.

"Don't suspect it matters much if I'm a little late. Do you?"

"Only if you're the crewman going off duty and supper is waiting," Nelander replied, forcing herself to sound amused.

"Speaking of supper, hurry up and get washed. I've got everything ready."

"I told you I would --"

"I know you did," Nelander interrupted. "But I figured you'd be tired after all that sawing and nailing and whatever else you did over at the Willingham place." He edged nearer and offered Nelander a hand down. She accepted because to refuse would have been rude. "Did McConaghie have a dog for Louis?"

"I did not see him to ask."

"Too bad. But maybe it was meant to be."

She did not like the tone. "Why is that?"

"I was just thinking he might have had some gossip."

This time, goose bumps prickled the back of her neck.

"He is not the sort of man... with whom I freely associate."

"Don't blame you. Dirty lookin' fella; or so I've heard," he added, rubbing Blaze behind the ears. "Being a townsman, I thought he mighta heard sumethin' off the telegraph. I'll take care of that, brother. You go into the house and set at the table."

Seth refrained from unbuckling the harness but made no move to leave.

Norman continued to talk while guiding horse and wagon toward the barn.

"Heard the news outta Missouri? Place called Carthage. That's west of Springfield. Know it?"

"Know of it. Never been there. What happened?"

"Ain't that far, really. Along the Neosho River. Federal forces attacked those of Claiborne Jackson. Sixty or seventy dead. Too bad your soldier boys from town didn't have time to get there." His eyes glistened. "Mighta stemmed the tide of battle. It was the cavalry who outflanked Sigel; caused his blue boys to fall back."

"Cavalry: men on horses." The implication became clear. "Oh, my God. That's who those men were -- the ones who burned Mr. Willingham's farm. Rebels."

"Confederates. Makes sense, doesn't it? Cavalry ride horses. Horses get shot, just like men. They gotta be replaced."

"But... this is Kansas."

"It's a war between the states, brother."

Nelander pursued another avenue.

"Seems you don't need Mr. McConaghie's 'gossip.' No one said anything about it at church. How do you know?"

"I'm like an Injun -- always got my ear to the ground," he casually replied, continuing to lead Blaze. "It was only a matter of time before someone fired the first shot." He chuckled. The enthusiasm did not appear contagious. "Like you and that fella during the parade, Seth. Tempers flare. Who knows what triggered the fight? Men will be men. It just happens, and then you've got a full scale conflict on your hands. Won't be any 'Six Weeks War,' either."

Despite Nelander's attempt to stop him, Seth went after his brother.

"What makes you sound so pleased?"

The younger turned back.

"Did I say I was pleased? Far from it. But you know me. I'm an old soldier. Can't help but be interested."

"Sounds like you've got your mind made up."

"Me? No, sir."

"That maybe you ought to go back to your unit and have a hand in this conflict."

"Didn't I tell you? I resigned, brother."

The fact should have been obvious from the start but Seth took the news badly.

"You're not... on leave?"

"I was. But not anymore. I said my company disbanded. What's to go back to? A man fights because he's with men he respects. For the honor of the company. For personal glory. That's all gone."

"I thought a man fought for his country and his flag."

Even in the gloom, Norman's teeth flashed white.

"Maybe I'll enlist in your cause, Captain Ward. Fight under your standards." He pointed toward the pole. "Under the Skull and Crossbones. Become a pirate and look for treasure. An' that black flag -- no quarter. That intrigues me."

Peter raced back, placing himself between the men.

"Are we gonna look for treasure, Uncle Norman? Now that you're gonna stay?"

"His treasure and ours are not the same," Nelander interjected, coming to get the child. "Go into the house. Right now."

"Yup," Norman agreed. "Supper's ready. Hate for it to get cold."

She anticipated carrying on the conversation, but he had finished talking. Using his task of unhitching the horse as an excuse, Norman disappeared into the barn. If he felt she had more to say, clearly he did not want to hear it.

During supper, Peter bubbled about the construction of Mr. Willingham's new house, the anticipation of Patricia's imminent return and his uncle's decision to quit the army. All were equally wonderful in his eyes. Ordinarily, Nelander and Seth would have enjoyed his chatter, but this night it put their nerves on edge. Fortunately, the activities of the day and anticipation of going to town wore down the young crewman and twenty minutes after finishing a second serving of Norman's brown sugar rice pudding, he fell asleep on the couch.

They might have left him there, but neither parent wished to take the chance he overhear what they had to say to Norman, so Seth wrapped him in his arms and carried him to bed. Returning empty-handed and hardly less wearily than his son, he slipped into his rocker.

Minutes ticked away before he finally demanded, "What about this fight? At Carthage?"

"I expect word will trickle down. Are they still printing a newspaper now that General Daly has gone?"

Seth sighed and rested hands on thighs.

"I don't know. How would I?"

"Thought maybe someone would have said something about the Gazette -- at church."

"Seems you've been in town more recently than either of us. You... know things."

More than you ought.

Norman let it go, forcing Seth to continue along the previous thread.

"So: what about it? Was the outcome bad for the Union?" The dragoon scowled. "You throw around names as if I ought to be familiar with them. I know Governor Jackson is a secession man. But I never heard of this Sigel. The Rebels won?"

"I guess you could say that. They had twice as many causalities. Lot of wounded on both sides. Good work for Doc McTree. I suppose that's where they scurried him off to."

The mention of their friend caused anxiety and consternation but laid emphasis on the greater issue.

"Does this mean the war's gonna be fought in Missouri?"

And, by implication, Kansas. Her border sister.

Norman easily deduced his reasoning.

"What I think is that the Feds wanted to sew up both states early; sort of take them out of the mix, so to speak. Didn't happen. There'll be a lot of unrest hereabouts; small skirmishes. Maybe some larger ones. But the greatest blood will be shed in Virginia."

Compelling Seth to ask, "Why?"

"Richmond is the capital, my boy. It's also a stone's throw from Washington. Take her down and you kill two birds with one stone. That's what you'll be hearing about."

"Soon?"

Norman reflected on the question.

"The armies are already gathering in the Old Dominion. Whenever some general decides it's time to impress his president he'll act."

"You make it sound so...."

"Political? Oh, it is. Take my word for it. Most soldiers don't have any idea what they're actually fightin' for. It's like you said: they think they're defendin' country and flag. But what does that really mean? What's a country but a set of rules and regulations? One is pretty much the same as the other. And a flag? Just a colored cloth. If they changed the Stars and Stripes tomorrow into a solid green background with black half moons, men would follow that just as empty-headedly."

Seth picked up an outdated edition of the Gazette and flipped through the pages. Not to read, but to give his hands an occupation.

"Appears to me not all countries are the same. They have different rules and regulations." Tossing the paper back on the pile, his head dropped back, giving him an unobstructed view of the ceiling. "The South wants slavery. The North doesn't. That's worth fighting for."

"Why? You don't own slaves. And neither do any of the good citizens of Lawrence who were so eager to join up."

"Negroes are human beings. They have a right to be free." Growing agitated, he reached down for the newspaper so recently discarded. "It says here that there are more Negroes in Sumter County, South Carolina, then there are whites. What if there was an uprising and the Africans took over? You suppose that gives them the right to make the rules? To hold whites as slaves?"

"I suppose that's what they worry about in Charleston."

"You didn't answer my question."

"There are some that hold that God made darkies inferior."

"What about you?"

"I never gave the question much thought."

"Think about it now."

Norman stretched his legs, then casually massaged his stockinged feet.

"I'm not what you might call a God-fearing man. Religion is something pa taught with a hickory stick. Goin' to church don't make you holy; it only makes you think you are. There's a difference."

"I turned out all right."

"You ever switch Peter when he said he didn't want to go to church?"

"No."

"Ever skip a few Sundays, yourself? Maybe after Belinda died?"

Roused to anger, Seth crumpled the paper and tossed it near but not directly at his brother.

"What are you getting at?"

"Religion is like solderin' -- there's lots of different reasons to be in either army: God's or man's. Some are better than others, but the ones who think they know the most are usually those who have a finger up their ass." Flushed and annoyed, Norman bent down and retrieved the paper ball. Using both hands, he crushed it flat. "Sorry. That's the soldier in me talkin'. And I'm not a soldier anymore. Got to get over the habit of usin' bad language.

"I'm tired of takin' orders, big brother. That's really why I got out. If I had to stand in front of 'General Daly' an' salute, I think I'd upchuck. He's not an officer. He's a jackass with money who bought u-ne-forms for his boys. Don't get me wrong. It's the same on both sides. I don't really care who wins. But just once, I'd like to do something for myself. For Norman Ward."

"That's what being a farmer is all about. I plant what I want --"

"Oh, hell. Don't give me that. You're dependent on what will sell. And you're tied to the land. Might as well be shackled to it. You bend the knee and pray for rain and the sky's as empty of clouds as if God had forgotten how to make 'em. You owe your soul to the bank and when times comes you can't make a payment, they repossess what you spent your whole life working for. You might as well live with a noose hangin' over your head. That's not what I want."

He got up and paced to the window.

"What do you want?"

He laughed and the noise surprised them all.

"Money." Leaning back, he rested against the sill. "The kind that don't 'grow on trees,' if you know what I mean."

"Can't say that I do."

Norman relented and the blood drained from his face.

"Well, that makes two of us. I think I'm for bed." Prodigiously yawning, he shrugged and pushed off. "Sorry to have kept you folks up. I know you have to be up early and I'm no help to you. Maybe I'll get up at revile or whatever you call it on a pirate ship and go out in the fields with you tomorrow."

"We're going into Lawrence to pick Patricia up in the morning."

A brief expression of regret passed over his wan countenance.

"That's right. I forgot. Must be some significance in there somewhere. Good night."

"Good night."

"Don't let the bedbugs bite."

Close, but not complete.

He left out the "Sleep tight."

For that, the godliness in Barbara Nelander gave thanks.

Chapter 24

Finger to her lips, Nelander enjoined Seth to silence.

"It is 1:30. Time I was going."

Shaking off the drunken effects of sleep occasioned by her extinguishing the lamps an hour past, he tried to blink himself into wakefulness.

"I wish you didn't have to go."

"So do I. But Norman is wrong, you know. People do have to stand for something."

He grimaced and averted his face so she could not follow his eyes.

"Tell me that again if I come home one day and say I've enlisted."

Because she could not otherwise bear it, Barbara turned it into a joke.

"That depends on which side you choose." His stomach muscles tightened and she felt his silent laugh. "I will be back before noon. And then we can go into town. Unless you want to go without me." As soon as she spoke, the idea appealed to her. "Maybe that would be better. If you leave early, Norman won't notice I'm not with you. That way, he won't miss me at breakfast."

"He sleeps in the barn, my love. I can hardly hope to hitch Blaze without waking him."

"But he may not get up to see you off. In that case, speak to me; say something and pretend I answer --"

"No!"

Startled by the vehemence, she demanded, "Why not?"

"Too much like talkin' to spooks. We've enough around here to last me a lifetime."

Meaning, If I speak to you when you're not here and answer for you, then it will be the same as though you are dead.

She could not disagree.

"All right. He'll just have to presume I went with you. No reason for him to think otherwise."

"I wish you weren't going."

She kissed him and slipped away.

Lacking any sort of instructions from Mathis McConaghie, Barbara took a cloak and cap. While her husband slept, she had also filled a canvas sack with leftovers from their meal, a small bag of beans, a pound of bacon wrapped in a cotton towel and a corked bottle, filled with drinking water. Just in case their passenger needed a repast along the tracks.

Slinging it over her shoulder, she looked back, blew Seth a kiss, then slipped through the door.

With only a sliver of moon, picking her way through the bushes which grew at the side of the strawberry field required care and minute attention. Fearing to make noise, least she warn whomever might be on the prowl, it required nearly the complete cycle of a "bell" to reach the trees. Once hidden in the low overhang, she grew stiller, yet, holding her breath to listen. No sound came to her ears.

"Wait," she whispered to herself. "Wait."

Five minutes. Ten. It could have been an hour, for the interior timepiece in her skull circled the clock face at ten times normal speed.

Wait.

Nothing.

She tried amusing herself by imagining who the conductor would have with him. Another young woman? A black man? Escaped from where -- St. Louis? Kansas City? Or nearer home? Fort Leavenworth? Had the slave broken out of jail? Had he been unjustly convicted of a crime?

What lawless act could it have been? The audacity to love a white woman? Her heart ached for Mrs. Dryfus, also known as Mrs. Giles. Barbara doubted she would have had the strength to watch Seth hung from a tree. Not without doing something.

Doing what? What could a mere woman do?

The suppression of her own gender raised hackles.

Damn this world and all those who seek to assert themselves over others. Damn men who speak blasphemy in the Lord's name. Damn those who choose violence over reason, hatred over acceptance, superiority over --

A hand came out of nowhere and wrapped itself around her mouth. Fighting off her first instinct to struggle, Nelander went limp. The action did not stop her mind from working, however. If that damned fool McConaghie thought she would scream if he came up too suddenly behind her, he had another thing coming....

"Quiet, now."

A familiar voice. He had been late. No more.

The hand loosened its grip. Before it had quite removed itself, a new identity registered.

A familiar voice. But not the one she had been expecting.

The shock almost caused her to scream.

"Norman!"

"Shhh! Quiet, I said. They are out there."

"You? You are the conductor?"

"Not I."

Cold sweat dripped from her forehead. Hatred welled in her breast.

"You have intercepted them? Those who were to come?"

The hand went back over her mouth. Another gripped her throat with Indian-like vice.

"I have intercepted you. That is the difference."

The hand relaxed once more. She spoke in a harsh, grating whisper.

"I will never turn them over to you. Nor will I give you the names. Kill me now before I shout warning."

"I know everything. You may keep your honor. And your life. Go home. You have no mission tonight."

"You are a bounty hunter --"

"Not that, either."

"Then how do you know... my plans?"

"Do not ask, for like you, I am sworn to secrecy. Let us say," he added, "secrecy sworn to myself. Enough. Leave this place. Quickly. You know nothing. If others use your property for illegal activities, it is unknown to you." He pushed her back. "Go! And say nothing."

"And if I scream?"

He grinned. The sight made her sick.

"I will tell those who come we were having a midnight tryst." He crudely patted his groin. "Your reputation will be ruined."

"Worse than being a woman helping a slave escape?"

"For that, they would slit your throat. Your choice."

"Who-are-you?"

"Seth's brother."

"I would have it otherwise. I liked you better... as a stack of letters."

"I am telling you to go, Mrs. Ward. For the sake of your husband. Others tonight have not been as lucky."

Swallowing the lump in her throat, Nelander abandoned her post. Without looking back and taking no care as to the noise she made, her footsteps took her unerringly home. Rushing into the house, she dragged a chair from the living room, placing the back against the knob. She had no illusions of creating a permanent barrier. But to do nothing would have been to accept defeat.

Seth met her before she had quite completed the task. Without asking for explanation, he wedged the chair into place, then grabbed her by the shoulders, bringing the deer rifle with him so the cold of the metal pierced the fabric of her blouse.

"Are you all right?"

"I am unharmed."

"Are they coming after you? Have no fear. I will shoot the first man who dares lay a hand on the knob."

"I would as soon you aimed it at the barn."

"They are coming to steal our horse?"

She could not blame him the innocence of the question. In his place, she would have thought the same.

"To sleep there."

He blinked, then lowered the weapon. Not from refusal but resignation.

"Norman?"

"He met me in the wood. Told me to go home: saying I had no mission this night."

"How could he have known?"

"He knows," she quoted, "everything."

Crossing to the window of his ship-under-siege, Seth drew back the curtain. Nothing moved. He no longer trusted his eyes. Or his heart.

"He followed us to church? Overheard McConaghie?"

"No."

"Then Mathis has talked -- or sold out."

"Not that, either."

Less convinced, he began, "I never trusted him --"

"He was not for us to trust. That bond existed between Mathis and Mrs. Dryfus. When she told us of her reasons, I accepted them."

He sucked air between his teeth. "Giles."

"Her own son, Seth? Turning on his own people. I think not."

"We spoke of a spy."

Legs too weak to hold her, Nelander sunk onto the couch. Seth debated holding her or guarding the entranceway. She relieved him of the decision by patting the cushion.

"Come away. I... over-reacted. No one is following me."

"But you said Norman is involved. Surely he will return."

"Surely he will." She inhaled the words as though imbibing them into her soul.

"He did not take his horse," came the insistent plea. "I will hide in the barn and shoot him when he comes in."

"You may eventually do that, but for better cause."

"What do you mean?"

"Soldier Ward was on the prowl tonight, but I think he found me by accident. It was not I he waited for but some other."

"I do not follow you."

"Another business. Not bounty hunting, although I would not put it past him. I think... whoever he came to meet ran across the Underground route by accident. Discovering it, they must have also reasoned others would be about -- searching for escaped slaves and those who would help them. They needed to put a stop to such activity."

"What has happened to McConaghie?"

She shrugged. Not from unconcern.

"Some evil."

Cradling the rifle for support, Seth stared gloomily into her face. Although he could make out few details, they told their own story.

"They would not have... killed him? Run him off, perhaps.... But cold blooded murder?"

"There has always been a license to kill those in the Underground Railroad, has there not?"

"We will have to tell Sheriff Bochner."

Nelander finally rested a hand on his, forcing him to lay down the rifle.

"Tell him what?"

"That my brother is somehow involved."

"By morning, Norman will be gone. Now that we know for certain he is up to something, he has lost his safe haven. It may be we never see him again. Bochner will never catch him."

"You speak as though you know."

"He has learned his craft well. From the Indians. A local lawman is no match for his skills."

"Then, he will go away? Leave Kansas?"

"I did not say that."

He groaned in misery and held his head in his hands.

"I am sorry I ever had a brother -- any brother."

For the moment, although the moment faded, she could not agree.

"He saved my life tonight. Had I been caught by his associates, I would not have fared so well."

"Southern conspirators? But what could they be doing which requires such secrecy?"

The answer came to her unbidden.

Money. The kind that don't grow on trees.

Which involved a war on an entirely different front.

With Seth and Peter waiting, Barbara hurried to change the baby. This last minute complication delayed their departure but it would be several hours before they got into Lawrence and performing the simple, yet delicate task on the trail held little appeal.

Adeptly removing the soiled cloth and depositing it in the covered pail for later washing, she stole a precious second to stare at her child.

"Ten fingers, ten toes," she whispered. Strong arms and chubby little legs with the power to knock an unwary caregiver into the next county. A beautifully shaped head, finely dusted with light brown hair, just curling at the ends. This last had been a recent edition. Seth had likened it to the development of feathers on a chick and meant it as a compliment. He had also noted Paula weighed "somewhere in the range between Miss Henpecker and Mr. Noise Box." Barbara had countered by more rightly comparing the infant's weight to a number averaged between "Bessie, the cow and Blaze, the horse."

"On accounta the fact you tote her more often than I," the proud father had laughed, "I defer to your expert opinion."

That had been a good time; a special moment. It seemed an age ago, yet in actual time, no more than two weeks. She wondered how many future opportunities would pass unnoted as the baby's parents worried more about national politics and battles encroaching on their ever complicated lives.

Using a damp sponge laden with soap, Nelander cleaned the affected area, dried the shiny pink flesh with a soft towel, then wrapped her squirming bundle in a fresh cotton cloth. Trying the ends with a sailor's knot used at sea to facilitate the unloosening of wet fastenings, she slipped a lightweight gown over the grasping fingers then stood back to assess the work.

"Pretty as a picture and tight as a drum."

Paula agreed by blowing a spit bubble.

Nelander popped it and the baby laughed. A good game.

"No time to play, now. We are going to get your sister. Do you miss her?"

Paula responded by widening her eyes into the size of a Spanish doubloon. The tip of her tongue played over pink gums.

"You look like your father," her mother decided. Of all the men she knew, only Seth would take that as a compliment. "Here we go."

Slipping the baby into her papoose carrier, Nelander deferred working her arms through the straps. Later, in town, she would carry the baby on her back. To secure this most precious bundle from being dropped. Or snatched away.

On second thought, she changed her mind. Wiser to protect against danger known, than prepare for a struggle only anticipated.

A paraphrase of the common expression, Better to stay with the devil you know than face another of uncertain evil.

In either case, Norman Ward served as the familiar threat.

Child in tow, Nelander hurried through the house and into the yard. Seth sat on the wagon seat, Peter standing behind, hand resting on his shoulder. Norman maintained a position halfway between them and the barn. Were

Patricia back from her sojourn as an art student, the child might have characterized the scene as Still Life.

The younger man took in the approaching woman with a flash of surprise and high-stepped before confessing, "Took you fer an Injun just now. Carryin' the babe that way."

"Does that make me the enemy?"

"Never shot a squaw. Or a runny-nosed brave." He lowered a hand to indicate height. "Some do, though. Women make young'uns, an' boys grow into warriors. You suppose I earned some credit, sparin' one or two?"

He meant her to make the inference.

"If you did, you've already spent it."

The rebuff forced a congenial grin. "Ah. Off to town?"

Seth answered. "We are going to get our daughter."

He pretended to have forgotten.

"That's right. It's Monday."

"You be gone by the time we get back?"

"Thought I would be."

"That's good."

"Where is Uncle Norman going, Captain Papa? Aren't we going to look for pirate treasure?"

"No, son. Our treasure is in the land. In what we grow. In one another."

"But I wanted to find buried coins. An' jewels."

"That's a pretend, Peter. Norman can't help you find what isn't there. Don't know that he can rightly find anything he's lookin' for."

"Why is that, sir?"

"He's lost his map."

Norman grimaced, but did not argue.

"Guess this is good-bye, brother. Don't expect to be seein' you around."

"You leavin' the state?"

"I'm disappearin'. Like a ghost ship. Sometimes they pop up in the most unexpected places."

"Carrying dead souls aboard," Nelander clarified. For the record.

The book chronicling profit and loss.

"Can I ride Rum one more time before he goes?"

"No, Peter. That's a... cavalry man's horse. It's not for boys playing games."

"Are you going to war, Uncle Norman? Like Dr. McTree?"

"War is where you find it, nephew."

"What does that mean?" None of the adults cared to clarify the statement. "Are you comin' back? After it's all over?"

"That depends."

Peter shook his father with both hands. "You want him back. Don't you, papa?"

"He's going his own way."

The child gasped and reeled back.

"Does this mean you're a Rebel, Uncle Norman?"

"Would that bother you?"

"Yes, sir! Rebels want to hurt Blind Betty and Mute Thomas. They want to see 'em made slaves. That isn't right, sir!" He jabbed a finger. "You can't believe that! You can't want to hurt my friends! They're pirates," he added, tears coming to his eyes. "Pirates don't never turn on one another."

Norman tried an apologetic smile.

"But I was never officially made a pirate. Remember?"

"But you're pa's brother." No one chose to answer. "I'll give you the oath."

"Oh, no, boy. I've taken too many oaths in my life. Don't want to break another."

Peter's lower lip protruded. "A man should never break his word."

"That's why I won't give it, now. But maybe I'm a pirate in other ways. Say good-bye to your sister for me. I hope Mrs. Dryfus taught her how to paint. Give the old lady something to do, now that she's outta that other business. Good thing, too. It's dangerous. Like I said: I never shot a squaw. But others might."

"I'll tell Patricia. But she'd like to hear your good-bye for herself."

"You... shake her hand for me. Can you do that?" He winked. "Note that I didn't say, 'Kiss her on the cheek' for me. I don't suppose boys like to kiss girls for any reason."

Nelander put an end to the conversation.

"Seems you don't know a lot about boys, either."

Which served as a "good-bye" without the traditional "God bless."

Or even, "Fare thee well."

Which, in a roundabout way, had a great deal in common with bed bugs biting.

Chapter 25

The Wards encountered no sentries on the road. The campgrounds for the competing armies had been abandoned. No flags fluttered from atop eagle-crested staffs. Yet all was not quiet. Even before reaching the outskirts of Lawrence proper, the overwhelming sense of something wrong raised the hackles.

Seth did not turn to his wife and say, "Perhaps the raiders have struck again."

Nelander did not suggest, "News of Carthage has reached town."

Both knew that whatever lay behind their queasiness held far greater import than anything they could imagine.

A group of men had gathered outside Anson's Dry Goods. Having already discussed, digested and spit the news out, they had all but worn themselves to a nub. The arrival of newcomers, however, reanimated their spirits.

"Seth! Over here."

Reluctant to respond, for he wanted to retrieve Patricia and be gone without delay, refusal to heed the summons reeked of bad manners. Worse, it inspired the snubbed to question how someone might already know the grim tidings. Living alone on an isolated farm, knowledge with such events implied complicity.

"What's up?" he inquired, hoping the tremble in his voice did not betray him. In actual fact, he did not know the news. Just as true, he would as soon have lived in ignorance.

"Mathis McConaghie's been murdered!"

"He was found hanged by the neck until dead."

The unconscious rendition of a judge's pronouncement added an additional level of horror to the scene.

"Oh, dear God."

Nelander uttered the words. The fact her shock had to do with events of last night and Norman's dire prediction, *Others tonight have not been as lucky,* was overlooked as being uttered by a female.

The onlookers attributed Seth's blanched face to breeding.

"McConaghie.... Dead?"

"Face as dark as a blueberry when they cut 'im down. Tongue lollin' outta his mouth."

The speaker meant to shock. Having won a hand of make-believe poker with the woman's outburst, he hoped to trump his own game.

"Who.... Who did it?"

"Don't nobody know. Sheriff's been out all mornin'. He ain't been back, yet, but when his new deputy come in to borrow a wagon, we all know'd sumething were up."

"He didn't want to say what, at first, but no one'd loan him a wagon till he said why he needed it."

"Tinker bein' gone an' all. That's where Will usually goes fer a wagon. But the smithy's closed."

"An' Doc McTree's gone, too. No one to certify the body."

"Guess it don't need no certifyin', innyway. Bochner knows Mathis as well an anyone, an' if he says that was Mathis, you can bank on it."

"Have they... come back? With the body?"

"Not yet. They're on their way. Guess Will'll take it over to the undertakers. Ginnis can write out a death certificate, I reckon. He's done it before."

Seth presumed their obsession over "certifying" and "certificates" came from having already beaten other salient details into the ground. Swallowing hard, he asked, "Where did this happen?"

Not because he wanted to know. Because he already knew.

Out by your place.

Say, that's right, ain't it? Not very far from your strawberry field.

It's a plum amazement you didn't hear innythin'. You didn't, did you? No hollering? No shootin'?

Wonder what ol' Mathis was doin' out that way, anyhow?

You wasn't exactly friends, was you? Some say you had an axe to grind with him.

Mebbe you outta stay in town. Bochner'd be sore at us if we let you go. Reckon he'll have a heap of questions fer you.

"Behind the old Windsor farm. Some ol' black boy found the body 'round daybreak. He cume in fer the sheriff."

"Black boy?"

"That dumb wit. What's his name?"

"Mute Thomas," another supplied.

"That's right. He was out shootin' squirrels wid his slingshot an' stumbled acrost it. Musta scared the heebie-jeebies outta him." The speaker chuckled. "He was durn near white as a ghost when he cume in this mornin'. That's goin' some fer a tar baby."

The others laughed at the crude joke.

"Where is Thomas now? Has he stayed in town?"

"No, sir. Went back wid Will. If he weren't a'ready deaf an' dumb, this'd done it, sure."

"Who would have wanted to hurt Mathis?"

Death bred familiarity.

The answer came with whiplike rapidity. "Bounty hunters."

"Bounty hunters?"

"Way we figure it, Mathis was out trackin' a runaway. Likely caught up wid 'im, too. There was others after the same game. Them from the Simpson Agency. Heard of 'em?"

A flat "Yes."

They continued as though he had not.

"That outfit moved in here 'bout six months ago. We're what you call fertile ground. Guess there's -- what you call it? A way-station 'round here. Whites what help darkies move along. Send 'em up north."

"Mathis an' his boys been slavin' fer years, but these fellas, they got class. They know how to git to the bottom of a thing. 'Spect they cume up on the nigger at the same time an' there was a scuffle. Mathis got the worst of it. They hanged him as a lesson for his kin. Stay away. It's our territory, now."

Knowing better, Nelander inquired, "What about them? The boys? Dick, Bill and Douglas. None of them were...?"

"Hanged? No, ma'am."

One scratched behind his ear.

"Ain't seen 'em around, though. Wonder if innyone tolt 'em what happened to their pa?"

"They'll be riled, a'right."

"Cain't be sech a bad thing, though. If them McConaghies had it out wid the Simpsons, might be they'd chase 'em off. A little dabblin' in slave catchin' on the side is one thing, but them Agency men -- we don't need 'em around here. Dirty business. If I seed one around here, I'd tell 'im to git out. 'Specially after what they done."

"Them's Rebels, a'right. Don't have the stomach to go off an' fight like the rest. Talkin' secesh around town but hidin' out in the hills where it's safe. We don't need that kinda thing. Lawrence's a free town."

Notwithstanding their approval of a little dabbling in slave catching.

"I've got business," Seth said. "I'm sorry about the news." And then, lower, "I never liked him but I wouldn't have wished this on a dog."

"Dog" having a double meaning.

Maneuvering the wagon around the group, he drove off, listing to the side nearest his wife. She put a hand on his knee.

Nothing else to do.

Seth broke the silence. "I suppose she knows." Meaning Mrs. Dryfus.

"Of course. Mute Thomas never came in town looking for the sheriff. If he were the one to find poor... Mathis... he would have gone straight to Blind Betty. And she would have directed him to the -- Big House."

"You don't think he was --?"

It required less effort to talk than think.

"The one to find the body? Not unless he habitually followed McConaghie, which I doubt. There would be no reason; he was well-trusted. Well versed in the routes to take." On his look, she added, "He quoted me chapter and verse. All the way to Canada."

"McConaghie was the one who... charted the course?"

"Certainly not. I doubt he was ever farther west than the Kaw River."

"Who, then?"

"Blind Betty."

Blind Betty? But she cannot see!"

"No. But Thomas can. I am sure the two of them poured over maps like thieves, she telling him what was required, he tracing the routes."

"And then making their own. I have seen them. Markings burned into leather scraps. Written in code. Follow the drinking gourd."

Nelander nodded. "A reference to the north star. A seaman's best friend. Keep that in your sights and you will never get lost."

"You really think Betty ran this whole operation? From the Windsor house?"

"She started plotting the escape routes before they came to work with us. Ironically, we aided and abetted the Cause by giving them a more secure home. One out of the way of prying eyes. If there is a spy in Mrs. Dryfus' home, it must be a Negro. One who works there and probably lives in Nigger Hole. By moving out, we allowed Betty and Thomas to work in relative security."

"And Mrs. Dryfus went along with this?"

"Why not? You heard her story. She and Betty are very close; almost like sisters. Betty raised her son, for God's sake. And, obviously, Betty needed a white person to act as the contact in Lawrence."

Craning her head back, Nelander stared into the sky, following the clouds north. "I didn't think of it before, but it all fits together. And gives us the date this all began; at least the groundwork."

"Tell me."

"Mrs. Dryfus said she and her husband did a lot of traveling after they were married. Where did they go?"

"To Europe."

"Yes. Afterwards. But in the beginning? What did she say? She chose the destinations. St. Louis and Alton -- along the Mississippi-Illinois Rivers. Topeka, and all points leading to the Finger Lakes. Undoubtedly, she used those excursions to meet like-minded folk; people who could be trusted. That explains why she came home from Europe. She had work to do: creating outposts; laying the... tracks." Nelander paused, visualizing a young Victoria Dryfus playing a dangerous game behind her new husband's back.

"She -- and Betty and Thomas, and even Mathis -- joined a very select company. Depending on where the runaways were located, they were sent under cover -- hidden beneath wagon tarps alongside fine furniture bought in Charleston, and sometimes openly -- acting as a valet for a young gentleman. They were taken to the Big House, or to Little Lawrence until it was safe for them to continue their far-reaching journey to freedom."

Seth frowned. "And now, we are all out of business. You were the one who mentioned Norman 'lost his pirate map.' In truth, what he has done is placed 'X's' by Mrs. Dryfus' house and Betty's and ours. 'X,'" he explained. "Meaning we are known conspirators."

"Our identities have not been revealed."

"But Norman -- he knows."

"Norman may use that information for his own ends, but I do not believe he is a traitor -- not to his big brother. Despite what either of us think of him, I trust his loyalty to you."

"You heard him speak with contempt about Rick -- and of how I read books and loved the land."

"He would do much that is dirty and despicable for gain, but he would only betray you out of desperation."

"If he is not a bounty hunter, then what is he?"

"A marauder."

He groaned and slapped his leg.

"Sweet Jesus! He is one of those devils who burned out Louis Willingham?"

"Not personally, for we know his whereabouts at the time of the fire and he was not there. But on his orders? Without doubt."

"I cannot believe it." And then, accusingly, "You said nothing of this last night."

"It has come to me in a flash." Loosening the straps on her shoulder, Nelander repositioned the backpack. The motion awoke Paula, who reached out and grabbed a fistful of her mother's hair. Rather than disentangle the little fingers, Barbara left them, for the pain clarified her thoughts.

"I should have put it together before this. The incident in town -- at the parade. That Confederate officer speaking to you in such a way as to imply some kinship. Then later that evening -- the soldiers going through the woods. They called you captain."

'That is what I am called."

"By me. By the townspeople. But those men were not from around here. In the heat of the altercation and by the dark of night, they thought they recognized you. Not as a farmer named Seth Ward but as the former dragoon, Norman Ward. Their captain and leader."

His knee jerked and the horse, taking the frustrated gesture as one of command, picked up its pace.

"Norman, a Rebel?"

She considered, then slowly shook her head. "Norman is a man who has learned how to work both sides for his advantage. You heard the stories he told: about the padre selling guns and liquor as a sideline. How his lieutenant abandoned that infantry colonel to fend for himself against the Indians? In neither case did Norman express regret. Becoming a soldier did not make him patriotic. I doubt he ever held such sentiments."

Her lip curled in disdain. "He considered it a job -- a learning experience. A way to survive while always looking for an edge -- an advantage. A means of making his fortune. There isn't any money to be made as an enlisted man or even as an officer, so the war has no appeal to him. But as a private contractor -- a man who may disregard the laws of the land by pretending to favor one side or the other -- that fit the bill."

The second before Seth turned his head away, Nelander knew she had gone too far. Quickly trying to make amends, she began a softening of the harsh assessment, but he would have none of it. Jaw quivering, corners of his eyes shiny from the condensation of internal dew, he aborted her effort with a stiff jerk of the hand.

"I don't know why I'm sad -- why your words upset me. I never knew Norman. Not really. He said it. We grew up in different worlds. He -- or I, for that matter -- might just as well have been adopted. We're that different. What he did with his life is nothing to me." Words tumbled out over one another, some commingling, others standing alone in stark contrast, so that Barbara had trouble sorting through the jumble.

"Once I accepted the fact he had joined the army, I put him out of my head. Well, that's not completely true, but you know what I mean." He sniffed, debated whether to blow his nose, then settled for wiping the clear mucus away with the side of his pointer finger. "I never thought of him as ambitious. Rick -- now, he was ambitious. He was like pa -- had his finger in everything. Business. Politics. Farming. Money lending; I don't know.

Rick followed in his footsteps. Norman and I never could understand either one of them."

She considered stopping Seth but in the end, did not.

"I wasn't much with people; it was the land that spoke to me. Belinda and I had our dreams of a farm and that was enough. Norman drifted away about the time we were married. He wasn't more'n sixteen but he was headstrong and that made him seem older. I can't say I missed him. In fact, his going was a relief. In an odd sort of way, it tidied things up."

"How, Seth?"

"By cutting my strings with ma and Rick. I might of kept in touch if Norman had stayed on -- just to be sure he had a place to stay or money for a pair of boots. He'd have told me all about them -- how Rick was doing, what he was messing with, his dealings," he spat. "Might even have come to stay with us -- Belinda and me. That woulda been hard -- harder than it was now."

"Why do you say that? Didn't she like him?"

"It wasn't her -- it was me. I didn't like him."

"How did I make the situation easier?"

His lips twisted in a grin. "You didn't like him, either. I could tell right off. That sorta put me in the position of defending him; as a means of assuaging my conscience."

She gave him a shove with her shoulder.

"I see. I supplied the suspicion while you played big brother. But I knew that, all along."

"You did?"

"Certainly."

"Oh. Well, damn." He finally regained control of his emotions and slowed Blaze down. "You figured he didn't go home, didn't you? Norman, going to see ma and Rick's graves. Saying a prayer over them. It just didn't figure."

This time, Nelander disagreed.

"No, Seth. I was willing to go along with his story. It was you who thought otherwise."

His eyes shifted. "He stayed in town, didn't he? Recruitin' his outlaw gang. It was a ruse -- to give him time. If we thought he was in another county, we wouldn't look for him. That way, he could always come back to me. Keep an eye on things. He knew we were working for the Underground Railroad, didn't he?"

"I suppose he suspected as much."

"How'd he find out?"

"That's a good question. But I was sure Norman was onto us after he brought me the letter from Hoskins. Pete Erlinger never gave it to him. I doubt Hoskins even wrote it. Norman just wanted to see what we'd do."

"But you said he's not a bounty hunter."

"Not in the traditional sense. But word gets around. He probably heard the story from the McConaghie boys or those agents from Simpson's while they were sitting around Tankard's Draft. They didn't put it together but he did."

"He was only funnin' us?"

"Maybe it was a test. Who knows? He wanted to see our resolve." She stared at her hands. "More likely, he wanted to flush us out; confirm his suspicions. Try and figure out who else was involved. Mrs. Dryfus is a wealthy woman. If he tied us with her, he could always try blackmail."

"Threaten to report her to the authorities?"

"That, certainly. Even if Sheriff Bochner dragged his heels bringing charges against her, Norman could shut the whole operation down. She wouldn't want that."

An expression of strangulated agony set into Seth's features.

"My own brother. He's not so different than Rick, after all. Doesn't care about human suffering -- just making money. Break up the Underground Railroad; steal another man's horses. Burn a house. Shoot a dog." He shivered. "Just like pa."

The second captain aboard the Pirate Treasure bit her lip. Breakfast churned in her stomach. She had a feeling they had only touched the tip of the iceberg. Noting the grim expression, Seth worriedly inquired, "What is it?"

Barbara Nelander seriously wondered whether he really wanted to know. Had she the option, she would have placed herself in the same category.

CHAPTER 26

"Papa! Captain Papa!"

Patricia ran down the path, arms extended. Three feet from her father she propelled herself into the air. He caught his daughter, staggered back, then burst out laughing.

"A whale! Look, everyone! I've caught myself a whale!" Kissing her cheeks and forehead, Seth settled the child back on her feet with a large huff of expelled air. "Who ever said we don't have any whales in Kansas?" Arching back, he studied the beloved face. "Grow'd an inch since last Friday. An' put on ten pounds. Hardly recognize you!"

Pausing to reflect on the compliment, Patricia reluctantly decided he exaggerated.

"I missed you so much."

Dodging Peter, then succumbing to her brother's own demonstrations of affection, she kissed him back, then smartly saluted Nelander. The adult returned the salutation, then offered her own brow to be kissed. Those wet ones exchanged, the girl darted behind her.

"Bend down so's I can reach Paula."

Doing so gladly, they waited for a fourth round of kissing to be completed before following her up the inlaid steps to the house. Instead of finding Giles there to open the door, Mrs. Dryfus offered her personal greeting.

"Good morning and welcome. My young protégée is glad to see you but I confess I am less so. Her company has been a delight."

Guiding them indoors, the matron's sparkling orbs and rejuvenated countenance bore testimony to her words. In four short days she had transformed from a woman barely alive to one of vibrant health and cherished expectations.

"Wait 'till you see what I have painted. I have worked ever so hard, papa."

"And not been any trouble?" he sternly inquired. Mrs. Dryfus spoke for her.

"Not a bit of it, sir. I would steal her from you in a moment."

Taking Patricia by the hand, the two new best friends led the way into the parlor. If their eyes did not drink in the changes wrought, the re-instilled sensations of present and future joy would have conveyed their own story.

The room had been entirely redecorated. In place of the imported yet lifeless furniture, a new couch sat by the fireplace. Covered in a soft, golden red, the cushions invited a long comfortable stay, rather than the former stilted formality. Gone, too, were the high back chairs, replaced by six overstuffed, mismatched seats, each boasting padded arms, leg rests and brightly hued pillows of crimson, forest green and three shades of blue.

Instead of the Oriental carpet, a fresh rug with a high nap had been spread nearly from corner to corner. Patricia pointed to it with pride.

"Put Paula down," she begged. "It's softer than grass. When she's ready to crawl, it will be comfortable on her hands and knees."

Barbara eagerly did as directed, propping the baby up against the sofa. She promptly toppled over, giggled at herself, then began an exploration with fingers and toes.

"You may come to regret this, Mrs. --"

"Victoria, please. Or Vickie, if you prefer. Patricia and I have dispensed with formality. This is to be a room for fun and imagination. No more brooding."

Given the state of affairs outside the mansion, Nelander forced herself to consider how much information had reached the ears of those who dwelled within. In honesty, she had anticipated quite a different reception. One which not even a twelve-year old girl with oil paints could brighten.

Inadvertently giving herself away, Victoria Giles quickly responded.

"We will speak later, Captain."

Whatever subtly she intended shattered quickly as Peter promptly filled in the blanks.

"They hung Mr. McConaghie."

Patricia gasped and grew still, leaving it for others to comment. The more experienced of the two officers, taking a cue from the elder, promptly changed the tone of the discussion.

"*Hanged.* Curtains are hung; men are hanged."

Peter surprised them all with child's wisdom.

"Yes, sir. I know that. I just thought if I used the wrong word, it wouldn't sound so terrible."

Seth cried and engulfed the boy in a bear-like hug. Wiggling from beneath the powerful arms, Peter pointed upward to the space over the mantel. Four pair of eyes followed the direction.

"There sure has been some improvement! Did you paint that?"

Gone were the portraits of Mr. Dryfus and his young bride. Two others flanked the stark, leafless tree.

"I did the one of Vickie," Patricia supplied, stiffening a foot and making a small circle with it across the rug. "My teacher did the other. They're not finished," she hurried on. "We didn't have time to get them down. And the oil's not dry, so don't touch them. But we wanted to surprise you."

Awed by the power of the artwork, Seth and Barbara drew closer, eyes riveted at one and then the other of the new additions. Swallowing the lump in his throat, Seth addressed his daughter's artwork first.

"You did that? Of Mrs. Dryfus?" Left without an adequate compliment, he stumbled, "I can recognize her!"

Smiling broadly, the subject of the painting stepped nearer to allow for closer inspection.

"An excellent likeness, to be sure. And a great achievement for one so young, who has never worked in the medium or had professional tutoring."

"Tell us... how you did it, Patricia," Barbara requested.

Bashful and proud, the girl stepped forward.

"At first I didn't know what to paint. I thought about doing the valley with the strawberries in bloom but my mind wandered all over the place. I didn't know where to start. Then, I thought I'd paint the flag in front of the house -- the Jolly Roger. But it got all out of...."

"Perspective," Mrs. Giles supplied.

"That's it. I made it too big so you couldn't tell where it was flying." Hands in her pockets, she added in an undertone, "I wasted a lot of paint."

"Never wasted, my child. I told you that."

"I know, but they're god-awful expensive." Her head shot up. "Do you know where Vickie's paints come from, Captain Papa? All the way from France."

"Do tell," which meant she had succeeded in impressing him.

"Yes, they came from Paris, where many youths go to learn their art."

"Did you study there -- Vickie?" Nelander asked.

"A bit. Not seriously. My mind was too dark. My tutors wanted me to use spring hues but all I saw were blacks and greys. My... husband bought me an artist's case filled with colors. They come in powders and are to be mixed with oil to produce a workable texture. He purchased easels and pallets and canvas in order to please me. He did not know how much -- or how -- his gift would be used." She indicated the centerpiece, the only remaining original from the previous grouping.

"It was my idea to take the others down," Patricia volunteered.

"But the one of Mrs. Dryfus was very beautiful."

"Yes, papa. But it was also hurtful. And that other --" Her face puckered. "That was ugly."

Shocked that she might have offended, he put a finger to his lips, but Victoria Giles stopped him with a merry sound.

"I wanted to burn it but Patricia had a better idea. Come." Leading the procession, she took them to a small antechamber off the parlor. Opening the door with a small silver key she wore around her wrist, light filtered in from the sides.

Amidst a clutter of unused or broken side tables, lamps and various decorative bowls, vases and small sculptures "hung" Mr. Dryfus.

Nelander chuckled in approval.

"As good a place as any for a ghost from the past."

"Locked in for good measure," Patricia announced. "Vickie and I blessed a strawberry and put it by the door to keep him in." Removing a tiny ornamental glass figure from a side table, she held it up for inspection. "We didn't have a real one, but I figured this'd do just as well."

"What is your opinion, Peter?" the matron addressed the expert. "Effective?"

He took the bauble and encased it in his small hands. Not satisfied, he lifted it to his ear and listened.

"Yes, ma'am. You did a right good job. This talisman hadn't never heard the Lord's Prayer before. That was a good blessing."

She withdrew in an amazement akin to shock.

"How did you know we used the Lord's Prayer?"

So simple a matter. "The strawberry told me. It was Patricia's choice but you went along."

"I was not so sure about 'forgiving trespasses.'"

"It's better that way, ma'am. Callin' on the devil to do God's work is a bad thing." He squinted wisely at the elder. "It confuses the spirits. They don't do the devil's work. They're on the side of the angels. Only devils do devil's work. And mostly, they're men an' not ghosts." The profundity carried the argument. He returned the charm to its resting place. "You're safe."

Carefully closing the door, leaving Mr. Dryfus to the watch of heaven, they went back into the parlor.

"Did you have Victoria pose for you, Patricia?"

"Yes, sir. Up in the garret. She was awful patient, too. She can sit still a long time!"

"I have had much practice. But there is much work to be done on it, yet. Many more sittings. You will let her come back and... finish it?"

"Of course. If she wishes."

"More than anything, papa."

"This other," Nelander pursued, referring to the portrait on the left. "You did not paint this, child."

"Vickie painted it," came the reverent avowal.

Mrs. Giles grasped one hand in the other, fighting emotion.

"I never thought to paint again. Ever. Once my... hanging tree had dried, I put away my paints and closed the room. It seemed an end.... A period. What else could follow so powerful a landscape?" Forcing her hands to relax, she took in a deep breath. "Teaching Patricia gave me new inspiration. I might have ignored it, but *she* would not allow."

The sentence had an accusatory ring.

"I said if we took down her portrait and replaced it with the one I painted, then we couldn't have ol' Mr. Dryfus there. That'd be -- ugly."

"Out of symmetry," Nelander observed, eyes fixated on the new portrait. "No one posed for this one."

"No.," came the low confession. "Not in the flesh. Out of my memory."

Unlike the girl's, which had been started in oil, this artist had blocked the face out in pencil, roughly sketching in a head and shoulders. Various portions had been darkened but most remained mere line drawings: the shape of the head, the set of the jaw. Above and below the eyes temporary lines extended past the ears, enabling the artist to keep them straight and in perspective.

Despite the incompleteness, a latent sense of life permeated the sketch, as if, indeed, the possessor of the face had imbued it with his essence.

"His eyes are following me."

A quiet, "Thank you," served as the greatest reward a painter could ever receive. "I thought so, too. For the first time in many, many years, I have felt watched. By a good spirit. No longer did I feel so... alone." Her voice choked. "He has come back to me."

"Marc," Nelander intoned in reverence.

"Yes. My beloved Marc Giles. My true husband."

"I can see the boy in him," Seth observed. "Antony. He has his father's -
-"

"Complexion?" she asked. Too fast.

"I was going to say resolution. His father's sentience. His bravery."

Ashamed, she bowed her head. "You do him honor, sir."

"It is you who do honor to his memory. And to your son."

Feeling a new presence in the room, Seth turned to see Mister Giles standing in the entranceway. A fleeting look of bitterness passed over his countenance before one of pride replaced it. He gave no explanation for the former as he joined his mother.

"I never knew him. I had no idea what my father looked like. Patricia has done both my mother and I a great service. She has renewed my mother's love of art and given me a precious insight into that which cruel fate has deprived me."

"I am so glad. For both of you." Unable to account for the sudden unease, Nelander turned the topic of conversation. "If Patricia is not an imposition, then she may certainly come again. But --"

"We have other things to discuss." Like Nelander, Mrs. Gile's tone hardened. "Peter, go out to the stables. Your filly has been looking for you."

"Has she? Really?"

"Indeed. Go and tell her you are here. Giles has some sugar cubes to treat her with." Addressing the solemn brown man, she requested, "Take the boy away and see him settled. Then come back."

"May I go, papa?"

"You may. But come when I call. We shall not stay long."

"Yes, sir."

Giles trailed after Peter, clearly the follower in this case and not the leader. The matriarch addressed the second innocent.

"Patricia, go upstairs. To the garret. I wish you to work on another painting. The one of the valley. With the strawberries in bloom."

"But I want to stay here --"

"And I desire for you to go upstairs. There is a picture waiting to escape your fingers. Do not put it off. Or you shall grow into a bitter old lady like me."

Going to Mrs. Giles, the girl tugged on her arm, indicating she lower her head.

"You are not old. And you are a wonderful lady. I love you."

Kissing her cheek, she solemnly obeyed the order, leaving the adult Nelander-Wards alone in the parlor with their host. Only too aware of the recent declaration that the refurbished room be a place for positive energy, all had the idea of leaving at the same time. A loud grunt of annoyance temporarily prevented the exodus.

"Paula! I almost forgot her."

Signaling she would retrieve the baby, the matron hesitated, then looked to its mother for approval.

"May I?"

"Certainly."

Scooping up the infant, then smoothing down the soft down covering Paula's head, the act brightened the older woman's mood.

"I would not have her subject to dark thoughts. You would, perhaps...? Let me show you."

Guiding the company out, she crossed the hallway and entered a spacious dining room. Gliding between the cherry-wood table and matching sideboard, she led them through a music room to a smaller chamber. A small stuffed toy hung from the handle.

Expecting it to be locked, the Wards held back and were surprised to find she merely turned the knob and entered. Inside, they beheld a small but lavishly decorated nursery.

"Another one of my... treasures. It will suit, do you not think?"

"Oh, Victoria, this is wonderful!"

Finding too much to take in at a single glance, Barbara rushed inside, mouth rounded into a wide "O," and eyes as wide as any child's. A small crib dominated the scene, crafted of light, nearly white wood. Highly polished, it shone as a beacon, augmented by lightweight blankets of pink and blue. A tiny pillow no larger than a loaf of bread perched at the head, embroidered with baby animals matching the color scheme of the bedclothes.

A child's table and two matching stools sat in one corner. Larger toys, an elephant wearing a leather harness and a dog with glass eyes and long black fur occupied the places of honor. Shelves along one wall held dolls, ranging from small, handmade corncob creations with mismatched button eyes to those nearly three feet high, designed of porcelain. Dressed in intricate wardrobes, matching shoes and beaded gloves, they gave so lifelike an appearance any one might have made a curtsy and welcomed the guests to their domicile.

Framed artwork covered the other three walls. As different from the hanging tree as night and day, the technique boasted the same hand created them all. One displayed a toy box overflowing with the gear of childhood: a large red ball, a disarrayed set of alphabet blocks; a jester's cap with a shiny bell on the tip; an Indian headdress and a wooden sword.

Another picture featured two foals standing side-by-side, staring toward an unseen onlooker. One had a foreleg up, the other whisked its tail. Behind them, more indistinctly painted, sat a dogcart, wheels of bright yellow, sideboards a sparkling royal blue with half moons rising toward the seat. A third painting depicted a straw basket filled to brimming with a litter of kittens. One had bits of straw caught in its fur; another poised to lick, a long strawberry-red tongue stealing out from between sharp pointed teeth. Oblivious to its mates, a fat tabby attempted to escape, grey paws and protruding tummy suspended over the edge.

"I feel as though I must grab that precocious one before it falls!" Spinning around, Nelander found too much to assimilate. "This is a child's dream."

"Call it my dream, if you will. Assembled many years ago and put away... until recently. If you think it fit, we may leave your darling Paula here while we converse in the dining room."

"Of course. But it is almost too precious to disturb."

"No, madam. On the contrary. It is too... special to remain unloved by some small life."

Placing Paula in the crib, Nelander propped the embroidered pillow behind her back. Standing on tiptoe to imbibe the scene, Mrs. Giles glowed.

"Here. Give her this to play with. It was given to me many years ago and I had not the heart to relinquish it." Taking a small rag doll out of a willow basket through which ribbons had been woven, she offered it to Paula. "From the godmother of my son." Tears in her eyes, she watched as the miniscule pink fingers grasped the toy. "Seeing this has made... my world complete."

Seth spoke for his daughter.

"She thanks you, lady. And she says you have made her world complete, for now she has another member to fulfill her family circle. It is a poor child who has but one grandmother. Now she has two. Miss Betty and Miss Victoria."

Putting a hand to her mouth, the old lady tried, unsuccessfully, to hide her brimming emotion.

"God bless you all. And to think -- it was strawberries which brought us together."

"Strawberries -- and your young man -- Mr. Antony Giles."

The gentleman, who had reappeared from his outside sojourn, gave a violent start. Not precisely in the manner anticipated.

"I do not want that-man's-progeny in my crib. I do not want him in my room. The room I was never allowed to occupy."

With a cry of despair, Mrs. Dryfus fell back against the wall and swooned.

CHAPTER 27

Allowing him his right, the Wards held back as he rushed to his mother. Grasping her before she fell, he tenderly steadied the woman in his arms.

"Come, mother. Let us leave this place." And then lower, but clearly meant to be overheard, "You should not have brought them here."

"Antony.... Antony, why?"

"Not-here."

Tugging with ill-disguised anger, he assisted her out and settled her in one of the dining room chairs. Seeing she would not slip off, he returned to the nursery and pointed inward.

"Take the child."

Nelander did so, holding Paula tightly to her breast. Once out, Giles slammed the door. Removing a lace handkerchief from her sleeve, Mrs. Giles wiped her face with a shaking hand.

"Tell me, Antony. What is this about? I asked your permission --"

"That was before I knew," he pouted, offering a menacing stare at Seth.

"Knew? Knew what? Tell me. My heart cannot stand such a shock. I am... you heard. The baby's grandmother. Betty and I --"

"Never! You have both been deceived. He is not what you think. He is like all the rest of the -- white trash."

Utterly disturbed and thrown off kilter, Seth assumed a defensive position, legs balanced for flight or fight.

"Say out what you think you know."

"Mathis McConaghie was betrayed. By you."

Seth anticipated some dire pronouncement but not that. His lips worked in silent denial as his mind struggled to work through the accusation. The result left him with only a weak, "Not I, sir."

Nelander had no better grasp of the situation but a fiercer temper.

"That is a bald-faced lie! How dare you speak to him that way?"

"Our plans were known to the enemy."

"Last night was an accident -- Mathis was discovered by no fault of ours. A tragic mistake; being in the wrong place at the wrong time. I know," she ended with a snarl.

Giles brushed the denial aside.

"McConaghie was hanged by bounty hunters. But it is not only of last night I speak. Two days ago there was another run." Barbara expressed surprise which he dismissed with a grimace. "Do not say you are in ignorance. The conductor was caught in the woods and the slave removed from his custody."

"We knew nothing of that. They did not come to our house --"

"He knew." A finger jabbed the air with cutting ferocity. "And a week before that another failed run. He -- your husband, madam -- has been privy to our plans." To cut off debate, Antony added, "I told him. To his face."

"Here?" Seth cried. "Here, at the house? That is impossible. I have been on the farm; I have not come to town."

"You speak falsehood."

"Someone has misrepresented --"

"I spoke to you, myself. On Miss Betty's word you could be trusted. We discussed the escape routes; the other people involved. And all have been caught."

"Not I. I swear."

"You are good at swearing -- Captain Ward." His face contorted in fury. "And better at collecting your 'finder's fee' from the Simpson Agency. Easy money for a farmer with few crops to sell. I suppose you will say you did it for your family. What is the cost of a darkie's life in exchange for your comfort?"

Seth rushed forward but Nelander intervened. Jaw set, eyes flashing, she startled Giles by thrusting the baby into his arms.

"Take her. If you believe what you say and will not listen to reason, dash that innocent life to the floor and stomp it out. Take your revenge if that is what you believe, without listening to my explanation."

The baby began to howl. Instinctively cradling it a moment, Antony recoiled, then moaned.

"I have given the explanation. Your husband's comfort. Take back this child."

"I will not. She is your adopted niece. Do with her what you will. As family, I trust you, though that trust does not work both ways."

He leaned forward, eyes protruding, cords in his neck swollen from tortured passion.

"I told Captain Ward, myself! There can be no mistake."

The horrible truth settled over the gathering like a black cloud of miasma.

"Dear God in heaven. You spoke to him."

Triumph held no sweetness.

"I did."

"If you spoke to a man purporting to be Captain Ward," Nelander articulated through clenched teeth, "it was not Seth, but Norman Ward, his brother."

"Oh, sweet Jesus!" Seth swore, words wrenched from tightened throat muscles. And then, more vehemently, "That bastard! The son of a bitch!"

Rising from her chair, Mrs. Giles leaned against her son. He shoved the baby into her arms before declaring, "I know of no Norman Ward."

"A man so closely resembling Seth they might be twins."

"You are making this up."

"Indeed, I am not. Few know of him. Norman has recently come from the army and has been staying with us." Her eyes closed as inner turmoil exploded throughout her body. "I suspected he was up to no good, but this...." She turned her eyes to Antony's red-rimmed orbs. "Seth and I spoke of a spy in the house. But never considered the possibility that person came from our own."

"He called himself by your name," Giles protested.

"Take a closer look. At Seth. Study his face. They are similar in appearance but not identical. The hair," she demanded, grasping at straws stolen from a kitten's portrait. "Seth is brown-haired. Norman's is lighter. Almost flaxen. Surely, you remember."

Giles drew nearer, trembling from the significance of his mistake.

"You are not he. But I thought.... I did not know you well. He spoke of his wife and children as though...."

"As though he were I. Details he has learned by living under my roof. That," Seth snarled, turning to Nelander, "is evil."

"I would not disagree."

The mulatto dropped back and began tearing at his hair. Unable to endure the sight and fully aware the mistake had been an honest one, Nelander quickly interceded.

"Enough! We need not beat up on ourselves. We have enemies aplenty who will do that for us. Say we have learned from our mistakes and move on."

"But those I betrayed --"

"No betrayal."

"Lives have been lost."

"Not the lives of brown men and women," she stressed, glancing at Mrs. Giles for confirmation. The lady nodded. "Only freedom."

"Easy for you to say," the young man spat, still trembling. "When that is all one has known, it is simple to overlook the torments of bondage for another."

"I say only freedom," she harshly corrected, "meaning their slavery as temporary."

"They will never again escape --"

"You are forgetting the War, sir." Pronouncing the word with an upper case "W," she succeeded in capturing his attention.

"But it is being waged over States' Rights."

"Aye, for now. But a Federal victory with subjugation of the Southern states will see great changes wrought. If President Lincoln does not free the Africans during the conflict, Congress surely shall once peace is declared. As punishment for disunion, if nothing else."

"And if the Confederacy wins?"

"Unthinkable."

Hands dropping listlessly to his side, Giles sagged and could not meet Seth's gaze.

"I am sorry, sir, that I doubted you. But it seemed.... When Mute Thomas brought us news this morning of McConaghie's hanging, I knew it must be you who sold them out."

"You told 'me' of his plans last evening?"

"No. I did not see 'Captain Ward' yesterday. Nor did I speak with Mathis. Had I, I would have warned him against you. He went on his own."

Nelander bristled. "So you thought Seth and I were traitors?"

"No. Not you. My second mother speaks highly of 'Nelander.' I would never go against Betty's judgment."

"She does not feel the same about Captain Ward?"

Caught in his own tangle, Giles shrugged.

"What was I to think? Since the body was discovered on the Windsor farm, I could see no other explanation." He sighed and the confession took the wind from his sails. "In any case, I spoke openly of McConaghie's work to you -- to your brother, rather. I am responsible for his death."

"And by so doing, saved my life."

Giles' eyes narrowed. "What are you saying?"

"Norman sold your information to the Simpson Agency, but he was content to let it go at that, without implicating his sources. Last night was an entirely different case." She hesitated, then shuddered. "Norman is the... captain... of the gang raiding the farmers hereabout. Their rendezvous last night had nothing to do with bounty hunting. The meeting was held near our farm, I presume, as a convenience for Norman. His men stumbled across Mathis and his passenger by accident. Or, perhaps it was the other way around. Mathis thought it was I coming through the woods and revealed himself. He either recognized one or more of them, or they feared his knowledge would somehow endanger Norman's... cover. So they killed him."

"But how did that affect you? You... saw it?"

"No; nor learned of his murder until this morning. I went to keep my appointment and waited behind the strawberry patch. Mathis never came -- but Norman Ward did. *Since he knew my reason for being there* he warned me to go home and say nothing."

"Then, you are still in danger."

"I think not. If Norman had chosen, he could have turned me over to his men then and there and they would have hanged me alongside poor Mathis."

"Evil bastards, as you say," Giles finally remarked, shoulders squared. "It is a lesson. Trust no one."

"No, son. Take care in those you call friend. Nelander and Captain Ward have proven themselves. They are family."

Acknowledging the truth of her words, he suddenly began shaking. "Damn me for a fool." Taking Paula, he rested a brown hand on her forehead in a form of blessing. "I offer apology; and ask your permission to return this... niece of the Giles' to her room."

Although desiring to return home as soon as possible, refusal would have been tantamount to a slap in the face. Sensing approval, Antony brought the baby back into the nursery. Paula began crying when he put her down, but the doll placed between two tiny hands quickly diverted her attention and the sobs faded into gurgles of delight.

"You will stay, then? For coffee?"

"Thank you."

Settling in around the great table in the dining room, Mrs. Giles rang and ordered refreshment. Another servant quickly obeyed, bringing the beverage on a silver tray, along with bread, butter and a plate of honey comb. To break the uneasy silence, Seth noted the sweetener.

"I see Mute Thomas has brought you a present."

"Another benefit of your generosity," Mrs. Giles agreed with a smile. "Although I would prefer strawberry jam, this is an acceptable alternative. Now: we were speaking of Patricia." They were not, but no one objected to the change in topic. "I am most impressed with her. You have raised her well, for I never knew a more polite child. Or a more intelligent one. She speaks knowledgeably on many subjects."

"That is Seth's doing," Barbara spoke before he could throw credit on her. "She and her brother were already well schooled before I came."

"But Nelander has given them a wider breadth that I could have done with my books. She has seen the world and made it come alive for them. Opened their horizons."

"They are very fortunate to have two parents who care. That is a gift of inestimable value. And her talent as an artist: you must let me help develop it. Not only with lessons, but by introducing her to men with influence. Her work must be seen and judged by art critics. In the future, a display of her paintings. In New York. Or Philadelphia, or perhaps Chicago."

The enormity of the suggestion stunned.

"You think she is that good?"

"I do. It is about time the west is represented in the eastern galleries. For too long we have been presented to the masses by sketch artists from the newspapers and magazines. We all know how they lean. To the sensational. The outlaws and the lawmen. I would have it otherwise." Her voice trailed off before she quickly rapped on the table with the handle of a butter knife. "I have it!"

"What, Mrs. Giles?"

"Victoria," she corrected with a smile. "There are two ways to fight a war. With bullets and with words. Let us add a third: images. You say, Nelander, there is a chance President Lincoln or the Congress may free the Africans. Hope is not enough. Let us give them ammunition. Portraits of slaves. Faces of hope and fear; tear-stained countenances. Expressions of resolution; anger. The terror of those recaptured. Men, woman and children willing to risk everything for freedom."

"Do you think that possible?"

"Why not? We shall create a public uprising in the North for emancipation. Make this war stand for more than the preservation of the Union. It must wipe out the old and sweep in the new. Only that may justify the terrible loss of life our country faces."

"How to get Patricia's paintings north?"

"You forget, Captain Nelander, I am a very wealthy woman. Between the very rich, doors are always open. And note: it is easier to smuggle a painting through the lines than a slave."

Her listeners cringed but could not disagree. Only Seth had a disparaging note.

"But to leave her here? I will miss her."

"Although that would be my preference, for I have grown so fond of her company, I cannot deprive you. I will prepare a paint box for her to take back to the Pirate Treasure. No," she decided as suddenly. "She must do her oils here for she is not advanced enough yet, to blend and capture highlights. And oil takes too long to dry. We require immediacy. She will draw in colored pencil. Those may be rolled and hidden in a valise or a carpetbag. And we shall call them... 'Sketches Along the Underground Railroad.'"

Nelander caught her breath.

"A new 'Drinking Gourd.' This one directing our Cause to follow the eastern stars."

"In the night sky," Giles added. "The black horizon."

His poetry carried the motion and the four freedom fighters raised their cups in toast.

Same war.

Different front.

Clutching her box of colored pencils, Patricia bounced in the back of the wagon.

"Hurry, Captain Papa. I am eager to get started."

"What shall you draw first?" he asked, ignoring the request for more speed.

"Miss Betty and Thomas. And their house. I like the way it looks; the baskets hanging on the walls. And the smoke house." Her face reflected sadness. "And I want to draw Miss Theresa and baby Samuel. How they looked that night they came to the Pirate Treasure. And the elephant! Remember that? The spirit of the elephant and how she said she was going to call the baby Samuel Elephant!"

"That is a good beginning."

"And you, mother," she added, touching Nelander with her address. "How brave you were, hiding them in the outhouse."

"No braver than your father; or either of you," she added, affectionately glancing back at her children.

"And Nigger Hole: the people there."

"But you must not call it that," Seth winced. "That is a slur."

Being twelve-years old gave the child wisdom lost by an adult.

"Yes, papa, but it is real. Calling it 'Little Lawrence' is a lie."

"A white lie," Nelander observed. "She is right." Tapping him on the arm as he drew the reins to the left, she asked, "Where are we going? Through the fields, again?"

"No. I have a stop to make before we go home."

He did not elucidate and she did not ask.

Maneuvering through the streets, occasionally nodding to an acquaintance but more often keeping his eyes lowered, Seth brought the wagon to a stop outside the undertaker's shop. Handing the reins to Nelander, he jumped down.

"I will only be gone a minute."

Hands in his pockets, Seth strode to the boardwalk, trod heavily on the rickety wooden slats, then pushed open the door. Inside, he stopped, too suddenly, fortified his nerve and forced himself to peruse the display of coffins Ted Ginnis had added to the interior decoration. While a customer could expect no less upon entering such an establishment, the too patent reminders of death caused his stomach to churn.

"Hello?"

"Back here!" The reverend, who carried the title from adoption rather than pedigree, appeared from the rear, wiping his hands on a cloth. Recognizing the visitor, he affected a twisted grin. "Grim business. But someone has to do it. We're all mortal, you know." Piously raising his eyes, he inspected the ceiling. "But there are better ways of meeting your maker than hanging. Ugly death."

"They brought Mr. McConaghie here?"

"Sheriff did. About an hour ago. Come to pay yer respects? Didn't think you an' he got along so well."

Seth dragged his foot over the floor, creating a small pile of loose sawdust.

"Death has a way of erasing old wounds. I'd like to see him... if that's allowed."

"Don't see why not. Ain't like he's gonna have a bevy of visitors." Ginnis shrugged. "Seen his boys around. Even they ain't been in. But Mathis ain't pretty."

"I know death," the farmer stated with terse, one syllable words.

The undertaker continued as though he had remained silent. "No one's gonna pay to have him fixed up. Nor buy a buryin' box, either, much less any service. Mebbe you feel the way you do, but most don't, I reckon."

Brushing by, Seth shot him a warning.

"Leave me alone with him."

Ted Ginnis busied himself behind the counter.

Slipping sideways so as not to have to touch the back door, Seth removed his hat and crept up to the body. It had been laid out on a wooden slab. The clothes had been removed. Seth covered the remnants of a man with a sheet, granting him the last final dignity of passing.

"I'm sorry for what happened to you, Mathis," he whispered. "I don't know if you were a good man or a bad man, but you had a goodness in you I never thought. I guess I owe you for that.... And for what you did for Mrs. Giles." Speaking the name aloud in a strange, unprotected place gave him the shivers and he hurried on. "Some things you might have done differently, but I don't hold them against you. Now."

Creeping closer, he tried to avoid staring at the bloated face, instead fixing his attention on a hand which hung below the sheet. He cleared his throat.

"You said you were afraid of ghosts. I hope you know better, now. Peter says there aren't any bad spirits. Those you mighta been scared of have probably come to take you away. I'm glad for that. I don't expect you'll have anything to say to my boy and that's just as well. Leave him be. We'll pray for you."

Sinking slowly to his knees, Seth knit his fingers and bowed his head. After completing a prayer, he got up and sidled to his right.

"Good-bye, Mathis." His voice cracked. "I hope you can run those dogs of yours in heaven. Go after those coons. Chase 'em up a tree. But no shootin', remember? There's no killing up there. Every creature's got a right to the afterlife. Coons. Squirrels. Hounds. Even men whose wives got a disease and go wanderin' in the night. I'm hopin' there's forgiveness for everybody. Up in the Lord's country, maybe we forget the pain we got down here. That'd make it just about right."

Fighting tears by biting his lip, he gave a solemn farewell.

Returning to the office, Seth reached in his pocket and took out a coin. It felt warm from the heat of his body.

"This is for your trouble," he said, handing it to Ginnis. "I want him buried proper. Dressed up. In a nice... coffin. With a prayer service. This cover it?"

Ted Ginnis took the money, eyes wide.

"More'n enough. Buy him silver handles for the box, too. And a satin pillow. I 'spect he'd like that. Mathis was always one who wanted to be a fancy fellow. Stay here; I'll write it up."

"No need."

"But don't you want change? A receipt?"

"I trust you. Keep whatever's left. For the next... poor bastard who comes in."

Ginnis hitched a shoulder, only too happy to comply. But he could not give up the explanation so easily.

"Never took you for one who absolved so completely, Seth. Not when he's been hurt like you was. And to pay up for a funeral."

The captain farmer had no more to say.

Like as not, were Reverend Ginnis to die, he would find no coin in his pocket to defray the expenses.

As much as some things changed, others remained resolute.

"Good day."

"I'll hold service in the morning. At the graveyard behind the church."

"Never been there."

Which ended the conversation as surely as innocents found God.

With or without consecrated ground.

Stepping out into the bright sunshine, Seth squinted, then shaded his eyes. Despite the heat, he felt a chill. Nelander slid over so he could resume his seat.

"Had something I had to do," he said.

"All right."

"Had to get rid of Norman's coin. The one he gave me to buy a dog for old man Willingham."

"A hound from Mathis," she acknowledged.

The cold he felt transferred to her.

"Louis'll have to find his own dog."

It would come from neither Mathis McConaghie nor Dr. Hank McTree. Both were out of the dog breeding business.

CHAPTER 28

It would have been different if they came in the night. Sneaking around like thieves, doing their stealing under cover of darkness. Men who were afraid of being caught; men who dared not show their faces. Not from shame, perhaps, but fear of the law.

Much had changed in so short a time. Lincoln's "Six Weeks War" died an ugly death at Bull Run and might have proven Nelander's "unthinkable" prediction dead wrong right then and there if Confederate leaders had not held Thomas Jonathan Jackson back from charging Washington with his victorious brigades.

As July turned to August, tall stalks, heavy with wheat, ripened. Silk on the ends of fat ears of corn turned brown. And men, neither laborers nor soldiers, came to take what was not theirs. In the light of day, without bothering to cover their faces. Some wore slouch hats, either broad-brimmed or with one side pinned to the crown. On several, tassels in the shape of acorns or bullets dangled from leather straps. Others sported kepis or forage caps, high in back, low in front. One or two had straw headgear with ribbons around the circumference. Always black, the bands lent a festive air to the harbingers of death.

These were not government agents, not in the regular sense. They were bandits, bent on supporting one side or the other. Sometimes, it did not matter. They robbed for money or a quick turnaround on what they stole. The newspapers called them "guerrillas." The townspeople styled them murderers.

Seth and Thomas had the wagon more than half full with corn when they appeared over the horizon. One man leading, the rest following. They halted on the crest of a hill and watched the harvesting.

Thomas clapped his hands to catch Seth's attention and pointed their way. The farmer gave grim acknowledgment.

"I see them."

The freeman arched an eyebrow as much as to say, What do we do, now? Seth shrugged.

"We can't fight them. There are too many." Thomas touched his own face. "Yes. I know. I've seen them around, too. What does it matter if we can identify them? Sheriff Bochner doesn't have any deputies. They've all gone off to war. Or resigned their positions. He can't fight them alone, either."

As if hearing the discussion, although they were too far away for the softly spoken words to travel, the leader raised a hand. Military style. As though he were directing a troop of dragoons against a band of helpless Indians. They moved forward in columns of twos. They had been well trained, if outlaws could be said to have discipline.

"Mornin'," the man on the front horse greeted.

Seth took off his hat and fanned his face.

"Morning." The suffix good would be left for another time. One more appropriate to the occasion.

"Looks like you've got a good crop this year. Better'n most. Corn. And wheat, too. Make a lot of meal and flour to feed hungry men."

"That's why I grow it. To feed men, woman and children."

He must have said something amusing for a few snickered.

"Planning on taking it to market?"

"I am."

"Must be figurin' on makin' a pretty penny. Corn and wheat is sellin' high these days."

"That's the idea."

"Well, I'm afraid I'll have to disillusion you."

"How's that, then?"

"You're donatin' it all to the cause."

"what cause would that be, then?"

"Our cause."

"You're not army."

"Wouldn't matter if we were. There's all kinds of quartermasters out this way on the same mission. Buyin' for the troops."

"You're buying, then? Come to give me a fair price? If you are, I'm willing to dicker. Take some off if your boys are willing to help Thomas and I do the picking."

The man smiled. He had crooked teeth and a slow drawl. Not from Kansas. Missouri, Seth guessed. The Boothills. Missouri had gone for the

South but it remained bitterly divided. Kansas had sided with the Union. Shared borders rendered most politics moot.

"We'll do the pickin' all right, but I'm afraid all I have to offer you is your life. How much you figure it's worth?"

"Three fields of wheat and two of corn?" Seth guessed.

The officer liked his answer.

"You'll be sensible, won't you?" He pointed a stirruped foot at the farmer's musket.

"That's for shooting varmints."

"There's some call us that. Unwanted pests."

"You don't do yourself credit. You're much more than that."

The rider leaned forward. "You a smart talker?"

"I'm a man who's about to lose his livelihood."

The answer appeased. "You'll make do."

"Don't see how. I got a mortgage. Bills to pay."

"You ain't alone. Your neighbors are in the same fix."

"Thanks to you."

"Might be better if you just joined up and went off to fight. Give you something constructive to do." The robber's smile widened. "But then, if you did that, who'd plant the crops we come by next year to raid?"

The joke elicited rough guffaws.

"Think you'll be around, then?"

"Don't see why not. Who's to stop us?"

"Maybe the Union boys."

"Why would they? We're doin' their work for 'em. Saves them the ill will of the people, stealin' your crops the way they do."

"I heard President Lincoln's representatives paid for the corn and wheat."

The officer stood in his stirrups and gave hand signals to his men. They dispersed, some crossing to the wagon, others drifting away to the wheat fields, long sickles hanging from their saddles.

"What they pay this year they won't next. That's a fair statement."

Seth reached down and slowly picked up his weapon. No one made a move to stop him. He cradled it in the crook of his arm.

One man against twenty. Not much of a contest.

"Leave my horse and wagon alone."

"Gotta have some way of totin' off the crops, Mr. Stiff-Upper-Lip."

Hopelessness gave birth to resolution.

"You've got your own. Over the hill. Outta sight. But they're there. Leave my horse and wagon, I say."

"Had that old crow bait long?"

"Since he was a colt. He's old, now. No use to you. But he's mine an' I owe him."

"Turn him out to pasture when he breaks down?"

"That's the idea."

"Expensive proposition, isn't it? Feedin' a horse that's outlived its usefulness?"

"Men get old. Doesn't mean we shoot 'em."

"You shoot me if you had the chance?"

Seth raised the gun and aimed it. The man on horseback did not flinch. The farmer spoke while staring down the barrel.

"No. But I wouldn't hire you, either. From what I've seen of other men's fields, you and your boys do a mighty poor job of clearin' 'em off."

Third time the charm.

One last smile.

"Put down the weapon."

"You're not taking my horse and wagon."

"You'd give your life for a horse when you wouldn't fight for your crops?"

"They were meant to go. The horse stays. I told you. I owe him. A man's gotta stand for something. If he gives up on a dumb beast, then he's lost everything."

"Your wife consider that a fair exchange? You dyin' for a horse we're gonna take, anyway?"

"I don't speak for her."

"What's the horse's name?"

"Blaze."

"You figure she'd rather have Blaze in her bed than you, farmer-man?"

"I figure she'd rather shoot you between the eyes."

Several of the hooligans began circling around Seth. Thomas made a move to stop them, but one rested a pistol against his temple and he froze in his tracks. The fire did not go out of his eyes, however, and another raised his rifle at him for good measure.

The officer patted the neck of his mount. In case it was skittish at the sound of gunpowder igniting.

"You wouldn't shoot me but she would?"

"You've come to it."

"I'd like to meet her."

"No. You wouldn't."

The flat denial finally wore the marauder's patience. Snapping gloved fingers, he indicated the hills where they had come.

"Doohand, go get the wagons. Bring 'em up and get 'em loaded. The sun's hot. We gotta be done by nightfall."

"What about ol' Blaze, here, lieutenant? We're short on walkin' stock and this here boy's got a lot of corn."

"Leave him." He pointed toward Seth. "You and the darkie go sit in the wagon and wait. Don't shift around. Don't stand up to piss. Don't talk." He had almost finished, before adding, "Leave the musket." His lip curled in derision. "Unless you 'owe' it, too."

Seth dropped the weapon, turned his back and motioned Thomas. Together, they went to the wagon. Blaze flicked his tail at them as they passed. Seth did not scratch his ears and he went back to grazing. The pair settled in the back and did not move again.

By evening the thieves had stripped the field bare. Piling their ill-gotten gain into wagons, they covered the tops with tarps, then the leader directed they "Get a move on." The one named Doohand saluted.

Mounting what might have been a dragoon horse were he a proper military man, the leader rode toward the farmers.

"You said you wouldn't shoot me, mister. And you wouldn't hire me. I've been wonderin'. What would you do with me?"

Seth had had a long time to contemplate his answer.

"Send you to the front lines."

The reply intrigued.

"Which side?"

"It doesn't matter. Rebel or Yankee: a sharpshooter's a sharpshooter."

"You'd have another man do your killin' for you?"

He nodded. "To make your death count for something. If I shot you, you'd just fill in an empty hole of consecrated ground. In Virginia, I hear the worms are hungry. Everything's gotta eat. That'd be your worth."

The soldier who fought for no side but his own made a low retching noise. Spurring the flank of his mouth, he made a circuit around the wagon and rode off. Whatever last words he might have had he kept to himself.

The high-pitched, unearthly keening traveled on the wind with piteous abandon. Reaching a crescendo, it drifted aimlessly for a torturous beat, faded, then began anew in an ancient version of a timeless song. Combining infinite sorrow with supreme agony, the sound might have originated from Mother Nature wailing over the needless slaughter of a herd of buffalo, the destruction wrought to a mountain blasted away for the Iron Horse, or the irreparable damage done to a dammed river.

Following the scream came silence. Of the kind usually heard at kirk yards, choked by weeds of disillusion and shattered faith.

One minute. Two. Then sharp ringing noises, one following another with arrhythmic symmetry.

From the house, Peter Ward clutched his mother's hand. Even in the darkness of unbroken night, the paleness of his flesh glowed with an unearthly sheen.

"What is papa doing?"

"Chopping wood."

"At night? There is no light to see by."

Asked by youth to age. To explain the inexplicable.

Nelander had no obligation to reply. She did so to assuage the future. One day, some small voice would ask the same of him.

"He does not need light."

"He may cut himself."

"This is a special occasion." Where angels protect the corporeal form of Man from wanton self-destruction.

"When will he come in? Supper is on the table."

"Soon."

Patricia came beside them and laid a hand on her brother's shoulder.

"Papa Captain is angry," she said. Easier for her to explain. Treading the line between child and adulthood, she possessed the vocabulary to transcend both worlds.

"Because those men stole our corn?"

"Because he didn't fight them. He is taking it out on the wood."

"Oh."

The universal acknowledgment of having reached a consensus, however obscure.

A spark from the blade flared, briefly illuminated the night, then faded. One tiny firefly amidst a star-studded sky. Impotent by itself, time suspended as the pseudo-insect waited for others to follow its example. None did.

Symbolizing the eye of a lighthouse being forever extinguished.

A curse, followed by the disruption of shadow: one black form moving within another. A gesture of violent upheaval, the movement of air, then in the distance, a thud.

Seth had picked up and thrown a piece of firewood. In so doing, a splinter had jammed itself under his fingernail. Blood flowed in sacrifice. Pain briefly engulfed his universe. It served to sever past from present. Rage subsided.

Shaking his hand, then biting out the splinter with his teeth, he drove the axe head deep into the chopping block, paused to consider the damage he had wrought, then jerked at his shoulder where a suspender had slipped down his arm. Putting himself to rights, he cursed again because it meant nothing, and came inside.

Peter tried to rush forward but Patricia held him back. Dardanelles, the orange runt, arched her back and hissed. Herman woofed and Squash, wagging its tail, came out from underneath the table to sniff the new arrival. Seth made no attempt to pet the dog, instead staring at the space recently occupied by the feline.

"I hate cats."

He meant, I hate myself, and Nelander said nothing, fully aware cats needed no defense and the man's anger had burned itself out.

"Supper is getting cold."

"I am not hungry."

It would be a night of negations.

They went to the table and Patricia doled out the portions. A simple meal of cornbread, cheese and apple slices, it did not take long to consume. Afterward, Barbara made tea which Seth left untouched until it had grown tepid. Slumping in his chair, he held his head in his hands. She correctly read the signal to speak.

"There was nothing you could do. Twenty against two. You saved the horse and wagon. No one could have done more and most appreciatively less."

"They took it all -- the corn and the wheat. We have nothing left."

"All right."

"It is not all right. First, there was the damned drought and then the flood. Now, we have a war on our hands where men may steal with impunity."

Although not meaning to catch his eye, Nelander grinned.

"It appears I am bad luck."

His head shot up before the expression had quite faded.

"What do you mean?"

"In the four years I have been here, you have suffered drought, flood and war. Your own checklist," she ticked off on her fingers. "That is a very poor track record. If I were a ship, I would have earned myself a bad name. I would be a jinx ship. No one would sail on me."

"It has nothing to do with you. You are completely blameless."

"Ah. Just as you are completely blameless for what happened today."

His nose flared which drew back his upper lip. "You set me up for that."

"I was merely stating facts."

His mouth worked as if he were chewing tobacco.

"You have been a very valuable addition to the... crew."

"I work for free," she agreed. "Inasmuch as you never paid me a wage. That is a compensation, I suppose. But I eat and take up space."

"You have given me a daughter."

"Not without some assistance on your part, sir. Or we have a miracle on our hands."

He huffed. "You are trying to make me feel better."

"If I plead guilty, is that another black mark against me?"

"Without crops to sell, we have no money."

"Back to that, again."

"This time, you have no savings and it is a long way to the next strawberry harvest. Even if that were a saving grace. I suppose they will steal the fruit, too, when the time comes. I should have shot the bastard."

"Why? So Patricia and Peter could have planted him in the ground? What crop do you suppose he would sprout?"

"You could have used him for fertilizer."

"I am not a Pilgrim." She paused to contemplate. "Interesting. The word is pronounced 'pil-grum,' yet it is spelled with an 'i' and not a 'u.' As in 'pil-*grim.*' As if spelling were some sort of pre-destination."

He crossed his legs, one foot shaking in nervous agitation.

"Yes. I am Seth Ward. 'Ward,' as in cell. I am ready for the madhouse." When she did not disagree, he demanded, "What does 'Nelander' mean?"

"'Landers from the country of 'Ne.'"

"You made that up."

"Of course."

His chest shook but he could force out no laughter.

"What are we going to do?"

"There is only one thing we can do. Send banker Provost off as a soldier. And while we're at it, we might as well recruit his entire bevy of shareholders. That will make a clean slate of it. If we ask politely, perhaps 'General Daly' will supply them with uniforms."

This time, she elicited a grunt.

"Can't they afford their own?"

"Certainly. But men of finance are more accustomed to spending other's money."

Aware that he had recently held this conversation before, Seth asked, "What side shall we recruit them for?"

"Not the Rebels, that's for damned sure. Rebels never have enough to eat. Provost's constant whining will only inspire more raiders to steal from farmers. He must be a Yankee."

"I am sure he has no idea how to discharge a weapon. And his shoes -- they will be worn out in a week of hard marching. He will make a poor soldier. How can we expect to win the war with men like him in the ranks?"

Patricia had the answer.

"I think we out to make him an ambassador. That way, he can go to England or France and never be heard from again."

He finally convulsed, feet landing on the floor to stead his shaking body. "Motion carried!"

The unanimous agreement did not really solve their problems, but it opened the door for a night's rest and a renewed fortification for the morning. Temporarily putting off the consignment of the 'landers' from 'Ne' into a 'ward' of the madhouse.

"Someone's coming, Captain Papa."

Ceasing his walk around the living room which had worn a path in the rug, Seth went to the door. Picking up his musket which the thieves had left in the stubble, he checked to be certain it held a charge, then peered out over the pane.

"One rider."

Nelander joined him.

"Who is it? Can you make it out?"

"Not from this distance."

"It is Rum," Peter identified. The horse, not the man. Seth stiffened.

"I will shoot his brains out." The man, not the horse.

Jerking the door open, he strode into the yard. Choosing a place under the Skull and Crossbones, he made his stand, waiting patiently for the rider to reach accurate shooting distance. Seeing the intent, Norman slowed his mount to a walk. Seth waved him forward.

"A little nearer so I may be assured to put this bullet between your eyes."

"Never there, big brother. Even a sharpshooter cannot always strike a target so small. Aim for the chest. Not as spectacular when a body is hit but just as deadly. And that is the point, is it not?"

"What do you want? You were never to come on this land again."

"And I meant to keep my word. But circumstances changed. May I dismount and speak to you?"

"No. We have nothing to say to one another."

Taking that as tacit permission, or disdaining the idea his brother would shoot him in cold blood, the former dragoon slid a leg over the saddle and landed lightly on his feet.

"We have, or I would not be here. I do not come... lightly. Will you invite me in?"

"Why should I?" Seth shifted the rifle from one hand to the other. "You do not need an invitation. You do what you want and take what you want."

"We have things to discuss. I am here -- to make an apology."

He knew his way through the door just as surely as his brother's heart. Seth slowly lowered the weapon.

"It will not take long? I have work to do." His voice tightened. "Fodder to gather for the winter."

"No. It will not take long."

"Tie your horse at the railing. Peter, do not touch it. Let it be."

A disappointed, "Yes, sir," preceded a lowering of his head. Scuffing his foot, he brightened as a new idea occurred. "I have another horse. Her name is Fleet, Uncle Norman. I got her from --"

"The filly is not yours," his father interrupted, more for the sake of cutting off the name Peter meant to speak than denial.

"Oh, come. We are all friends here." Spreading her arms, Nelander bade Norman welcome. She did so with a sour expression, conveying their full and complete comprehension that the visitor knew well to whom Peter referred. Ignoring the sarcasm proved easier than he imagined.

"Thank you. I would like to think so."

Assuming first rights as a guest, Norman crossed the threshold then hesitated, unclear whether they would allow him to sit and where. The Wards answered his doubts by staking a place just inside and going no further.

"What have you to say that will not take long?"

"A mistake occurred yesterday. I had issued standing orders that your farm was not to be touched. There was apparently some... confusion. Barnaby and his troop should have bypassed your fields but did not. Thank God," he added in an undertone, "there was no violence. You did well, Seth, not to resist."

"Yes. I know. I can be counted on to be a coward. I am not like my brother, the great Indian fighter. The -- captain -- of a band of lawless outsiders."

Norman's pupils dilated as he glanced around the interior, darkened by drawn curtains meant to keep out heat.

"No coward, sir. They would have killed you."

"This is your apology?" Sweating profusely, Seth stood back a foot from the door. "Very well. You have said your peace. Your orders were disobeyed. I add only, that is the mark of a poor commander."

"They will be punished --"

"Yesss," Seth drawled. "The same way pa punished us with a hickory stick when he thought us behaving in... unchristian ways. That, as you can see, had mixed results."

"You never liked him, did you? I always thought that. I'm not sure you were any fonder of ma. And certainly not of Rick. Between the two of us, I was the more faithful son."

"What of it?"

"I don't know. Just thinking out loud." He hooked both thumbs under his cavalry belt. "I never understood you. Barnaby told me you refused to give up your horse. That was brave."

"If you have said all you have come for, I ask you to leave. And remember your promise. This time, do not break it. Never come back, or next time I will shoot you. Whether you come alone or in the company of your renegades. You are an abomination."

"Because I am tired of risking my life for nothing but another's glory? Of earning less than a stage driver? Of sleeping on the prairie with no roof over my head? Or of my failure to stand tall for a flag which has done nothing for me?"

"For stealing my identity and using it against oppressed people."

"Ah. That. So little a matter. No one was harmed by my little deception."

"If you do not consider being returned to bondage 'harmed,' then you are lower than a snake."

"Now who is abandoning principal, brother? I was merely carrying out the law and making money on the side. Supplying the Simpson Agency

with ill-gotten information aided them in bringing criminals to justice."
Tugging on an ear, he added, "McConaghie was not my fault."

"Your men hanged him."

"Because he was where he should not have been. Had I known there was
a slave transfer in progress that night, I would have called my rendezvous
for another place. Giles said nothing of it and so I presumed all was quiet."

"'Mr. Giles' to you, bastard."

He shrugged. "Very well. I have said my piece. Now I offer restitution."
Reaching into the pocket of his short leather jacket, Norman produced a
tightly wadded roll of money. "I am here to pay for the corn and wheat."

"That which was stolen?"

"Yes."

"Have you also made restitution to the others? To Louis Willingham?
To Abe Benshaw and Joe Wilkie, who also had their crops stolen?"

"No. Of course not. They are nothing to me."

"Then I cannot accept your guilt money."

"Call it what you will. I am offering you twice what you would have
gotten at market -- and throwing in the free labor."

If he meant to jest, the humor fell flat.

"I do not want it."

"Are you so rich, then, you can afford to refuse me? What of your
obligations to the bank?"

"We shall be like all the rest. We shall default."

"What foolishness is this? What pigheaded stupidity? Take the money."
He thrust it out. "It is yours. Fairly earned."

"You sold it, already?"

"I have sent it on its way. Across the river. To Missouri. The money will
come back to me. Does that satisfy?"

"No."

Norman finally leered at his older brother. "What is it which makes you
stand on your high horse? The fact your precious corn and wheat is to feed
enemy soldiers? What if I told you it is to go to the Union? They pay in
gold."

"They did not pay me."

"I am acting as the middleman. Surely," he addressed Nelander, "you can see that?"

"What I 'see' and you do not is that Seth and I and the children live here. Willingham and Benshaw and Wilkie and the rest you stole from are our neighbors. If we were to come out... ahead on the deal while they suffer... there would be hard feeling. Resentment. Is that plain enough language even you can understand?"

"So... Nelander, if these good people found out your brother-in-law paid you while stiffing them, they would burn you out. Hardly what I would call friends."

"They are no worse than others and better than you. Your men would have murdered Seth in the field, had he resisted. You said so, yourself. Therefore, you are equally guilty of intent if not deed. Your men murdered Mathis McConaghie. What threat was he? That he could identify your 'boys'? Say 'yea' and I will know you for a liar. The men who came yesterday wore no hoods. Seth could describe each to Sheriff Bochner. Before yesterday, I thought they feared recognition. Now, I know otherwise. They committed murder from sheer wantonness. After your own image, sir. Molded on the frontier fighting Indians under that flag you profess to hate."

Angry and thwarted, Norman thrust out the money.

"Take it. Pay the damn bank. Or give it to your damn neighbors, for all I care."

Tossing the wad to the floor, he stopped to watch it roll under the kitchen table. Squash, the hound puppy bred by Mathis McConaghie, the Underground Railroad conductor, went after it. Suspecting a new game, he barked, madly wagged his tail, then poked it with his wet nose.

By the time he decided the toy had no prospects for fun, Captain Norman Ward had disappeared.

Proving the dog to be a prestidigitator of sorts.

Chapter 29

The roll of money remained under the table two days. On the evening of the third, Seth got on his hands and knees and fetched it out. Slightly soggy from dog saliva, with assorted indentations indicating at least two pair of teeth, the wad remained otherwise intact.

With no thought of saving the string which held the bills together, Seth slit the binding with the blade of his pocketknife. Taking care to wipe the steel against his pant leg before snapping it away, he made a wry face.

"Don't know where it's been."

Nelander, closing observing the action, nodded in harmony. Care should be taken. Not from Herman and Squash but from whatever residue of psychic poison Norman Ward had inadvertently contaminated it with.

Straightening the paper proved a more difficult matter. Having been bound into the shape of a fat cigar for at least 72-hours, the individual bills re-curled immediately after being unpeeled. Grunting in annoyance, Seth tried bending them backward. The effort succeeded but only temporarily, finally forcing him to separate the denominations and hold down the edges with the salt cellar and pepper grinder.

"How much?" Nelander typically had a better eye for counting from a distance but the constant rolling had distracted the tally.

"Ten one-hundred dollar bills."

"A thousand dollars. So: his conscience bothered him that much, did it?"

Air emerged through her husband's nose, representing disgust.

"Say, rather, he is making such a good 'livelihood' that he can afford to be over-generous. I give him no credit for having a conscience. I don't think he ever had one. I used to think him... what is the word I want to say? Dull?"

"Immoral?"

"Ah. Yes. Or a combination of the two. As a boy, he never expressed affection for anyone or anything. Have you ever been acquainted with anyone like that, Barbara?"

The use of her first name conveyed the depth of his own emotion.

"Yes; several. Once or twice my father made a mistake and hired on a man as you describe, but more often I saw them ashore. Thoroughly despicable."

"What are we going to do with all this?"

"Spend it on something foolish. Personally, I would like a surrey -- with an overhang to keep your hot Kansas sun off my head."

"Wear a hat," he grinned.

"What would you like?"

"We have already played that game once." Sighing in resignation, he carefully re-rolled the money so meticulously straightened and shoved it in his pocket.

"I suppose we ought to turn it in to the sheriff."

"We could do that. And have it tied up in a legal morass. In the end, it would probably go to the state. That doesn't seen right."

"We can't keep it --"

"-- unless we agreed Norman gave it to us for some other reason. Rent, for example. And food. While he stayed here."

"That makes the Pirate Treasure a pretty expensive boarding house."

"Or, we could say my mother sent it to me from Canada. That much money would go a long way toward paying what we owe on both our properties."

"Your friend, Pete Erlinger, would be the first to say you never received a letter from Nova Scotia."

"All right: hand-delivered from some wandering messenger."

"He would have to be a pretty stupid messenger not to recognize the feel of cash money in an envelope."

"Surely he wrapped it around a jar of -- pickled herring."

"The herring being more valuable than the money?"

"Canadians are all wealthy. Everyone knows that. Or, more truthfully, we could say my mother finally got the money owed her from my father's estate. That which the good magistrate in San Francisco withheld from me, being as I was only a female."

"So is your mother."

"True. But legally, she was Captain Ned Nelander's heir. I suppose by this time she has gotten the proper papers signed and sent off. It has been four long years, Seth. And a lot of starvation in between, I wager."

"Do you really think so? That she has gotten the money from the sale of the Bottom Dollar?"

"Actually, until this moment, I had not given it a thought."

He frowned and joined her in the living room, pulling his rocking chair closer to where she sat on the couch.

"How much was it worth?"

"The ship? Twenty thousand, easily. She was well-maintained, with a good reputation. Those... devils... in San Francisco sold it for $10,000 and then took their cut off the top. I have no idea how much that would have been. And then, Mrs. Nelander would have had to pay legal fees. God knows what that set her back. Another thousand? Men are greedy bastards, Seth."

He cringed, not from the cuss word but her hurt.

"They can be."

"I suppose when it was all said and done, she may have collected five or six thousand. Not much when you consider the lifetime of work my father put into it and the fact she will have to live on the inheritance the rest of her life."

He settled down but not comfortably.

"You have never written to her."

"I have not."

"Don't you suppose she wonders what happened to you?"

"About as often as I wonder what happened to her."

"Some of that money was rightfully yours."

Grasping the direction in which he headed, Nelander slowly shook her head.

"Only if you consider my father meant to bequeath the ship to me -- on the understanding I continue to support my mother. Which I would have done, had things worked out as they should. Since the Bottom Dollar was sold and therefore can no longer bring in any income, whatever she got belongs to her."

"And if she dies? Then, whatever is left is yours as her only living kin. If no one knows how to contact you, it may sit in a bank --"

"Stop it! Put it out of your mind as I have done. I will never write her, I will never go back there and I do not want an inheritance. What I wanted was the ship. Since I did not get it, that is an end to the story." Shaking from anger, she forced herself to take a sip of tea before reverting to the original topic.

"There: I have said it. The bank. I think we ought to take this thousand dollars and bring it to Mr. Provost. To make a deal."

Leaning forward, Seth pretended to fix his gaze on the floor.

"What sort of deal?"

"So far as we know, there have been four farms raided by Norman's bandits. There have probably been others. Will be others," she amended. "That means few if any of us will be able to meet our obligations this fall."

"Just as it was after the drought. When they foreclosed."

"Yes. But this is different. The bank and its shareholders cannot expect immigrants from Boston or any other northern city to flock here and buy up the land. Not with a war in progress. That would be foolhardy. Besides, they got what they were seeking. Kansas came in as a free state and civil strife will determine, once and for all, if slavery is to be prohibited."

Getting up, he paced around the room before ending up at the dining table. Removing the cozy, he poured himself a cup of tea, stirred the warm liquid with a finger, then returned.

"What deal?"

"One thousand dollars, divided five ways. That is two hundred from each of us, to be used as full payment for this year's obligation."

"He will never accept that."

"Those are the terms. Accept partial payment as full or receive nothing. What would you choose?"

"I-am-not-a-banker."

"No, but you are a businessman. Receiving partial payment is better than incurring the ire if not the outright hostility of the people he must associate with. The man lives in Lawrence, for God's sake. You know how short tempers are. Throwing five families out on the street is more likely to get him shot than anything else."

"And next year -- if Norman is still around?"

"We will have to worry about that when the time comes. Perhaps the war will be over by then and some semblance of order restored."

Finishing his tea in several long swallows, Seth wiped his lips with the back of his hand.

"All well and good. But where do we say we got the $1,000 from? And why are we being so generous?" His hands wrapped around the cup. "I like your idea. You are a good-hearted soul. And a clever one. But if I show up with folding cash, people will know damned well where it came from -- my brother. The thief. They will wonder how much else he gave us. Or if I am somehow involved with his scheme."

"Not everyone knows you have a brother -- much less that he is the leader of an outlaw gang pillaging Douglas County."

He waved away the objection. "Let us presume they do."

The truth hit like a tidal wave. Barbara slumped back, eyes shut.

"You are right, of course. I had not thought of that. I guess I expected Provost and the others to take our story on face value without looking a gift horse in the mouth."

"Then we must say the money came from Mrs. Dryfus."

The tiny voice, coming from the hall, caused ripples of surprise. Both adults turned to the child.

"Patricia -- what made you say that?"

Padding into the living room, the hem of her nightshirt trailing across the floorboards, the girl made a slight motion with her hands.

"I didn't mean to overhear, but I couldn't sleep. It's too hot."

"That's all right. Your idea is a good one. But we would have to ask Mrs. Dryfus before we use her name. Do you really believe she would approve?"

"She doesn't think much of the townspeople but she's already decided to be a patron of the arts. That's me," she added with shy pride. "Might as well go all the way and be a patron saint."

"When you put it that way, I don't know how she'd refuse."

Patricia thought about it a moment before agreeing.

"I wouldn't mention any names to her. There are those she'll never forgive; she'd rather see the whole county burn than do any of them a favor."

Seth bit his lower lip. "That woman has hated for a long time." He did not elaborate on whether he meant she ought to bury the hatchet or rake the fires. Whatever Nelander held for Mrs. Dryfus, she did not grant Seth freedom of choice.

"Someone hangs you the way they murdered Marc Giles, I won't waste my time on hate. I'll go after them with the vengeance of the Archangel Gabriel. With or without God's permission."

Repulsed both by the scenario of death and his wife wreaking havoc, Seth waved the future back where it belonged.

"We will go into town in the morning."

Mrs. Dryfus not only found the proposal agreeable, it tickled her funny bone. She allowed them to "Do what you will with my name," and asked no further questions. The most obvious of which would have been, Where did you get one thousand dollars? Not knowing granted permission to think what she cared without becoming bogged down by details.

The fact she guessed correctly had no bearing either way.

Asking to see Mr. Provost at the bank, the clerk waved them away with an imperious air.

"If you've come to beg, I'm to say he isn't in."

Seth glanced at Nelander.

"I told you we ought to have brought that mounted artillery your mother sent from Canada."

"Yes, I know, but I remind you again it would not have fit through the doors."

"Then you aim at the hinges and shoot them off. What's the problem?"

"So much noise will wake the baby. If she begins crying, you will have to console her while I drive the caisson into the bank."

Regretting the pretend part more than he ought, Seth extracted the roll of money from his pocket. Waving it under the clerk's nose, he forced the employee to retreat.

"Will he see us, now? Or shall we deposit this somewhere else?"

"Come right this way, Captain Ward, sir."

The "sir" being in reference to riches instead of rank, he earned himself no credit.

Eliminating the usual prerequisite of announcing customers, Mr. Lanley took them directly to the president's door. Knocking loudly as befit the bearer of good news, he turned the knob and ushered them through. Annoyed at the intrusion, Ronald Provost glowered, striking Bab'ra Nelander with a blow of deja vu. Once before she had crossed this threshold and although on a mission of a different sort, the memory stung.

In 1857 she had been a penniless traveler on a mission of retrieving money rightly her own. His lack of trust and sympathy then left a scar barely healed which present circumstance rudely reopened. She would not play polite penitent a second time.

"What is this, Lanley?"

"They have come to make a deposit, Mr. Provost."

In tribute to his breeding, the banker's face registered no expression. He did, however, bade them welcome.

"Come in. Have a seat. Good to see you, Seth. And you, Mrs. Ward." Allowing the count of three for his assistant to depart, the officer laid his hands on the table, palms down. "This is true? You have cash money to deposit in the bank?"

Seth tossed the wad onto the desk, forcing the banker to cut the new string and count it. He did so with professional calm, using the sides of his fingernails to pry the bills apart.

"One thousand dollars. A great deal of money. Where did you get it?"

If he meant to be rude, he succeeded.

"From Mrs. Dryfus. She wishes Captain Nelander and myself to open a... trust?" Adding a questioning inflection, Seth turned the discussion over to his partner.

"Yes. A Trust. For the farmers of Lawrence. If certain conditions can be met."

"Victoria Dryfus wishes to be philanthropic?"

"As I say: if you are willing to be the executor of her gift."

Color spread into Provost's cheeks and his fingers tapped on the desk blotter.

"Of course. Certainly. If I may be of assistance. But I must know more."

"And there is more to tell. She has offered this great sum of money to be divided fairly between those unfortunates who have suffered at the hands of the renegades: the raiders who are stealing farmer's crops and thus depriving them of their rightful incomes. With which they would have met their obligations to the bank."

He caught on quickly.

"There have been seven to my knowledge." Peering over the top rim of his spectacles, he added, "Or is it eight? Are you among them?"

"We are. Yesterday a band of outlaws came and ravished our fields. They took all the corn and wheat."

"I see. I am sorry. This situation is unendurable. You have spoken to Sheriff Bochner?"

"Yes; we reported it before coming here. But as you know, he does not have a force anywhere near equal to the task of preventing these thefts. He had called upon the army and the troops at Fort Leavenworth for help, but has received little by way of encouragement."

Provost's face darkened further.

"It is a disgrace. What good are soldiers if they cannot protect the citizenry? The militia recruited from Douglas County should have been left here. Personally, I have no interest in what happens in St. Louis. Let their own volunteers handle matters."

Neither of the Wards needed be privy to the banker's political views to shudder at the comment.

"One thousand dollars. To cover all debts owed for the year 1861."

Provost coughed into his hand, then reached for an embroidered handkerchief. Running the linen over his forehead before crossing it under his nose, he put it away with deliberate care while speaking.

"That is hardly enough to cover two farms, let alone eight."

"Not eight, sir: all future farmers who may yet suffer the same fate."

"If this is Mrs. Dryfus' terms, then I cannot accept." Aware of what he stood to lose, Provost picked up the individual one hundred dollar bills and ran them through his fingers. "Where did she get this money? Not from her account here. I have not been informed she withdrew so substantial an amount. I trust she is not keeping so much cash on hand. I am against such a practice. Too dangerous. If she likes, I shall place this in the safe, which I assure, is completely theft-proof."

"She does not like. In fact, we are to say that if you do not agree to her charitable terms, she will withdraw her entire fortune and place it elsewhere. Fort Leavenworth, for instance."

"That would be inconvenient for her foreman who must pay the factory workers --"

"We are not here to argue her position. We are merely attempting to carry out her wishes. If you cannot not -- will not -- adhere to the terms set forth, then you will kindly return the money and we will be on our way."

Beads of sweat collected along the edges of his muttonchops.

"Seth -- Captain Ward -- be reasonable. You, she, is asking me to take one thousand in exchange for four times what is owed."

Resting his hands along the back of the chair he had disdained taking, Seth's eyes narrowed.

"Say, rather, you have the unprecedented opportunity of making one thousand times more than nothing."

Fidgeting at the desk, the banker abandoned all hope of distracting himself and leaned back. The hinges on the oak chair squeaked.

"Why is she doing this? I have never known her for a generous woman."

"Perhaps war has opened her eyes to the suffering of those around her."

"She can afford more."

"Out of consideration for our past acquaintance, I will not tell her you said that."

"Surely, four thousand --"

"We are not here to dicker. Make your decision, for Captain Nelander and I do not wish to return without your answer."

"One thousand for eight...."

"For all who may be ruined."

A small light shone from behind Provost's eyes.

"What if these outlaws are captured and money recovered? What then? Who gets it? Come," he pleaded. "I must have something to tell my shareholders; some glimmer of expectation. The situation we now have is unendurable. The army will come. Or the war will end and the men will return home. Then Bochner will have enough deputies to catch these hooligans."

Nelander made the final determination. Not from pity for the banker and his shareholders but from the absolute conviction no money would ever be recovered.

"Very well. You will put it in writing while we wait. All debts outstanding for the year 1861 to be declared paid in full and no further action taken against any farmer until the fall of 1862 after the next crop has been harvested. If any illicit money is recovered, one half goes to the bank, the remainder divided evenly between the farmers, so they may meet whatever other debts are owing."

"That is not what I said."

She effected surprise. "Captain Ward, have I not stated that which you understood to be the 'deal'?"

"You have." He tapped a finger on the desk. "And I'm gettin' tired of standing. My feet hurt. I might just have enough patience to wait while you commit the deal to paper: two copies, naturally. We'll bring in Mr. Lanley to witness the transaction. Then you'll put a seal on both 'deeds' with red wax. You file yours in the safe and we'll return a copy to our benefactress."

The banker tried one last ploy.

"Seth, with one thousand dollars, you could buy yourself free and clear. No one has to know but you and I."

Captain Ward bounced on his toes.

"You know, I mighta taken you up on that, but for the sorry fact you don't consider Captain Nelander a party to this transaction."

If he had said, *She is only a woman,* Mr. Lanley would have had to write the pact in Mr. Provost's place.

Taking out a pen shaft, the president affixed a silver nib to the end, then dipped it in the ink well. His hands shook and a drop fell onto the blotter. It looked like blood.

Black blood.

And indeed, it might well have been.

For those farmers relieved of the spectre of bank's henchmen appearing on their doorsteps with orders to vacate and "No Trespassing" signs to beat into the land, life resumed a modicum of normalcy. This select group included the Nelander-Wards. In a better position than the rest for they had their strawberry money to fall back on, they "paid down" their obligations to the merchants in Lawrence, laid in "supplies for a rainy day," and kept to themselves. With talk revolving around the War and which way the signs pointed after each successive skirmish, Seth and Barbara decided, without undue consultation, to "batten the hatches and steer clear of trouble."

Their isolation occasioned little note, for after the flurry of gratitude over Mrs. Dryfus' initial generosity died down, the townspeople's interest directed itself at Ron Provost. Since he had been the one to announce the terms of the Great Compromise of 1861, without ever mentioning the Wards' status as intermediators, they applied directly to him for similar deals to carry them through the fall and winter months. At first pleased with the new-found status and then annoyed by the constant stream of petitioners, the banker finally appeared at Mrs. Dryfus' mansion, requesting an audience.

Presumably his idea had been to rework the original terms of her grant while receiving a second, more lucrative bequest on behalf of the citizens. A black man, known around town as Giles, answered his summons. Dressed in livery and effecting a stiff, chipped dialect, he informed the businessman, "The lady of the house is not receiving," and politely closed the door in his face.

On the few occasions Provost did glimpse Seth in Lawrence he tried to broach the subject but received a cold shoulder.

The same Mr. Giles who shunned banker Provost came regularly to the Pirate Treasure and became their primary source of intelligence. How he came to possess certain knowledge of the War the crew did not ask and he never volunteered.

Waiting for Patricia to gather her sketches together for her biweekly trip to visit her tutor, Giles accepted a glass of warm mint tea sweetened with honey and settled in on the porch.

"There has been a battle at Wilson's Creek," he began, brushing away an interested fly.

"Where is that?" Seth asked, hands on his knees.

"In Missouri. General Lyon led 5,000 troops against the rebel Benjamin McCulloch. He was killed and his forces moved back to Rolla. That is southwest of St. Louis. Two hundred Union dead and seven hundred wounded. The troops are now to be led by Major Sturgis."

"A loss for us?"

He nodded. "A significant victory for the South; second only to the battle at Bull Run. The secessionist papers make much of it, as they were outnumbered three-to-one, although the editors did not dwell on the high number of causalities they sustained. Over 400 from what I hear, with over 1,000 wounded. That is high attrition; numbers which cannot be sustained if they expect to carry on this conflict through the winder and into next year."

"So long." Nelander clenched her hand. "Norman was right. He said it would be no Six Month War."

"President Lincoln has declared that all slaves who are compelled to fight for the South shall be freed."

"A step in the right direction. But... we must win the war to make it permanent. And it goes badly."

"It goes, Captain Nelander, slowly."

"I had hoped otherwise. A quick resolution." Giles made no comment. "Have you heard any news of the militia from Lawrence? Were they involved?"

He shrugged, indicating little interest.

"You have not seen or heard from Captain Norman Ward since his last visit?"

Seth growled. "He is not welcome here. He knows that. I will shoot him on sight." A maniacal grin worked its way over his darkened features. "And pick his pockets. If he has brought more money, so much the better." He suddenly grew suspicious. "What have you heard? It has been quiet around these parts, lately. Or so I am led to believe. No more raids."

"He has taken what he could from hereabouts and moved on."

"Out of state? To Kansas? It seems he has more friends on that side of the river. Or into the Territories?"

"Northward," Giles agreed. "Where there is even less law. Easier for him to steal crops, cattle and horses."

"Someone will stop him. Vigilantes. God."

The black man offered no opinion on which, if either entity, might have the upper hand.

"How are Miss Betty and Thomas getting along?"

"Well. We have enough baskets for the spring strawberries and larger ones to sell. We bring them to church and Hector Anson takes them to sell in his shop. They have an account there."

"Ah. I had not heard. That is well. You are good friends."

"Family, sir. We are family."

Giles turned his head sharply, considered, then smiled.

"So you are. I have heard it said a man cannot pick his family but only his friends. In this case, you have managed to combine both. I am most grateful."

"We included you in the category of family, Antony," Nelander stated, daring to use his first name. "And Victoria."

"I will faithfully repeat what you said. She has grown very fond of you. And the little miss." Crossing one leg over the other, he took a drink. "She has sent one of the sketches away. For consideration."

Nelander and Seth perked up.

"Which one?"

"I do not know. When she hears back I expect she will summon you." He might have said more but Patricia emerged, ribbon-tied portfolio under her arm. Making a small curtsy to the guest, her face alit with fondness.

"Good morning, sir. Would you like to see what I have done?"

"I would."

Placing the large cloth-bound cover on her father's knee, the girl unfastened the bow and removed several sketches. Using her mother as an easel, she displayed the first.

"Miss Theresa and baby Samuel."

A deep intake of breath indicated the viewer needed no introduction. Bending closer, he stared keenly at the likeness of the young Negress and her baby. The colored pencil portrait depicted a head-and-shoulders visage of two faces, the older staring adoringly at the younger. Luminous brown irises, highlighted by a stark white background conveyed an overwhelming impression of love and pride. The infant, tiny lips puckered in a crooked oval shape, appeared to laugh. Across his small, rounded shoulders the artist had drawn a colorful, hand-knit red scarf to protect his neck, while a floppy cap, drawn at an angle, covered one ear. Behind parent and child, against a blue-black background, rose a bright yellow-orange moon. A small grey elephant, trunk extended, legs splayed, flew over the celestial orb.

"That is to indicate their flight to freedom," Patricia explained, although the adults readily grasped the implication. "Do you think it too... obscure? If one does not know the story, they may think Miss Theresa... foolish." Her lower lip protruded. "Elephants do not fly."

"I think it inspired." Giles' hand shook as he positioned it near but not touching the artwork. "You have captured the spirit of the Underground Railroad, Miss Patricia. Miss Victoria will surely put a caption to it so others will grasp the meaning." Withdrawing, he pressed his heart. "You have managed to convey a...." His voice choked. "A humanness." The word came out harder than intended. "So many... whites... do not consider us human. You have put a face and a dignity to the African race."

"I wanted everyone to know what war should really be about: people sacrificing for people. Not fighting over boundaries or distribution of wealth."

"This must go...." He did not finish the sentence. Sniffing away the unspoken, he rested his tea glass on the porch. "You are ready?"

"Yes, sir."

Reassembling the sketches and tying the ribbon, Patricia kissed her parents, then ran to the wagon.

"I am off, Captains Papa and Nelander."

"Take care, child. Have fun."

"I will."

Perched on the seat beside Giles, she waved, in one gesture capturing the enthusiasm of youth and the wisdom of age. Her parents waved back.

"She is growing up so fact," Seth whispered as the wagon disappeared over the hill.

"Would you have it otherwise?"

"Yes. And no."

Which conveyed Barbara's sentiments exactly.

CHAPTER 30

Sheriff Will Bochner swore, leaned both elbows on the cluttered mess strewn across his desk and contemplated the telegram he had just received. He might have held that position all day but for a perverse stream of sunlight, sneaking under the half-drawn shade, piercing his eyes. He cursed again, this time for effect. The fact it "effected" on no one in the otherwise empty office bore no relevancy on word choice.

Jerking his head back in annoyance, he jabbed a hand around his shirt collar to stem the tide of rolling perspiration. He succeeded merely in dampening his fingers. In an effort to dry them, he waved the offending digits in front of his face and blew on them. That feat accomplished, he pushed away, gave the old chair on flat wheels a kick for good measure, then affixed his eyes on the large, hand-colored map directly across from him. Depicting what the war lords had designated as the "Trans-Mississippi Region," his eyes took in two adjoining states: Kansas and Missouri.

"General Fremont declares martial law across Missouri," he parroted from the text. The next sentence he extemporized. "Wonderful. Just what I need. All them damn pro-secessionists fleeing into Kansas to get away from that Union general's damn rules."

Working his shoulders to remove the kinks, a habit developed from long periods of tense inactivity, he then stomped his left foot which had gone to sleep.

"Fremont wouldn't know the smell of gunpowder if it seared his nostrils." He liked the analogy and forced a grin onto his otherwise relentless features. "I shoulda been a newspaper editor."

As soon as spoken, he regretted the comment and quickly retracted the idea. "Never mind. If I had been, I'd of joined the militia and got myself voted general."

And then what? Marched across the border to confront enemy troops? Hardly an occupation which suited his taste.

Absently wondering what had become of "General" Jim Daly, Will shuffled over to the window. Stooping low to peer out, his tired eyes took in the scene of Lawrence. The weather being hot and humid, few loiterers were to be seen. Those men not engaged in farming or business concerns holed up at the Tankard's Draft. Little work offered itself and those without gainful employment spent their time discussing "the war." Lacking even the five cents for a beer, they did little more than take up space.

The lawman did not like loiterers or would-be drunks. Men with nothing better to go represented trouble. Whether or not they could read, news from the front traveled quickly. It had not been good. Not for a Union sympathizer. That clown John Fremont, mapmaker and presidential candidate, had gotten himself appointed commander of the mid-west. Proving inept as an officer, he had descended to the level of aggravating citizens. Declaring St. Louis and the adjoining cities suffering from the "helplessness of civil authority and total insecurity of life," his edict had made matters inestimably worse.

As Missouri went, so followed Kansas. A steady stream of lost battles and bungled opportunities in the former had drawn pro-Southern sympathies out from under the bed. With the addition of those fleeing the Union officer's threat to confiscate property of any who aided or abetted the Confederacy, Bochner had problems on his hands. Ones he did not appreciate.

Moving to the map, he pointed at all the areas in southwestern Missouri lost to the Union. Dug Springs. Wilson's Creek. Lexington soon to follow if his sources were right.

Colonel Mulligan has been hung out to dry.

Fremont doesn't know any better. He'll never reinforce Mulligan. He wants the Yanks close at hand to protect his own sorry ass.

After Lexington, then what? Springfield? That brought the war mighty damn close.

To make matters worse, Fremont had issued his own emancipation proclamation. Slaves belonging to those with pro-Southern leanings "are hereby declared free men."

What right had he to do that? If the wealthy former senator from California had any sense, he would have left that problem for the higher-ups: those in Washington. But Fremont fancied himself playing God without ever having won a single skirmish.

Taking his hat from the "out basket," Bochner jammed it on his head. No need to strap on a gunbelt. He never took it off. Not at night. Not even when he soaked his feet in Epson salts, stripped down to his drawers. No telling when the shooting would start. Or some hayseed from the hills would come in and tell him another farm had been burned, horses stolen, crops taken.

They looked to him for help and he had none to offer.

"I'll ride out in the morning," had become, "I'll make out a report."

It had not taken long to go from lawman to paper-pusher. Only the end of August, and he no longer bothered with the formalities. What point? He had no one to send a report to. The department in Topeka? The governor in Wichita? They had other things to worry about. The troubles of a sheriff in Lawrence hardly rated a raised eyebrow.

He did not have to witness the conversation to hear what transpired.

"Tell him to do the best he can."

"Tell him he's on his own."

"Write him a letter. Say we're keeping close track."

A useless admonition. The mails were not running. Not with any regularity. They might as well lie and tell him they're sending in the army to restore order. No harm in that, knowing the letter would never arrive.

Like the army.

Lost in transit.

Will supposed their conscience bothered them or they would have done it.

Even in war, lying came hard.

He reckoned they collected their pay vouchers, though. More than he could say. He owed fifty-five dollars at Anson's Dry Goods. Told Hector to "Put it on the bill and send it to Topeka." Anson had refused him further credit.

If he did not make rounds and stop in for a friendly chat at one of the local houses, he would have starved to death by now.

All things considered, that remained a viable option.

He wondered what Abe Lincoln had for dinner. Not that he begrudged him. Just wasn't feeling too charitable at the moment.

Licking dry lips, Bochner went out into the street. A furnace blast of air struck him full force and he nearly staggered. Smoke from the factory hung in the air in long, dark columns. At least Mrs. Dryfus still had that up and running. Gave men work. Kept them off the street by producing tinware. Sold it to the army. Even in times of trouble the rich managed to get richer.

Odd, she had suddenly becoming a benefactor. Ron Provost, the banker, had told him all about it. Gave $1,000 to keep the farmers from losing their land. Those whose crops had been stolen by partisans. Provost had used the word. "Partisans." It had been a new one to him. Bochner called them raiders. In low moments, "damn thieves." Partisans had the ring of respect. As though they actually stood for something. Taking a stance; defending a principal.

The name Jeff Thompson came to mind. He had heard about Thompson. A Virginian who had come west. Settled in St. Louis. Got himself elected mayor some years back. Now he had banded together a bunch of "partisans" to defend Missouri from the "invaders." For that, read Federals. Union men. Thompson was making a name for himself. He had an allure: drawing in all the outlaws. Making his own rules. Paying in gold.

Sheriff Bochner had heard his "own" set of raiders sold their stolen horses and crops to the Union. That had been early on. None of that going on much, now. Likely, they had joined the ranks of Thompson or those of similar ilk. Stealing. Murdering. Stirring up trouble. General unrest. Those sort had taken the news of Fremont's emancipation proclamation bad. Shot a few Negroes in protest. Little Lawrence looked to him for protection. But he was only one man.

They buried their dead quietly. Africans were a quiet people. He liked that about them.

He did not like Ron Provost. But was beholding to him for his job. Sheriffs were elected and blacks did not vote. Provost carried a lot of weight. That's why he made his rounds at the back twice a day, morning and nightfall. To look like he was performing his job. If the partisans took a fancy to the bank, there was not much he could do about it. Lose his life defending other people's money didn't seem worth it.

But a man had to have a job.

Gave him a reason to get up in the morning. Even if it didn't pay.

Brushing away a black horse fly -- the same one, he swore, which had been following him around for a week -- he started walking. Up one side, down the other. His mind wandered. He wondered about Seth Ward, too. Provost had said it was Seth who had brought in the proposition from Mrs. Dryfus. Reasoning fell short on that one. What did a dirt farmer have to do with the wealthiest woman in Kansas? What quirk of fate had crossed their paths?

Word got around. Not in taverns and saloons where men gossiped about weather and crops and who was shacking with someone else's wife, and crooked politics, and how Lincoln really got himself voted in. Word from the back alleys and off the prairie. Seth Ward was involved in smuggling niggers. Took 'em in, passed 'em on. Dangerous occupation for a dirt farmer. A man could get himself killed.

Bochner had never known Seth to get in a fight. Well, once or twice, but there had been circumstances. He had held his own but he was no match for professionals. That's what the bounty hunters were. Men who killed as soon as look at a fellow.

Bounty hunters had a lot in common with partisans. He expected a man with sense to steer clear of both types.

Shaking off his doldrums, the sheriff completed his early rounds, purposely completing the circuit -- as far as he intended to go -- at the gate of Dryfus Mansion. The place did not actually have a name; he called it that for the sake of clarity. Others had different choices.

Tinplate House.

Coffeepot Shanks.

The Widder's Hidey Hole.

The Rich Bitch's Place.

"Bitch," he supposed, because it rhymed with "rich." And because Victoria Dryfus *nee* Dillinger was a female. Had she been a man, they would have styled it "The Rich Old Codger's Place" and foregone the rhyme.

In the course of his duties, some of which occasioned electioneering, he had called upon the widow-woman. Not that she could vote, but her opinion carried a lot of weight. One word and all the eligible males in town who worked for, or did business with her, did their darndest to see her desire come to fruition. It therefore behooved him to stay in her good graces.

Hat in hand, he had stood at the door and explained himself to Giles, the manservant. Talking polite to a Negro came easy for Will. As a peacekeeper, he had always found it wise to treat everyone with respect. It didn't matter the color of a man's skin. A darkie could shoot just as straight as a white. Besides, standing in good stead with the residents of Little Lawrence kept incidents from getting out of hand. Once in a while, when trouble reared its ugly head, he had gone there and quieted things down. They listened because they trusted what he had to say, knowing full well there were always worse men who could take his place.

Most of them had even lived long enough to remember the time when "Big Lawrence" had been a hotbed of hatred for the dark race.

That had been before Will's time. Not a lot before, but some. Moving from Westport, Missouri on the border of the newly opened Kansas Territory, Sam Jones got himself mixed up with some shenanigans, destroying the ballot box at Bloomington. That made him famous -- or infamous, depending on one's political persuasion -- and the acting governor, Daniel Woodson, had appointed Jones the first sheriff of Douglas County. That had been March, 1855. Sheriff Sam lasted fewer than two years but he left behind a legacy of bloodshed and some said murder.

Will had been appointed to fill out the tern, then been elected in his own right.

He had not been an insider and had not been an outsider. More like a man caught somewhere in the middle. Like most of the folk in Lawrence. Most he knew by name when it came time for electioneering. First time he ever spoke to Giles, though. He had seen him about on his mistress' business but there never had been any reason for sociability. Talking to him at the door had been an experience.

He must have said the right things, for the man let him in and bade him wait in the parlor. For that matter, he had never been in a parlor. Not a proper one, done up with stately furniture, pictures on the wall and a rug on the floor. Mrs. Dryfus had come in but she never invited him to sit, so they stood there talking.

"I've heard things about you," she said, failing to add whether they had been good or ill.

"I'm runnin' for sheriff, ma'am," he had replied. "I'd like your support."

"Why?" meaning, *What's in it for me?*

He had been hard-pressed to come up with an answer.

Will Bochner knew something about Victoria Dryfus; more than some, less than others. He knew what other men talked about. Stinking rich father. The tutors who drifted in and out to give her a proper education. The arranged marriage to Stanley Dryfus.

And something about a hanging, coming in between.

There were other rumors, too. About a baby, born out of wedlock. One of those half fish-half fowl infants no one wanted. Smothered at birth. Or given away. "Rape," ran the street chatter. Behind closed doors or under the influence of whisky, they called it by a different name.

Miscegenation.

He doubted the truthfulness of the assertion. No one in Kansas rightly knew the meaning, much less how to spell that ten-dollar word. With those two factors against it, the rest had to be trash.

Strung up a Negro for it. But that had been before his time.

Dismissing it that way, it didn't count.

In answer to her question, Will replied, "I don't hold with vigilantes." He didn't know where the sentence came from. Hadn't been planning on saying anything like that. He had meant to say, "I'll uphold the law." Or, "I'm an honest man." But that other had come out.

He forgot what she said in return. Something like, "I am a woman and don't know much about those things." He had gotten her support, though and won the election.

After that, he always felt he owed her.

In the beginning, he had always made it a point to patrol around her property. Made himself conspicuous. Just to be sure she understood his appreciation. Then, one day Giles appeared out of nowhere. Hat in hand, the servant made a deferential bow and explained that "Mrs. Dryfus says to tell you she respects the fact you're watching over the town but she hires men to see to her own property."

He took that to mean the mistress didn't want him hanging around in either a literal or figurative sense and he had stopped going anywhere near the mansion. Finding himself at the foot of Dryfus Mansion now represented a breach of protocol. Shifting uneasily, he glanced up, hoping no one watched from an upper story window. No reason for him to have specified "upper story" in his mind, except for the fact he always imagined older people occupying the second or third floors of dwellings. For safety sake. Or perhaps because it gave them a better vantage point on the world they had segregated themselves from.

The greater danger came from Giles. More of a watchdog than a butler, he might be lurking behind a curtain, staring out through a peephole or standing guard behind a tree or the side of the building. Men in Lawrence didn't like Giles. Didn't trust him. Bochner figured that stemmed from the fact he rarely talked. Or that he had a wealthy mistress who'd set the hounds on anyone who gave him a hard time.

That, and the fact he was a product of miscegenation.

Men, he reckoned, were jealous of other men who lived a better life than they. Even if he were a Negro.

Will Bochner knew more than he liked to admit. In his bones, he harbored the belief Mrs. Dryfus ran a way-station along the Underground Railroad. Not that he had any proof of her involvement or even if such a place existed in Douglas County. Folks hereabouts were a bit off the beaten track, Will liked to think. Just quiet souls: farmers and shopkeepers and men who made tinware for a living. All minding their own business. Keeping their eyes down, not looking one way or the other. Only got riled up some when election years came around. Majority voted for the Union. They were against slavery, most of them. But didn't say so too loudly.

He had been surprised, therefore, when more than a handful had joined the Rebels. Hadn't expected them to go against the Founding Fathers. Not many were involved in commerce outside the state and none owned slaves. Especially after the Kansas Constitution came in against it. One or two, maybe. Men born and bred in Missouri, who had drifted over. But not enough for a company or a brigade.

He had expected the McConaghies to side with the dissidents. They were big talkers, especially the boys. Made a few dollars chasing runaways. Cozied up to those Simpson Agency men when they came round. Anything for easy money. The others had surprised him.

"Goin' to fight fer Jeff Davis," one had told him. That had not cleared up the problem. Who the hell ever heard of Jeff Davis before all this started? Why would a Kansas boy care what happened in Virginia or South Carolina, for that matter?

Wearing a uniform and marching under a flag was one thing. But seeing that new rag they flew -- the one with the circle of stars -- it evoked no sentiment. Not like the good old Stars and Stripes.

He understood the raiders better. They didn't wear uniforms and they didn't salute any flag. They were only out for themselves. Partisans. Just a fancy word for outlaws. Yet no one hereabouts had wanted to join forces with Will to root them out, as if the marauders were doing something noble. Before this so-called civil war, he would have had ten, twenty men volunteer as deputies. They wouldn't have stood by while a gang of thieves robbed them blind.

What had turned men into scardy cats? He wished he had the answer. If he had, he would do everything in his power to counter their fears. But no one would speak up.

He supposed the success in Missouri had something to do with it. The Confederates had made fools of the Union boys. Former governors and mayors had turned out to be better soldiers than trained military officers.

Don't stick your noses into our business or we'll come and get you, too.

Maybe that was it. But it did not sit well with the sheriff.

He did not like being a man straddling the fence between the law and the lawless.

With a shudder, he felt a pair of eyes on him. Maybe from the second story of the house. Maybe from behind a tree. He could not be certain. His stomach turned. He should not have come this way. Didn't know why he had. Tipping his hat, which might have been mistaken for an effort to ward away the bright sun's rays, he moseyed on.

Just passing by. Don't mean anything by it.

But he had and he figured the watcher or watchers knew that, too. Had he come to warn them, in a polite sort of way, to stay out of the slave transportation business? Or maybe to plead for the mistress to up the ante on her gift to the farmers? Just to make banker Provost happy?

Had his wandering footsteps taken him to the forbidden gate to remind them he needed allies against the local terrorists? Or to plead with them to leave Seth Ward alone? The man had enough troubles.

Some men knew his brother was a partisan. No amount of intermediating between the wealthiest woman west of the Mississippi and the farmers who had their crops stolen could mitigate that.

The men in Kansas might not band together to protect their own interests but they could damn sure turn their anger against one of their own.

Such things had been known to happen.

And Sheriff Will Bochner had sworn he didn't hold with vigilantes.

CHAPTER 31

A chill in the air made the warmth of Miss Betty's fire feel especially good. Nelander learned toward the flickering flames, hands extended.

"Are we going through a cold snap or is winter upon us?" she asked of her friend.

Summer had turned to fall, and now, as October snuck upon them, it seemed as if the warm months had been ages ago. The former maritime officer supposed the reason for that lay in the fact July, August and September had been filled with tension. War news, always at a premium, filtered in slowly, in bits and pieces. News mostly came in the form of letters.

Jim Daly, the former editor who had been sent to Missouri, proved the mainstay of information. Writing to his wife in the style of a reporter, he detailed the situation, as he saw it, from the southeast portion of the state. She, in turn, posted the pages on Anson's bulletin board for the curious to read.

Daly described how the soldiers lived in tents and took turns cooking their meals over a contraption called a "spider," which meant a sort of stove. Food had been adequate, if tasteless, and he had lost ten pounds the first month. Their unit had been incorporated into another from Kansas and his rank reduced. Bitterly chastising the "higher ups who don't appreciate a man's worth," he threatened to resign before being reminded that he had signed up for a year. "Leaving for home," he added, "meant desertion." That prompted him to stay, but the light, somewhat bombastic tone of earlier letters turned sour and begrudging.

"We have marched over every hill, dale and prairie in Missouri," came the more terse description, "and the soldiers' shoes proved inadequate to the task. When my own recruits applied to me for replacements, I informed them that as we were now under the control of the Federal government, they ought to look to Washington for redress." Apparently none were forthcoming for in another "Bulletin From the Front," he repeated, almost word-for-word the complaints.

He saw "no good" in marching, repeated "sanitized" soldier's expressions of contempt for "Granny Fremont," and then described in vivid detail a heroic piece of action he performed in "Jefferson County."

On September 1st, at a place called "Cape Girardeau" (pronounced Ger-ar-dough, the writer explained), Daly heard General Ulysses Grant had assumed command of Federal forces. Obtaining special permission to go there and get an interview, he had discovered, too late, the general had moved his headquarters to "Cairo, Illinois." In the margin Daly added a second pronunciation: "Ill-a-noy, although some say Ill-a-noise, depending on their place of origin."

"Talk is rampant about a shift in emphasis toward the Mississippi and the Kansas boys are none too happy with the situation. They say they joined to fight in Kansas and not some 'durn' river with so many 'S's' in it no one can keep them straight." Thereafter, the editor-turned-soldier launched into great detail about the "strategic value" of New Orleans and how, if he were still a general, he "would surely take it from the rebels, but not with troops from Missouri, who are ill-trained and 'suspect' as far as loyalty goes."

On September 25th, the latest bulletin received, the author described in great detail how "Granny Fremont had the audacity to close the office of the St. Louis Evening Gazette, and arrest the editor for daring to criticize the general about his failure to reinforce the nobel Mulligan and thus force him to surrender Lexington (Missouri)."

According to Thomas, who regularly went to town to read the news, much had been made of this, not so much because an editor had been arrested, but from the circumstance of Mr. Daly misspelling "noble."

Word, too, had come from Dr. McTree. Having no family in Lawrence, he wrote to Reverend Ginnis, who read the letter aloud in church with all the pomp and bluster of one being the chosen to receive such proprietary information.

After inquiring about the locals, some of whom he mentioned by name and expressing the wish his dog be well cared for, McTree described the "Medical Corps," the word "corps" being pronounced without the "s" sound, he had added in parenthesis. The doctor wrote he had treated "causalities too numerous to count" and "done the best he could for them."

However, it seemed his physician's bag had been stolen on the march from Lawrence to Kansas City and he had inferior tools with which to work. "Doctors from this state," he added, "use common wood saws to amputate limbs and on any given day, a passerby could see piles of discarded arms and legs waiting for the undertaker, the burial squad or a family from the Bootheels to come and claim any which they might desire for interment elsewhere."

The physician added that "Many of the corpses were bloated on account of the heat and ungodly humidity, and were unrecognizable." He doubted not that an unwary father buried a body "resembling but not actually his son," and that "after any skirmish, the lines at sick call the next day were twice that of the previous."

The major complaints were sore and blistered feet, stomach ailments and constipation, for which he prescribed a substance known as "blue mass," which cleared the bowels nicely and "sent an infantryman back to the ranks with alacrity."

There were, apparently, several passages describing the "deplorable sanitary conditions, owing to the fact no officer had the slightest idea how to dig a latrine, much less enforce the custom of using one," but Reverend Ginnis discretely omitted reading them aloud as being "Unfit fer church and ladies."

That also held true for the concluding paragraphs which made mention of the soldiers' penchant for "going down the line," which the minister brushed aside and failed to elaborate on.

Turning her head, lowered lids stung from the waves of heat radiating from the fireplace, Betty clucked her tongue.

"Ah 'spect it'll be an early winter dis year. We seed da las' ob da warm days. Thomas a'ready took mah baskets don' to da valley an' put 'em ober da strawberries durin' da night. Dat way, we keep 'em safe from frost." Picking up a sock she had been knitting, her sighted fingers worked the needles with precision.

"But how could you have made so many?" Nelander asked, finding her attention mesmerized by the activity. "There are over three thousand plants there."

Proudly pausing to draw up a strand of yarn from the large ball at her feet, the Negress smiled.

"Ah make big'uns; dose long 'nuf to cober a whole heap at a time. Not heaby ones, but light, so deys kin be taken off in da mornin' so da little ones kin drink da sun. Dey wilted, Nelander, but cum spring, dey perk up right 'nuf. Yuh git Capt'n Ward to cober yuhrs wid straw. Dat be good 'nuf 'till Ah makes yuh some baskets fo' da patch behind da house."

Wondering how much, if any, of their effort would be rewarded by selling the fruit in the spring, Barbara pulled her coat closer around her shoulders.

"If those raiders come again, they will take the strawberries for their own use."

"Mebbe dat brudder ob Capt'n Ward's will leabe money ag'in."

The comment elicited a shudder and the younger woman drew back in surprise. Although close to the older, she had never spoken of Norman, or the fact he had paid them for the stolen corn and wheat.

No one knew the truth but Mrs. Dryfus and that realization silenced Barbara as she considered. It should have been obvious that whatever passed between the Wards and the grand dame on the hill would inevitably be told to her oldest confidant, but until this moment, the idea had never germinated. Nelander did not resent the sharing of a secret but it nevertheless caught her off guard.

Taking a slow breath, she carefully considered her words.

"No. I think that will not happen again. Nor do I believe Norman's so-called protection will last. I keep hearing his voice in my mind: how he cared more about money than anything else. Perhaps an army will have less need of fruit than that which can be made into bread, but some quartermaster will pay him for it. And he will take what's offered."

"Dat may be so. Yuh hand meh da red yarn?"

Reaching into Betty's sewing basket, Nelander took a ball of red yarn and placed it in the wrinkled hands. Adeptly working the new thread into the sock, she began a bright band around the top.

"Ah cain't see da colors, but Ah habe a sense ob dem. An' I like to make what I do pretty. Yuh pretty, Nelander."

The compliment caused a blush to appear on her cheeks.

"Thank you."

"Dat babe ob yuhrs be pretty, too. An' tall; tall an' willowy like her pa."

"She is growing so much. It is hard to believe Paula is already seven months old. I feel as though she has always been with me."

"Dat a good way to feel." The band of red on the sock grew like the cresting of a crimson wave after a storm raked the bottom of the sea. "It be gettin' dark?"

"It is."

"Den yuh mus' be off. Ah don' wan' yuh out in da night. Der's trouble in da wind." The chill in the room deepened as the fire burned down. Nelander went to add a log but Betty stopped her. "No need. Ah don' feel da cold like odders do. It don' bother me." Her hands slowed but only for a second. "It reminds meh ob da grabe."

"That's a depressing thing to say."

"No, Nelander. It be da truth. We all gonna die. Ah look forward to it. Da Lor', He's waitin' fo' meh. Ah'm an old woman. Ah don' want to wear out mah welcome. Ah been alibe fo' a good many years. Da chariot been waitin' on meh. A glorious chariot, Nelander. Wid four white horses an' an angel, dressed in white linen."

"Please. They can wait a little longer. Seth and I and the crew -- and Thomas need you." Her voice broke. "What would we do without you?"

"Yuh git along."

"I refuse to listen." Putting her hands over her ears like a small child, Barbara attempted to block out the sound. She need not have bothered, for Betty had finished speaking.

They sat in silence until a pocket of sap burst in the hearth, sending an arch of orange sparks into the air. More like a rifle shot than the effect of boiling liquid, both women jerked in response. Betty tied off the row she had been working on and Barbara hugged herself.

"All right. Time for me to walk home. But you will take care, won't you? And remember what I said? About us needing you." She cleared her throat. "It is more than that, mother. We love you."

"An' Ah lobe sweet Jesus."

A statement which held little comfort for the listener.

"You will not do anything foolish? It has been quiet lately, but Seth says he does not think the raiders have gone. There are those in town who do. They say they have moved away; joined forces with that man Thompson in Missouri. Or gone west. Seth read that the Confederates were recruiting Indians to fight for them in the Territories. He thinks Norman might have gone out there."

"Dat what he says?"

"That is what he hopes."

"Den Ah hope so, too."

"But you do not believe it. And neither do I."

"Da Lor', He works in mysterious ways, Nelander. Sumtimes we git what weh hope fo' an' sumtimes we don'. Dere are none ob us who see da Plan. Only da Lor'. He knows what's best fo' His chil'run."

"I would rather say the Lord helps those who help themselves."

She had not meant to be humorous but a wide smile spread over the old slave's face, lighting the area around her sockets as though she saw through an inner spark.

"It all turns out da same."

"Well, if He is soliciting opinions, I would rather have it my way than the other."

"Now, yuh make me laugh." Betty did, in fact, chuckle under her breath. "Dat's what Ah a'ways seed in yuh, Nelander. A faith an' a stubbornness. Yuh cum outta dis a'right."

"It appears you and I, mother, have a different idea as to what is 'all right.'"

"Mebbe weh do, mebbe weh don'. But in da end, weh all fall on our knees an' praise God fo' His blessin's."

Not caring to debate the matter further, Nelander stood and rested a gentle hand on Betty's shoulder.

"You will take care? Knowing how much you mean to us? Make me this one promise."

Blind Betty set aside her knitting and rolled the loose ends of yarn back into balls. Carefully shoving the basket behind her, she got to her feet. Waiting until her friend's hand slipped away, she took a step back.

"All be well."

Accepting that as the only avowal likely to be given, Nelander fastened the buttons on her coat and crossed to the door.

"Good night, then. And God bless."

Nothing happened on Nelander's walk from the Windsor place to her own and although she woke several times during the night, muscles tensed, ears straining, she heard nothing. A sense of wariness pervaded her mind throughout the day but aside from spilling a glass of milk when Squash began a series of rapid, high-pitched yelps, the hours passed without justification for suspicion.

Seth had remarked, "You're jumpy as a cat. It's only an early-rising raccoon," after the incident at the table and let the dog into the yard. She went to stop him, too late. Responding to his surprised expression, a mumbled, "I can't stand the thought of anything getting hurt," prompted him to call the animal back. Afraid he might quiz her further, Nelander set about the task of replacing the soiled tablecloth. A hand on hers stayed the action.

"It's all right. I feel the same way."

Infinitely relieved, she flashed a smile and the matter dropped.

October turned to November and November to December. Stray bits of information reached them about outlying farms being attacked, but for the most part life settled back into a routine. Seth spent most of his days chopping firewood, Nelander gave the children their school lessons and baby Paula developed an astounding strength that promised to wreak havoc around the house when she learned to crawl.

One morning, early, Seth rattled the "egg jar" over the hearth.

"How much do you suppose we have in here?"

Supposing he already knew, to the penny, Nelander answered, "A little over two thousand dollars."

He grunted. "More than enough, then, for a trip into town."

The actual amount being closer to twenty dollars, Barbara cast him a look.

"What is it you had in mind to buy?"

"Christmas presents. Won't be much, but maybe some store-bought candy for the crew and a bottle of rum for our holiday toast. We ought to buy Mrs. Dryfus something, too. Don't know how we're ever going to be able to repay her for the kindness she's shown Patricia."

"And Betty an' Thomas," Peter chimed in, overhearing the discussion.

"Them, too."

"All right, then. Who's coming?"

"We'll all go," Nelander decided. "Might do us all good to see some new sights. Do you suppose they've decorated?"

"Hope so. It's baby's first Christmas and I want her to have some fun. She won't remember it," he teased, poking Peter, "but it'll always give us the opportunity of reminding her what went on." His eyes sparkled. "Snow glistening over the fields, trees lit up with ice catchin' the sun's rays. The boughs over the railings an' the big winter scene Mr. Provost puts up outside the bank."

Stroking his chin in a manner meant to be infuriating, he continued. "The year... 1851, it was. Oh, you shoulda seen Lawrence. Red ribbons everywhere, a big ol' spruce tree in the town square and Tinker Taylor decked out like an English lord, passin' out paper sacks full of rock candy and tin soldiers and squares of homemade fudge wrapped in green cloth. Patricia was two at the time an' after she got done eatin' her feast she looked more like a tar baby than a little girl." He winked at his son. "You recall that, don't you, boy? We all had a good laugh over it. Powerful funny."

Peter drew his upper lip back in annoyance.

"No, sir, I don't remember it!"

"But you were there --"

His foot stomped. "I was only six months old!"

Seth's good humor improved.

"But you were there, right enough. Strapped on my back."

"I hope, sir, I pulled your hair."

"Seems to me Patricia got two sacks of treats and ate yours, too."

Barbara easily caught his drift and help up her hands.

"I see. All of this is planned to torment our daughter when she is old enough to remember what she missed!"

"That's one way of putting it."

Still greatly amused, he went into the bedroom, laughing. By the time he bundled up the smallest Ward, the others had hitched Blaze and were waiting outside. Passing over the carefully wrapped bundle to its mother, Patricia attacked Seth with the only salvo at her disposal.

"Seems to me, Captain Papa, it was you who ete Peter's candy. Me bein' only two, I don't see as how I coulda gone through all that rock candy an' fudge. Them tin soldiers, now -- I do seem to recollect you traded 'em to Jed an' James for a bag of horehound they had stashed away. Claimed your throat was raspy, but mama said it was candy, just like fudge an' you had the biggest sweet tooth she ever saw."

He pouted and rolled his eyes.

"You made that up."

"Oh, we're all good at tellin' stories in this family."

With a "Gee up!" and a roll of his head, the wagon lurched forward.

The iron-rimmed wheels made good time over the frozen road and the steady clip-clop of the horse's shoes sang to them, making the trip seem faster than usual. Arriving just after ten o'clock, Nelander got her first glimpse of Lawrence, decked out for the holidays.

No one dressed as an English lord met them with sacks of candy, for Tinker Taylor had gone for a soldier, but other efforts quickly lifted the veil of what might have been a sad omission. True to expectations, green pine branches had been woven around the hitching rails outside the dry goods store, Tankard's Draft and the sheriff's office, while festive red and green ribbons grew in profusion from the dressmaker's shop. Other merchants had decorated their windows with cheerful clippings from old periodicals, adding the visages of package-filled sleighs, bell-bedecked horses, snowy landscapes and candle-lit London townhouses to the scene.

If anything were different this holiday season on 1861, the only reminder of the war were a score of small paper Union flags, crisscrossed among the greenery or tacked to door frames.

Pulling up outside Anson's, Seth took Paula so Nelander could get down, then scooted the walking variety of child through the entranceway, taking care to close the door behind. Stamping his feet, he greeted the proprietor with a wave.

"Cold out there."

Hector grinned and indicated a high stack of blankets, mufflers and other winter accouterments.

"Then you've come to the right place. I've just the items you need to put under your tree, Captain Ward."

"Free, are they? Being given out as Christmas presents?"

"On sale, just for you."

Watching while Patricia and Peter pressed their noses against the glass to inspect the wonders of penny candy, he kissed the baby on the cheek then turned to his wife.

"The selection isn't exactly what you'd find at the Crystal Palace, but it'd be my pleasure to buy you a present, ma'am."

The reference took her aback.

"How do you know about that?"

"1851; London. There was a whole spread in Harper's. Lot's of illustrations. For a while, we had them up on the walls. Gave the place a... cosmopolitan feel."

"Really? Did you?" He nodded. "What became of them?"

"Curled at the edges and got yellow after a while. But they were nice to look at in the beginning. Must have been a wonder, all those countries coming together to put out their finery. And all the scientific exhibits. Bet a man coulda walked around there for a week and never seen everything. Sure would like to have gone. You didn't see it, by any chance?"

Her eyes rounded.

"The Industry of all Nations," they called it. What I remember best -- aside from the sheer magnitude which overwhelmed the senses -- were the nautical items. Two barometers in particular: The first was Gothic, with an elaborate dial plate depicting the four circles of weather. And the words, of course: Chance, Fair, Stormy and Rain. The other was designed for the Sailor's Home in Liverpool with a fac-simile patent anchor and braided chain."

"You were there," he whispered in awe. "You've been everywhere."

"The Industrial Exhibition in Hyde Park; the exhibition on the Vegetable Kingdom -- you would have loved that." Her expression saddened. "But at the time, I had little interest in botany. The Harmony of Colors; the

Science Exhibition. Statues and tapestries. And the food -- dishes and spices from every country in the world."

"Did they have chilies?"

"I don't remember. But such things as saffron and paprika."

"How is it I have never heard of this before -- your adventures?"

"For the same reason I never heard that you put the illustrations on your walls. Our life together has hardly started, my love."

He grinned and kissed her.

"Got mistletoe if you two intend to carry on like that," Anson supplied, rapping his fingers on the counter.

"I expect we need some of that! And molasses -- that jug you ordered come in?"

"Got it right here waitin' for you."

Hector hefted a large crock sealed with bright red wax and set it out.

"Add ten pounds of coffee and two pounds of tea. China tea," Seth added with importance.

"And you, my husband? What is it I can buy you?"

Passing Paula to her mother, he dug hands in his pockets. Patches of crimson appeared on his cheeks.

"Saw what I wanted, last time I was here. Shall I show you?"

"Please."

"You won't laugh?"

"I will not."

Taking baby steps, Seth wound around the various oversized articles sticking out from shelves, taking her to a small display of toys. Eagerly pointing toward a royal blue velvet bag tied at the neck with gold thread, he whispered, "That's it."

Using her one free hand, Barbara hefted the small treasure, did not immediately identify the contents, then shook it. Failing to recognize the slight clink, she handed it to him.

"Show me."

Carefully untying the bow, Seth spilled out a handful of small glass spheres. He puckered for a whistle.

"The best I've ever seen. These are 'match' beauties. The kind you use when you're playin' with the best. Perfectly balanced. And look at this one," he indicated, pointing out the largest. "Black. A perfect 'pearl' shooter."

"Marbles."

"Marbles. The kind I always dreamed about owning. From way back, when I was a boy. I had a set, of course. But they weren't matched. Just catch-as-catch-can. And all chipped. These are perfect."

"Then you shall have them."

Indicating he bring them to the counter, her eyes fell on another toy in the display. Unlike the marbles, this was crafted from balsa and paper and encased   in   glass.

"Ship in a bottle," she sighed. "Oh, my God. A four-masted schooner. It's beautiful."

Hurrying back, he inspected the treasure.

"Wasn't here last time. Or I woulda bought it and surprised you."

"I am surprised, now. May I have it. Oh, Seth, look at the detail; the tiny people manning the deck."

"That's you and I right there," he decided. "The fleet captain and the captain. This one's Patricia and Peter's up here --"

"In the crow's nest!"

"And look! There's even one who could pass for baby Paula."

The smallest figure of all sat on the deck, legs splayed, a bucket between them.

"All covered in sand! To scrub the planking. But in our case, we shall say, playing in the sand. Our whole family -- right there in a bottle."

"But where's Miss Betty and Thomas?" Patricia asked, tearing herself away from the candy to stare at the vessel.

"There -- and there! Miss Betty by the wheel, piloting us in times of peril. And Thomas standing lookout." Lowering her voice, she added, "And even Mrs. Dryfus -- right there with her hand on the mast."

Taking it to the counter, Seth reverently set it down.

"How much?"

Anson scratched behind his ear.

"That one's a bit pricey. Two dollars. Come all the way from New England. Had it in the back and forgot about it. Just found it the other day when I was cleanin' up."

"Two dollars, it is."

"And this bag of marbles," Nelander added. "And an entire dollar's worth of candy for the crew. Peppermint sticks and spearmint chews and sour balls and molasses taffy. And rock candy chunks. What else?"

"The bottle of rum!" Peter demanded, least they forget.

"The bottle of rum. That comes from the saloon." Nelander tapped her head. "I have it right here on my list."

"And what about Paula?" Not forgetting his father's story about the great celebration they had had when he was six months old, he did not wish her left out.

Hands behind his back, Seth led the procession, each examining specific items that might just do. In the end, the baby, herself, found her own present. Reaching out from her mother's arms, she grabbed a painted gourd affixed to a stout handle.

"A rattle!"

Without waiting for the official holiday, they gave her the toy and she began a vigorous shaking, laughing at the sound. Seth sighed and assumed a command face.

"Just as long as we all agree right here and now she doesn't take it to bed with her. Or we'll never have another quiet night again."

The proposal carried without a dissenting vote and they added it to the growing list of presents accumulating by the molasses, coffee and tea.

Selecting a knife for Thomas and a fine bonnet with a ribbon tie for Betty, that left only Mrs. Dryfus.

Three turns around the store proved futile and Seth grumbled, "You shoulda bought her a Japanese vase at the Crystal Palace."

"That would have only set me back five hundred dollars. A mere pittance. Ah! Here." Indicating a set of one dozen small jars, Nelander nodded. "For making jam. So that she might have the taste of strawberries all year round."

Compared to a Chinese vase that did not seem like much. But coming from the heart, and with remembrance of another time, the Nelander-Wards hoped it would just suit.

CHAPTER 32

A joint resolution of the crew of the Pirate Treasure, taken in the back of the wagon, accepted the notion of inviting Mrs. Dryfus and Mr. Giles to Christmas dinner. This year, with the addition of Miss Betty and Mr. Thomas, they could have quite a gathering.

The motion had arisen spontaneously from Patricia, noting that the presence of new guests might somehow make up for the absence of Beth and Terrance Windsor and the twins. Although her parents found the topic difficult to discuss, Peter had further risen the specter of their former neighbors by adding, "Even if they ain't welcome no more, we can still pray for them, can't we?"

With an abrupt "Yes" to both, Nelander hurried back into the Dry Goods store and borrowed a piece of paper and a pencil from Mr. Anson. Failing to give the shopkeeper any explanation, she quickly wrote the invitation and sealed it with a straight pin purloined from the outside bulletin board.

Since mailing it seemed odd, given they were already in Lawrence, Patricia volunteered to run up and hand-deliver the missive in person. The suggestion carried and the family waylaid their trip home for a brief diversion to the mansion on the hill.

The grand dame answered the door herself, effecting surprise at the caller.

"Patricia Ward! Is it your day for painting lessons?"

"No, ma'am. I've just come to hand this over. I expected Mr. Antony," she bashfully concluded, offering up the letter.

Breaking with tradition and manners, Mrs. Giles removed the pin without offering to bring the child inside. Reading the contents with a thoroughness hardly necessary for so short a note, her lips moved as she formed the words. Finishing it, she began again at the top and completed a second perusal before speaking.

"This is most kind of you. But I am afraid I am otherwise engaged on Christmas day." Immediately noting the child's crestfallen expression she hastened to soften the denial. "Might Mr. Giles and I come sooner? Say, the 24th? Would that spoil your plans?"

Considerably brightening, Patricia shook her head.

"No, ma'am. That would be all right. Papa Captain's got a goose from Mr. Weezer. He traded firewood for it and it's coming just that day. All plucked, too, 'cause Nelander said she didn't have a taste for eating a bird she had known intimately. That means," Patricia added with all seriousness, "she doesn't want to eat a bird she's been tending, even for so short a time."

"I see. How does Nelander reconcile cooking one of your chickens for Sunday supper?"

Patricia pretended horror and covered her face with spread fingers.

"We never have had chicken on Sunday since Nelander's been with us. At least not one of our own hens. If papa wants a nice fat drumstick, he buys one that's already been 'trussed' after church when there's a bazaar."

"What does he use for trade?"

"Fish from the pond."

"Who cleans them, then? Is Captain Nelander squeamish about boning fish?"

"No, ma'am. She says she had a reckoning with all creatures from the sea long ago. She takes only what she needs and always says a sailor's prayer over what she catches."

"But she had no... reckoning... with chickens?"

"Apparently not."

Mrs. Dryfus finally smiled and tucked the invitation up her sleeve.

"Kindly tell her we shall be most pleased to visit on the 24th. At what hour?"

"Five o'clock."

"Thank you, child."

Waving a happy good-bye, Patricia skipped back down the path. Leaping into the wagon, she faithfully repeated the acceptance.

"That's all right, isn't it? Having them come a day early? It will still be like Christmas, won't it?"

Casting a glance at Seth, Nelander replied, "It will be exactly like Christmas. For me, anyway, it will seem even more so."

"Why is that?" Seth asked, turning Blaze and setting them on a homeward course.

"At sea when the weather is bad and we are expecting a storm which might require all hands on deck, the captain often decides to move the holiday up. That way, the crew may celebrate the day without being interrupted and the cook does not fly into a rage that all his preparations have gone for naught."

Seth flinched a little and stared down at his gloved hands.

"I thought you were going to say the captain ordered the feast early in case one of the seamen were washed overboard in the storm and he wanted him to have one last big meal before going to his reward."

"If that really were his reasoning, I would not have said so."

"Oh."

Guilty of having cast a pall over the day, Seth said nothing the remainder of the trip and went into the barn to work after their arrival home. He uttered no more than monosyllables the rest of the afternoon and evening and only when he and his wife prepared for bed did he string a sentence together.

"I hope I did not spoil anything by what I said in the wagon," he began, awkwardly sitting on the edge of the mattress in his union suit. Nelander fussed with the baby before taking her own place opposite.

"Not at all. You made a good point."

"Which one of us was more accurate?"

She laughed and turned down the covers.

"If you had any familiarity with ship's 'doctors,' my love, you would know the answer to that, already. They are a temperamental lot, prone to fits. No one willingly crosses the cook. I have known brassy sailors who would speak back to the officer on watch but quail before the Master of the Galley."

"Why is that?"

Slipping her legs beneath the covers, she waited until he had blown out the lamp.

"Because many of them are former able-bodied tars; disabled in one fashion or another. A badly mended leg; weak lungs which prohibit them climbing the mast. Loss of good eyesight. Or old age. I suppose that is the most common. No one will hire them on as deck crew so they accept whatever they can get."

She waited for him to ask the obvious: Why don't they just retire and live off their savings? Or go to a seaman's home? But he did not. Instead, Seth rolled into bed and put his hand in hers.

Which made up for and went beyond mending the taboo he had broken earlier.

Greeting their honored guest with a name more proper for the setting and the occasion, Nelander rushed out into the yard, breath forming in clouds as she spoke.

"Welcome, Mrs. Giles! Merry Christmas! And to you, too, Mr. Giles."

"Season's greetings, Nelander," the elder countered. "And now that we have dispensed with the formality, it is 'Victoria' and 'Antony.'"

"Come in, quickly. It is cold. Peter will take care of your horse and buggy. It is so good to have a boy around the farm," she added in delight. Having observed Peter's eyes bulge at the sight of presents, delaying the inevitable by calling on his gender caused both women to grin at one another. "Patricia: help carry in the packages."

"I can help," Peter tried, eagerly shoving his nose under the protective tarpaulin to have a better look. "Before I take the horse into the barn."

"No need. Your sister can manage. Not too heavy for a girl, are they, Victoria?"

"Indeed not."

Giving a yank, Peter unhitched his four-legged charge and hurried him along while the three females took the wrapped packages inside.

"You, Antony, come in out of the cold. It is going to snow and I do not want you outside. Men," Nelander winked. "They have less sense than dogs. And far less intelligence than cats."

Arms spread around bundles, they rushed through the open door and into the living room where a bright, cheery fire welcomed the newcomers. Seth, who had been standing with the baby in his arms, stuck out one to Giles.

"Welcome, old man," he greeted. "Take off your coat and gloves and make yourself comfortable." With a nod of recognition at having overheard the outside conversation, a wink followed the observation, "Good to have womenfolk around to do the toting."

At first shocked and then guardedly bemused, Giles removed his outer garments and hung them on a hook over the door. Before he could trot obediently after Mrs. Giles to take her wrap, Seth dragged him toward a chair.

"No introductions necessary? You know Miss Betty and Mr. Thomas?"

Lovingly accepting the hand of her stepson, Betty bestowed it with kisses before shoving him away.

"Ah been suspectin' da captain ob dis house been imbibin' freely ob dat rum I smelt on da table, an' now Ah knows fo' sure dat's what's causin' his loose tongue. An', suh, no matter da occasion, or da liberty granted, it be 'Miss Victoria' to yuh. An' plain 'Thomas' an' 'Antony' fo' da boys. We all fambly here, an' I sho' neber called my chil' Mista Thomas befo'!"

Seth huffed. "Well, then, make yourself useful, mother." Dropping Paula into her arms, he stomped over to the kitchen table, wrapped his fingers around the bottle of spirits and rattled it against the set of eight variably-sized glasses already set out for use. "Who's for a drink to celebrate the holiday?"

Speaking as the elder, Mrs. Giles put an end to that errant expectation.

"The rum goes back on the table, Seth Ward. And you may take your place beside Antony. I see my rocking chair is vacant and I intend to sit there directly."

As Patricia put her fingers around her throat to simulate choking, Seth sputtered, "My... my... captain's chair? You intend to sit... there?"

"Indeed I do, youngster. As senior...." Lacking the word, she raised an eyebrow at the other command officer. "What am I, exactly?"

"The commodore, sir."

Well satisfied, Victoria laid her handful of presents under the tree and stately glided toward The Chair.

"I expect, Captain Ward, you would not think of having The Commodore sit on the floor? Or the couch?"

Scuffing a foot as though he would have it otherwise, Seth could do nothing but agree.

"Please, sir. The place of honor is yours." And then, with a twinkle, "But beware the seat. It may not be as soft as you are accustomed."

Alas for the senior captain, Mrs. Giles had her answer ready.

"That being the case, I will have you sit there -- and I will perch on your lap."

Nelander and Patricia clapped and Seth backed away, as bashful as a ten-year-old.

"If it is not to your liking, ma'am, I will fetch a pillow."

She settled in, rested her arms on the sides and sighed in satisfaction. Not content to let him off so easily, however, a snap of the fingers brought him around.

"A footstool, Captain Ward."

When nothing close to fitting that description met his eye, he grinned and dropped to all fours, presenting the flat of his back for the support of her legs. She gladly took advantage and kept him there a full minute while Herman, stunned by the new arrangement, galloped up to lick his face.

Thomas signaled to Betty and she interpreted.

"He says da dog jest got his Christmas present!"

More applauding and a round of petting for Herman sealed the deal. Peter, quickly returned from his chores, opened a new chapter.

"Well, now that that's settled, when are we gonna open the presents?"

More clapping, followed by knowing smiles between the adults.

"That, sir, comes after Christmas dinner." Nelander winked at the commodore. "He knows his father has bought him a candy store's worth of sweets and wishes to stuff himself before feasting on goose."

The senior-senior officer concurred.

"Help with the table, boy. Antony and I --" Her brows furrowed. "What is his rank, by the way?"

"First officer."

"Ah. Good. First Officer Antony and I are famished. In preparation for our visit, we have fasted since last night. Understanding the goose to be a very large one!"

The original four members of the landlocked sailing vessel "hopped to it," and soon the room filled with a vast assortment of pleasing aromas. Amidst the clatter of serving dishes, the steel-on-steel of a knife being sharpened and the barely suppressed chatter of the participants, the meal was soon laid out.

"Your feast awaits," Seth pronounced, offering a hand to Mrs. Giles. Antony performed the same service for Miss Betty and the two ranking ladies were seated, one at each head of the table. Nelander and Seth sat opposite one another, Antony and Thomas by Barbara and Patricia and Peter next to Seth. Not to be left out, Paula sat by her mother in the highchair.

After a simple grace, the commodore exclaimed in delight, "Fit for a Queen!"

"It's been a long time since I had so many at the table," Fleet Captain Ward admitted. "Maybe too long. The children and I lived a lonely life before a seafarer drifted off course and landed in our front yard." Lifting his glass of water in toast, eyes sparking with the jewels of emotion, he finished, "To you, my love. For bringing us all together."

Amid cheers of "Here, here!" and "To you, Captain Mama," which elicited matching tears from the recipient, the extended family clinked glasses.

"We have all been too isolated," Mrs. Giles observed, daubing at her own eyes. "I had almost forgotten what it was like to invited out to dine -- or even to enjoy myself in company. This is surely the greatest -- and the most special banquet I have ever had the honor of attending. Friends and family not even Her Majesty, the Queen of England, could boast."

"Well, fewer children," Nelander ad-libbed as Paula let out a loud avowal of approval. "Hurry, Captain Ward. We are all hungry."

Doing yeoman's work, he quickly carved the magnificent bird, detaching both drumsticks before slicking thick slices of breast meat.

"Who wants what?" he demanded, licking his lips. Thomas quickly signaled to Betty.

"He says, dere be too many men an' not 'nuf legs." Clearing her throat, the elder shook her head and repeated herself in an entirely different voice. "He says, there are too many men and not enough legs."

Momentarily stunned by the change in vernacular, Betty savored the reaction before continuing. "Miss Vickie taught me how to speak properly and I will not disappoint her on so auspicious an occasion, least she think I had forgotten. Or that I had taught our own sons improperly. Captain

Ward, some of that juicy white meat for me and Thomas. A drumstick, if you please, for Antony and yourself."

Peter pretended to pout.

"What about me. I'm a man, too, aren't I?"

"You, child, are a small fish in a big pond. Some of the dark meat from the underside for this warrant officer. And you, Navigator?"

"The same for me," Patricia grinned.

Seth doled out the portions and Barbara passed around the bowls, letting each choose from the vast array of onion and spice stuffing, boiled potatoes, green beans and mashed pumpkin.

The first to "set to," Peter smacked his lips.

"If we hurry, we get to the sweet potato pie that much sooner," he explained, a rivulet of gravy dripping from the corner of his mouth. "Miss Betty brought it," he explained, eyes sneaking toward the oven where it had been put on to warm.

"It appears since I have been isolated from civilization nothing has changed," Victoria primly noted. "I wonder why you bothered," she added to Nelander, "preparing this fine meal when at least a portion of your crew desires only the dessert."

"I often question that, myself. But I have never found the anticipation of pie a deterrent from the main courses."

"Ah ga gaga."

All heads turned on Paula.

"You see," Seth explained with a lopsided grin, "the apple does not fall far from the tree."

Dipping his finger in the gravy, he offered it for Paula's inspection. Toothless gums and a soft pink tongue eagerly sampled the delicacy.

"It will not be long before she assumes her rightful place at the table. She knows a good thing when she tastes it. No disrespect, ma'am," Antony continued, addressing the child's mother, "but it is hard to do better than goose gravy."

Enunciated in precisely the same style as Miss Betty, his three complete sentences -- the longest any of them could remember hearing him say -- brought grins and nods.

"True. And I, for one, will not rue the day."

Banging the ends of their silverware against the table in a slight breech of etiquette, the crew "dug to," and made short work of the meal. When everyone declared themselves either "satisfied" or "stuffed to the gills," depending upon personal preference and age, they leaned back to contemplate their stomachs.

"I suppose we are all too full for the final course?"

Peter patted his tummy before shocking the assemblage by pulling up his shirt.

"Right here," he indicated. "I've been saving a spot."

"Then, we shall fill it, sir. Coffee or tea?" Barbara asked the others.

"Tea."

The commodore settled the issue and Nelander placed the kettle on to boil while the rest gathered in the living room. Resuming the captain's chair, Mrs. Giles finally had time to assimilate the holiday decorations.

A large pine tree, reaching to the ceiling, occupied center stage. Covered in handmade decorations of wooden sleighs, cows, horses, dogs and cats, brightly colored balls, paper cutouts of sailing vessels and glass icicles, it presented a festive, cheery aspect. Other Christmas ornaments lined the mantel. Arranged in chronological order, the pieces represented the development of skills as Patricia and Peter's artwork progressed through the creative stages of childhood. Standing like a family portrait, the decorations symbolized not only the advancement of age but the promise of life to come.

Two large yellow tallow candles burned at each side and the warm, red-orange-blue fire, burned down to a ruddy glow filled the room with inviting comfort.

"I spent the Christmas season in England one year," Victoria remarked, finding it hard to tear her eyes away from the homemade scene. "The trees there -- and it was a new custom at the time, mind -- were covered with small lights. Each home had rich Brussels carpets, polished silver lamp bases, ornamental vases and statues, boughs with holly berries and cachets of dried flowers to give the rooms a floral scent. There were servants dressed in livery to wait on us, imported French wines and chocolate, mint candies of pink and green and paper bells strung by gold and silver cords."

She sighed but not wistfully. "In many homes there were full orchestras which played music for gentle contemplation or dancing. Gentlemen in black suits and ladies in ball gowns. Children," she underscored, "were to be seen but not heard. They were presented for admiration and then dispatched to the play room." Clasping an embroidered handkerchief to her lips, she slowly shook her head. "I would not trade one minute here for all that finery."

"But it must have been grand," Barbara decided, serving the pie with heaping piles of fresh white cream.

"Grand? Ostentatious, it was. A way to brag of one's achievements; or rather, the accomplishments of one's husband. What money can buy holds no merit when placed beside the wonders of loving hearts."

"Thank you."

Sipping her tea, Mrs. Giles pointed toward the ornament on top of the tree.

"I expected... an angel. Or a jolly old man in a white beard and red suit. Pray, explain the fish."

"I made it," Patricia whispered. "We never have had anything to put there and I wanted something that represented the season as well as the Pirate Treasure. Since we are celebrating Jesus' birthday, I knew He was a fisherman of Men. And Nelander is from the sea. She always says we ought to give thanks to those who give us sustenance. I thought it would be a way of remembering all our blessings."

"And so it is, child. It is perfect."

Bowing her head, the old lady offered a silent prayer. After communing her own thanks to the many spirits listening, she snapped to attention.

"Now -- it is time for presents."

Another blessing on a day of rekindling past with "present."

CHAPTER 33

"Who goes first?"

"Me!" Peter cried, racing to the tree. Breath still warm from the rich flavors of sweet potato pie and China tea, his boyish fingers probed the multitude of gifts distributed by family and friends. "Here is one with my name on it!"

Seth momentarily quelled his spirit with a stern, "Youth before beauty, my lad." Bouncing the baby on his knee, he pointed to a gift clearly marked "Paula."

"Oh, all right." Effecting a pout as real as pretend, the boy gathered in the gift and pressed it into the tiny pink fingers. "Make quick work of it."

Proving herself adept at asserting her place as well as her temper, Paula grasped the package, eying it with clear joy. Instead of tearing off the wrapping as an older child would, she gummed the corner. Peter threw up his hands.

"Oh, please! Somebody help her or we'll be here all night."

He had not meant to elicit laughter, but succeeded, nevertheless.

Taking pity, Nelander slipped the red ribbon off the corners, then removed the checkered green and white cloth used as wrapping. Dipping her fingers between the layers of cotton bunting used for packing, she grasped a thin chain. Holding it out for inspection, the close-clustered gathering beheld a brass disc, the size of a walnut, suspended from the links.

"A necklace!" Mrs. Giles guessed, somewhat puzzled by the plain adornment.

"Say, rather, a teething ring," the seaman corrected. "I am assured by our resident expert that there is nothing better than brass for a baby to chew on when her gums are sore. I am also informed this useful metal has a tangy taste, highly approved of by the crawling set."

Attention turned to Seth, who sheepishly grinned.

"That's what I used when I was a boy."

Peter effected real astonishment.

"You remember that far back, papa?"

"Thank you, son. That just missed being a compliment." Spreading his hands, he demonstrated by how much. "Yes: I remember that far back. All the way to the Revolution. In fact, while in short pants I assisted George Washington survey the Virginia Valley."

Eyes expanded beyond the need of sextant and line, Peter whistled.

"Really?"

"No."

Disappointed, the boy held out his hand for the present. Delicately draping it over Paula's head, he stood back to observe his handiwork.

"What was it for? The brass circle, I mean."

"Primary as a washer," Nelander explained. "Placed between two larger objects to ease friction and facilitate removal when the equipment was cleaned or lubricated. Brass is an essential metal aboard ship. Who can tell me why?"

"Strength?" Patricia guessed.

Seth tried "Malleability?"

Mrs. Giles took another track entirely. "Because it is inexpensive?"

The seaman laughed. "All good answers but none exactly correct. Brass is an alloy of copper and zinc. The principal benefit is that it does not conduct electricity. It neither causes or transmit sparks," she elucidated. "Very important when your world is made of wood and fire is the most dreaded word in a sailor's vocabulary."

"I thought," Peter pouted, "that was 'The rum cask is empty.'"

"That is four words," Nelander teased. "Be reasonable. Which is more frightening: a conflagration or being without grog?"

Eyes rolled around their sockets as he weighed the equation.

"A fire may be put out, but when the rum's gone, that's it!"

She tussled his hair, then playfully shoved him away.

"I found it in my kit bag when I was going through it the other day. I don't know why I packed it; it may have just been on the table when I scooped everything inside. Or I may have planned on using it as a sinker -- for fishing. Being unfamiliar with fresh water creatures, I supposed them to be as large as what we caught at sea."

Somewhat mollified by his parent's misconception, Peter admired the gift.

"Paula's too young to drink rum, anyway. I expect she'll get more use out of it as a teething ring."

"And when she discovers that by banging it against the rattle we bought her at Anson's, she can make a great noise, it will have an added benefit: that of keeping us in a constant state of alarm."

"Yes, well, you were the one, I believe, who spoke with such -- eagerness -- of expanding our crew."

Nelander's risqué comment drew laughs from the adults and the captain shrunk under their jibes.

"Let us move on or we shall be at this all night!"

Patricia and Peter unwrapped their trove of penny candy, then Nelander and Seth opened the packages they had given one another. The ship-in-a-bottle went on the mantel and the marbles were eagerly shown to Thomas.

"I'll teach you how to play," Seth promised his adopted brother. "We can buy a bag of marbles for you, too."

"He means, so you will have some to lose when he beats the pants off you," Barbara interpreted. Thomas signaled his approval.

"I never really had anyone to play with. Rick, my older brother was more interested in cards. Poker and the like. He always thought marbles were for boys and not men. To hear him say it, he was always grown up. He wanted to play games for money, never understanding my fascination for bits of polished glass."

Without mentioning his younger sibling, a lapse not unnoted, Seth held a marble to the light, eyes glistening. "This one is almost translucent. Pale blue. When you look through it at the sky, it almost acts as a.... Well, not a telescope, exactly, but it seems you can see things through it you can't with the unaided eye. Those are the ones I always tried to win. Other boys liked the solid colors; they thought they shot straighter."

"Did they?"

He hedged and then hitched a shoulder. "Maybe. But their intent was winning; to capture as many of the other boy's marbles as possible. Wealth," he added in a lower voice, "meant the most marbles. Winning, to me, meant having the finest collection."

"No one here would argue with you." Nelander kissed him on the cheek. "Now, you have a fine set -- and a new playmate. I am afraid, Thomas, your evenings are now taken. When you and Captain Ward are late for supper, Betty and I will know what you are about: squatting around a circle shooting marbles at one another's pieces."

She painted a pretty picture. One applicable only for the moment. But for the moment, it satisfied and Thomas clapped his hands before writing on Betty's palm.

"He says he will create his own marbles: from amber. He knows where to find some and he'll make a set of nice round ones. Then, he'll play with you and see whose marbles are better."

Challenge accepted, they went back to unwrapping presents.

Betty and Thomas had brought exquisite baskets for the children: a toy box for Paula, a treasure chest for Peter and a paint box for Patricia, partitioned off for brushes and small jars. Seth received a large basket for holding tools and Nelander's was meant to store spices.

"Big enough for chilies, paprika, nutmeg and cinnamon!" she declared in delight. "With room, besides. What a wonderful gift."

Betty smiled and indicated two rings on the top.

"Mista Seth can hang it up for you. I put hooks on the bottom. You can hang fresh herbs from it so they can dry."

"A wonderful idea."

Miss Betty received her bonnet with joy and entertained the gathering by putting it on and parading around the room like a grand dame.

"Dis be da finest hat Ah eber did habe!" she declared, before winking at her former mistress. "One that would rival those fancy people you met in England."

Mrs. Giles laughed and clapped. "You are a far better looking woman than any of them, Betty Ward. They thought themselves attractive with their French gowns and pearls, but all the adornment in the world cannot make up for natural beauty. Or grace. Or even," she added with a flash of anger, "breeding. The African race has an astounding variety of facial features and symmetry of form. You embody that and more. To say nothing of intelligence and loyalty. Two qualities I find nearly lacking from the Caucasian family."

"I think the Lord is colorblind, Miss Victoria. Those made in his image are not so fortunate."

"He might have done a better job." Sucking back a pout, Mrs. Giles attempted to lighten the sour mood she had inadvertently brought on. "Come. I, too, have brought presents." Handing Peter a thin envelope, she watched with anticipation as he tore it open. The look of astonishment proved the worth of the gift.

"A bill of sale. You are giving me -- you are giving me Fleet for my very own?"

Gasps of astonishment followed the pronouncement. Seth laid a hand on the boy's shoulder.

"Madam: that is very generous of you but we cannot accept so valuable a gift."

"I want Peter to have her. The filly does me no good. I have abandoned riding in my advanced old age."

"Then, you must sell it, ma'am, for she is worth a great deal."

"She is horse, like any other. No more or less valuable for all its bloodlines. My groom tells me he can do nothing with her -- that she is too high spirited and uncooperative. But 'Fleet,' as you say, has taken to Peter. She will make him a good riding horse." Noting Seth's distressed look, the matron hastened to add, "But we all agree the horse will be stabled at my home. At least until Peter has thoroughly trained her. And earned enough to pay for the saddle and bridle. You see," she emphasized, "I am not that generous. You must work to pay for the tack. Such accouterments do not come cheaply."

"I will be glad to, Mrs. Giles. Anything. Just say the word."

"All right, then. When your father brings Patricia for her art lessons and you are not needed on the farm, I will set out tasks for you. Cleaning the barn. Mowing the hay. Exercising the other horses. Shall we say... two years?"

Two years for the war to be over. Two years for enough blood to be shed that men will come to their senses and settle their differences. Two years for law and order to be restored. Two years until the slaves are freed and all people may walk the streets without fear of bounty hunters or prejudice.

"As many as you say! Oh, Papa Captain. I have my own horse! Say it is all right. Say I may keep Fleet as my very own!"

He hesitated, clearly caught between the value of the gift and a little boy's heart.

"We will speak of it again in two years."

Satisfied that his argument had carried the day, Peter ran for another present under the tree.

"Here, Miss Victoria. A present for you."

She withdrew, not having expected a gift.

"Surely not...." And then, with forced levity, "A bribe?"

The child did not understand. "For Christmas."

Ashamed at her cynicism, Mrs. Giles took the box.

"So heavy. What is in here, I wonder?" Fingers shaking, she explored the wrapping. "It is too pretty to open."

"Go ahead," Patricia urged. "You may keep the wrap if you like. It's only a bit of cloth. We use it over and over. Nelander says she has seen presents wrapped with colored paper and big, fancy bows, and that people just throw it away when they're done. That seems such a waste." Her chest puffed out in pride. "Ours has history. I can remember all the presents I've ever got and they've been wrapped in that same cloth. It makes everything more special when you do it like that. And it's less wasteful. I use that one under the lamp in my bedroom. As a sort of a doily. It's cheerful and it makes me happy. But when we need to wrap a present, I take it out again."

"Then I most certainly will not keep it. But that is a wonderful tradition."

Barely able to suppress emotion, she meticulously unknotted the string, then draped away the cloth. Lifting the lid of the box, her breath caught as she identified the contents.

"Jam jars."

"For making strawberry jam," Peter explained. "We thought that next spring, in case you can't eat all the strawberries, you can make jam."

Inexplicably blushing, the lady bowed her head.

"Something I have been giving much thought to." Salt droplets pooled at the corners of her eyes and softly trickled down. "Yes. Perhaps.... I don't know." Hand to her lips, she finished, "This is very thoughtful. The best present I have ever received." Handing the box to Giles, she brushed a hand across his. "For both of us."

Misunderstanding, Peter quickly intervened.

"No, ma'am. We have something else for Antony."

"Yes, we do," his sister insisted. "It's a sort of family gift -- from all of us. We talked about it. Something from the heart so he'd know we care."

Making a nod at her brother, he bent down and scooped up Squash. Taking awkward steps for the puppy wiggled in his hands, he offered out the hound.

"He's yours, now. You ain't got a dog and he's a right fine one." Antony's nose crinkled as he struggled with mixed feelings. "We got him from Mr. McConaghie. He said the pup wouldn't hunt and he traded us for some strawberries. But papa says he will hunt and that he's a fine animal."

Antony turned luminous orbs on the adult.

"What does this mean, sir?"

"Squash is a bond between us. He was... bred to track Men, but he will never do that. Mathis really gave him to us because he knew the dog would not bark if he came in the dead of night. And for that, the dog served his purpose. We were recruited, sir. And remain dedicated to the cause. But we have old Herman, here, to guard the crops and another from Hank McTree for the strawberries. Thomas has a dog; now, you do, also. For companionship."

"You give me a... dog?"

"From all of us. With full and complete expectation that you will one day be seen around Lawrence with the best hound in the state."

"Maybe we can go riding, together, Mr. Antony. Me on Fleet and you on one of the other horses. With Squash runnin' ahead of us, scarin' out rabbits."

"I... do not know," he faltered. "We shall see."

"But you will take him? As our present?" Peter began to tremble. "Otherwise, we won't have anything to give you."

The young man looked to his mother, clearly torn. She made a snap decision possibly overruling one made seconds before.

"Yes, Peter. Antony will be pleased to accept your most generous gift. And thanks all of you," she added, making a point of establishing eye contact with all the Wards.

Uncertain how gracious she sounded, even if her intentions were sincere and appreciative, Mrs. Giles bustled through an opening in the semicircle which had been created around her and drew a large, flat gift from beneath the pine. Clasping it tightly, she positioned herself as a general might, back to an impenetrable fortress of sharp needles.

"I saved this for last. It is for you, Patricia." Before giving it over, she held back, running a hand over the narrow top. "You see, I cannot be accused of wastefulness in my choice of wrapping, for I have used the same paper with which it came."

"You... bought me something?"

"In a manner of speaking." She brushed aside the objection and lowered her voice in imitation of Captain Ward. "You need not worry, Patricia. The present itself cost me nothing. No obligation incurred."

Seth grunted as the rest grinned.

"Now, you are making fun of me."

"My father would have called you stiff-necked. Which would not necessarily have been an insult."

"If Mr. Dillinger called me that, I would necessarily have taken it as an insult."

"Good man," she approved. Once more running a hand over the top of the package, Mrs. Giles gave it a loving pat. "I have said I paid nothing for the present. This is true. What small cost I incurred came from.... You shall see. It is not rightly a present at all and I meant to give it to you sooner." Ending with a gush, she thrust it forward. "Here it is, then."

Patricia took the gift, felt around the edges, then hesitated.

"What is it?"

"It ain't a paint set," the ever assertive Peter forwarded. "It ain't a horse. It ain't --"

"Enough of your 'aint's,' young man," Nelander sternly reproached. "What it 'ain't,' is, it ain't yours. Let your sister discover for herself."

Too eager to bear the suspense, he began bounding around the room. Nelander quieted him by pressing the baby into his arms.

Pulling one of the long ends of white butcher's string which held the paper in place, Patricia delicately removed the fastening, then tucked it in her pocket before lifting away the covering. She beheld an ornate gold picture frame, plate glass protecting the article beneath. With the back to her family, they could not see what it held. The expression on her face, however, conveyed a momentous surprise.

"Show us."

Mouth agape, the child slowly turned the frame so that it faced outward.

"Jumping jehosophat!" Seth mildly cursed, bringing a hand to his chest. Barbara rocked back on her heels, then rushed forward, doing him one better.

"Oh, my God, what is this?" Near enough to read the banner from where she stood, closer proximity only increased her awe. "Harper's Weekly. Your painting, Patricia! You have been published!" Spinning in the same motion, she confronted Mrs. Giles. "How is this possible?"

"I sent Patricia's painting to a gentleman I know: Mr. Wendell Phillips. A renowned abolitionist. I briefly explained the circumstances and asked his opinion. When he did not write back, I questioned whether he had ever received it. He travels so much, speaking in our cause," she explained. "I feared he might have missed it, somehow, on his journeys."

"Or that he did not like it," the artist supplied.

"Never that. It is exquisite. And then one day I received a package by special delivery. I did not think to look at it right away as I often receive Northern newspapers and periodicals. It sat a week or more before I had the chance to sit down and read." Her entire body glowed with pride. "Imagine my delight."

Clearing his throat but failing to disguise his emotion, Seth nodded. "We can imagine. Something of what we are feeling, now."

Reverently tiptoeing nearer, he read the print depiction of Patricia's work. "Miss Theresa, baby Samuel and the little grey elephant jumping over the moon." Tipping sideways to avoid the glare of firelight, he read the caption. "A runaway and her babe captured at a way-station along the Underground Railroad. Not captured by bloodhounds or human bloodsuckers but by a Girl whose initials I only dare give as 'P.N.W.' The Elephant, a creature originating in Africa along-side the Subjugated Race, symbolizes a jump for Freedom."

"'P.N.W.'" Nelander breathed. "Patricia Ward."

"Patricia Nelander-Ward," the girl corrected.

"This is too much to believe. Too... wonderful. Our daughter, Seth -- published in so distinguished a paper."

He swallowed hard and scraped his foot. "We have you to thank for this, Mrs. Giles."

"Indeed, you do not. It was the child's own work. I merely passed it along to good people. They did with it what they would."

"But we could never have hoped -- and you gave her lessons."

Victoria Giles brushed away her own part.

"There is a letter from Mr. Phillips. Shall I read it?"

"Please do."

They rapidly settled down, each leaning forward so as not to miss a single word. Mrs. Giles took the letter from her handbag.

"Dear Mrs. Dryfus: this is the most extraordinary Painting I have ever had the pleasure of setting eyes on. Your Artist has captured the Humanity and the Inhumanity of Slavery on one bold canvas.

"The eyes of the young mother staring adoringly at her babe -- so like those of any white mother. And the babe -- Righteous Mankind's hope for the Future that he Thrive and Grow in Freedom, unshackled by the cruel irons of Slavery. The imagery of the Elephant jumping over the moon is sheer magic. It ties the Dark Continent in with the Celestial Body which leads Our Brothers and Sisters out of Bondage.

"God bless you for all your Efforts and an especial blessing for Miss P.N.W., whomever she might be." She hesitated, then read on. "Although I suspect you are the creator of this magnificent painting. I enclose the newspaper which extolls the Fruits of your Labor and assure you it can only Forward the work of your Friends. Your obedient servant, Wendell Phillips, Esquire."

Folding the letter, Victoria steadied herself. "I immediately wrote back to correct his misconception. He replied, saying you have a divine talent, Miss Patricia, and he would be honored to accept more of your artwork."

"More!" Seth gushed. "Did you hear that? He wants more."

"He wrote other things besides, but they are a matter for another time. You are pleased, then?"

"Pleased? We are astonished." Seth looked around in anticipation. "We must hang this somewhere special. Over the mantel by Nelander's map --"

"Yes, Captain. You must. But not now. When times are safer. Theresa and the child would be recognized by the McConaghie clan. Or by Brian Clement or any of that Simpson gang," she added with disdain. "Helping slaves escape is still against the law. Better I keep it." Her voice hardened. "No one dares enter my house without permission."

His face fell but truth willed out.

"Of course. You are right. In my excitement.... I wanted it here." Punching a fist into his palm, he scowled. "When will this damned war be over?"

"I don't know, sir," Peter piped up. "But this calls for a celebration. By Mrs. Giles taking it back, it's almost like we buried treasure. That's a pirate tradition if ever there was one. I'd say rum is in order."

On his father's nod he scrambled for the bottle and glasses. Nelander went with him and put on the kettle so they could make a hot toddy of spirits, sugar and water. Serving it in tall glasses, the crew of the Pirate Treasure drank to Patricia's great achievement and the hope that like-minded Brothers and Sisters saw the war to its proper and everlasting conclusion.

CHAPTER 34

Suppressing a yawn with no success at all, Seth stretched, scratched an itch behind his knee, then kicked off his shoes.

"Sure you don't want another game of marbles?"

Thomas, whose own eyes were half closed, reluctantly shook his head. Pointing to Peter, who had curled up on the floor just beyond their hand-drawn circle and lay fast asleep, he indicated the same state of weariness.

"You're right, I guess. I don't want the day to end, that's all. It's been a perfect Christmas." He tapped the floor where he had stretched out, catching Nelander's attention. "What would you say? The best Christmas?"

She playfully brushed the question aside.

"It could have been better."

His eyebrow arched as he unconsciously braced himself for a lecture on the values of judging events as "best."

"We ran out of rum too early."

He gently kicked Peter with the tips of his toes.

"Not for this little crewmember. Nor the other, either, I wager. Where is Patricia?"

Barbara edged aside, revealing a second sleeping child, this one under a blanket on the couch.

"You sent her to bed. Remember? When she used your 'shooter' to knock your marbles out of the ring, or whatever you are supposed to do to win."

"Beginner's luck."

"How many did you win, Thomas?"

He held up his fingers. Four.

"We weren't playing for 'keeps,'" Seth groused.

"Yup. The best Christmas, ever." Arms and legs barely responsive, Nelander worked her way into a sitting position. "Do you suppose Antony and Mrs. Giles made it home by now?"

"Asleep in their beds as snug as bugs in a rug."

"Considering all the cat fur, dog hair, 'children's toys' and such we drag over our rug, I'd rethink that, if I were you."

He flashed her one of his lopsided grins and patted the small carpet upon which he sprawled.

"I don't know. Right now, it feels pretty comfortable."

Miss Betty, who, until that time had been dozing in the Captain's chair, forced her eyelids apart.

"Weh bes' be goin', Thomas. It be a long walk acrost da fields."

"Why don't you stay here? It must be past midnight. No sense going from the warm out into the cold. It's freezing. You'll get a chill. We have plenty of room."

Betty considered, then reluctantly waved him off.

"No, suh. When an old woman has her own home, it's a mighty fine feelin' to return."

Correctly reading the radiance of her features, he could not disagree. Kicking his feet to work out the kinks, Seth get up and padded toward the kitchen.

"Let me at least put some coals in the hand warmer for you."

Grabbing a metal rod, he began to stir the ash in the cook stove when a loud, peeling sound arose from outside. Frozen as surely as though an Arctic blast had broken through the windows, his head shot up. All attentive, it took only a second longer to identify the tolling.

"Fire bell!"

Stomach muscles tightened, he dropped the poker and raced for the door. Hand on the knob, he stopped as quickly as he started, cold sweat popping up along the collar line of his shirt.

"Fire bell?" Dread replaced fear. "That's impossible. The only alarm we can hear across the fields comes from Betty's place."

"And no one is there," Nelander finished. Turning to Betty, she demanded, "Is there?" For once, words failed. The Negress slowly shook her head. Barbara pressed. "No one you're moving along the Railroad?"

Again, a negative shake.

"No one you're expecting?" Seth pressed.

"No, suh. Da only conductor left in town is Giles, an' he jes' been here. Wouldn't habe had no time to go home, find a po' soul dere waitin' an' bring 'em back. An' sho', not cume here." Her face puckered in disgust. "Wouldn't be ringin' no fire bell, neither."

"Then... who is it?"

"More to the question, what do they want?"

Slipping off the couch, Nelander replaced her shoes and joined Seth. Opening the door an inch, both pulled back from the icy draft. Forcing themselves to acclimate, they tried again.

"Can't see anything," Seth complained. "Too far. No one in our yard."

"I suppose if he were here, he'd have rung our bell."

"Who?"

The single syllable choked coming out, sounding more like tortured gibberish than a question he wanted answered.

"Someone who's up to no good." And then, more angrily, "Someone who is issuing us the royal summons."

"Us? Why us? You said if they wanted us, they'd have rung our bell."

"All right. Someone who is commanding you to make an appearance at the old Windsor place."

The "you" caused the sweat to roll down his back. The unpleasant feeling only augmented his anxiety.

"Why me? Why there?"

She answered the second, presuming that would cover the first.

"A person who has been banished from our property. Someone you threatened to shoot, should he ever show his unwelcome presence at the Pirate Treasure. "

"Norman." Issued as a snake hiss. For a moment, hope displaced reason. "But it is Christmas."

"Very early Christmas morning," Nelander agreed.

"What does he want?"

Wakened by the noise and sudden activity, Patricia sleepily came up and took hold of her father's hand.

"Maybe he wants to give us presents."

"That devil does not give gifts, he only steals what others have received."

Seeing the girl stiffen, Nelander had a better answer.

"Perhaps you are right, darling. Christmas has a strange way of effecting people." Pushing the child back, she hurried her over to where Peter still slept on the floor. "Take your brother and go to bed. Bring Paula with you and keep her in your room. Go now."

"Yes, sir."

Rousing the boy, she led him away, baby tucked between her arms. When the four adults were alone, Seth attempted to work off the effects of rum by shaking his head and forcing his eyes wide.

"I'll have to go see what he wants. If I don't, he'll come here, all right. With a big, toothy grin on his face, saying 'I tried to call you, brother, but you didn't come. So I had to show up here. Hope you don't mind.' Happy holidays and all that."

Voices so similar, Nelander clearly envisioned Norman's deceitful countenance.

"Yesss. He is up to no good, all right. Or perhaps he has gotten himself all liquored up and is... playing a game."

"Either way, he is still dangerous." Motioning her away, he reached for his coat on the hook behind the door. She stopped him.

"I am going with you."

Even in the dimness, Barbara read his horror.

"No. You stay here. Protect the children."

Sweeping an arm across the living room, her answer carried with it a finality.

"We have Thomas and Betty for that."

Hearing his name and finally feeling free to speak, the black man began a series of rapid hand signals. Even without the key, both Wards readily interpreted his intent.

"No, Thomas. If there's going to be trouble, I don't want you mixed up in it." The signaling continued, this time more frenetic. "How would it look?" Seth reasoned. "A Negro involved in an altercation with a white man? Folks in town wouldn't stand for that, even if Norman is an outlaw. That's a line you're not allowed to cross. Christ, they'll all be up in arms and next thing you know, a mob would attack 'Nigger Hole' to prevent servile insurrection. And then pass goddamn ordinances allowing brown women and children to be locked up."

The man's shoulders slumped, hands dropping listlessly to his sides.

"Nelander and I will go. Besides," he added, not without truthfulness, "I'd feel better with a man here. Watching the children. No matter what happens, I have to know they're safe." His throat constricted. "If anything bad happens.... If we don't come back by dawn, you hitch Blaze and take them to Mrs. Giles' house. She.... She is to keep them."

Betty spoke. Her words, coming in the vacuum of his statement, rang louder and with more insistence than the fire bell.

"Yuh won' be back by dawn."

"Then follow orders," he snapped. "Nelander, get the deer rifle."

She obeyed, checking the charge after removing it from the wall. Nodding in conformation, the pair dressed quickly and left without further argument.

The cold night air stung, making breathing hard. What little oxygen penetrated the warmth of their lungs acted like a whip. Lunching ahead, bend by pain, it took a quarter mile before the sensation passed and their exhalations exploded into clouds of mist about their heads. Stealth being impossible as brittle grass crunched beneath their feet, neither attempted quiet. Nor did they speak. The time for speculation had ended.

Gone the way of Christmas past.

A light burned inside the Windsor house. Tethered to the hitching rail, a cavalry horse lifted one foot and then the other, attempting to mitigate the cold. Hearing them come up, it turned its head, ears flattened, tail swishing. In its short life, the animal had learned humans meant no good.

"Rum."

Not a comment referencing the toddies lately consumed. Or even the effects of mild inebriation both had felt before setting out. Exercise across the fields had mitigated that. Rather, the name of the animal.

Bestowed by an innocent boy, filled with the joy of being a pirate and recruiting new members into the service.

It seemed a long time ago since the court martial.

Lacking any cohesive plan, and driven more by instinct than battle preparedness, Seth strode across the yard, regardless of the target he made. If Norman desired to shoot him in cold blood, he would. No amount of care would delay the inevitable. A civilian had no chance against an old Indian fighter. Not one who left the bodies of the slain to rot on the prairie.

Rapping hard on the door, he turned the knob and entered, Nelander right behind. Betty's rocker had been turned so it faced the entranceway. Norman sat in it, feet propped on an upturned crate. His rifle balanced on the wooden arm.

"Good morning!" he greeted in cheery welcome. "Merry Christmas. A bit early, I agree, but I wanted to bestow the blessings of the holiday on you."

Seth looked around, playing a dangerous game.

"Where are Miss Betty and Thomas? What did you do to them?"

Hands went out, palms up.

"Didn't do anything. They were gone when I got here. Suppose they heard my horse and hightailed it into the woods. Reckon they're squattin' on their haunches wondering when I'm gonna leave." His hands folded. "They won't have long to wait. That's what I'm fixin' to do. Leave."

"You're going away?"

Easily lowering his feet, Norman settled into an effected ease.

"That's right. Heading west."

"West?"

He nodded pleasantly. "Received a commission from the government." Patting his thick overcoat, Norman smiled. "You are addressing a colonel." His tongue clucked. "Not as ostentatious as being a general of militia, I grant, but mine is a commission in the regular army."

"The Confederate States army," Seth growled.

"Correct."

"But why? What ties have you with slavery" Or States' Rights?"

Norman dismissed the concern with a wave.

"None. Absolutely. Military men are not political. They don't give a -- fig," he added out of false deference to Nelander, "for sovereign nations or boundary lines. What they want is power."

Stepping in further, Seth attempted to rationalize.

"I thought you said you were only interested in money."

"One begets the other, big brother. They go hand-in-hand. Not that you would know." Norman's lips curled. "Always satisfied with living hand-to-mouth. You're chicken feed, Seth. Never had any ambition. Me, I always wanted more." Getting to his feet, he paced away from them. "Soon, I'll have everything I ever wanted."

"How is that? Are they paying you that much to buy your loyalty?"

"Indeed, not. The Confederacy holds its gold close. They're not gonna spend money bribing me."

"Then what changed your mind? You found stealing from farmers a well gone dry?"

He shrugged. "There's always spring. And the Union pays well. I never minded playing both sides against the middle. But my services have been recruited." He puffed his chest. "I've been to Richmond."

Seth blew air through his cheeks.

"That's why it's been quiet around here. I thought you had pulled up stakes. Maybe gone into Indian Territory."

"Close," Norman leered, "but no segar. I took the boys with me; spoke to the Secretary of War, himself. Made out a case." Norman bounced on his toes. "If the Confederacy don't act quick, they're gonna lose the entire southwest. They've got a man out there, but he's not an Injun man. Not like me. I speak their lingo."

"I never heard you say that before."

Norman laughed. "I lied a little. Don't matter. I know how to approach the red man. What they like. Fire water an' blankets. Canned meat. Rifles. Promise 'em their own land and mebbe give it to them, too."

"In exchange for what?"

"Supporting the Confederacy. I've been authorized to negotiate with the Injuns. Not the rag-tag bunch who fought for the South at Chusto-Talash a few weeks back and made such a mess of it. The Creeks. Them who threw their lot in with the Union. Tenacity, they got; believe all the clap-trap 'Father Abraham' give 'em about how it's in their best interest to fight for the Union. I'm gonna tell 'em otherwise."

Feeling it better to keep Norman talking, Nelander asked, "Where does the money and power come in?"

He pretended astonishment and guffawed. "Use your head, woman. With the authority of ol' Jeff Davis behind me, I'll be a big man. After I get the Creeks on our side and lead 'em against the Yanks, the South'll control everything from Texas to California. That'll mean a generalship for me. General Norman Ward. An' after the war, Davis promised I'd be appointed Territorial governor. How'd that be?"

"I don't know," Seth confessed. "You tell me."

"You are a babe in the woods, aren't you, big brother? Never looking at the big picture. Territorial governor? How many ways I got then of making money? Tribute from the Injuns. Bribes from the settlers. Land fees; protection rights. Then the railroad comes through; but only on my say-so. They got real money to spread around."

He began pacing, hands behind his back. "This is my chance. No more chewin' dust, no more saddle sores. No more, 'Yes, sir, no, sir.' I'll be the 'sir,' and men will take orders from me. Not just soldiers, but bankers an' businessmen."

"Then, I wish you well."

Seth meant it for a lie and made no bones about conveying the sentiment.

Norman stopped, rubbed his chin, then grinned. The drag on his cavalry sword scraped the bare floor, making a dull grating noise. He adjusted the belt and glowered at Seth. For a moment it appeared he would continue to blow his own horn but something stopped him and he veered off on a different track.

"You never did believe I went to see Rick and ma's graves, did you?"

"No."

"Why not?"

"I couldn't imagine why you'd care."

"You was wrong. I did go. Wasn't all that far. No skin off my teeth," he added as though needing to justify the effort. "Wanted to make sure they were really dead. You know? People say one thing, truth might be another. Since you never checked it out, I figured someone had to," he added in accusation. "Can't trust anyone. Men are born liars."

Many things were becoming clear to Nelander. Like her husband, she saw profit in keeping the renegade talking, somehow feeling that time weighed in their favor.

"What you really wanted was to see if Rick left a will. Maybe in your favor, but more likely in Seth's. You wouldn't have told him, though. You look enough alike. You'd have presented yourself to the magistrate and said you were Seth Ward, finally come to collect your inheritance. Not even a childhood friend could have spotted the lie."

Norman chuckled at her intentional confirmation of his assertion. "Now, I always figured you for a wise one -- Nelander. Wouldn't a hurt nothin'. What Seth didn't know wouldn't have made a tinker's dam." He rattled on without waiting for a reply. "Rick didn't, though -- leave anything to me or Seth. Left it all to his business partner, whoever that was. Imagine? A business partner instead of his own flesh. Bastard."

"What about his wife?"

"She ran off with the partner. Guess I can't blame her. I asked around. No one knew where they went." He shrugged. "Maybe it wasn't true. Maybe the mayor took everything for himself."

"But you went to the graves."

I did. Even put flowers on 'em. Not because I cared." The point seemed important. "To put an end to it."

She stiffened. "Is that what you intend to do, now? Put an end to it?"

"Don't take your meaning -- ma'am."

"Put an end to Seth? To your own brother? See him in the grave, too? So you can leave with a clean slate?" Norman appeared shocked. "You didn't summon us out here to wish us Merry Christmas."

"It's the 'us' what bothers me. Wasn't expectin' you both. Shoulda known, though. You two share the same shadow."

"Don't imagine you'd have any qualms about murdering a woman." Her eyes narrowed. "Having so much experience with 'Injuns' -- squaws and children."

"You learn your lessons good -- Nelander. That's the mark of a true officer. Guess you coulda captained yer own ship. Too bad you didn't stay at sea."

"Unlike some people, I have no regrets."

Norman crossed to the window and parted the curtain. Meaning to appear casual, he conveyed the opposite.

"Meaning me? I have no regrets."

"Oh, I think you do."

"How's that?"

"Your men; the gang you recruited. They were fine for the work here -- robbing and killing. You were their captain and they your soldiers; 'Yes, sir. No, sir.' just like you always imagined. Them, something better came along. The deal you brokered in Richmond. All of a sudden they became a burden."

"You're tellin' the story. Go on." Although dividing his attention, Norman followed her reflection in the glass, hand resting on his sidearm. "Put that deer rifle down, do you mind, ma'am? There -- away from you. That's right. Wouldn't want it going off by mistake."

He set her up for the retort, If it goes off, it won't be by mistake. Therefore, Nelander did not offer it.

"They knew of your promotion and your plans. Naturally, they figure they're entitled to a piece of the pie. Whatever bribes and tribute you manage to collect. Just like you wouldn't have shared with Seth if collected on Rick's will, I can't see you splitting your take with them."

"That seems a reasonable assumption."

"I've been wondering why you bothered coming back to Kansas. You could have gotten rid of them along the way to the Oklahoma Territory. You know the country; they don't. By the time you got established, it would have been an easy matter to... dispatch the Indians against them. Do your dirty work for you."

"Right enough."

She moved a foot to her right. His gaze followed her image in the glass.

"So I'm thinking you had to have a reason to go so far afield. That led me to the idea of booty."

Raising an eyebrow, he savored the expression. "Booty? I like that. A pirate word." He rolled the sound around in his mouth. "Boo-ty."

"You like more than the word. You like the entire concept of being a pirate. Peter got to you, didn't he? With all his stories of adventure on the High Seas and how buccaneers buried treasure. That's why you came back -- because you wanted to be like him and play a child's game. Before leaving for Virginia, you and your gang dug a hole and hid your blood money for safe keeping. There was no sense taking it with you, in any case."

Norman, the pretend pirate, bounced on his toes.

"That's just what we did. We drew us up a map with skulls an' vultures an'...." His eyes flashed. "And drinkin' gourds on it. Like we was... land pirates. And hid our booty."

"And now you've come to retrieve it. Have dug it up," she corrected, pointing toward a still-damp encrustation of mud on his boots. "Only, you don't plan on sharing any of it with your fellow thieves. You're taking it all with you."

"That'd be a mighty dangerous thing to do, ma'am."

"It would be, if you figured on getting caught. But you have a plan."

Norman's gaze shifted from her reflection to stare through the window. His leg shook, which he quickly quieted with a slap against his thigh.

"Tell me."

"It's Christmas. I bet you ol' boys did some mighty fine celebrating last night to ring in the holiday. Got drunk. Or, at least, they did. Drunker'n skunks. And while your boys were laid out, you slipped away. Dug up the money and came here. Then summoned Seth."

"He's family. Wanted to say good-bye."

"The same way you said good-bye to Rick and your mother? By laying flowers on their graves?"

"Hard to do, seein' Seth is still alive."

A noise in the distance temporarily distracted Norman and his breath froze on the window as he leaned forward. Finally convincing himself it was nothing, he bade her continue.

"They're out there, aren't they? Your cutthroat 'crew.' Woke up from their drunken stupor and found their captain missing. First thing they would have done is follow the map -- and discovered an empty hole for their trouble. They must be rip-roaring mad. They're tracking you, right now. And those tracks will bring them right to this place. Only they won't find you -- they'll find a man who looks like you. They'll shoot 'Captain Ward' for betraying them and then tear this house down, looking for the treasure. They won't find it, of course, but in the time it takes for them to realize they shot the wrong brother – if they ever do, that is -- you'll be long gone."

A low, cutting grunt broke from Norman's lips.

"It seems I'm a better pirate than you, Seth."

He checked the horizon again, this time with keener interest. Despite the light banter, a nervousness had crept upon him. Outside, the wind had picked up, whistling the age-honed adage, Time waits for no man. Either Norman felt sand running out of the hour glass, or he expected an interruption. One he would rather not face.

Only a fool placed himself in a position of having enemies behind and before him.

Norman Ward proved himself a fool.

Turning slowly around, he looked toward where he supposed his brother to be. But his attention had been too long on Nelander. The real Captain Ward had moved.

It took a second for the fact to register. Pulse surging, Norman lunged, but Seth, who had maneuvered close to the rocking chair, bounded for the army-issue rifle. Fingers outstretched, muscles tensed, he grabbed the weapon. Leveling it waist high, he offered a severe countenance. One not without irony.

"Oh, I don't know about that. You forgot the principal of good strategy. While you were engaged with my decoy, I confiscated your weapon. A move Blackbeard would heatedly approve."

Hands up in apparent surrender, the false captain appeared to capitulate.

"Damn me if that ain't true. I underestimated you, brother."

"No, you didn't. You didn't consider me at all. But I don't mind. You have been out of my thoughts these many years. I guess that makes us even."

"Only if you have the guts to shoot me. Otherwise, I just walk out the door, get on my horse and ride away. Nelander's right, brother. They're out there. Comin' close. I can feel them. Only by the time they get here, they won't find me, they'll find you. So my plan works, after all."

Making good his threat, he dashed toward the exit. Nelander would have blocked his path, but the man with the rifle, whose time had finally come, reacted more violently. Barely touching the trigger of the finely honed weapon, he fired a warning shot over Norman's head. The bullet missed by an inch, splintering the door frame. Cold air, doing service as spouting blood, poured in through the gaping hole. The temperature in the room dropped faster than mere weather could explain.

Seth clucked his tongue. The discharge of the rifle left his nerves tingling. The sensation elicited memories.

"You know, there was a time when I thought I could look a creature in the eyes and tell when it was ready to die. Believed I had the courage to put it out of its misery. I didn't, though. Got talked out of it."

Norman clutched at straws.

"What do you see in my eyes?"

"Nothing."

He bounced on his toes. Seth did not react. Working his hands, Norman thought about, but did not raise them a second time.

"I'm not gonna rush you -- not going to give you the excuse."

"You already have."

"You can't shoot me in cold blood."

"Brother, my blood's been hot since I first learned how you tricked me. I welcomed you into my house and you turned, like a snake. Think I can forget that?"

"It's still murder."

"No one calls it murder when you shoot a rabid dog."

Inexplicably confronted by death, Norman Ward, dragoon, Indian fighter and marauder-turned Confederate agent, gasped. Skin tone turning parched white, tongue protruded from bloodless lips, he retreated a step, stunned by the metamorphosis before him. He no longer saw the companion of his childhood; the middle brother with whom he had stolen a peek at their older's risqué playing cards. Gone the boy who had fallen in love before old enough to shave. Transformed, the man who loved the land and never minded living hand-to-mouth.

Before Norman finally stood an image of himself. One with no compunction against taking his life.

"No," he pleaded. "Look into my eyes. I'm not ready to die."

Seth responded, but not in negotiation. As judge and jury, he had already consigned Norman's fate to the executioner.

"I didn't shoot a cow and a horse when maybe I should have, but I loved them. I don't love you. To me, you're nothing but a...." He struggled, but not hard, for the word. "A disease. It's been a long time since I wanted to kill a cancer. A Lupus, " he added with a grimace. The weapon felt featherweight in his grasp. "Know why they call it that --Lupus? Dr. McTree told me. It's a Greek word. Because the cancer eats flesh away like a wolf." His contempt deepened. "I killed one such disease. Cold-blooded, you could say. Thought I had taken it out of the world -- my world. Until you showed up."

Seth raised the weapon high, by his face. Aimed it the way Norman must have when hunting Injuns. Eyes closing, he whispered, "God forgive me," and pulled the trigger. The blast came close to shattering his eardrums. Spun around by the recoil, he staggered, caught his balance, then dropped to one knee, rifle back in firing position should Norman move. He did not.

The mate of his earliest days lay sprawled against the wall, back propped up so that he appeared to be sitting. Except that his head drooped at an unnatural angle. Blood dripped from the side of his face. The place where his ear had been now resembled the hole in the door. The difference being, no air slithered through Norman's brain.

Barbara Nelander bent to inspect the wound. She feared her stomach would turn, but it did not.

Not as bad as expected. Norman Ward was not a cow or a horse, after all. Not one of the beloved. Not one of the family of pirate.

"If you intended to hit him between the eyes, you're a lousy shot, Captain Ward."

"Is he dead?"

"No. The son of a bitch only fainted. Imagine that." Disdaining to touch the body, she braced herself then reached under Norman's shirt. Grasping a length of latigo, she swung the weight on the end, then tossed the talisman aside. "Do I get to finish him off? So we can both have a hand?"

"Don't want you involved."

On the surface, the statement had the ring of being ridiculous.

"I see. Want the reward all for yourself, do you?" They eyes met. "'Wanted: Dead or Alive.' That's what the poster on Sheriff Bochner's bulletin board says. The sketch of Norman wasn't a very good one: hardly recognizable. But Bochner will take our word we shot the outlaw leader. I've a hankering to buy a new frock with my share. What you gonna do with yours, pardner?"

She made him laugh. A great testimony to both their set of jangled nerves.

"I meant to kill him."

"We're gonna need to replace Betty's door, too. That'll cost, some. Better speak up. I'm whittling the reward money down fast."

"A new cow," he said. "And a horse."

"You didn't kill Bessie or Blaze, either. And ol' Herman's still around. The farm's full up with critters."

"I meant to kill him."

"You didn't kill Belinda, either."

His leg shook. The horse named "Rum" whinnied. The muscles in Seth's neck stiffened. In desperation came resolve.

"Go out the back. Now."

In the distance, the sound of hooves. A company of soldiers.

"The shots," she identified. "Easier than following tracks."

"Won't be long until they get here. Get out."

She tasted fear. "You're not staying here? Inside. Why?"

"Gonna finish it up." He stared at Norman's insensate body. "Put an end to the... Lupus, once and for all."

"I'm staying with you --"

This time, he screamed. "Get out! He's my brother."

Nelander did not know what he meant. Only that she must obey.

"I'll go out back. Not far."

He did not hear. His attention had gone ahead. Via a route along the underground railroad which took him to the past.

When his eyes cleared, she had gone.

Dragging Norman away from the door, he created a trail of blood. Not much of one. Zigzag; the way a sidewinder moved. Removing the military coat from his brother's limp arms, he slid his own through the sleeves, then jammed the cap atop his head. The uniform made him feel odd. Like a killer. As though he had to live up to the shiny brass buttons and the gold, intertwined catgut.

"Captain Ward? Captain Ward, you in there?"

"I'm here," Captain Ward truthfully called.

"We heard shootin'. You all right?"

"Just doin' a little bounty huntin', boys. There's a pair of niggers live here. Thought they might be worth sumthin' to the Simpson Agency."

Resting the rifle in the crook of his arm, he opened the door. The idea of playing his brother was not a new one. It had come to him in the field after the Independence Day celebrations. As though Fate were putting him on guard. Only the question of time and circumstance had puzzled him. Now he knew. To keep Norman's soldiers occupied while Nelander got away.

He opened the door.

In the gleam of starlight he presented a stately figure. Norman Ward always appreciated a good appearance.

"You git 'em, sir?"

"Two shots. You heard."

The mounted men exchanged glances. There were ten. Or twelve. The officer could not be certain. Not in the dark.

"How much you think you'll git fer 'em?"

Easy chatter. To set the stage for a killing.

"Not much. Fifty dollars." He grinned. He remembered the way Norman grinned. The tow-headed boy with a smile. Stealing a look at Rick's French picture cards. The same way he must have grinned standing over their graves.

Just to be sure.

"You mighta told us where you was goin', sir. When we come to, you was gone. Didn't look good."

"Had some business to finish."

"All done now, Norman?"

"Nearly."

One of the troopers dismounted. He, too, wore a uniform. His lacked the brass buttons and the convoluted catgut. Perhaps that was why he hesitated.

"We looked for the saddlebags, Norman. They weren't there. Only an empty hole. You got 'em?"

"Thought mebbe I'd re-bury them. For safety's sake." He remembered Norman had once been a pirate. But his tenure had been brief.

"Without tellin' us?"

"I woulda told you. The sheriff's been messin' around. Didn't want him to stumble onto camp like that damn nigger-runner McConaghie."

"We'd a hung him, too."

"Not if he'd a come with a posse. One of you boys mighta got shot."

"Makes a nice story, Capt'n. Now, why don't you step on out with those saddlebags nice and high so's we can see 'em. Then, we'll know it was a mistake, you runnin' off with our money. And we can all go on to the Oklahoma Territory together."

Seth raised the rifle and shot the man. This time, he aimed for the gut. The robber cried, clutched at his innards, then toppled back. A horse reared. Captain Ward ducked back in the house and slammed the door.

Over his head he heard a pinging sound. At first he thought it was hail. Being only a farmer, and not really a soldier, he could be forgiven his ignorance. Bullets. First, desultory, then a volley. Smashing through the door; shattering window glass. He fired back, this time settling himself for the recoil. Because he wore the uniform, the aftershock did not seem so severe. He supposed that is what happened. Men got acclimated to killing.

Until it became second nature.

He fired again. More shots followed.

"Come on out, Norman."

"We got you surrounded, sir."

"Jest give us the money. No one's lookin' for your blood, sir."

"Don't have to be this way."

But it did.

Norman Ward's plan had come to fruition. Seth Ward had taken his place.

The ending would be different.

Scrambling under the tattoo of bullets, Seth reached the hearth. Using his foot for a scoop, he scattered the coals. The smell of wood smoke filled his nostrils. More bullets. He did not fire back because he did not know how many shots Norman's rifle held.

Ripping the grey wool coat from his shoulders, he dropped it over the coals. First a curl of smoke and then flame.

He yelled to hold them back. Like wolves, they would not commit to a frontal attack until sure the victim had been disabled.

"Sorry, boys. But what's mine is mine. I recruited you an' now I'm disbandin' you."

The mutinous pirate.

Not Norman Ward. He remained oblivious to the end.

Saved the ignominy of walking the plank by diving directly into hell's flames.

The fire caught. Seth threw the woolen Afghan onto the flames. The threads burned quickly. He tossed coals toward the windows. The curtains went up.

"We're comin' for you, Norman."

He supposed they were. And hoped they found him.

But not before it was too late.

Paper money burned.

Hunched over, shoulders low, he stumbled in the flickering light, fell to his knees and crawled out of the growing inferno. In the back of his mind, Seth recalled Norman had rung the fire bell. Little had he guessed the necessity of so casual an act.

He made it out back just as the soldiers broke in the front. He heard them inside. Shouting. Cursing. Discharging their weapons.

"Look for the saddlebags."

Captain Ward did not know where Captain Ward had hidden his treasure. He hoped he had done it well. So that he might take it with him. To pay the Ferryman.

Outside, he gasped for air. Cold, fresh air. It stung his lungs in a different way than the acrid gunpowder and the thick, black smoke. Good to be alive. Good to be just a pirate captain, again, and not a soldier.

Hearing a trooper come along the side, Seth scooted toward the smoke house. Tripping on an outcropping of tree root, he stumbled and fell, crashing through the door. In the confusion, no one heard. His chin landed on something soft. Leather.

No time to think. Or just enough. He hoisted himself up, using a meat hook. Stood. Looked down. And then dashed away.

Empty handed.

Nelander met him in the brush. Taking his arm, she steadied him.

"You all right?"

"Yes."

Instead of "Yup." That had been laid to rest.

They scurried away. Not like rats deserting a sinking ship. Like sailors, returning home to sea.

Ahead of them, the dawn broke.

CHAPTER 35

The house went up in a blaze of glory. All the way across the fields Nelander and Seth felt the red glow at their backs, rivaling that of the emerging sun. Neither paused for a glance over the shoulder. What will be will be, their attitude seemed to suggest. Where once a home stood, cold ash would reign.

All things considered, the trade-off had been worth the price.

Marching into the yard, snowflakes began to fall. Blowing on his hands, Seth looked for friendly signs of habitation and saw none. Aside from the briskly blowing flags, no sort of motion caught his eye.

"They have gone," Nelander reminded him. "Our instructions. If we did not return by dawn, Betty and Thomas were to take the children to Mrs. Dryfus'." Being in the open, she unconsciously reverted to the socially requisite surname.

"That seems an age ago." His shoulders rounded. "Betty was right. We did not get back before first light. I wish we had made it eight bells: 8 o'clock, instead."

"You may, but I do not. Knowing them safely away gave me courage." On his look, she added, "Dollars to doughnuts, pard', they left shortly after we did and are now tucked in bed."

"On Christmas morning? To be sure not. Peter is in the stable with Fleet and Patricia is in the garret, already working on her next painting for Mister -- what was his name?"

"Wendell Phillips. I meant," she drolly amended, "Betty and Thomas."

"Ah. You know what this means, don't you?"

Tempted to reply, *A pot of boiling hot coffee and then a dive into bed,* she set her resolve. "A brisk walk to town."

Glad she did not verbalize that which he might have been tempted to agree, Seth shoved hands in pockets.

"A mere twelve miles. We can be there by tea time."

Not wishing to put off the onerous trek, the pair abandoned any thought of fortifying themselves with breakfast and began the trek. The snow worsened as they walked, accumulating an inch in a little over half an hour.

Visibility remained adequate, however, and they navigated without difficulty, although soon losing the road to drifts.

Keeping conversation to a minimum in order to conserve energy, the sun had reached its zenith before Seth broke the mutual silence.

"Is it all over, do you suppose?"

Open ended, he let Nelander choose the subject.

"Yes. I suppose the marauders searched and did not find the money."

"And Norman?"

"Left him behind."

"Is he... gone?"

She did not mince words. "They either shot him, which I consider most likely, or left him to burn in the fire. Either way, he is 'gone.'"

"Why did he turn out the way he did?"

She hesitated, but the pause had nothing to do with debating the merits -- or lack thereof -- attributed to Norman Ward.

"Ask rather, why did you turned out the way you did. I see Norman as no different than your father or your older brother. You were the... red apple in a field of green."

"Red," he intoned with reverence. "Like strawberries." And then, "What about the house?"

"One of the last pieces to fall in place."

The reference made no sense. He tried harder.

"Explain what you mean. Will we rebuild it?"

"Of course. Not as fine, perhaps, but from the ground up. Henceforth, no one will call it the Windsor Place. It will have a new name."

"What shall it be?"

Nelander stopped, turned back and took at their twin tracks, rapidly becoming obscured by ice crystals. From there, her eyes turned upward. Even through the clouds, she saw the celestial bodies.

"The Drinking Gourd. One way-station on the road to freedom."

"I like that." He shivered, but not from cold. "The Pirate Treasure, bordering the Drinking Gourd."

"With Strawberry Fields in between."

According to plan, they arrived in Lawrence at eight bells: 4:00 P.M. Cold, weary and wet, the pair plowed through the knee-deep snow, eager to reach their destination. Passing the Sheriff's Office, Nelander indicated they go inside. An arch of Seth's eyebrow asked the reason why.

"I said the burning of the house was one of the last pieces to fall in place. I propose to finish the puzzle."

He followed her. Will Bochner looked up from where he had been playing checkers with himself. The sight of them caused concern.

"What have you two been up to? Sit down -- you look all done in. I'll stoke the fire and put on a pot of coffee."

Barbara spoke for them both.

"Walked all the way from home. Please don't bother. We only stopped by to report a death." Seth stiffened and tried to catch her eye. He failed. "You may take down one of your wanted posters."

"Which one?"

"That of Terrance Windsor."

Seth fell back against the door. Will stood and offered to help, but he waved him off. Barbara Nelander-Ward continued.

"He came back to his old home: wanted us to meet him there. To make peace. Exchange some small gifts before he and Beth and the boys left the state for good. They received a letter from Beth's family. In California. Things are going well and they need an able-bodied crew. Growing grapes."

Resting a hand on the table to steady herself, she absently moved a checker. A red one. "There was an accident. A window blew out and the wind pushed over a lamp. The house went up in a blaze. Seth and I barely escaped. We tried to save Terrance but he went back in -- for some item of sentimental value he had left behind. The roof collapsed." She started to tremble and could not stop. Will Bochner understood she and Beth had once been best friends. "There was nothing we could do."

"That's all right. I'm sorry. I know how hard this must be for you. Don't worry. Once the storm lets up, I'll go out there. Take care of things."

"That would be kind."

Patting her on the arm, Will drifted toward his desk. Removing a stack of posters, he riffled through the stack until finding the right one. With a sad shrug, he opened the belly of the stove and placed it inside. The edges curled, the printed ink image turning brown, then black, before imploding in flame.

"That's an end to it, then."

Seth came and directed Barbara away.

"Merry Christmas," he said.

They stepped outside, shutting the door behind them.

Presents all distributed, they needed do no more than collect their crew and go home.

Mrs. Giles greeted them at the door. While their appearance could not have come as a surprise, for both Nelander and Seth saw the black man in the garden signal their imminent arrival, she nevertheless grasped them with arms stretched to the limit.

"Here, at last! I have been so worried. As soon as Betty told me what happened, I sent Giles. But by that time...."

"The house had burned."

Weariness fell from Nelander the way a snake shed worthless skin. Accepting the invitation to enter, she allowed Antony to take her coat and the mistress to guide them into the parlor. Miss Betty and Thomas awaited them. Both rose as they entered.

"It be fine to see yuh."

"You said we would not be back before dawn and you were right."

"Weh took da chil'run. Dey be out an' about. Yuh want meh to fetch dem?"

"No, no. Leave them to their pleasures. There is something I must say -- "

Mrs. Giles interrupted by wrapping her knuckles on the end table for attention.

"This is my home -- my ship, if you will -- and we will have decorum. You will all sit and partake of refreshments. It is Christmas, after all, and we will honor the day."

Looking around for the first time, the two bone-tired travelers saw the large green pine placed by the hearth. Reaching to the ceiling, the tip bowed from the weight of a small golden angel. Other glass globes, some of cut crystal, reflected the glow of tiny beeswax candles, delicately placed in small brass holders. Baubles of cranberry red, royal blue, forest green and snow white were evenly spaced between silver icicles. Surrounding them, deep brown chocolates and fudge brownies helped form a magnificent re-creation of the four seasons.

Several wrapped gifts lay beneath, set atop a snowy quilt.

Glad to settle into soft cushions and rest throbbing feet, the Wards eagerly partook of steaming mugs of sweetened cocoa and small, delicately designed finger sandwiches, held together by festive silver picks, each with a different holiday design.

Hand suspended over the selection, Barbara identified the hand-painted shapes.

"Christmas tree; bottle of champagne; a dress-up chest; a bouncing ball; a silver chalice; a china princess; a hobby horse; a speeding engine; a jack-in-the-box. How wonderful. Did these come from England?"

"I suppose so; but I did not purchase them. They have been in my family for generations. This is the first time in many seasons I have taken them out."

"Exquisite. I never thought to be served with such finery."

Victoria Giles laughed and the sweet ring of joy filled the room.

"You admire the trinkets, yet say nothing of the sculptured tray or the gold coffee service. They are worth one hundred times the others."

Nelander pretended to wave away the objection.

"When you have seen one tray and coffee service, you have seen them all. But these -- trinkets -- as you call them are unique."

Seth blew on his cocoa, then look a deep swallow.

"Where have you seen trays and gold coffee services?"

"Nowhere," came the blithe confession. "But they are easy to imagine."

He grinned and began on the food. Eating one delicate creation in two brief chews, he licked the pick and handed it over. "You may admire the hardware, Captain, whilst I eat your portion."

"I shall do both."

She matched him swallow for swallow for several minutes, then with the sharp bite of appetite appeased, they leaned back in comfort. Mrs. Giles took that as her cue to speak.

"Last night during our celebration, I did not give the two senior officers of the Pirate Treasure their gifts, thinking to save them for another time. That hour has arrived. But first, I offer a small explanation." Stooping down, she took up one of the small, wrapped gifts. Cradling it lovingly for a moment, she wiped her eyes. "When you so kindly invited me to Christmas dinner, I said I had other things planned for the day and you obliged me without intruding of my motives. You thought, perhaps, a private party? Select guests? The wealthy and influential of Kansas?"

Her guests made small indications that may have been the speculation. For a moment, Mrs. Giles' expression turned harsh.

"No such thing. Since my return from Europe after Mr. Dryfus' timely demise, I have, on occasion, been... forced to entertain those you might consider elite, but never at Christmas. This time I reserve for myself. And Marc."

Fingers caressing the present, she brought it to her lips, kissed it, then held it out. No one made a move to accept it, rightfully comprehending they were not the recipient.

"He and I spent only one Christmas together and that time stolen from other obligations. I presented him a watch with a chain and a fob to dangle from his vest. He gave me a bottle of rose water brewed by his own hand. In the years since, I have reserved this holiday for he and I -- his spirit and my body -- to spend together. I wear a sprinkling of his perfume as a reminder of a gift from long ago, and offer him a present." Her face wrinkled and in the flickering candle light, she suddenly looked old.

"Africans are a very spiritual people and they have many tales of ghosts inhabiting the places they knew in life. Mind, I do not say haunting. They return on special occasions to celebrate their life with the ones they love. Thus, I have an excuse for my eccentricity, lest you think me mad."

Seth crossed his legs without meaning to be impolite and sighed.

"If you anticipate an argument, you have invited the wrong people. We are the parents of a boy who speaks to spirits."

"On a somewhat regular basis," Nelander agreed, copying his freedom by stretching out her legs. Victoria bowed her head in reverence.

"Thank you. This is my present to Marc; my husband."

Delicately unwrapping the gift, she neatly deposited the wrapper on the arm of the sofa before holding it out.

"A jar of strawberry jam," Barbara gasped.

"His last request. One that I shall endeavor, for the rest of my life, to fulfill." Waiting a moment for the spirit of Marc Giles to accept her offering, the matron turned to her guests of flesh and bone. "Every year I must buy a jar of strawberry jam for his present. Every year it is a matter of grave concern to me." The purposeful use of the adjective struck home, although no one moved. "I worry I will not find something exactly right." Her voice strengthened. "This year, you have alleviated that worry. The jam in this jar was made from those berries grown in your strawberry fields."

Moving away from the tree, the wrinkles disappeared, restoring a vibrancy to the old lady's features.

"You see now why I paid fifty dollars for the lot? Why I sent Giles to pay $500 for that which you would harvest? So I would always have a ready supply of strawberries with which to make jam."

"Nelander clapped. "How extraordinary!"

"Ordained by God," came the stern qualification. "A stranger, cast off course, settles in Lawrence. She buys strawberry plants because her husband's boyhood dream was to cultivate them in a valley which came into his possession by an act of good will, gone awry. Another quirk of God's Divine Plan. The unexpected need for you to hire help; the... awesome fact you reached out to the two most sacred living people in my life."

Hands shaking, Victoria steadied herself and forged ahead.

"Having Giles buy the strawberries might have been enough, but you brought them to my doorstep. Hand delivered the fruit. And at the same time introducing me to one child with the talent and the grace to reach out and rekindle my spirit -- and another who... as you say... speaks to spirits. So many blessings, I am nearly... stunned.

"Stunned," she repeated, tears gently cascading down her cheeks. "Rejuvenated. Re-invigorated. Inspired."

Replacing the jar under the tree, she smiled.

"Every year I perform this ritual on Christmas morn and by afternoon the jam has disappeared." She glanced at her son with tenderness. "I am a good one for rationalizing. I suspect it is Antony who takes it." He protested but the effort proved unnecessary. "Perhaps it is; perhaps it is not. I am at peace."

Mrs. Giles began walking, working her way by the boughs of the tree and around the room.

"You have marked what I said: that every year until this one, I have worried myself almost to death over procuring just the proper jar of strawberry jam. One that is perfectly suited to my needs. This year, in answer to a prayer, my problem has been solved. For all time."

Tarrying behind Seth, she gently petted his head.

"Last spring, I gave you $500 for next year's crop. I acted hastily, to ensure myself an adequate supply of strawberries. I have since rethought my position."

"If you want your money back --"

The pained offer went unfinished as Victoria brushed a finger over his lips.

"What I want is something greater. I spoke of assurance. I used the words, 'For all time.' I mean to have your strawberries but I will not dicker. We shall not go through this process year after year. Both families -- yours and mine -- deserve the stability only a union between us can achieve."

Speaking rapidly, the significance nearly went unnoticed. It took Nelander to decipher the plain English.

"A partnership?"

"Yes." With effort, a smile worked its way over the woman's features. Never before had she entered into a business contract so willingly. Or with more at stake. Stooping for one of the few remaining gifts, she started to hand it over, thought better of it and made a small, low noise. "I had meant for you to take this home -- to speak of it among yourselves, but now I change my mind. A woman's prerogative."

Still stunned by the revelation and by what Mrs. Giles' suggestion implied, Nelander resorted to her officer's demeanor.

"Only a block of wood refuses to change his mind when presented with facts contradicting his original position."

"Thank you. I have been accused of many things, but never that." Breaking the seals, then discarding the envelope, Mrs. Giles produced a sheaf of papers. Moving closer to the illumination, she positioned her body to accommodate the light.

"I wrote this myself, without benefit of legal representation. You may wish to have it examined by a lawyer."

"Or a banker." Nelander felt giddy. "Mr. Provost, perhaps. "Although he is a bit on the dour side. Nothing, it seems, is either possible or practical in his eyes. Although I do not know why I am so down on the man. Were it not for his persistent negativism, I might never have sought a job as governess with a strange fellow and two peculiar children."

Seth grimaced. "Remind me to go in and thank him the next time we pass the bank."

"I was thinking, rather, of pizzoning him with chilies at the next Eatin' Contest."

"That, too."

Mrs. Giles let them play out their nervousness, then made her sales pitch.

"This is my idea. We form a corporation for the purpose of commercially manufacturing strawberry jam. You provide the fruit and I the factory."

"But how --?"

"A simple matter of expanding my present operation. The plants I inherited from the late Messrs. Dillinger and Dryfus produce tinware and glass. The former I maintain ownership of. But the latter -- the glassware product line -- may easily be converted to the production of jars of a size and shape amenable for the packaging and sale of jam. These many years I have handled the business side of the operation; labor, contracts and investments. That will be my contribution.

"I have little experience in advertising, however. Putting a product across. Getting shop owners to carry our brand, and eventually finding distributors who will enable us to expand into other states. East and west.

Nelander-Ward, I would expect you to assume that task. Among us three, you are the best in dealing with people. Of putting your point across."

Flattered and excited by the prospect, Barbara readily agreed.

"Does this mean I get to flog those who do not cooperate?"

Seth turned his head and addressed the wall. "Took the words right out of my mouth."

"As to that, I leave to your discretion. Mr. Nelander-Ward, you are the farmer. Your assignment is to monitor the crops. See to their proper fertilization; watering, weeding. Whatever is needed. Eventually, as the business prospers, we will require more land; additional plants."

"Something," he guardedly admitted, "Barbara and I have already discussed. In our dreams."

"You are awake, now. Can you do it?"

"With Miss Betty and Thomas' help."

Exactly what she wished to hear. "Excellent. But then, they are already part of your crew? Able-bodied hands?"

"Tars," Nelander clarified. After a stunned silence, all burst out laughing.

"'Tars" it is." Mrs. Giles turned to Antony. "The factory will require a supervisor. As long as we are choosing apt words, you shall be our... overseer."

"I am still a Negro."

"The war will change that."

He evinced surprise. "Father Abraham may affect many changes, ma'am, but I doubt even he can alter the color of my skin."

Realizing the mistake, Victoria chuckled, then grew serious.

"I would not have him do that. We are what we are. Having our brethren convince him to end slavery is enough. The rest will come. Will you do this?"

Clasping hands behind his back, Antony's chin jutted as he worked his jaws.

"Being an overseer has a pleasing ring to it, but I rather fancied myself a lieutenant."

"As indeed you shall be," Barbara declared. "A commissioned officer in our new enterprise. Peter is already a warrant officer: we will appoint him boatswain. His responsibility shall be as inspector, for all operations, generally. Patricia will be our resident artist and create labels for the jars. But what shall we call our product?"

Speaking from the stairwell where she had crept down to listen, the artist supplied the next-to-last piece of this new jigsaw.

"Gawd's Strawberry Preserves." Four pair of eyes turned in unison. "G-A-W-D: 'G' for 'Giles' -- Marc 'Giles.' 'A' for 'Antony.' 'W' for 'Ward.' And 'D' for 'Dryfus.' That's the first name we knew you by, Victoria. The 'Strawberry' is for Nelander, of course, because she brought them to Kansas. And the 'Preserves' is for a just and lasting peace."

"Gawd," it went without saying, represented the Lord.

Spoken in dialect.

Which covered a multitude of blessings.

Seth had one last question.

"What about Paula's contribution?"

"That's easy." Peter came in from the stables, bits of straw lining the exterior of his coat. "Won't be long now -- by the time spring comes around, again -- that's she's eatin' people food. Everyone knows how fussy babies are. She'll be our taste tester."

The motion carried unanimously.

Business woman.
Advertiser.
Farmer.
Able-bodied tars.
Lieutenant.
Artist.
Boatswain.
Spitter.
Spirit.

All working under the jurisdiction of "Gawd."

The End

GSFE

ALSO BY: S.L.KOTAR AND J.E.GESSLER

A character based historical 1950's courtroom based murder mystery entitled "**The Hugh Kerr Mystery Series**"..

- Book I   **The Conundrum of the Decapitated Detective**
- Book II   **The Conundrum of the Absconded Attorney**
- Book III   **The Conundrum of the Sins of the Fathers**
- Book IV   **The Conundrum of The Two-Sided Lawyer**
- Book V   **The Conundrum of the Clueless Counselor**
- Book VI   **The Conundrum of the Loveless Marriage**
- Book VII   **The Conundrum of the Executed Defendant**
- Book VIII   **The Conundrum of the Jettisoned Jury**
- Book IX   **The Conundrum of the Perjured Pigeon**
- Book X   **The Conundrum of the Haunting Halloween**
  - **Party**
- Book XI   **The Conundrum of the Tuneless Tunesmith**
- Book XII   **The Conundrum of the Meddling Motorcar**
- Book XIII   **The Conundrum of the Blundering Bear**
- Book XIV   **The Conundrum of Shooting Fish in a Barrel**
  -
  - **To Be Continued!**

Next a series is "New Beginnings" a 1950's medical drama.

- Book I   **The Believer**
- Book II   **The Heretic**
- Book III   **Arrow Song**
- Book IV   **Peas In A Pod**
-
  - **To Be Continued!**

"the ReproBate saga" is a character-based series in the 1860 American Civil War

- **Book I**   **Beneath the Rose**
- Book II   **skull and cRossBones**
- Book III   **Redefining Bastions**
- Book IV   **thicker than Blood**
- Book V   **prioR Battles**
- Book VI   **Requited Blasphemy**
- Book VII   **The waR Between**
- Book VIII   **To Richmond or Bust**
- Book IX   **carrying Battlescars**
    - **To be Continued**

"the Hellhole saga" is a character-based series from the American West

- Book I   **First Draw**
- Book II   **Audition for a Legend**
- Book III   **Strange Bedfellows**

"The Kansas Pirate Series" is another character-based series from the American West

- Book I   **Pirate Treasure**
- Book II   **Strawberry Fields**
- Book III   **The Drinking Gourd**

Stand-alone novels include:

- **Catman** *He was every man; he was no man*

- **ONE** Science Fiction space travel

- **Shepherd of the Kingdom** a modern-day horror classic

Non-Fiction

"**The Kepi Magazine**," A publication specialized in the Civil War and 19th century life.:

- **The Kepi Volume I and II**
- **The Kepi Volumes III and IV**

www.ingramcontent.com/pod-product-compliance
Lightning Source LLC
Chambersburg PA
CBHW031609260626
47154CB00021B/1872